HEIST

HEIST

ROBERT SCHOFIELD

ALLEN&UNWIN
SYDNEY·MELBOURNE·AUCKLAND·LONDON

Allen & Unwin
83 Alexander Street
Crows Nest NSW 2065
Australia
Phone: (61 2) 8425 0100
Email: info@allenandunwin.com
Web: www.allenandunwin.com

Cataloguing-in-Publication details are available
from the National Library of Australia
www.trove.nla.gov.au

ISBN 978 1 74331 520 0

Set in 12.5/16.5 pt Bembo by Post Pre-press Group, Australia
Printed and bound in Australia by Griffin Press

10 9 8 7 6 5 4 3 2 1

For Emma and her beautiful mother

ignis aurum probat
Seneca

ONE

'What the fuck am I doing here?'

Ford didn't talk to himself unless he was alone and out of earshot, but it was a question he asked himself every day. Leaning against the handrail, he looked down at the frothing leach tanks beneath him. He stood here every morning. It was the highest platform in the processing plant and the first place to catch the dawn sun. He looked up to the east, where the sky was glowing pink, to the point between two distant hills where the sun would soon appear from below the earth's sharp edge.

He knew the answer to his question: he could follow the chain of events that had brought him to this empty place in the Australian desert, but knowing how one event had led to another did nothing to explain the inertia that had prevented him from changing course at any point.

He felt the first stirrings of a breeze from the east, cool air being pushed ahead of the rising sun. On the rare days when the wind was from the west, he imagined he could detect a sea breeze, a hint of salt-water freshness from the Indian Ocean, blown across six hundred kilometres of desert. He knew it was wishful thinking. All that was caught in the air was red dust

1

blown off the bush, and wafts of cyanide and xanthate from the tanks beneath him. The smell always seemed to hang in the air. Lingering, not quite distinctive, it was more a metallic taste than a smell, something always on the tip of his tongue, like a half-forgotten memory. When he became aware of it, he wanted to wash it away with a cold beer, which made it worse.

The moon was still shining silver in the west, and below it he could make out Orion dipping to touch the horizon. Its stars seemed closer than the nearest town. As a kid in Manchester, it was the first constellation he had learned. Now it was one of the few he recognised in what felt like an alien sky. He was still not used to it being upside down, hanging there as proof that his world had been turned on its head. He scanned the landscape, measuring the isolation. There were no lights to be seen except the pool of yellow sodium around the processing plant and the white light spilling from the pit.

The sun broke through the gap in the hills. Ford checked his watch. It was a few minutes earlier than the day before, and a day closer to summer. He tried not to think of the heat and the flies that would bring. He preferred the nights when he could sleep without the rattle of the air conditioner. These dawn moments were the most peaceful of his day, but far from silent. He had worn ear protectors on the climb up through the machinery, but by the time he reached the catwalk the noise had faded to a dull clatter and he was able to slip them down around his neck. The steady vibration from the mills came up through his feet. He found the din comforting. It drowned out his thoughts.

He heard the diesel roar of an ore truck straining up the incline in the darkness beyond the plant. Its headlights appeared over the rim of the pit, and it kicked up a cloud of dust as it accelerated along the haul road towards the stockpile. Beyond it was a pair of drill rigs tall enough to catch the first horizontal rays of sun.

Ford reached into his pocket and pulled out a phone, his cigarettes and a lighter. He looked at the phone's blank screen, shook his head and put it back in his pocket. He tapped out a cigarette and put it between his lips, then leaned over the handrail to check if there was anyone around.

Turning his face to the sun, he lit up and inhaled. He took out the phone again and studied it. The third button he pressed brought the screen to life. Beyond the pit he could see the radio mast with its blinking light, sharing a hill of bare red rock with a water tank, but he still checked the signal strength. The range of the mast was a few kilometres and beyond that the phone would be useless. In its memory he found the only number stored there. He selected it, created a new message and tapped in four digits.

Taking a drag on his cigarette, he stared at the number. He held the smoke down until he could feel the nicotine building, and then he exhaled. The smoke folded itself around his hand. His thumb hovered over the send button.

A couple more deep drags finished the cigarette. He stubbed it out against the handrail and put the butt in his pocket. His hand strayed to his throat and fished inside the neck of his shirt till it found the gold chain around his neck. With a practised motion he pulled it from his shirt and his fingers easily found the small misshapen lump of gold hanging from it. Without moving his eyes from the phone he rolled the small nugget between his fingers.

His thumb moved to the cancel key and he scrubbed the four numbers one by one. Then he punched in the words 'fuck you' and hit the send button. He waited a beat for confirmation that the message had been sent, reached out over the handrail and let go of the phone. He watched it fall, the sodium light glinting off it as it tumbled, until it vanished into the bubbling slurry in the tank. By the time the tank was next drained for maintenance, the acid would have done for the phone. He tried not to think about what state he might be in by then.

Putting his ear protectors back on, he headed down. Now it was light he could do his inspection round. His eyes ran automatically over the equipment as he went down the stairs. When he reached the ground he cut across to the cluster of office units. Stopping at the breathalyser unit fixed to the outside wall, he took a straw from the tray and stuck it into the hole in the machine. He blew and waited for the beep. The readout flashed a row of red zeros, and he wrote three noughts on the pad beside the machine and added his signature. He opened the office door and stamped the dust from his boots.

In the chair opposite Ford's desk sat Werran with a smirk on his face. Ford knew what was coming. He took off his hard hat and hung it on the back of the door. Then he took off his safety glasses, found the cloth in his pocket and slowly wiped the dust off them. He avoided eye contact until Werran gave up waiting.

'I saw you up there,' Werran said. 'Third time I've seen you this week.'

It was still cool in the office, and would be until the sun rose higher, but Werran's forehead shone with sweat. He took off his baseball cap and wiped his brow with his sleeve then slicked back the thin red hair across his scalp. He was dressed the same as Ford, in yellow work shirt and jeans, the Gwardar Gold Mine logo embroidered on the pockets. His plastic identity card hung from a clip on his breast pocket. Werran was the only staff member Ford knew who was smiling in his mugshot. Ford's eyes were drawn to the neat creases in the other man's shirt, and he wondered whether he spent his evenings ironing. His own shirt was faded, frayed at the cuffs and mottled with a dozen types of stain. He idly poked a finger through a cigarette burn in the sleeve. A clean shirt was the uniform of a bludger.

'I thought you quit?' said Werran.

'One vice at a time.' Ford took the butt from his pocket and flicked it at Werran, who flinched as it bounced off his cheek. 'Bag it and tag it. Exhibit A.' He slumped down into his chair. 'You missed your calling. You shouldn't be wasting your talents chasing health and safety out here. Should be in the city, a big-shot parking inspector, making a real difference to people's lives.'

Werran reached into his pocket and produced a brass key. He held it out across the desk. Ford stared at it. He had seen it before, but not this close.

'You're second key man today.'

'Don't want it. Try someone else.'

Werran shook his head. 'Take the fucking key.'

Ford reached across and Werran dropped it in his palm. It was heavier than he'd expected. 'Where's Marco?' he asked.

'Left for Kalgoorlie yesterday, soon as his shift ended. Supposed to hand the key over to you before he went, but you were nowhere to be found.'

'Out in the workshop all day. He drove?' Most of the men had flown out on Tuesday for the race round in Kalgoorlie.

'His choice. Scored an invitation to the corporate marquee for the Cup, so he won't be slumming it with the boys. He'll be drinking McCann's champagne, rubbing shoulders with management in a tent full of office girls. All big hats and skimpy dresses, getting rat-arsed six hundred klicks from responsibility.'

Ford looked at the key in his hand. It changed everything. 'You had a week to tell me. Why wait till now?'

'Don't look like you're getting a bloody medal. Stevo was supposed to be doing it, but he pulled some bullshit stunt about compassionate leave and drove out yesterday arvo.'

'Drove to Perth?'

'Fuck no. He's in Kal. I reckon the only one seeing any compassion from that mongrel will be one of the lovely ladies of Hay Street. You're the last man standing.'

'When's the milk run?' asked Ford.

'Not going out on the plane today. There's too much. Truck's coming.'

'Today? What time?'

Werran checked his watch. 'They'll be here at eight, in time for the lock. Got a text real early, telling me the van left Kalgoorlie at five. I'll see you in there about ten minutes before.' Looking pleased to have caught Ford off-balance, he hauled himself out of the chair and left the office by the internal door. Ford craned his neck and watched him loiter a few minutes in the corridor, fussing over some safety messages on the noticeboard, and then head towards the crib room.

Ford turned on his computer and stared at it for twenty minutes, unable to focus on his work. Eventually he grabbed his hard hat and went outside to sit on the bench under the shade cloth. He lit a cigarette and looked at the rusted oil can full of sand, overflowing with butts, that marked the smoking area.

On the far side of the plant, parked among stacked containers on a broad stretch of gravel designated as the storage yard, were two low-loaders hooked up to a pair of battered prime movers. They were empty, apart from some equipment under a tarp on the front of each trailer near the cab. Maybe the drill rigs were moving out.

Ford burned through two more cigarettes thinking over his options. None offered him much hope. He pulled a shred of tobacco off the edge of his lower lip and opened the pack to see if a third would help. It was empty. He thought about opening the packet in his top pocket but checked his watch. It was time.

He put on his hard hat and safety glasses and walked across the yard towards the refinery. It was tucked up against the tallest part of the plant and surrounded by a chain-link fence. He punched the four-digit code into the keypad beside the electric gate and it slid open. He walked past the large roller door and stopped at the personnel door beside it. The corrugated-steel door had an identical keypad, and the video camera on a bracket above it covered the gate and the approach to both doors. Ford keyed in the number again, tilted his face towards the camera and waited for the buzz.

Once inside, it took him a moment to adjust to the darkness and the heat. There were no windows. The furnace was cold and the equipment stood idle, but the room held the heat from the day before when there had been a pour.

Two men were already in the room, waiting for him. Werran stood at the long bench beneath a pair of dusty TV screens monitoring what was going on outside. He had a clipboard and was pointing out some figures to Bill Petkovic. They didn't interrupt their conversation to acknowledge Ford. He looked nervously around the room, checking the equipment out of habit. His eye was drawn to the vault in the corner. Its concrete walls filled nearly a quarter of the room. As he looked, its steel door buzzed for a moment and then emitted a soft click. Ford checked his watch. It was eight exactly.

The noise snapped Werran to attention. He straightened his back and pushed out his chest. 'Time lock. We're on. Front gate rang a minute before you arrived, Ford. Van just checked through. Let's open up.'

He went to the vault and concentrated on the combination wheel in the centre of the door, the dial as large as his hand. He twisted the wheel, leaning close to see the etched numbers and to hear the soft clicks, his lips moving as he remembered the sequence. Ford shifted his weight from one foot to the other. Petkovic was scraping the dirt from under his fingernails with a pocketknife.

At the next click, Werran released his breath and pulled down on the lever above the wheel. The door was clearly heavier than he'd expected and he had to grab the lever with both hands and lean back to swing it open. The vault inside was dark. He

7

reached in and turned on the light switch and a single neon tube pinged and stuttered.

It was the first time Ford had seen the inside of the vault, and it was only just large enough for the three of them to fit inside. A plain wooden chair stood on the concrete floor next to the small steel safe. On the safe sat a child's piggy bank.

Werran held up his key. 'Ford, show me your key so Bill can witness that both key holders are present.' Ford rummaged in his pants pocket and produced it. 'Bill, could you please confirm both keys?'

'Do you want a fucking salute as well?' Petkovic muttered as he parked himself in the chair next to the safe.

A horn sounded outside. Ford and Werran stepped out of the vault and returned to the monitors. They could see the armoured van backed up to the mesh gate and a guard standing in front of the camera grinning at them. Werran pressed a button next to the monitor and the electric gate opened. The guard returned to the cab and the van reversed through the gate. Once the gate was closed, Werran pushed the second button and the roller door at the front of the refinery ground into life. Sunlight flooded into the room and Ford put a hand over his eyes. Once the van was backed in, the door rolled down behind it and the room returned to dim artificial light.

The driver killed the engine and the cab's doors swung open. Both uniformed men got out, leaving their helmets on the seat.

'Glad to see we're not the only sad bastards having to work during the race round,' said the driver, yawning and scratching his head. 'What did you losers do wrong?'

The guard was engrossed in a form on his clipboard. He was taller than the driver, with heavy shoulders that sloped as if being pulled down by their own weight. He walked over to Werran and thrust the clipboard under his nose. 'Check the docket and let's get on with it.'

Werran looked at the clipboard, then turned to Ford and nodded towards the vault. They went back inside and Werran inserted his key into a hole on the left side of the safe's door. He looked jumpy, but Ford found the bare cold space calming. 'Where does mine go?' he asked.

Werran sighed and pointed to the matching keyhole on the right. Ford slid in the key and turned it. He heard the click as the lock disengaged, and took out the key and put it back in his pocket. Werran yanked the handle and swung open the door. Petkovic didn't move from his seat, but the other four men gathered in a semicircle and bent down in unison to stare at the stack of gold bricks in the safe.

'Why so much?' asked Ford. He counted eight twenty-kilo bars on the floor of the safe. He did the mental arithmetic: with the gold price running as high as it was, there was more than eight million at his feet.

'They've been holding back for a while,' said Werran. 'McCann's putting on a show for some investors during the races. Marco reckons he's going to park the van in the middle of his corporate marquee and lock the buggers in the back one at a time. Five minutes alone with this little pile and the greed will be sweating out of them.'

'Are you going to keep staring at it or are you going to load the fucking stuff on the van?' Petkovic asked the driver. 'Your mate in the back is probably getting a bit lonely.'

Ford looked back at the van and heard someone moving about inside it.

'Don't worry about him,' said the driver. 'He sits in there all day with his little murder mystery novels, his headphones plugged into his music. I think he likes it in there.'

Werran bent at the knees, lifted the top bar from the safe and handed it to the guard. Ford took the next in both hands. He followed the guard to the van and, copying the other man's actions, put the gold bar into the deep steel tray mounted in a recess in the side of the vehicle. The tray slid back and the bar disappeared. Metal banged on metal as the man inside stacked it with the first bar. Petkovic grunted impatiently behind him, so Ford turned away and went back to the safe. Werran handed him another bar, and he stood waiting while the men ahead of him loaded.

The driver smiled at him. 'So, who'd you upset? Why aren't you in town with your mates, drinking, gambling and rooting?'

'I volunteered,' said Ford. 'Better off here, as far away from Kalgoorlie as I can get. Away from all that temptation.'

'You're holding twenty kilos of gold. What kind of temptation you worried about?'

Ford tried to shrug, but the weight of the bar made it difficult.

The driver looked as if he was about to give Ford some advice, but he was interrupted by a piercing siren outside the building. He and the guard both turned towards the door.

'Don't panic, just the cyanide alarm,' said Petkovic. 'Probably a spill, or just some idiot pushing the wrong button.'

Werran came out of the vault at a canter, his eyes wide, and rushed to the camera monitors. Ford stood frozen to the spot. Werran reached for the door handle, but Petkovic shouted, 'You know better than that, mate. We stay in here till we get the all-clear. Shouldn't be more than a few minutes.'

A flicker of movement on the screens above Werran's head made Ford look up. Four figures were approaching the personnel door of the gold room. He heard the short sequence of tones as the code was punched into the keypad and the click as the lock released. The door opened and four men strode into the room. They were dressed in orange boilersuits, their faces hidden by mirrored safety goggles, respirator masks and hard hats. Ford didn't notice the guns until a pistol was levelled at his face.

TWO

As soon as they entered the gold room, three of the men fanned out, their guns held high. One headed towards the vault, another to the front of the van and the third to its rear doors. The fourth man closed the gold-room door and stood in front of it. He was wearing a red hard hat, where the other three had white ones, and he held a pistol in an outstretched hand. His other hand grabbed at the stopwatch hanging around his neck. He looked at it, then let it swing again. From his belt he took a silver baton; he flicked his wrist and it telescoped out from his hand. He swung it at the camera over the door, and glass and plastic shards rained down onto the concrete.

'Get down on the floor, now!' he shouted, his voice echoing off the bare steel walls. 'Get down on the fucking floor!'

Ford stood holding the gold bar, his legs slightly bent and the weight resting on the top of his thighs. He stared at the man's dust mask, which moved up and down as he spoke. It was a half-face respirator, with a circular filter on either side and a smaller vent over the mouth. The vent was open, the man clearly not concerned about any cyanide leak or about muffling his voice.

11

The first guard from the van reached for the phone on his belt, but the man who had headed towards the vault saw him move and sprinted across the room, bringing his shotgun down butt first in a swinging arc that thumped into the guard's hip, smashing his hand and knocking the phone to the floor. The guard doubled over and the gun came down a second time on his head, dropping him to the floor. The butt of the shotgun came down for a third time and the phone broke apart on the slab.

Werran and Petkovic stood frozen beside the driver. As the second armed man approached them, all three retreated until their backs were against the van. The armed man walked past them and reached inside the cab, taking the driver's radio and the guard's handgun from the seat, and removing the keys from the ignition.

'Everyone drop their phones and get down!' yelled Stopwatch from the door. 'On the floor! Get your hands behind your back! Don't move or you're fucking dead!'

Petkovic and the driver dropped their phones and sprawled on the floor, but Werran stayed standing. The blood had drained from his face. The second man, a head shorter than the others, stepped forward and raised the muzzle of his gun to Werran's eye level. Ford could see the gun clearly for the first time—a stubby black assault weapon with a distinctive curved clip, an AK with a short barrel and a folded stock.

'I said get down on the floor!' Stopwatch screamed.

Werran was stiff. Ford watched his bottom lip quivering and then noticed the dark stain spreading across the front of his pants. The armed man in front of him noticed it too, as he lowered the gun to point at Werran's groin. He shook his head and stood back.

Coming to his senses, Werran put his hand in his pocket and limply held out his phone. The man pointed to the floor. Werran dropped the phone, put his hands behind his head and slowly lowered himself to his knees, then lay face down.

Ford was still standing on his own in the centre of the room, cradling the gold bar. Stopwatch stepped away from the door with his pistol still raised and walked towards him until the barrel rested against his forehead. 'Drop it,' he said.

Ford spread his fingers and the gold bar dropped. It landed on his foot with a dull thud. He closed his eyes, inhaled deeply and waited for the rush of pain, but it didn't come. He let out his breath in relief, silently thanking the steel toecaps in his site boots.

Stopwatch leaned forward and spoke slowly into Ford's ear. 'Now lie down on the floor and put your hands behind your back.' Ford dropped to his stomach as fast as he could, putting his hands behind his head. Stopwatch leaned over him and patted down his pockets. 'Where's the phone?'

'I don't have one.' Ford blew dust across the floor as he spoke.

'Don't shit me. Where's the fucking phone?' He rolled Ford over. With the pistol in his face, Ford could feel his shirt pockets and pants being patted down.

Finally, Stopwatch stood up straight and gave Ford a swift kick in the ribs. This time Ford felt less appreciation for the steel toecaps.

'Think about your family,' Stopwatch hissed. 'Tell me where you've put it.'

'I don't have it.'

A second kick in the ribs made Ford curl up on his side hugging his knees, his cheek against the cool concrete, his face turned towards the van. The third kick hit him in the left kidney and the fourth found the other one. He kept his eyes open and forced himself to stare through the pain, breathing hard, trying to ignore the sinking, sucking feeling of hopelessness in his chest.

Stopwatch went into the back of the van and checked the door to the secure compartment. He stuck his head out and nodded to the other three, and then jumped down.

The alarm stopped. Everyone in the room was motionless.

Stopwatch was the first to move, stepping up to the small window at the side of the van. He tried to peer through the mirrored glass, put his ear to it and listened, then walked around to the other side of the van, where the driver lay.

'Tell your friend to come out.'

The driver lifted his head off the floor and turned it to speak. 'He can't come out. He's locked in there.'

'Then get up there and open the fucking door.'

'I can't.'

'Tell us how to get him out, or we're going to hurt you. We know where you live. We know how to get to your family. We know where all your families live. Tell us the combination to the compartment.'

The driver had evidently been trained for situations like this. He spoke slowly and clearly. 'We put him in there an hour before we get here and set it on a short-term time lock. The door won't open for another hour, when we're back out on the road. I can't open it, and neither can he. If we need to get him out in an emergency we need an override code from the despatcher back at headquarters.'

Stopwatch went into the vault. He came out and made a circuit of the van, scanning the floor as he went, circling back to stand over the driver. 'Three bars in the vault, one on the floor here. How many in the van?'

'Four,' said the driver.

Stopwatch stopped and thought about that, and everyone waited. He seemed to make up his mind and signalled to the other three. The man nearest the cab took off his hard hat and replaced it with the guard's helmet. He peeled off the boilersuit to reveal a shirt that was the same as the driver's. His back was to Ford, but when he took off the hat Ford noted short dark hair matted with sweat. He was a thin man, of similar build to the driver. Before climbing into the driver's seat he took off his work gloves and Ford saw he was wearing tight-fitting leather driving gloves underneath.

The other two men gave their guns to Stopwatch and jogged into the vault. They reappeared with a bar each, which they laid on the floor in the back of the van. One of them made a second trip and all four bars were loaded. After retrieving their weapons they walked over to Werran, Petkovic and the driver and levelled their guns at them.

'Get up!' said Stopwatch.

The three men staggered to their feet and were jostled into the vault. The guard was still unconscious on the gold-room floor, and the two armed men grabbed his ankles and dragged him to join the others. Ford turned to watch as the men in boilersuits closed the vault door and turned the steel handle, which made a solid click as the lock engaged. He knew there was a vent into the vault so they wouldn't suffocate, but he was thinking about why he'd been left outside.

'Up!' yelled Stopwatch.

Ford went to move, but he was stopped by the pain in his chest and back. The kicking had winded him, but it felt as if it may have cracked a rib as well. The two men in white hats grabbed him under the armpits, dragged him to his feet, and then threw him into the back of the van. There, Ford curled up into the foetal position again and tried to catch his breath. There was still a stabbing pain in his side and he realised he was lying on the gold bars laid out on the floor. He pulled himself up onto the bench at the side and tried to sit upright to relieve the pressure on his ribs.

The two men in white hats had disappeared from sight. Stopwatch climbed into the rear of the van and closed both doors behind him. He secured them with the long flat steel bolts, one above and one below the two small windows in the doors, and sat on the bench opposite Ford, ignoring him. Again he checked his stopwatch, and then unzipped his boilersuit and slipped the pistol inside. For some time he stared at the door to the internal secure compartment. Ford followed his gaze. There was no sign of movement through the small wired glass window in the door.

Ford's thoughts strayed to the man on the other side. He too must be sitting in fear, trying to picture what would happen next; or perhaps, like Ford, he was forcing such thoughts from his mind. If he had a phone he would have used it by now. The nearest police were in Leonora, sixty minutes away; in any case, Ford doubted local country cops would take on an armed gang. There would be an armed response unit in Kalgoorlie, but they were three and a half hours away by road. Even by chopper—assuming they had one ready to go—they would take an hour to intercept the van, and Ford thought that whatever was planned would happen in the next thirty minutes.

He heard the roller door rattling open, and then the van start up. They rolled forward. As they passed out of the building into the mid-morning desert sunlight, the brightness made him squint.

He watched the roller door close behind them, then the outer gate. The two other men appeared from around the side of the building and walked behind the van as it went through the gate. They then cut off diagonally, out of sight of the rear window. Ford turned to watch them through the side window. They were walking towards the two low-loaders he'd noticed earlier. One of them carried a black canvas bag over his shoulder, and its bulky shape suggested it held their weapons.

Ford put his face up to the small window and squinted left and right. He expected to see a few of the emergency response crew trying to find where the alarm had been triggered. A crowd of men were standing over by the offices at the emergency muster point. They were all looking casually in the direction of the van as it drove slowly across the yard. Some of the people from the offices had brought their coffee cups with them and were chatting. Mostly they looked bored. They probably thought the alarm was a drill. Ford thought about trying to signal out the window but remembered the van glass was mirrored.

The two men on foot had split up and each was heading to one of the low-loaders. As the armoured van passed out of the yard and turned onto the road, Ford moved to the rear window and watched the low-loaders start up and pull into line behind them. The van didn't seem to be picking up any speed; it just bumped along at a relaxed pace. A kilometre further down this road Ford knew they would reach the gatehouse and the barrier.

He looked back across at Stopwatch, who continued to pay him no attention. He was holding a mobile phone and his thumb moved over the pad. Ford suspected that whoever the text was being sent to would be waiting on the other side of the gatehouse.

He took a good look at Stopwatch and tried to take an inventory. When he'd been standing in front of Ford, holding a pistol to his head, they had been the same height, six foot exactly. He held himself upright and, broader than Ford in the shoulder and chest, looked like he kept in shape. All Ford could see of his face behind the respirator, the mirrored glasses and the hard hat were his ears and forehead. His skin was pale, and his hair, as much as could be seen, was straight and dark. His ears were small and had no lobes. In the left ear Ford noticed two piercings, which looked enlarged and elongated, as if he usually wore heavy studs. In front of his ears Ford could see the start of sideburns behind the straps to his respirator. Scanning his clothing, Ford recognised the boilersuit as the same style they kept in the stores at the mine, as was the red hard hat. The hat looked new, but the boilersuit was slightly faded and had been worn before. Stopwatch's boots were the same brand as Ford's but a couple of sizes larger. They were scuffed. His gloves were also the same type issued on site, and were new and clean.

The van slowed and Ford knew they must be at the gate. They stopped briefly and then moved off. Out of the rear window he watched the low-loader behind them stop at the gate. The driver leaned out of the window and swiped a security card, and then the gate lifted and the truck pulled away. The guard at the gate waved casually to the driver as he passed.

The gravel road that left the guardhouse stretched out straight to the horizon, where it joined the highway. The whole of the road was visible from the guardhouse, so Ford knew that in a few more minutes they would be out of sight and onto the blacktop.

He tried to recall Stopwatch's voice. He had been the only one to speak: the other three had communicated with gestures. The accent had been Australian, but Ford didn't think he could identify any regional accent, if there was such a thing, and this man's voice was neither refined nor coarse. He was completely anonymous.

The van swung left onto the bitumen highway and headed south. This would take them to Leonora, and towards any police response. Ford worked through possible options for their next move, and couldn't think of any that looked good for him.

He looked down at his hands and stroked the long scar that ran the full length of his index finger. It sparked a memory. It was on a stretch of road like this, late at night in his first year in Australia, that he'd swerved to avoid a kangaroo and left the highway. The car had veered into the ditch beside the road and flipped. He'd come round hanging upside down in his seat-belt. He remembered the sense of dislocation, and he had that same feeling now. In the crash his flailing arm had smashed the windscreen and the glass had carved open the back of his hand. His forehead had been cut on the steering wheel. Adrenaline had flooded his system and he'd been surprised by how calm he felt. He had crawled out of the car, and opened the boot to retrieve his flashlight. A passing road-train driver had seen the car's tail-lights in the ditch and stopped to pick him up. Ford couldn't remember his own name, or where he was going, but he felt relaxed. He had sat in the cab of the truck and looked at the blood and torn flesh on his hand, and felt no pain.

One of the low-loaders overtook them and pulled out ahead, while the second one dropped further back. The country passing by outside the small windows was flat and featureless, red dirt spotted with mulga and saltbush. There were some rock outcrops to the east, but otherwise the road receded behind them as a straight black line across the desert.

Ford looked again at the man opposite. He still didn't seem to want to acknowledge Ford's presence and was motionless except for occasionally glancing at the stopwatch. Through the window behind the man's head Ford could see a salt lake stretching west several kilometres. The road was built up on a causeway. There was a patch of water in the centre of the lake—the remnants of winter rain, a mirror reflecting the sky. It was circled by a ring of white salt.

The water reminded Ford of the beach, and he couldn't think of the ocean without picturing his daughter, Grace. He closed his eyes and her face appeared, lit by sunshine, her golden hair awry and matted with salt water, her blue eyes gazing into his. Her expression was quizzical, and he had no excuse for his stupidity. He knew that he had failed her, and it now seemed there would be no opportunity to put things right. He would not get out of this. He would not get back to her.

THREE

Ten minutes after turning onto the highway, Stopwatch reached inside his boilersuit. Ford held his breath, but the man withdrew a two-way radio not much larger than a phone. He extended the aerial and adjusted the controls, then spoke into it. 'Alpha One, this is Mobile Three, over.'

There was a hiss of static, the radio turned up loud over the rumble of the van, and a voice replied, 'This is Alpha One, over.'

'Alpha One, this is Mobile Three, be advised we're at Papa Zulu. Confirm visual, over.'

'Mobile Three, affirmative, visual confirmed. We're ten klicks north of your position and closing, over.'

'One, do we have company? Over.'

'Three, you're clear south and two trucks approaching from north, estimate ten minutes, over.'

'Bring her in.'

'Wilco.'

'All mobile units, disperse, out.'

Ford turned to look out of the rear of the van. The low-loader rig was now a long way behind them and had pulled off the road. He watched as it turned in a wide arc across both lanes of the highway and stopped, blocking the full width of the road. The rig had kicked up a cloud of red dust, which swirled into the sky behind it and was whipped into sharp eddies as a plane flew through it only a dozen metres above the road. The twin propellers carved a path through the cloud and large spirals flicked off the wing tips.

Ford watched small puffs of smoke spit out from under the plane's tyres as they touched the bitumen. He heard the roar as its engines reversed. The armoured van was still moving, but the plane was travelling faster and the gap between them closed rapidly until he could see the pilot. It was a small twin-engined Piper Aztec; Ford had travelled on similar four-seaters on charters to remote mine sites. As the plane came closer he saw that the pilot's face was hidden behind sunglasses and a wrap-around microphone and shaded by a baseball cap.

A phone rang in the van and Stopwatch again reached into his boilersuit, this time bringing out a mobile. He read a message on the screen and then pulled out the radio. 'All units, Leonora police are mobile,' he said. 'Repeat, Leonora mobile. Fifteen minutes mark.'

Ford felt the van slow as the plane got closer, and they decelerated together until they came to a stop only twenty metres apart. When he turned away from the window to look at the man opposite, he found the gun pointed at him again. Stopwatch opened the rear door of the van and, with a sweeping wave of the gun, indicated to Ford to get out.

As he stepped down, Ford squinted in the bright sun and felt the heat of it on his shoulders. The plane hadn't killed its engines, and Stopwatch made no attempt to speak over the noise. Ford felt cold steel pressing into the back of his neck. He followed the direction of the nudges and walked around to the shaded side of the van, where the muzzle of the gun pushed his face against the vehicle's hot metal panelling.

The van's front door opened and the driver got out, still wearing the guard's helmet, his face hidden behind the dust mask and sunglasses. His AK was in one hand and in the other he carried the guard's revolver, which he handed across to Stopwatch. Ford heard a metallic click, and then the rattle as the cylinder of the revolver was spun and snapped back. He closed his eyes and waited.

Nothing happened. He opened his eyes and turned his head to see both men walking around to the back of the van and out of view. The plane was still sitting with its engines running, the pilot flicking switches in the overhead panel. It was nose-on to Ford and he couldn't see any markings. With the armed men out of sight, he took a few steps backwards to spot the aircraft registration on the side, but it had been crudely painted over, and the rest of the fuselage appeared to have been recently resprayed plain white, the finish uneven.

Behind the plane, in the distance, the low-loader was still parked across the road. A motorcycle was halfway between it and the plane, travelling towards him. The sun was behind it, and in the heat haze shimmering off the bitumen the bike was a silhouette hovering above the road. Ford turned to look in the opposite direction and saw the second low-loader blocking the road at a similar distance and another bike approaching. He remembered the tarps he had seen on the truck beds: he had assumed they were covering mine equipment. The second bike was closer, and Ford made it out as a tall off-road machine with large panniers front and rear. The rider had changed his boilersuit for black fatigues and a full-face helmet.

Ford scanned around him. The gravel shoulder of the road dropped away steeply, sloping down to the salt lake. There was no water at the edge, but it looked wet and soft. It ended near the truck to the north, where the shoreline rose slowly until it became bare red gravel with a few scrubby bushes that would offer no cover, even if he could run that far in the open. He edged to the front of the van to look across the road. The embankment was as steep on that side, but the desert rose gently away from the road and the scrub was denser. In the middle distance was a low hill with a rock outcrop. He doubted he could run that far without getting picked off, and even if he made the cover of the rocks, the dirt bikes would run him down. Returning to the side of the van, he pushed his forehead against the metal and stayed still.

Stopwatch and the driver came out of the van, each carrying a gold bar. They walked slowly past the wing tip and disappeared around the far side of the plane where, Ford knew, the rear door was. They returned at a jog and repeated the trip with two more bars, and then disappeared into the van again. The two dirt bikes had now arrived, and the men dismounted, the big one with the shotgun slung across his back and the short man with the AK strapped tight across his chest. Ignoring Ford, they looked in through the back doors of the van. Then they turned and ran past him, slid down the embankment and lay face down on the sloping gravel. The other two men burst out of the van and flung themselves down the slope as well.

Ford was still considering whether to dive after them when the explosive inside the van detonated, the pressure wave rippling the wall of the van and knocking him backwards off his feet down the embankment. By the time he had gathered himself, the other four men were on their feet scrambling towards the van. Ford crawled after them, then stayed down on his hands and knees at the side of the road, watching.

From the outside the vehicle didn't appear damaged, except for a few bulges in the wall panels and roof. A small cloud of white smoke blew out from between the open rear doors. They had blown the internal door to the strongbox. Ford thought about the guard inside.

The four men went into the van one at a time, each coming out with a gold bar and walking it over to the plane. That meant all eight bars taken from the vault were loaded, and they were done.

Three men remained by the plane while Stopwatch walked back towards Ford with the guard's revolver in his hand. This was it. Ford considered putting the van between them, but that wouldn't buy him much time. He looked again at the rocks in the distance, but his ribs still ached from the kicking and his head was ringing from the explosion. He doubted he could even start to run.

His mouth was dry. He had to make up his mind how to think about this, how to accept it. He tried to picture the movement of the gun, the hammer arching back, the cylinder slowly turning. Waiting for the release, for the end of things, he was surprised to feel relief.

He tried to imagine the darkness, but instead found himself thinking of the sunlight in her hair. And then it came to him that he had someone to get back to. She was all that stood between him and death.

He made himself take a deep breath and let it out slowly. There was only one place left to go.

FOUR

Stopwatch was still ten metres away when Ford pushed himself to his feet and ran in a crouch for the back of the van. He threw himself inside and turned to close the doors. Stopwatch raised the gun to fire, and Ford pulled the first door towards him, flattening himself behind it. When a bullet punched through the door a hand's breadth from his head, he discovered the rear compartment wasn't armoured. Ducking low, he reached for the other door, and pulled it closed as a second and third round came through the door. He slid the bottom bolt across. As he reached for the upper bolt he looked out of the rear window.

The three men who had stayed by the plane were now sprinting towards the van, fanning out and unslinging their weapons. Stopwatch was still walking calmly towards him with the revolver raised. He saw the muzzle flash and the glass in front of him cracked. The fifth bullet ripped through the door and he felt a hot stab in his shoulder. He looked down to see a tear in his shirt with blood blooming around it.

Ford dropped down onto the floor of the van as the other three men opened up. The AKs punched lines of holes through the sides of the van and a shotgun blast peppered the rear doors. They were aiming high. Ford crawled on his belly down the narrow gap between the bench seats towards the armoured compartment. A second burst of automatic fire hit the van. This time they were aiming low, but Ford was protected by two toolboxes that had been pushed under the benches on the other side.

Halfway down the van was the partition to the armoured compartment. Its door hung open, ripped, buckled and scorched where the locks had been blown, but still attached by its top hinge. Ford crawled inside the compartment and pulled the door behind him with his foot. The guard lay slumped sideways in the far corner, his knees to his chest and his head down. Ford couldn't see his face, but he saw the trail of blood from his ear. He was younger than Ford had expected, his face boyish and his hair long and sunbleached. There were shredded pages of a book scattered around the compartment, and Ford wondered how long it had been since he left school. He wasn't sure if the man was dead or unconscious.

A third burst of gunfire hit the van and Ford heard it ricochet off the partition. He tried to calculate how long he might be safe here if they had any more explosives. They wouldn't wait around trying to get to him, he knew: they'd want to get themselves and the plane out of here as soon as possible.

Vibration through the floor told him that the van's engine had started. There was a small window into the cab and he risked a glance. Stopwatch was in the driver's seat. Ford felt the van lurch into reverse and turn. Stopwatch was getting it off the road to clear the way for the plane, Ford assumed. It swung ninety degrees and then he was thrown backwards as it tipped over the edge of the road and down the embankment. As the van hit the bottom of the slope and ploughed into the salt lake he was slammed against the compartment wall.

He pulled himself upright and looked out of the side window. The three other men stood in a line at the top of the slope with their guns levelled. Ford again threw himself flat against the sloping floor of the van as the rounds hit, but then realised they couldn't penetrate the strongbox. He pulled himself up once more and put his face to the window.

One of the motorcycles was still in his field of vision. The man with the shotgun ran to it and lifted a plastic jerry can off the rear pannier. They had no more explosives, it seemed, so they were going to burn him.

The man scrambled down the slope and then his shadow moved around the front of the van. Ford smelled the petrol and, soon after, the smoke. If he had poured the fuel over the sides of the van, Ford knew, it would soon burn itself out, but if it was over the scrub grass under the van and over the tyres and the seats in the cab he wouldn't have long before it ignited the fuel tank. He smelled burning rubber.

Looking through the window, he could see the two men mounting their dirt bikes. The other two would be leaving on the plane, he guessed. The pitch of the plane engines increased. All he could see was the nearest wing tip; it started to move and he switched to the other side of the van to watch it disappear down the road and then lift into view. The whole plane came into sight as it rose off the road. As soon as it was airborne it banked steeply and headed off low to the west.

The bikes headed north along the road. When they reached the end of the salt lake they ran down the bank and headed west along the shoreline in the same direction as the plane, soon disappearing into the scrub.

Ford nudged the guard, who didn't respond. He felt the man's neck for a pulse but couldn't find one. He pushed open the partition door and slid down the floor to the rear doors, drew back the bolts and kicked them, but they wouldn't open. Peering out through the shattered windows he saw that the van was buried in the salt lake to a level above the rear fender and the doors were wedged shut by the muddy salt. A milky sludge was oozing under the door. He put his hands flat on the door to push and then quickly snatched them back. It was too hot to touch.

Smoke was seeping into the rear compartment and Ford coughed. He looked around to see where the smoke was coming from and noticed a gap in the wall where it joined the strongbox partition. The explosives had blown the weld along the wall and the two sheets of metal had parted. Ford saw his chance.

He pulled the two toolboxes out from under the benches and opened them. One was empty, but the other had what he'd hoped for: a tyre lever and a small flat hydraulic jack. He scurried up to the middle of the van, thrust the tyre lever into the gap in the wall panel and leaned into it. The gap widened and he could see daylight. The wall of the armoured compartment was thick plate steel, but the adjoining panel of the rear compartment was lighter, and when he thumped it with his fist he saw it move. He worked the tyre lever along the seam, opening it like a can of beans, and then levered open the gap until it was wide enough to jam the jack through.

The jack had a hand winder, and he started cranking. The smoke was thick and black now, but he could still see what he was doing. The smoke burned his throat and he coughed, tasting the burning rubber. His head throbbed, his ears were ringing, and the wound on his shoulder burned, but he thought only of the fuel tank and how long it would take for the fire to reach it.

As the jack widened the gap, the weld on either side split and the side of the van opened like a zipper. When the jack reached its full extension the gap looked big enough for his head and shoulders. He lay down on the bench and put one arm through the gap and forced his head through. The sun blazed directly into his face, its heat indistinguishable from the hot steel and the smoke from the burning tyres. Kicking against the bench with his feet, he inched himself out until his fingers found purchase on the outside of the van. Then he pulled himself forward, twisting his shoulders as they went through the gap, the jagged edge of the steel scraping the bullet wound. No adrenaline could mask the pain and he let out a scream.

With his head and shoulders out of the van, he twisted and squirmed, but the gap wasn't big enough for his chest. He braced one knee against the wall and pushed, and kicked his other leg until his foot wedged against something firm. He exhaled as much as he could to flatten his chest and gave it everything.

The raw edge of the wall panel scraped down his back and he could feel his shirt tearing, but he was moving. One more push and his chest was clear. His feet found the end of the bench and he pushed his hips out and fell into the scorched grass of the embankment. He felt the burning through his shirt and yelled again.

An acrid smell reached his nostrils, more pungent than the smell of gasoline. It was sharp and sulphurous, and he recognised it as burning hair. He looked at his arm and saw that its hairs were opaque yellow. Then he felt the stinging on his scalp, and slapped the palm of his hand on his head to pat down the tufts of burning hair. He rolled sideways until he felt the heat subside from his shirt, and lay on his side coughing into the dirt.

As soon as he'd caught his breath, he started crawling up the bank. When he reached the road he remained on his hands and knees, coughing, his chest in spasm and pain searing his ribs. The roar of an explosion engulfed him, a rush of heat hit his back and he turned to see a wall of flame engulf the van. The fuel tank had ruptured. He hauled himself to his feet and staggered to the far side of the road.

Crouching, Ford looked around. Most of the van was out of sight down the embankment; only the roof of the cab, and a rising column of smoke edged with flame, was visible. A road train was now pulled up behind the low-loader to the north. He scanned the sky to the west, but the plane was gone. Then he looked for a sign of the bikes, expecting to see a cloud of dust on the far side of the salt pan, but there was nothing. They couldn't have got too far away. He hoped they weren't somewhere nearby watching the fire.

A burst of gunfire answered his question. A cloud of dust rose from the edge of the lake and the buzz-saw noise of motorcycle engines cut through the ringing in his ears. They were four hundred metres from him and travelling fast.

'Oh, for fuck's sake!' he groaned, then turned and ran towards the outcrop.

The rocks were a hundred metres away uphill, and the bikes had to travel four times that distance to the road. Right now he figured he was at the limit of their guns' range, but the causeway was between him and the bikes, and they wouldn't see him again until they reached the road. If he could get among the low bush in time, he might be able to keep out of sight.

He ran. His lungs burned from the smoke, his ribs ached, and he thought his left leg might give way. He pumped his arms, concentrating on lifting his knees, keeping his eyes on the low line of saltbush ahead and listening for the bike engines. Just as he reached the bushes his left knee buckled and he sprawled in the dust.

'Get up, you daft bastard!' he muttered. 'You're not going to let yourself die out here.'

He got up and ran on, but his leg was cramping. He was fifty metres into the bush before a burst of gunfire came from behind him and he heard a bullet career off a nearby boulder. He looked back. The men had reached the causeway, their bikes silhouetted against the sky. There was another burst of fire and he turned and ran to a small stand of bottlebrush, where he stood panting, doubled up against the trunk of a tree. He felt safer among the trees until another volley shredded the trunk, wood splinters peppering his neck.

Looking down, he realised he was still in his site clothes—a high-visibility fluoro-yellow shirt, blackened and torn but the reflective safety strips still intact. The sun was now high in the sky and he would be glinting like a signal mirror. One more dash and he could be among the rocks. He ran. Two more bursts followed him, chopping up the dirt around his feet as he weaved between the trees. Ahead he saw a sandy depression behind a broad boulder: he threw himself towards it face down and lay there for a few seconds, blowing hard into the dirt.

He crawled forward until he found a gap in the rocks that gave him a view back to the road. The two riders were still side by side on the causeway, talking with their heads close together so they could hear each other through their helmets. Ford turned to look behind him and saw the bigger outcrop of rocks further up the hill. The men would be coming after him soon, and although they would be slowed by the sand and the trees, it wouldn't take them long to run him down. The rocks held the chance of a cave or an overhang where he could hide to buy himself some time. Recalling the close attention Stopwatch had paid to the time, he figured they wouldn't be able to risk staying here much longer.

Just then he heard three long blasts on a truck horn, and looked to the northern roadblock. The cab door of the road train was open and Ford could see the driver above the door. He stood with one arm on the roof of the cab and one on top of the door, leaning at a strange angle as if he was working the horn with his knee. Ford thought the driver must be looking at the van on fire, the column of black smoke now high enough to be visible to the horizon. He would have seen the two bikes, but Ford didn't know whether he had seen the gunfire.

The two riders looked towards the truck. One checked his watch. They looked back towards Ford, but he knew he was well hidden now. They shook their heads and revved their bikes, then turned and took off west.

Ford slumped down into the shade of the rock, sucking air. He rested his forehead against the cool sand, waiting for his ears to stop buzzing.

FIVE

He stayed low behind the rocks in the shade until his heart rate had dropped and the sound of the bikes had faded. Then he crawled back to the gap and looked towards the road. A plume of smoke still rose from the van. There was no wind and the smoke was climbing in a straight column. The driver from the road train stood in the middle of the road, a tiny figure two kilometres away, keeping a safe distance from the van. He turned slowly and scanned the desert in Ford's direction, his hand shading his eyes in the sun.

Ford checked his watch. The face was smashed and it had stopped at just past nine. That was three hours since he had stood watching the sun rise, trying to find a way to avoid what had just happened. He asked himself whether he could have done more to prevent it. He wasn't sure he had done much at all.

He listened again for the bikes, but heard nothing beyond the drone of flies and the thumping of the blood in his ears. He sat looking at the broken watch. It had been a gift from Diane, the only time she'd bought him something expensive. Soon after that she was pregnant and they'd agreed not to spend money on each other. He undid the strap and threw it over the rocks.

He tried to picture what would happen next. If the guard in the armoured compartment had been carrying a satellite phone or had triggered an emergency transmitter, the security company was probably alerted as soon as the men walked into the gold room. Its staff would be able to track the van. The robbery team would have known the response time for the police by helicopter and car and, as Ford had seen, they had been alerted by phone when the Leonora police mobilised. That meant they had a spotter outside the station, and it was likely they had people watching at the airport in Kalgoorlie to advise when the police were alerted. The men on the bikes would have stayed until the plane had taken off, but left themselves with enough time to get a head start across country before the police arrived. Ford had slowed them down by locking himself in the van, and those few minutes had been crucial.

He wondered how long it would be before the police arrived, and what he should do when they did. They would know from the men at Gwardar that he had been in the van; if they didn't find him there, they would assume that he had either left with the others or was still in the vicinity, breathing or not. He thought again of what the trucker had seen.

Ford considered returning to the road and waiting for the police, and tried to calculate how long they would keep him in custody while they pieced together evidence from the mine and from the van. Then he added the time to get statements from the men who'd been locked in the vault, and for forensics to examine the guard cremated in the van, but his mind wandered to what might happen to Grace during that time. Standing up, he turned his back on the van and started walking.

He kept the rocks between him and the van and was soon over the crest of the low ridge. Stumbling down the far side he turned south and struck out on a course parallel to the road but hidden from it by the rocks. He took a bearing from his shadow and picked another outcrop of rocks ahead. They would be high enough to give him a view of the road and by then he might have an idea of his next move.

He tried to increase his pace to a jog, but a stabbing pain in his ribs forced him to stop and breathe hard. A coughing fit racked him and he doubled over. He remembered the kicking he'd been given in the gold room. His breathing was laboured, his lungs still choked with smoke, and pain was building in his head and his shoulder, a sign that the adrenaline from the chase was wearing off. His knuckles were grazed and bloodied from scraping against the jagged metal as he'd pulled himself from the van. The rest of his body must bear similar cuts. He would have time to look at them later. The ache behind his eyes was a combination of the explosion and the smoke he'd inhaled, now made worse by the sun beating on the back of his head. He had no hat, no sunglasses and no water. Pushing on at a brisk walk and trying to put some distance between himself and the van, he concentrated on putting one foot in front of the other and tried to ignore the pain.

A cloud of flies collected around him as he walked: fearless, slow-moving bush blowflies that settled on his face, seeking the moisture at the corners of his mouth and eyes. They crawled across his hands searching for blood. Waving them away, he kept walking, his eyes focused on the scuffed toes of his boots, raising his head every few minutes to check his direction.

As the ground started rising towards the rocks, the yellow spinifex got higher. His thoughts turned to snakes. He didn't want to escape the guns and then die a lonely, stupid death from a bite. He didn't want to end his life here, in this place, in the quiet brightness.

He rested in the shade of a twisted blackbutt and scanned the rocky ground for a fallen branch. Finding one long enough to reach from the ground to his shoulder and strong enough to lean on, he broke off the twigs until he'd made a crude staff. He set off again, beating the grass ahead of him. Sweat ran down his forehead, and when it reached his eyes he wiped it off with the back of his hand. His hand came away smeared with blood. Another wound he didn't remember collecting.

His breathing became laboured again as the slope increased, but it was only a short climb and he hoped to find some shade among the red outcrop of rocks on the crest. His mouth was dry.

The rocks when he reached them were smaller than they had looked from a distance. There was no shade, but he wedged himself into a sandy gap between the two largest boulders. From there he took in the view to the west. The hill wasn't high, no more than twenty metres above the road, but it was the tallest point in the landscape and offered a view down the road in both directions. The road passed two hundred metres from him, through a broad gap between his hill and a lower one on the far side. He reckoned he had been walking for over forty minutes, which would put him about five klicks south of the van.

It was an unfamiliar vista. For all the time Ford had spent at the mine, he had never driven in on this road. He was always fly-in, fly-out: dropping out of the sky onto the airstrip in an air-conditioned turboprop, an hour's flying time from Perth. The flight had masked the mine's isolation.

The desert scrub spread out all around him, a broad red circle reaching from horizon to horizon, bisected by the road, so flat and bare that he could sense the curvature of the earth. In all the expanse of land he could see he doubted there were more than a handful of people, and he knew he was the only one on foot. Nature had put nothing in this landscape except gold. No mountains, no valleys, no rain and no rivers.

The road was an unbroken line receding north to his past

and the mine, and stretching out south between Ford and his future: between him and Grace.

There was no traffic on the road to the north. He could make out a pale strip across the road in the distance, which he took to be the second low-loader forming the roadblock. A thin spiral of black smoke arrowed downwards to indicate the position of the van. In the other direction, however, he could see two vehicles approaching from the south, their headlights visible even in daylight, both with blue and red flashing lights on their roofs. He tried to gauge their speed, but they were too far away. He lay on his belly and waited for them.

They passed him quietly, without sirens, just the rushing wind as they cut the air along the road. Two Land Cruisers, each with a driver. Two officers from Leonora.

Ford sat up and leaned his back against the rock. He looked at the blood on his knuckles, now mixed with red dust and streaks of black soot. He twisted his wedding ring and picked at the dried blood caught underneath it, and the flies took the opportunity to crawl across his fingers and probe the cuts. He shook his hands but the flies hung on, so he tried to brush them away. At the last moment they would rise quickly, and then drop back to the same spot. He passed a hand over his scalp. His hair was matted with sweat, scorched and sticky in places. He winced as his fingers found several deep scratches on the top of his head. Both sleeves of his shirt were torn and dark with blood from his shoulder. One leg of his jeans was ripped across the knee, and he pulled apart the fabric to find a deep gouge just above the joint with threads embedded in it. He unbuttoned his shirt. There was a broad purple bruise across the rib cage on his right side, some of it already black. He walked his fingers slowly across each rib, applying pressure till he cried out. They were bruised but he didn't think any were broken. He laid his fingertips gently on the cut in his shoulder where the bullet had clipped him. His wounds lay open to the kisses of the flies and the sun.

He felt in his jeans pockets, then fished around in the breast pocket of his shirt and emptied their contents on the flat rock in front of him. His wallet held two twenty-dollar notes, his driver's licence, a bank card, a credit card and a scrap of paper with the names of some racehorses on it. There were four coins, which brought his wealth to forty-four dollars, plus a disposable lighter, a crushed packet of cigarettes, and a pair of reading glasses with one lens cracked and an arm hanging loose. His mine ID card was missing. He could feel something deep in his hip pocket, digging into his groin. It was the brass key to the safe. Turning it over in his hand, he thought of the trouble it had unlocked. He dug a hole in the sand with his fingers, threw in the key and put a stone on top of it.

He checked his wallet one last time and under a leather flap found a small photograph of Grace. She was smiling into the camera, squinting in the sun. They had been at the park, and Grace sat at the highest point of the climbing frame, waving triumphantly. He recalled the day clearly, because it was the last time he could remember when they were still a family. Diane had been away on her first long trip to Indonesia, and he had taken Grace for a day at the park. When she'd finished posing for the picture, she had followed an older boy to the end of the climbing-frame platform and watched him as he slipped through a gap in the handrail and leapt into space. The drop would have been three metres, and he landed safely in the sand and went into a roll. It looked like a move he had practised before. Ford still had his attention on the camera or he would have recognised the look in Grace's eyes as she passed through the gap in the railing.

He lifted his head just as she launched herself. He watched her fall, her arms spread wide, her hair blown up above her head. She landed stiff-legged in the sand and fell backwards;

Ford heard the thump as her head met the edge of the concrete path. He ran and scooped her up before she started to cry, and when he saw the blood on the back of her head he carried on running. He ran all the way to the car, and in five minutes they were in Casualty.

At first Grace had sobbed quietly, but when the doctor touched the cut on her head she started screaming and kicking. The doctor and a nurse wrapped her in a sheet to restrain her, and Ford squeezed her in his arms to keep her still while they cut the hair away from the wound, then glued the sides of the gash together and dressed it. He could remember the look in her eyes. She had been angry rather than upset, furious at her loss of freedom and at the doctor. It wasn't the first time he had encountered her defiance.

Diane came home two days later to find her daughter with a strange new haircut and a dressing taped to the back of her head. That had started the argument that ended it all.

Ford opened the cigarette packet and emptied it. All of the cigarettes were crushed, ripped or broken in pieces. One was almost complete except for the filter. He pulled a few loose strands of tobacco from the torn end, put it in his mouth and lit it. He noticed that his hands were shaking. His mouth was so dry that he struggled to form a seal around the end. When the smoke hit his lungs, he fought the urge to cough and held it down. He closed his eyes and felt the buzz hit his bloodstream, imagined it coursing through his body to each site of pain.

He reckoned the cops would have reached the van by now, and tried to guess how long it might be before they cleared the trucks from the road and allowed traffic to pass. He was still about eighty kilometres from Leonora, with no settlements or water between, and Kalgoorlie was another two hundred beyond that. He wouldn't be able to walk all that way in his current state and without food or water. His best chance would be to hitch a ride south at the first opportunity, before the police started looking for him. Traffic going south would have already gone past the van and the police, but while any driver on this road would stop if he saw another car broken down by the side of the road, a man on his own, away from his vehicle, was odd. He was alone, enveloped in the monstrous silence of the desert. Free and alone, without assistance and without excuse.

A shadow passed over him and Ford flinched. He scrambled onto his knees and looked for cover, conscious that he was out in the open in a reflective shirt. He had heard nothing approach— maybe the plane was too high. Squinting up towards the sun he caught a shape moving, but couldn't make it out in the brightness. It banked and dived; as it came lower, he recognised the shape as a wedge-tailed eagle. After circling around him it glided gently down to the road, fanning its tail and angling its wings. It landed on a dark streak on the road, the putrefied carcass of a dead kangaroo. Two crows that had been tugging at the roo flapped their wings in half-hearted defiance and hopped away. One rose cawing into the air and flew in a wide arc towards Ford. He watched it as it landed on the rock above him and cocked its head, staring at him from one black eye. Ford held its gaze.

He remembered a creation myth he had read in one of Grace's picture books, a story from the Wongutha people of the local area, of how the salt lakes in this part of the desert were formed from the dried tears of the crows, crying over their loneliness. As he looked at the fathomless eye of the crow he couldn't imagine anything bringing it to tears.

'I'm not dead yet,' he said. 'Shoo, ya bastard!'

The crow let out a long falling cry, ruffling the feathers at its throat and stretching its neck towards Ford. It hopped off the rock, plunged and swooped back down to the road and landed on its shadow. It walked slowly around the eagle, waiting for an opportunity to rip at the blackened carrion.

Ford stubbed out the last of the cigarette and found half a cigarette in the dirt with the filter still attached. He lit it and felt a sudden lightness. It wasn't just the effects of the smoke this time, it was a feeling of elation. He remembered this feeling from before, from when he was a kid, touched by the solitude and the proximity to infinite things. Closing his eyes he turned his face to the sun. He felt the heat on his eyelids, the hot breeze stroking his cheek. A strange intensity burned within him, and he had the impression that, for the first time since childhood, he was now seeing objects clearly. Life was suddenly there, and he was in it.

The sun was overhead and the light was so strong that it bleached the colour from the desert. He smoked, watching the birds squabbling and tearing at the roo, until all three raised their heads and looked up the road. Ford followed their gaze and saw the road train approaching. It was the same driver he had seen leaning on his horn, and he was followed by a small convoy of cars and utes, the first to be let through the roadblock.

Ford lay down on his stomach as they passed, waiting to pick his ride. A few lone cars followed at increasingly large intervals. None of them suited Ford. They were mostly haulage vehicles, or mining company utes with short-wave antennas mounted on the bull bars. The traffic thinned so that he could only see one car on the road at a time between him and the distant point where the road disappeared into the heat haze.

The tenth vehicle travelling south looked like a solid bet. A ute moving slowly, no aerials, no bull bars, no lights on the roof. All mining fleet vehicles were white, but this one looked a dirty orange, and old. It only had one working headlight shining towards him, and that decided it.

When it was still a kilometre away, he pulled himself up and slid down the slope. He stumbled through the scrub and up the shoulder of the road, then stood astride the white line, facing the oncoming ute with both hands raised. The sun was directly above him and he cast no shadow on the road. He saw the hood dip as the driver applied the brakes, and it came to a stop ten metres from him. It was an old Toyota, and Ford thought it might have been red once: it was difficult to tell what was sun-bleached paint and what was rust. It sat low on whatever was left of its suspension and the dust on the windscreen was so thick he couldn't make out the driver.

Both side windows were already open and Ford walked cautiously to the driver's door. There were three people sitting in the cab, shoulder to shoulder across the bench seat, black faces under baseball caps or beanies. In the tray sat two young Aboriginal men with a child wrapped in blankets, only a mop of ragged black hair visible.

The driver looked at Ford with sharp eyes but seemed in no hurry to speak. He looked to be the same age as Ford, his broad face framed by his hair, which hung in dreadlocks from his green knitted hat. His round belly stretched the material of his blue singlet and pressed against the steering wheel.

'Where you headed?' said Ford.

The driver didn't answer. The old woman next to him said something quietly, but Ford couldn't make it out, and wasn't sure if it was English or her own language.

'Can you take me to Kalgoorlie?'

The driver turned and looked at the old woman, who shrugged. Looking back at Ford, the driver nodded, and then tilted his head towards the tray. Ford went round the back, cocked a leg over the tailgate and winced as he pulled himself up. He tried not to put any pressure on his ribs as he went over, but mistimed it and fell, sprawling sideways into the well of the ute. He looked up to see the child laughing at him.

SIX

The ute moved slowly. Ford looked through the rear window into the cab to see the speedo, but the needle was stuck at zero. He wedged himself against the side of the tray well and tried to make himself comfortable, but the metal was hard and his bones ached. There was no suspension left and every jolt in the road sent a stabbing pain through his ribs. Despite the sun he felt cold, and wondered whether he was in delayed shock. There were a few bags and sacks scattered around the back, and Ford picked up a couple of coarse grey blankets and an old baseball cap.

He looked questioningly at the young guys and they nodded, so he balled up one blanket and placed it behind his back, wrapped the other around him and pulled the brim of the cap down low over his eyes to cut out the sun. He pulled his knees up to his chest and rested his head on them. The blanket smelled of campfire and stale sweat. Ford sniffed his own shirt. The sweat was fresh, but no more pleasant.

He felt someone nudging him and raised his head. The child was holding out a clear plastic bottle with an inch of water in the bottom. He could see now that it was a girl, not much older than Grace. Her brown eyes held no expression. Ford smiled at her as he took it, but her face remained impassive. He sipped at it slowly until it was empty. She pulled another bottle from inside a carrier bag and passed it to him. It was warm from sitting in the sun, but he took a long pull and swilled it round his mouth, then nodded silent thanks.

Between the three heads in the cab he could see along the road. He glanced up from time to time, looking out for roadblocks. The two men facing him sat motionless, their eyes locked on him.

'Where have you come from?' Ford asked.

The younger one extended an arm to the east and said a word that Ford didn't catch.

'My nan's country,' the other said.

If they had come from the east they might have been travelling on dirt roads and only joined the bitumen close to where they picked him up. They might not have passed the police. Ford allowed himself to relax a little.

The featureless desert bush didn't change as they passed through. Only two vehicles overtook them travelling south, and Ford counted only a dozen travelling north. Then, after half an hour of slow progress, he saw more flashing lights approaching fast. As they came closer he saw they belonged to an ambulance escorted by a patrol car. They passed in a rush of wind and Ford followed them until they disappeared from sight. Watching the road was hypnotic rather than monotonous.

Distance markers counted down the kilometres to Leonora, and Ford felt his heartbeat steadily increase as the numbers got smaller. The bush stopped when they reached the rail yards at the edge of the town, and the ute slowed down further as it passed the speed limit sign beside the first weatherboard houses.

The town wasn't much more than a single broad main street and a handful of side roads. There was a short row of shops and a pair of handsome pubs, colonial relics from the gold rush that had been recently restored, but the street was deserted. The ute crawled down the main street and Ford hunkered low, peering out from under the peak of the cap. He spotted a pair of public phone boxes next to the post office and thought about who he might call.

At the edge of town they pulled off into the roadhouse and rolled towards the shade of the canopy. The engine stalled as they came to a stop in front of the diesel pump. The driver got out and started filling the tank. Ford looked around nervously. There was only one other car getting fuel, and two parked up by the road-house. Two big rigs were pulled up around the corner. The drivers would be inside getting lunch. He saw the camera above the door of the roadhouse with a field of view across all the pumps.

Ford turned to look up the street and froze when he saw the police station directly across from the roadhouse. It was a modern building with a curved steel roof and a single glass door at the front. Ford couldn't see inside. To its left was a parking area, but it was hidden behind a solid steel security gate and he couldn't see how many vehicles were there.

'I'll be back soon. Got to make a call,' he said to nobody in particular and vaulted over the tailgate. He walked briskly up the street to the payphones, trying to look purposeful rather than shifty. Both phones were new, mounted on perforated steel booths, and they took credit cards. He slotted in his card and dialled Diane's number. It rang six times before going to her answer machine, so he hung up and tried her mobile number, which went straight to voicemail.

He dialled her office number, and it was picked up immediately. 'Walsh Bonner Associates, Michelle speaking.'

It hadn't bothered him before that Diane had used her maiden name for her business, but now it jarred.

'Is Diane in?'

'No, she's working from home today.'

'I just rang there, I got no reply.'

'Have you tried her email?'

'Not from here, no. When are you expecting her?'

The receptionist paused, and Ford heard the swish of paper moving. 'Her diary says she's travelling next week. You can contact her through the Jakarta office, although the phones may not be connected up there yet. Would you like me to give you the number?'

'Is Matthew Walsh there?'

'He flew up to Jakarta on Wednesday. Who's calling? Would you like to leave a message?'

'Do you know when Diane is due to fly?' said Ford.

'She's due in Jakarta next Wednesday, but may be going to remote sites soon after she arrives. If she can't get mobile phone coverage, then email would be the best way to contact her. Who's calling, please?'

Ford hung up. There had been a time when Diane was a geology postgrad putting together her thesis and he had been the nine-to-fiver paying the bills. It had taken her three years after getting her doctorate to exceed Ford's earnings, and she never acknowledged that fact until she became pregnant.

He tried to remember when he'd last seen her business partner. Matthew Walsh had been sitting at Diane's kitchen table six weeks previously, the last time she had let Ford take Grace out for the day. Walsh had thanked Ford for giving him and Diane the afternoon free to discuss expanding their practice into Indonesia. Ford had bit his lip and swallowed hard. Walsh was supposed to be a good geologist, better than Diane, with contacts at the university, but he didn't have the confidence to run his own practice. He'd needed Diane to find the clients and close the deals. Walsh was better looking than Ford, but shy enough not to realise it. He was tall, with smooth skin, a full head of hair and a floppy fringe that Ford had wanted to grab hold of.

Ford thought about walking into the police station and getting them to track down Grace and Diane. He couldn't think of
any way that he might still be a threat to the men with the gold,
but giving himself up felt like giving in. He pulled his card out
of the phone and walked back to the roadhouse. He decided he
would make his way to Perth, find his daughter, and never let
her out of his sight again.

The driver of the ute was leaning with his back against the
cab, staring into the middle distance.

'My name's Jack,' said Ford, holding out his hand. 'Thanks
for the lift.'

The other man's grip was firm. Ford saw him read the mining company logo on his shirt.

'I'm Donovan,' the guy said. Ford smiled, and Donovan
shrugged. 'I was born in the sixties. My mam was a big fan.'

'So do they call you Mellow Yellow?' asked Ford.

'Not if they want to ride in my truck. You got any money
for fuel, Jack?'

They walked together into the roadhouse. There were a
few tables to one side, and a couple of truckers eating off big
plates and watching a small TV screwed to the wall. The girl
behind the cash register raised her head from the magazine she
was reading and then leaned to one side to look past them at
their ute. She looked from Ford to Donovan, waiting for a sign
as to who was going to pay. Ford wondered how suspicious
he looked, blackened and sunburnt, bloody and torn, but then
reflected that his shirt was cleaner than the truckers'.

The girl wore a shirt with the name of the roadhouse
embroidered above the breast pocket, and a matching cap. When
she read the total from the register her accent sounded Irish, and
Ford thought it was a strange place for a backpacker to end up.
He asked for two packets of cigarettes and a new lighter.

'Me mam's run out of durries,' said Donovan.

The girl looked at Ford and he nodded.

'Me too,' said Donovan, as she reached for the drawer.

The girl raised her eyebrows. Ford nodded, and she took out a fourth packet.

'Maybe some lollies for the kids,' Donovan suggested.

Ford saw a shirt the same as the girl's hanging over the door, as well as caps and stubby holders. Next to the shirt was a security camera. He smiled into it. 'You got one of those shirts in large?' he asked.

She disappeared into the back room, then returned with the shirt. She punched it all into the register and Ford gave her his credit card.

When they got back to the ute, Ford stripped off his torn shirt and threw it in the garbage canister by the pump. As he pulled on the new one he caught Donovan looking at the bruises across his ribs, and the cuts across his arms and shoulders.

'You look like you been in an accident, but we didn't see no car,' Donovan said.

Ford looked away.

'You got trouble?'

Ford nodded. He watched Donovan's gaze swing across to the police station and then back. His face remained blank. 'Monarchs catch up with us all sooner or later, bro. Better get you to Kalgoorlie.'

Donovan got back in behind the wheel and started the engine, and waited for Ford to climb into the back. As they drove off, Ford watched the gate to the police station. It remained closed. After a hundred metres the town ended and the bush began again, and the distance markers started the countdown to Kalgoorlie.

For the first hour after leaving Leonora, Ford's eyes stayed on the road behind them, looking for flashing lights. Then he started looking ahead, waiting for roadblocks. The others in the tray were slumped against each other, asleep. They passed through Menzies and saw nobody. As they edged further south the bush started to get taller, with occasional stands of salmon gums as evidence of seasonal watercourses.

The first sign that they were close to Kalgoorlie was the smoke stack from the Gidji Roaster. It towered above the trees, a long streak of white smoke drifting east. The road ahead was blocked by two patrol cars, their lights turning. Two officers stood on the road, one holding a stop sign. There were no vehicles ahead of them, no way to turn off, and the police had a clear view down five kilometres of straight road. As the ute slowed, Ford hunched into the corner by the cab, drew the blanket around himself, pulled his cap down over his eyes and pretended to be asleep like the others.

When they came to a stop he strained to hear any conversation between the police and the cab, but there was none. They were on their way again almost immediately. As they picked up speed, Ford risked a glance back. Both officers had their backs to him and were looking at an oncoming van. He realised he had been holding his breath. When he let it out, it triggered a coughing fit that left him curled up on his side.

When he finally lifted his head he saw that they were on the edge of town, passing the spoil heaps. He banged on the roof of the cab, and Donovan's head appeared out of the open window.

Ford leaned out to be heard. 'Drop me at the top of Hannan Street,' he said. Donovan nodded, and the ute began to slow. It pulled off the road at the sign pointing into town, and Ford climbed over the back.

Before he could turn around to say his thanks, the tyres crunched the gravel and spun. The Toyota was away. Ford lifted a finger to the peak of his cap in salute and hoped that Donovan had seen it in the mirror.

SEVEN

Hannan Street stretched away from him, four lanes wide and dead straight. The streets had originally been laid out wide enough to allow the camel trains—once the only link to the coast—to turn, but now the road was choked with cars parked diagonally up to the kerb. To his left he could see the headframe of the Mount Charlotte mine, still turning. The mining wouldn't stop for the races, and there would be men working shifts day and night through the weekend.

The sun had already dipped below the post office, and the facades of the grand old buildings on the east side of the street were bathed in orange light as the shadow of the clock tower grew longer.

Ford walked slowly down the footpath, keeping to the shadows under the verandahs on the west side. He had never seen the town so busy. The last of the shoppers were on their way home and the stores were locking up. Men just finished work for the day were going for a quiet drink before heading home to wash, while groups of people already dressed up were stepping out for the night.

As Ford neared the crossroads at the heart of the town, he spotted a police patrol car parked by the traffic lights. He stopped and stepped into a doorway. Two officers stood on the footpath in front of the car, talking to a pair of girls in short skirts and high heels, shiny handbags clutched under their arms. Two young men in silk shirts, their hair waxed into spikes, walked up to them. The girls laughed and the four walked on together. Satisfied that the police were just making themselves visible on the busiest night of the year, Ford continued along the street.

On the corner of the footpath diagonally across from the police he stopped and looked at the four grand buildings that fronted the crossroads: flamboyant hotels with wide verandahs. Opposite him, above the policemen's heads, an electric ticker sign was scrolling across the front of the Palace Hotel, its moving red dots reporting the news headlines, the weather forecast and the daily gold price. Ford remembered the first time he had come to Kalgoorlie, when the gold price had tanked and the town was in a slump. The owner of the Palace had turned off the sign, worried that the negative news was bad for business. The sign now showed the price at a record high. The global financial crisis had hurt everywhere else, but it was in Kalgoorlie's contrary nature to swim against the stream: while economies crumbled and currencies crashed, the gold price went up. Others' misery was Kalgoorlie's joy. The town had always stumbled from boom to bust and back again, and the rollercoaster was currently climbing steadily skyward.

Above the ticker the date of the hotel's construction was built into the facade: 1897, just four years after gold was discovered. The ensuing gold rush had built this town in the bush, with its grand hotels facing each other at the crossroads.

Opposite him stood the Exchange Hotel, a rambling gothic pile of carved verandahs, chimneys and gables, with its squat tiled tower dominating the intersection. A steady stream of people were walking up to its double doors on the street corner. A pair of doormen dressed in black stood either side, a neon sign blinking over their heads; they nodded as people walked past them and pushed open the swing doors.

Ford didn't like being on the street, especially not so close to the police. Deciding to blend into the crowd, he crossed the street, ducking his head to conceal his face with the peak of the baseball cap. Just as he reached the far kerb, the streetlights came on.

Keeping his head down he made to walk past the doormen. The larger one was built like a wardrobe and looked as though he had difficulty finding clothes to fit him. The smaller one was lean and wiry, and raised his palm as Ford got near.

'You going to be staying long?' he asked.

Ford shook his head. 'Just a quick beer after work.'

'You been underground? You're black as a boong. You should've washed up.' He looked down at Ford's boots and stood on his toe, leaning into it. 'No steel toecaps and no soiled work clothes. You know that.'

'Only a couple of drinks, then I'll be gone,' said Ford.

'You just get off?' The doorman smiled, and Ford nodded. 'We're not busy yet, so you can go in. If you're still here in an hour when the evening crowd starts arriving, we'll drag you out. Go home and clean yourself up then, and you can come back.'

Ford nodded again.

'But when you come back, we'll be full.'

The big man stepped in front of Ford, blocking his path. 'Look me in the eyes,' he said.

Ford raised his head and looked at him. The doorman had small eyes, close together.

'You been drinking already, mate?'

'No,' Ford said.

'How many you had?'

'I haven't had a drink today.'

'Look at your eyes. They're like slits.'

'I'm sober as a judge, and drier than a nun's nasty. Can I get a drink?'

'Your eyes look half cut.'

'I get that a lot. I have sleepy eyes.'

The doorman walked around Ford, looking at his torn jeans, the patches of dried blood, and the cuts down his arms. 'Show me your hands.'

Ford held them out, palms up. The bouncer grabbed them and turned them over. Ford winced.

'What the fuck happened to you? You been in a fight?'

'I fell out of the back of a ute. Bastard drove off just as I was climbing out.'

'In Leonora?'

Ford looked down at the roadhouse logo on the shirt. 'My shirt got torn. Gravel rash. A mate loaned me this.'

The two bouncers looked at Ford, then at each other, and the small one's face broke into a broad grin. 'One hell of a day by the sound of it.'

'You're not wrong.'

'Get yourself a drink. If you cause any trouble, we'll make your day even worse.'

Ford pushed the doors open.

'Hope you have better luck with a horse tomorrow,' the big one said to his back.

The walls of the bar were lined with timber boards and hung with a collection of saddles and wagon wheels. An island bar filled the centre, with stools on all sides. The room was still far from full, but most of the bar stools were occupied. Ford counted only three women customers. The rest were men, their attention focused on the video screens above the bar showing sport and music videos. The most attention was being drawn by a large screen showing an AFL match, the preliminary final live from Melbourne. The sound was down because the music was up.

The men in the bar mostly wore black, but there were a few in checked flannel shirts, and younger ones in hoodies and baseball caps. Ford checked for beards and tattoos, but apart from a couple of goatees there was only one grizzled old guy with grey hair, and a long silver beard cut square in the prospector style that had stayed in fashion in Kalgoorlie since the gold rush. A few men watched him suspiciously. Ford thought they were just wary of a solitary drinker.

Those whose attention wasn't held by the football were watching the barmaids. Blonde, their hair pulled back into fierce ponytails, they each wore just a bra, panties and cowboy boots. The video screens over the bar announced that tonight's hot skimpies were Mercedes and Lisa. Ford tried to guess which was which. He thought the girl with less make-up must be Lisa, and that she might be wishing she had chosen a more exotic stage name.

He was relieved to see a group of mineworkers in dirty clothes like his. They were sitting in a line across the far end of the bar. He watched their heads turn in unison as Lisa walked in front of them. Just as she reached the end of the line, the first one raised his hand to order more drinks. As she passed back in front of them, their eyes followed her, heads turning with their mouths open like fairground mechanical clowns.

As the other girl passed him, Ford put up a hand. 'Pint of Vic and a whisky. Malt.' He had to lean in and raise his voice above the music.

She nodded and began pouring the beer. As she leaned over the pump his gaze fell on her cleavage, and he looked from one girl to the other. In a greedy town like Kalgoorlie, quantity always trumped quality, and he thought the girl serving him was likely to get more tips.

His attention returned eagerly to the pump as the level of the beer rose and the condensation beaded on the outside of the glass. The girl put it in front of him and he stared at it, watching the bubbles rise and the head grow. The foam overtopped the glass and a small stream of beer streaked down the side. Ford caught it with his finger and brought it to his lips. It was the first cold thing he had touched all day.

The barmaid had turned her back to him and was raising a glass to the whisky optic. She mustn't have heard him ask for a malt. He was going to correct her, but changed his mind.

'Make that a double.'

She put the whisky in front of him. 'Sorry, darl, no doubles during race round. Best behaviour.'

Ford raised an eyebrow, and she shrugged. He picked up the whisky and drank it in one. Then he took a long pull on the beer, drinking it quickly at first, swamping the dryness in his throat. He realised he hadn't drunk anything since the bottle of warm water in the back of the ute, and he got a sudden rush of thirst.

'Could I get another whisky now, then?'

She smiled and refilled his glass. 'Drowning your sorrows?'

'My sorrows learned to swim a long time ago.'

'Maybe that cold beer will cheer you up.'

'Unlikely. You are what you drink, and I'm a bitter man.' He opened his wallet and gave her a twenty. She ran it through the till and put a few coins on the bar in front of him. 'Are you Mercedes or Lisa?'

'Mercedes.'

'Thought as much. Is there a public phone in here?'

She shook her head. 'Used to be, but they took it out. Reckon there's one by the post office down the street.'

As she pointed towards the door where he'd come in, a third barmaid appeared, dressed in a sober black shirt and pants. She reached above the bar and rang a small ship's bell that hung there. A roar went up from the men seated round the bar. Mercedes gave Ford a wink, reached behind her back and undid her bra, then whipped it off. Her breasts didn't move, just stayed rigidly pointing towards Ford. She gave her shoulders a shake, to little effect. Ford's attention strayed to the other girl, who was smaller but all herself. Catching his eye, Lisa walked towards him carrying a glass beer tankard stuffed with money and waved it in front of him.

Ford scooped his change from the bar and dropped it in the pot. 'Puppies' noses,' he said.

'Thank you,' she said with a smile.

'No, thank you.' He drained the rest of the beer in a couple of long pulls, then raised his hand for another round.

'Easy, tiger,' Mercedes said.

'I'm trying to get unwound fast.'

'Same again?' she asked as she lifted the glass, and he nodded.

He knocked the top off the next beer as quickly as the first and felt something loosen up inside him. When he raised his hand again to get the barmaid's attention, he saw her looking over his shoulder, her eyes narrowed. He made to turn, but a firm hand on his shoulder stopped him. Instead he watched the barmaid's eyes, which remained fixed on the man who sat down on the stool next to him. When the hand was removed, Ford finally turned his head to look at the new arrival.

He was a small nugget of a man, dressed in board shorts and a loose batik shirt. Tattoos filled his arms, tribal designs spiralling up each corded bicep and disappearing into his sleeves. His dark hair was slicked back into a short ponytail, and his beard and moustache were clipped into a tidy goatee. He lifted the hem of his shirt to scratch his belly, revealing tattoos across his stomach and the butt of the revolver sticking out of the waistband of his shorts.

'Hello, Jimmy,' said Ford.

The man smiled and showed his small yellow teeth. 'They didn't believe me,' he said. 'Thousands of square kilometres of empty desert for you to disappear into, but I told them you'd show up in the middle of Kalgoorlie within twenty-four hours. That is, if you weren't still lying out there as food for the crows.'

Ford went to stand up but felt another hand on his shoulder, this time on the other side. The touch was firmer than before, the pressure forcing him back down onto the bar stool. He turned and looked up at the man towering over him; he was at least a head taller than Ford. His barrel chest was squeezed into a black T-shirt and the huge arms straining its sleeves were covered in ink. He had a broad flat face, emphasised by a broken nose squashed level with his cheeks. His head was shaved, and his long beard was hacked square in a spade cut.

Ford forced a smile, but the man's face didn't respond—it seemed paralysed. Ford looked at the hand on his shoulder. Its knuckles were bruised and swollen and it was covered in tattoos. They looked to Ford like prison work: most were badly drawn or written in crude lettering that was difficult to make out. A snake wound up his forearm, and a banner spread beneath it read DON'T TREAD ON ME. It seemed familiar. Ford looked back at Jimmy, whose attention was directed at the barmaid's chest.

'Five hours we've sat out there in the car watching the cross-road,' Jimmy said. 'Thirsty work. I could do with a drink. Pity we can't stay.'

'I was just getting settled in,' said Ford. 'I had plans to drink myself into a black dudgeon.'

'It does seem a bit ironic, after you making it across all that bush, that we're going to take you right back out there.'

Ford tensed. 'I'm no use to you now. You got what you wanted. You collected on your debt.'

Jimmy laughed, a high-pitched snigger through his nose and teeth. 'It was never about the debt, mate. I think you always understood that. You're a smart man, you can see there're still a few things to play out. You always knew the situation you were in, and we were able to discuss things in a reasonable way.'

'Reasonable? You were never reasonable. You followed my daughter to school, you sat outside my wife's home. You threatened my family.'

'No, mate, we never spoke to them. We just helped you to define the equations, let you calculate the angles.'

'Where are they?' asked Ford, rising from the stool. 'I need to know they're safe.'

Pulling a beer, Mercedes looked up at him, startled by the sudden movement. Ford caught her gaze and widened his eyes, pleading. She frowned and turned her head. The big man put his hand on Ford's shoulder again and pushed him down.

'You need to calm down a bit,' said Jimmy. 'There's no point you making a scene in here. The bouncers are mates of ours and the girls know when to look away. Finish your beer. I'm sure your mouth's a bit dry just now.'

Ford picked up the glass and drained it. He sighed again as he put it down and his shoulders slumped.

'There you go,' said Jimmy. 'You're accepting it now. Don't pretend you didn't think it would end this way. When you get into debt with someone like Frank, it's never going to end well.'

'I had an understanding with Frank,' said Ford. 'I've had bad streaks before and come out of them. Frank knows that. He's been a bookie long enough. I've taken money off him before. Last year I was up, this year I'm down. I already sold my car to pay off some of it.'

'Then it was pure bad luck on your part that you owed Frank just when he decided to do something stupid and upset us. You owed him, he owed us, and so we own you. You knew the risks. That's what the horses are all about, aren't they, calculating the odds? Frank said you had a nice little system going there. You should have stuck with it. The big plays never come off.'

'Tell me my wife and daughter are safe.'

'Why don't you tell me what you did with that phone we gave you?'

'I got rid of it.'

'Where exactly? We don't want to be spending all night clearing up loose ends.'

'I dropped it in a leach tank at the mine. A thousand cubic metres of acid slurry. Nobody's going to find anything. Where's my family?'

'We don't have them, mate. That was never what we were about.'

'Then where are they?'

'I don't know,' said Jimmy. 'Now, let's go.'

The big man put a hand under Ford's armpit and lifted him off the stool.

'Wait,' said Ford. 'I need to take a piss.'

'Don't be daft,' Jimmy hissed in his ear.

Ford looked him in the eye. 'I've been in the desert all day without water and then just skolled two beers in a hurry. I need to break the seal.'

'Whatever,' said Jimmy. 'I guess we don't want you pissing yourself and spoiling the upholstery on the Chevy.' He stepped back to let Ford pass and jerked his head at the big man to go with him.

Ford spotted the men's room in the far corner behind the pool table, and headed for it. As he walked to the end of the bar he felt the big man following close behind. He edged around a pair of teenage girls in leather, with dyed black hair and copious mascara. They whooped and started head-banging as a guitar riff kicked in on the jukebox, swinging their long hair around. Ford sidestepped to avoid being flayed.

The men's room was busy, and he had to wait for a space at the urinal. When there was room he wedged himself elbow to elbow between two of the mineworkers he had seen earlier. His stream was dark yellow, and he realised he hadn't taken a piss since he left the mine. The stream grew darker, and Ford stared as it became streaked with red. He sprayed it across the back wall of the urinal to get a good look at it, and traced the aching in his back to his kidneys.

He zipped up and turned away to the basin, catching his reflection in the mirror. His face was sunburnt, and the lines across his forehead and around his eyes were picked out in black soot and red dust. He took off the baseball cap and passed his hand through his hair to see how much had been burned and to brush out the ash, but it wasn't ash, it was his hair that was greying. He ran his hands under the tap and cleaned the cuts across his knuckles. He washed his face and around his neck, and splashed water through his hair. Lifting his shirt he looked at his blackened ribs in the mirror, then pulled the shirt over his head and tried to see the scratches on his back. The deep cut on his shoulder from the bullet had filled with black blood. A teenager in a flannel shirt stood at the urinal. He looked at Ford over his shoulder, but said nothing.

Ford pulled his shirt back down, slicked back his hair and replaced the cap. He thought about what he needed to do.

When he left the bathroom the big man was there, his arms folded across his chest. Ford walked around him and dodged the elbow of a girl playing pool. As her arm drew back to make the shot he snatched the cue from her hand and in one smooth swing spun around and drove the heavy end into the side of the man's head, striking him just above the ear. The man's head snapped sideways and he took a step to find his balance, then came at Ford. He telegraphed his first punch wild and high, and Ford ducked under it and stepped around him.

By the time the man had turned towards him, the pool cue was swinging again in a high sledgehammer arc and smashed into the top of his head. The cue shattered and Ford found himself holding half of it, the end split and jagged. The big man staggered backwards until he hit the bar, grabbing hold of the brass rail to steady himself. Ford crouched with the remains of the cue in both hands, the splintered end pointed at the man's neck.

Everyone in the bar had turned towards them; however, Ford realised they weren't looking at the expression of cool rage on the big man's face as he pulled himself upright but at the bar-maid behind him. Mercedes had vaulted onto the counter in a single lithe movement and picked up the heavy glass tankard full of tips. As she lifted it, Ford saw her biceps flex and the tendons in her wrist pull taut with its weight. She squatted low on her haunches, sweat glistening on her cleavage, and her bare breasts swung along with the tankard as she smashed it into the side of the bald man's head. The glass shattered and coins flew across the room in a rainbow shower of scattered disco light. The man's eyes rolled back in his head as he crashed sideways into the row of bar stools.

The girl winked at Ford and nodded towards the side door, then grabbed the rope hanging from the ship's bell above the bar. As the bell rang she screamed loud enough to drown out the pumping rock music.

Ford looked behind him. As the bouncers burst through the swinging saloon doors, Jimmy was scrambling off his bar stool and forcing his way through the crowd. Ford pulled down his cap, hunched his shoulders and made for the side door. It led to a large hallway with a broad wooden staircase leading up to the first floor. The hallway widened out to a large formal door, which had once been the main entrance to the old hotel. That exit would take him out too close to the street corner and the cops, so he pushed through the small door opposite and found himself in the restaurant. It was a long room with several bars, and with tall windows along the street frontage. A band was setting up on the stage next to where he'd come in. He was relieved to see that the room was crowded and all the tables were full.

He made for the furthest door onto the street, and came out at the far end of the verandah. The sun had now set and darkness had fallen. Looking back up towards the crossroads, he saw the doormen come out of the saloon door and look his way. He could hear slurred shouting and laughter coming out of the door. Keeping to the shadows, he walked away from the crossroads, and when he found a dark patch between streetlights he crossed the road and went down the alleyway opposite.

Once in the deserted alley he started to run. His ribs ached, but the whisky had numbed the pain somewhat and it was bearable. He ran a block and then turned back towards Hannan at the next side street, slowing to a walk as he came out under the streetlights. He stayed in darkness with his back to the brick wall of the building and watched the street for several minutes. The temperature had dropped with the sun, and he wrapped his arms around himself. Cars passed him, and people walked in twos and threes towards the Palace and the Exchange. He looked for a taxi, and saw one dropping off a pair of teenage girls on the far side of the street, where they crossed.

He had rejoined Hannan Street a little below the post office, and he could see the telephone booths beneath the clock tower. When the road was clear he crossed, feeling vulnerable in the wide empty street but resisting the urge to run. The taxi pulled away as he got close, so he made for a darkened shop doorway. The girls from the taxi had joined a line of people in front of a bar directly across the road. He looked back up the street towards the Exchange Hotel and made out the police still standing on their corner and the bouncers each side of their door.

The phone booths were empty, so Ford walked slowly up the street, keeping close to the shopfronts, his hands in his pockets and his head down. He scurried into the first booth and hunched sideways in the perspex cowl, his back to the intersection. He automatically checked his pockets for change and then remembered putting his few coins in the pot at the pub. Cursing himself, he slid his credit card into the phone. Diane's mobile and home numbers both went to voicemail, and Walsh's home number rang out. After that he couldn't think of anyone else to call who might help.

Stepping out of the phone booth he looked for a bank. There was an automatic teller on the far side of the street, but it was too close to the intersection and in clear sight of the police and the bouncers. He turned and walked the other way.

His side of the street was quiet and dark, away from the pubs and bars, where lights and music spilled onto the footpath. As he walked beneath the awnings he caught sight of his reflection in a shop window and initially failed to recognise himself. Unfamiliar shirt, his face shaded by the cap, head bowed, shoulders hunched, hands jammed deep in his jeans pockets against the cold: he looked thin and lost, far from home, and the pain in his chest was like a stab of unbelonging. The facades of the buildings opposite were reflected behind him, looking like stage scenery. Glancing down at his arms he noticed the gooseflesh between the cuts.

He walked on, looking for a taxi. Three passed him, but they were all full of people coming into town for the night.

A crowd was gathered on the footpath outside the town hall, mostly smokers huddled together. He thought about having a cigarette himself but wanted to get off the street first. He looked in through the doors to the foyer as he passed. The place was full. Signs announced that a poker tournament was in progress, and TV screens hanging from the roof showed green baize tables.

There was a bar at the back. He paused, wondering whether there might be a cash machine inside, but the crowd looked too thick to push through and he could see security staff in uniform.

He walked to the end of the building and stood beneath the traffic lights on the corner. Beyond the intersection the grand facades ended and Hannan Street changed into a featureless strip of motels, convenience stores and fast-food outlets. The side roads looked darker. Their streetlights were located in the centre of the median strip and spaced too far apart to light the footpath. He sat down on a large boulder set into the pavement on the corner to consider his next move. Beside him sat the statue of Paddy Hannan, father of the Kalgoorlie gold rush.

He noticed two men in suits looking at him from the doorway of the town hall, smiling as they smoked. They clearly saw nothing strange in a battered and bruised man full of drink sitting beside a statue. Just another Friday night in Kal. Ford smiled and nodded at them, but something else had caught their attention, and he glanced up the street to see what they were looking at.

Two men were running down the footpath opposite. They were still two hundred metres up the road but their size and shape left Ford in no doubt as to who they were. As they pushed their way through the crowd of people lined up outside a bar, Ford lost sight of them for a moment. Trying to keep calm, he rose and walked nonchalantly down the side of the town hall, and then sprinted down Wilson Street. He had a hundred metres until the next cross-street and was confident he could get there and lose himself before they came around the corner.

Halfway there he spotted an alleyway running behind the town hall and darted into it. He found himself at the back of a supermarket car park. It was close to full of cars parked for the night while their owners packed the pubs. He ducked behind a van and slunk down to the ground with his back against the door, breathing hard and hugging his ribs. He tried the door, but it was locked. Crouching low, he moved between the cars, trying his luck with the doors as he went, keeping an eye on the street.

He cursed himself for wasting time: if he found an unlocked door he would still need the key for the ignition, and even if he had some idea of how to hot-wire one of them, it would by law be fitted with an immobiliser. He knelt down, looking for a line of sight through the car windows.

When the two men appeared they were walking casually and turning their heads from side to side. Jimmy was talking into his phone. Ford dropped down flat on the ground and crawled under an off-roader. He lay on his stomach and turned his head in their direction, looking for their feet. He tried to control his breathing despite the pain in his ribs.

He stayed there for five minutes, wondering whether they would move on or be joined by others. Three cars entered and parked, and he watched their drivers' feet recede, then rolled out and crept back between the rows of cars towards the alley. He retraced his steps to the end of the alley and put his head around the corner. The road was clear. Hannan Street was too public, so his only option was to head in the opposite direction, down Wilson towards the station. It was too late for trains, but he might be able to find a taxi and a cash dispenser. He wished he had a better idea.

As he stepped out of the alley into the light he heard the roar of motorcycle engines. He looked to his left just as two bikes did a slow turn from Hannan into Wilson. The headlights swept the wall and he stepped back, turned and ran, following the alley along the bare concrete wall of the supermarket. He looked over his shoulder: they weren't following, but the engines were still rumbling in the distance. They must be cutting laps around the town, looking for him.

When he reached the end of the wall, he cut between two buildings and came out on Brookman Street. He kept in the shadow of the fence and checked up and down. Further up the footpath on his side, he could see the police station's illuminated sign. The glass front of the stark white building was brightly lit. He had run out of other options; he knew now that he should have sat in the desert and waited for the police to arrive.

The street was free of moving traffic, but there were cars parked diagonally on either side and under the trees down the median strip. He could still hear the rumbling of the motorcycles, but they sounded at least a block away, so he stepped out of the shadow and turned towards the light of the station.

As he passed in front of the blank white wall that guarded the police car park, Ford was caught in the beams of a car's headlights. He turned to see that the lights came from a car parked against the median strip under a tree thirty metres away, directly opposite the front door of the station. The light hurt his eyes and he could only see the car's outline. The driver's door opened and he saw the silhouette of a man get out and lean against it. The man stretched an arm out along the roof and Ford threw himself on the ground as the report rang out and the bullet thudded into the concrete behind him. The shot echoed off the facades of the buildings opposite.

Ford was up and running before he heard the second shot, staying below the tops of the cars parked at the kerb. The third shot shattered the window of a car ahead of him. He reached the alleyway again. Looking round, he saw only the headlights and the muzzle flash from the fourth shot, and then he was sprinting down the alley, his head back and his arms pumping. A moment later he heard the screech of the car's tyres and the roar of the engine as it accelerated down the road.

Ford came out onto Wilson Street just as the car came sliding round the corner, its rear wheels fighting oversteer. Under the streetlights of the intersection he could see it clearly now, a green Falcon with an air scoop on the hood. He waited until

the car had completed the turn and was heading towards him
before he ran straight across the street. He hurdled the median
strip barrier and sprinted across the other lane and into the alley
opposite. The car was now trapped on the wrong side until it
found a cross-street. He heard it accelerate towards Hannan
Street to make the turn.

Ford ran down an arcade fronting a strip mall and found
himself in an unlit loading bay. Leaning against its steel shutters,
he clutched his chest and breathed hard. His only possible route
lay away from the railway station and out into the dark suburban
streets. He thought about finding an empty house, but decided
he should keep moving. He walked slowly onto Brookman
Street again and checked both directions. The street was clear, so
he turned away from town and started walking.

Light was spilling onto the footpath from a building ahead,
and he realised he had reached the point where Brookman
Street turned into Hay. Ahead lay the brothels.

Ford had only been this way once before, when he came
to Kalgoorlie on a work junket with Diane for the race round.
They had done the tourist trail, standing together hand in hand
on the lookout over the Super Pit, watching the ore trucks crawl
up the incline from the base of the pit. They had driven out to
the two-up school in the bush, and sat in the ramshackle ring
watching the two coins turn slowly in the air and the old men
take their money. They had spent the afternoon at the races, and
he'd had a run of luck: a guy he drank with at his local knew the
owner of a grey mare running in the second race that he'd been
holding back in her last three races to keep the weight down,
and it came in second by a head at handsome odds, delivering a
windfall they'd spent on champagne. They had drunk their way
from one end of Hannan Street to the other and back again, and
then at midnight they'd taken a walk down Hay Street to gawp
at the working girls.

It had been Diane's idea. She'd been to Kalgoorlie many times but had been too shy to go past on her own. She'd driven there once, doing the slow kerb crawl common on that block, but she'd gone too early and all the doors had been closed. Now she had champagne inside her, and a chaperone, and she wanted to see things up close. They walked past the three houses arm in arm. The first two had retained the starting stalls from the old days—a row of half a dozen corrugated-iron stables with split doors fronting the street, girls standing in the doorways. Some were sitting wearily on chairs, while others were leaning out talking to the drunks emptying out of the pubs. Closed doors indicated that the girls inside were busy.

Ford had tried to act relaxed, but he found it unnerving. Diane had paused at each open door and looked at the woman inside. Some of them smiled back and one gave her a cheery wave. Ford had tried to move Diane along, but she was unsteady on the dress heels she had worn for the races.

'Would you visit them?' she asked.

'Are you asking me as a husband, or as a representative of the male race?'

She kicked his shin. 'I thought they'd be better looking,' she said. 'But you dodged the question. Would you ever come here?'

'The first mine site I ever went to was four hours' drive from here, out past Laverton. I only went there for a week, during a maintenance shutdown. Small place, run-down and hot as hell. The only women there were the manager's wife, the cook's wife, and two lesbian truck drivers who had knocked down the dividing wall between their rooms to make a love nest. For the week I was there, the only conversation I heard from the blokes in the wet mess was about racehorses, how they were getting shafted on their overtime payments, and how much they were going to drink and root in Kalgoorlie when they finished their roster. After a four-week rotation in the bush doing twelve-hour shifts, that lady there would look like Botticelli's Venus.'

Diane looked at the women in their lace, leather and fishnets, and asked, 'Does that dress-up stuff really work? Do you go for that whole fancy-dress slut look?'

'They seem to be doing good business.'

'I'm asking about you.'

'It might look different on you.'

'Really?'

'Try me.'

They'd walked back to the hotel and spent the rest of the weekend in bed. Six weeks later she was pregnant with Grace.

The thought of his daughter brought him back to the moment. Normally there were a few men strolling around Hay Street, looking nervously in the stalls, but it was still early and the road was clear.

As he passed a yellow house, he glanced sideways at the stalls. There were two doors open. The first girl caught his eye and smiled at him. She was blonde and pale. She opened her coat for him.

He heard the deep rumble of a V8 and whipped his head around to see the green Falcon coming around the end of the street, caught beneath the lights. There was no mistaking the air scoop on the bonnet.

Ford turned and tried to walk calmly towards the open door.

EIGHT

The girl smiled at Ford again, but her expression changed as he put his hands on her shoulders and pushed her back three steps through the doorway.

'Get your fucking hands off me,' she hissed.

'Sorry,' he said, dropping his hands and flattening himself against the yellow wall beside the door so he was hidden from the street.

'Jeez, you're in a hurry, sweetheart.'

On her face he saw amusement rather than anger. Up close she looked even younger, and he thought she might be pretty beneath the make-up. He looked into her eyes to see whether he could trust her. Trying to keep eye contact while he listened for the car, he realised he was holding his breath. The car rumbled past and then accelerated as it made the turn back towards Hannan Street. Realising it would be some time before it came around again, he released his breath and his shoulders slumped.

'That's it, love, take it easy,' the girl said. Her face broke into a smile and she had a look in her eyes that Ford decided he would take as warmth. She gave him a once-over. 'You look like you've had a hard day.'

'I've had better.'

'Let's see if we can help you relax a bit, shall we?'

'Can we go inside?'

'Not much of a talker?'

'I'm cold. I want to get inside.' Looking past her he saw that the door opened into a corridor that ran down the back of all the stalls and connected them to a foyer.

'Do you want a full hour or just the half?' She tilted her head and rocked on her heels.

'Just a half, maybe.'

She told him the price and he nodded. He leaned forward and reached for the wallet in his back pocket and thought about how he was going to pay, but she put her hand softly on his arm. 'Not me. In here.' She took his hand and led him down the corridor to the foyer, where she pushed a buzzer on the counter. Behind the desk another corridor led away into the depths of the building. The place smelled of cheap perfume and talcum, and underneath it the dark odour of damp towels and something more pungent.

He heard a door slam and the shrill bark of a small dog. The dog came scampering out of the corridor and ran a lap around Ford's legs, still barking. He couldn't tell the breed. He hated all small dogs, especially the yappy ones. The dog was followed by a small woman wearing a cardigan and house slippers. She sat down behind the desk and looked at Ford without expression. The dog ran round and sat at her feet. The woman must have been seventy years old. Her hair was styled in a neat perm coloured a brassy red. Ford wasn't sure what he had expected a madam to look like but he thought she would look more at home stirring a pot of risotto and gossiping about the neighbours. He gazed at his feet.

The girl leaned over the desk. 'Half an hour,' she whispered.

The old woman kept looking at Ford. He fumbled for his wallet and gave her his credit card. 'Is that alright?' he asked.

She nodded and swiped it into a hand-held card reader, which she then passed across the desk to him. He looked above her head and saw the security camera pointed at him before he punched in his number.

The madam handed the girl a key. 'Number four.'

The girl turned to Ford and smiled. In the brighter light of the foyer he could see that the blonde hair was a wig and she was wearing blue-coloured contact lenses. Maybe he had misread the look in her eye. She now seemed to be staring through him.

'What's your name, sweetheart?'

'Jack.'

'Mandy. Shall we go through, Jack?'

She walked down the corridor and glanced over her shoulder to make sure he was following. She went past several doors before stopping at number four. As she fussed with the key in the lock, he brushed past her and went to the door at the end of the passage. He turned the handle but it was locked.

'Where you going?' she asked.

'Is there a back exit?'

'Running out on me already?'

'This door locked?'

'They're all locked, darling. Wouldn't want anyone bursting in on us. First time here, is it?'

'I need to get out the back.'

'Don't worry, I won't bite. Unless that's your thing.'

She stood holding the door open and waited for him. The room was small, and almost filled with a bed piled high with pillows. There was just room for a bedside table, on which sat a lamp, a box of tissues and a stack of towels. The walls had been dressed with cheap framed prints, and above the bed a black lace costume draped with a pink feather boa and an outsized string of plastic pearls was displayed on a coathanger hooked over a mirror. He turned away from his reflection. Next to the bed was an electric oil heater, and the room was hot and airless. The smell was the same perfumed damp as in the foyer, only stronger. A door next to the bed was ajar and he could hear the thrumming of an extractor fan inside.

'I expected you to be busier,' he said.

'It's still early. It'll get rowdy later. There's more girls starting in an hour.'

She stood by the door taking off her coat. Underneath she wore a black bustier and silk French knickers. The gap of skin between the knickers and the top of her stockings was so pale it seemed to glow in the gloom. She struck a half-hearted pose for him, and he smiled.

'I need you to take a shower,' she said, pointing to the door by the bed. 'Then make yourself comfortable.'

He would stay for a shower, but could not think beyond that. He put his head round the bathroom door. The room was tiny, with a toilet, basin and small shower, which he turned on. He got undressed by the bed and left his clothes on the floor, then picked up a towel from the bedside table. When he stepped into the shower the hot water hit his body and the pain shot through him in a dozen places at once. He bent forward to let the water run over the cuts on his shoulders and looked down at his ribs, where the black bruising had spread. He gently rubbed the cuts on his knees and elbows. They started to bleed again, and looking down at his feet he saw the water swirling around the plughole turn red from the blood and desert dust. He soaped himself all over until he felt he was free of the filth, and then he stood, legs apart, with his palms against the tiled wall, and let the shower jet hit him full in the face. He stood there for several minutes, letting his mind go blank and forgetting about the girl.

Finally he killed the water and stepped out, reaching for the towel. He walked naked into the room, patting himself dry. The girl stood by the door listening to some noise in the corridor.

She slid a dead bolt across the top of the door. Ford tensed, cocking his head to listen. Voices were coming from the front of the house. Two male voices, loud and deep, and one woman, quiet and firm. He could hear the dog yapping.

The girl turned to him, her brow furrowing as she looked him over from head to foot. She stretched out a hand and put her fingertips softly on his ribs, running them over the bruises. Despite the lightness of her touch, he flinched.

The voices outside the door got louder, and then it was quiet. Ford and the girl stood side by side with their heads close to the door, listening to the silence. Loud rapping on the door made them both start.

'Mandy, it's Shirley. Open up!' Ford could hear the anger in the old woman's voice. He stepped away from the door as the girl unbolted it. Shirley pushed into the room, her eyes on Ford.

'Just who are you?' she asked. Her gaze moved down his body, taking it in.

'Jack,' he said.

'I don't want to know your name. I got that off the credit card. You might have thought about that before giving a fake name.'

Ford shrugged and reached for his pants.

'I want to know why there were two bikies out front looking for a skinny Pom from the Gwardar mine.'

'Did you ask them?'

She snatched the jeans from his hand and held them in front of his face, showing him the embroidered company logo on the back pocket. 'Gwardar Gold Mine,' she read out. 'Get out of my house!'

'I tried. The back door was locked.'

'You can leave the way you came in, right now.'

'Are they waiting out the front?'

'Not my concern. I want you out of here.'

74

'They'll kill me.'

She looked him in the eye and held his gaze. He tried not to look away.

'Call the police,' he said.

She put her hands on her hips, 'I don't want cops in my house.'

'Why didn't they come in and look for me?' said Ford.

'This is my house and I decide who comes in. I don't want cops in here and I don't want bikies. Eighteen years I've been here and I don't owe either of them. Put your pants on and get out.'

Ford took a step towards her. 'I need to get to the police.'

'They looking for you?'

'Yes.'

'And you used your credit card at my house? They'll be coming past here soon enough. I'm not having them in here. Not tonight, not during the race round.'

She threw Ford his jeans and sat on the end of the bed, resting her hands in her lap, thinking. Mandy still stood by the door, but when she reached for the handle as if to leave, Shirley raised her hand. 'You stay right here. I'm going to make a call. Keep the door locked.'

When she was gone, the girl bolted the door again and pulled off her wig. Her hair beneath was a cropped bob, dyed black. Ford thought it suited her better. She stood with her hip cocked against the door frame. He was still standing with his pants in his hand, naked and wet.

'How long do you think she'll be gone?' he said.

NINE

Ford lay dressed on the bed, staring at the ceiling, his eyes following the lines in the pressed tin panels. The pattern of squares, filled with embossed leaves and flowers, looked to him like the gridiron street plan of Kalgoorlie. He felt that if he followed the lines long enough he might find a way out of town.

In reality he knew there were only three bitumen roads out. One went north, the road that he'd come in on, and one went south to Kambalda. The third ran west to Perth: that was the road he wanted to get onto, but it was the easiest one to watch. To the east there was only bush, and the empty desert of the Nullarbor stretching a thousand kilometres across the continent.

Mandy lay on her side next to him, with the wig on the bed between them. They both listened to the slow steady thump of the headboard against the wall in the next room.

'He seems to be hitting his stride,' said Ford.

The bumping was joined by a high-pitched noise somewhere between panting and whimpering.

'That's Jade,' said Mandy. 'She does the whole three-act-opera thing. Starts with the little yelps and then works herself through some moaning and meowing. When the guy hits the vinegar strokes she'll give him her scalded-cat finale.'

'Walls are a bit thin for that, aren't they?'

'She knows the right volume. Sounds a lot louder when it's right in your ear. Anyway, Shirley likes a few animal noises coming from the rooms. If it's too quiet, she sometimes goes into one of the empty rooms and makes them herself.'

The rhythm from next door quickened.

'Here she goes,' said Mandy as a growling squeal came through the wall, followed by a single male grunt.

'What if the bikies come back?' asked Ford, turning to look at her.

'They won't get past Shirley. They'll believe her if she says she hasn't seen you.' Mandy sat up cross-legged on the mattress and started to pick at a toenail where the varnish was chipped. 'I was here last race round, and she found a couple of them hanging round the back gate waiting for one of the girls. They'd been taking money off her, had her tweaking on meth. Shirley went to the shed and came back with a garden fork. They were laughing at her until she put it through one of them's thigh. Missed his balls by a couple of inches. She shoos them out of the gate and puts the girl on the next train to Perth. Now she always makes sure the girls are clean, and makes sure the cops are sweet so they keep the bikies away.'

'She pays off the cops?'

'Fuck no. She just runs a good house and lets them check that the girls are clean.' She reached out and put a finger through the chain around Ford's neck, and pulled the nugget free of his shirt. 'I saw this little thing earlier. Not much to look at, is it?'

'I hope you're talking about the nugget.'

'Some bloke gave me a nugget one time, asked if I'd be his girlfriend every time he was in town. Was about three times the size of this tiddler. Told me it would be just like the old days, when the girls used to do the prospectors for gold. Then I had it valued in town and it was worth a lot less than I thought. Only paid for one night. Poor bastard had been out prospecting on his own and found bugger-all. He spent the night curled up around me just smelling my hair. The sad sack couldn't even tell it was a wig.'

There was a quiet knock at the door and the girl got off the bed and unbolted it. Ford sat up.

Shirley walked into the room with her eyes fixed on him. Behind her was a heavy-set man in blue overalls. He closed the door behind him as he entered, then took off his cap and ran stubby fingers through short hair. Ford noticed the grease under his fingernails and the tattoos across the back of his hand. The man put his cap back on and stood looking at Ford, scratching a bushy beard. It was long and cut square across, in a style Ford had seen too many times that evening.

'This is Banjo,' said Shirley. 'He's going to take you out of here.'

'He looks like a plumber,' said Ford.

'That's because I am a fucking plumber,' said Banjo.

Ford stood up. He was a good head taller than the plumber but gave away twenty kilos to the other man, mostly around the middle. It was cramped with four of them in the room and he didn't think he would be able to get past Banjo to the door if he tried. Mandy sat down on the bed, curled her legs beneath her and wound the wig around her hand.

'Where are you going to take me?' asked Ford.

Banjo turned to Shirley, who shrugged. 'Away from here,' he said. 'Far away. That's all Shirley asked me.'

'Can you drive me to Perth?'

'I didn't mean that far.'

'Can you take me to the police station?'

Banjo again looked at Shirley, and then took a step closer to Ford. 'I don't like judging people by first appearances, so I hope you're not going to act like an arsehole much longer. Shirley don't want any cops involved.'

Shirley waved the girl off the bed and straightened the bedspread. She picked up the wet towel from the floor. 'You're going to leave out the back door and Banjo's going to take you away in his van. I don't care where you go, as long as you're not around when the police show up looking for the damn fool that used his credit card here.'

Ford shook his head. 'Not sure I trust him. Been running away from blokes like him all day.'

Banjo's face cracked into a smile, showing a broad set of white teeth in his beard. His belly moved up and down as if he was laughing, but he made no sound. 'I don't care if you trust me. I'm not doing this for you, mate. I'm here for Shirley. You can take your chances out the front with the guys in the street as far as I'm concerned.'

'I trust him,' Shirley told Ford. 'He's the first person I call. I've never known Banjo to lie to anyone but the cops.'

'He works for you?'

'He's a friend. Helps out now and then.'

'He put the jacuzzi in the backyard,' said Mandy.

Banjo was still laughing. He held out his hand and Ford shook it tentatively. Banjo's grip was firm. He smelled of wood smoke and tobacco.

'What's your name, big fella?'

'Ford. Gareth Ford.'

'Mind if I call you Gareth?'

'Only if you want to sound like my mother.'

'You can't go outside dressed like that. You'll stick out like a rat turd in a bowl of rice.'

Ford looked down at his roadhouse shirt and his jeans with the company logo.

'They'll know what you're wearing. You got anything warmer?' asked Banjo. 'It's getting cold out.'

Ford shook his head and folded his arms across his chest. He felt himself shiver, even though the room was stuffy from the oil heater.

'Wait a mo.' Shirley brushed past him and out the door. Ford stood looking at Banjo. The plumber hadn't lost his smile. It stretched across his whole face, and he had a squint born of long hours in the sun.

Shirley came back through the door with a coat draped over her arm. She grasped its shoulders with both hands and held it out to Ford. 'All I could find,' she said. 'Been in the lost–property box for a while.'

It was a heavy full–length oilskin riding coat cut in the bush-man style, with caped panels over the shoulders. It was worn through at the elbows and the hem was frayed. Ford put it on, noting its musty smell. It was too large for him, and with only a shirt underneath he felt as though he was swimming inside it.

'This is supposed to be inconspicuous?' he asked, trying to shoot his arms out of the cuffs.

'It fits where it touches,' said Banjo, his belly heaving again and his shoulders joining in. 'At least it covers those work pants.'

Mandy snorted. 'You need a cowboy hat to go with it.'

'Someone stole your horse?' said Banjo, still chuckling. Then he got serious. 'Let's not hang about.' Opening the door, he made a sweeping wave of his hand out into the hallway.

Ford looked at Mandy and she nodded. He tried smiling at Shirley as he left, but her face wore the same expression as when he'd first met her at the front desk. He wondered what it took to make her smile. He checked the corridor both ways, then walked to the end and tried the door. This time it was open. It led to another corridor, past a small kitchen and a room full of clothes racks and with a glass door. After stepping through the door Ford found himself standing on a timber deck with a sunken jacuzzi. Banjo stepped out behind him.

'Nice work, huh?' said Banjo. 'I did the decking as well.'

'A man of many talents.'

'Not having much success with that arsehole thing, are you, mate?'

Banjo stepped past him and walked around the fence that screened the hot tub. Ford followed and came out into a small yard where an unmarked white van was parked. A wide steel gate separated the yard from the laneway running behind the house. Banjo slid open the side door of the van for him. Ford climbed in and sat on the floor among the tools.

'Keep your head down,' whispered Banjo, and moved to close the door.

'Wait!' said Ford. 'Where are you taking me?'

Banjo stopped. The light was behind him and his shadow filled the door. Ford couldn't see his face. 'Do you know who's looking for you?' said Banjo.

Ford nodded. He opened his mouth to speak, but Banjo held up his hand to cut him off.

'You serious about going to the cops?'

'Only safe place for me.'

'I can't take you there. If those men are watching the station, I can't let them see you with me. Can't let the jacks see me with you either.'

'You just going to leave me in the street?'

'No. Let me think.'

Banjo closed the door and went round to the front. Ford heard the gate grind open, and then Banjo got into the driver's seat and started the engine. They drove out and turned into the lane, not stopping to close the gate.

TEN

The journey was five minutes, long enough to drive to the other side of town. Ford spent it listening for the sound of Harleys or a V8. He was hunched behind the driver's seat, too lost in his thoughts to talk to Banjo.

The van pulled up and Banjo got out and opened the side door. Ford stepped out and looked around. The van was parked next to a ute with two dirt bikes lashed to a trailer. The yard was crowded with junk: scrap metal, lumber, roof sheeting and piping. Through a gap in the fence he could see a rambling brick cottage with a weatherboard extension and a verandah that looked as though it had been built using junk from the yard.

'Home sweet home,' said Banjo. He lit a cigarette, walked to the shed and swung open the door. The room inside was lit by the glow of a wood stove built from an oil drum. It stood against the far wall and an improvised steel flue snaked up to the roof. In the centre of the floor was a motorcycle.

'I was just polishing her when the phone rang.'

'You're a bikie?' said Ford, looking again at the tattoos across Banjo's hand.

'I'm a motorcycle enthusiast.' Banjo picked up the rag draped across the bike seat and walked over to a bench against the wall, which was strewn with tools and tins of polish.

Ford walked around the bike, admiring the chrome. It was the biggest thing he'd ever seen, and he was surprised by the badge. 'You ride a Triumph?'

'It's a thing of beauty.'

'I thought you all rode Harleys?'

'Rode a Harley for twenty years. Thought I'd change to something designed in the twenty-first century.'

A dog was yawning in a basket by the stove. It got slowly to its feet, stretched, then padded over to Banjo and pressed its head against his leg. Banjo bent down and scratched its ears. It trotted over to Ford and sat in front of him. A sturdy cattle dog as barrel-chested and grizzled as its owner, with a head like a bear, it looked at Ford and pricked its ears as if waiting for him to introduce himself. Ford put his hand in front of the dog's nose. It gave his fingers a single sniff and then, apparently satisfied, returned to the basket, curling up with a sigh.

Ford stepped up to the wood heater and warmed his hands. He had never got used to the way the temperature dropped at night in spring. He opened the coat and let the heat spread across his ribs. 'You got anything to drink?' he asked.

Banjo opened a battered fridge at the end of the bench and pulled out a couple of long-neck beers. He opened them on a vice bolted to the bench and handed one to Ford. Above his head a shelf was filled with empty bourbon bottles arranged shoulder to shoulder along the length of the wall. Ford's eyes went along the shelf until he spotted a half-full bottle of Jim Beam at the end, the rye with the yellow label.

'How about we take a look at that JB?' he said.

Banjo grinned and reached for the bottle and the pair of shot glasses next to it, and put them on the bench.

'Got any painkillers?' asked Ford, and Banjo raised an eyebrow. 'I'm pissing blood.' He lifted his shirt.

Banjo sucked in his breath through his teeth and reached under the bench. 'Why're they chasing you? Looks like they caught you already.' He took out a large plastic bottle and stood it next to the bourbon. He poured the Jim Beam, then shook a handful of large pink tablets into his hand. Offering his palm to Ford, he held out the shot glass with the other hand.

Ford looked dubiously at the pills. 'They're huge. What are they, horse tranquillisers?'

'There's a few ketamine in there, but you might want to give them a miss. There's OxyContin too. The pink ones are Brufen. Big bastards, four hundred mill. They'll sort you out. Got a mate who's a doctor of sorts. I've got a first aid kit and some iodine here, if you want to clean up some of them cuts.'

Ford could see the trademark written in bold letters on each pill so he decided to take Banjo's word for it. In any case, he was in no mood to argue. He took two, put them in his mouth and knocked them back with a slug of beer. He took the shot glass and drained that, and finished the beer in two gulps. As he wiped his mouth with the back of his hand, he caught Banjo watching him.

'So what's the story? Who's looking for you?' the plumber asked, sitting up on the bench, letting his legs dangle.

Ford handed him the empty glass and bottle, and shrugged. 'Some guys. I think they're bikies.'

'That much we know already. Why d'you think Shirley called me?'

'You known her long?'

'It's Kalgoorlie. Everybody either knows everybody else or knows somebody everybody else knows.'

Ford picked at the scab forming on the scratch across his hand. 'I met them before.'

'Why do they want you?'

'Bookie's debt.' He looked up at Banjo's face to see if he believed that.

'You got names?'

Ford thought about that, decided he wasn't sure how far to trust Banjo, so shook his head.

'What do they look like?'

'One's a big, full-grown bikie, maybe five inches taller than me. Shaved head, beard like yours. Flat face, broken nose, mean-looking.'

'Congratulations, you narrowed it down to half the bikers in the state.'

'Lots of tattoos. Bad ones. Self-drawn; prison, maybe. Has a big snake up his forearm with the words "DON'T TREAD ON ME" scrolled underneath it.'

Banjo rolled up his sleeve and turned his elbow so Ford could see the snake down his forearm. 'Like this?'

Ford stiffened, glancing between Banjo and the door, asking himself how he had ended up again with the big man between him and the exit. He looked Banjo in the face, trying to get a hint as to his intentions, and was surprised to see that the big grin had returned.

'Jeez, you're jumpy,' said Banjo.

'What's the tattoo?'

'Desert Vipers Motorcycle Club.'

'But I know that design.'

'Gadsden flag. American War of Independence.'

'Why use something American?'

'It's all American, mate, starting with the motorcycle.'

'I didn't think vipers were indigenous to Australia?'

'They're not. But Australian snakes don't have such sexy names, do they? They don't have sports cars or jet fighters named after them. What were we supposed to call ourselves, the King Browns?'

Ford looked to the door again. 'I thought that flag had a rattlesnake on it,' he said.

'Don't get me started. The desert viper lives in the Sahara and across the Middle East, not round here. Fuck knows what that snake on the patch is, but it's not a viper or a rattlesnake. Good job the guys know a lot about motorcycles, because they know fuck-all about snakes.'

'You're a member, same as him?'

'Don't know about him. He must be from Perth. I thought I knew all the Kalgoorlie boys. Used to ride with the Vipers, but I gave that up years ago.'

'I didn't think it was something you gave up.'

'Sure it is. See?' Under the snake were two dates, fifteen years apart. 'Date I got patched, and the date I left. They let me keep the tatt because I left in good standing. I'd had enough of rushing off to meet trouble halfway. Marriage and a kid didn't really fit with the life.' Banjo went to the bike and pulled out the electrical cable connected to the battery. As he stood up he rubbed at a smear on the tank with his sleeve. 'I don't ride with the club that often now, so I can ride what I like. The brakes on my old Softail were about as much use as putting your thong on the road. This baby will take off quicker and stop faster than any hunk of Milwaukee iron.'

'I'm more of a Vespa man myself,' said Ford.

Banjo looked at him and nodded as if that explained a lot. 'I've had the piss taken out of me for riding a fag bike, but you're on a whole different level. All starting to make sense now.' He went to the fridge and pulled out some more beer. 'You know, riding a scooter is like rooting a fat chick. It's a whole loada fun, until your mates see you doing it.' He passed Ford a beer. 'You relax and drink this, and stop looking at the door. If you want to leave I'm not going to stop you, but I'm the only one's going to help you. Now I'm going to the office to use the phone. See if we can't sort this out.'

'You're going to tell them I'm here?'

'Not yet. At the moment I'm still trying to put some distance between you and Shirley.' Banjo opened a door next to the end of the bench and disappeared into the adjoining room. Ford poured himself another shot and returned to the wood stove with a drink in each hand. He stood looking at the glowing logs, thinking.

By the time Banjo returned, Ford had drained both drinks and was considering helping himself to more. The pills had kicked in and the pain had dissolved to a dull ache with a buzz on top.

He was reaching for the bottle when the glower on Banjo's face stopped him. Ford stepped away from the stove and started inching towards the door. Banjo's eyes followed him. 'Your lies don't live very long, mate,' he growled.

Ford had reached the door of the shed and he looked out into the dark yard. He didn't know where he was in the town. He thought he could outrun his host, even with the bruised ribs, but if Banjo called in back-up they would soon run him down. He turned and waited.

Banjo opened a beer. 'Spoke to a couple of guys. They're pissed off. They already knew your name, told it to me without me having to tell them. Something's going on and they don't know what it is, but it's got them spooked, and they reckon their phones are wired. All I got from them is that the cops are coming down on the Vipers and they're looking for you. So I've got to go out.'

'What do I do?'

'You're not going out on the street. I'm not having you give my name to the first cop or biker you meet. You're staying here until I can figure out what to do with you.'

'If the police are out there checking on bikers, and the bikers are out there hunting for me, isn't someone going to show up here sooner or later?'

'That'll happen. My name will be on a list as a known associate. The police'll do the patched guys first and work their way round to me. I've got a suspended sentence hanging over me, so they'll reckon they've got some leverage. Better get you out of sight.'

Banjo put down his beer and walked over to the Triumph. He rocked it off its stand and wheeled it into a corner of the shed. Back in the centre of the room, he bent down and lifted up a broad sheet of plywood, splattered with oil and paint, on which the bike had been standing, then carried it over to the shed wall, where he leaned it against the fridge. In the centre of the floor, Ford now saw, there was a trapdoor.

Banjo prised out an iron ring that was recessed into the gnarled timber planking of the door and pulled it up. A cool blue light shone up through the hole. 'Follow me down,' he said. Banjo climbed down through the trapdoor. The entrance was narrow and he had to suck in his gut to get through.

Ford followed, searching for each rung with his feet. He found himself in a small basement, no more than three metres square. It was just long enough to fit the camp bed that ran along a bare stone wall. The opposite wall was made of glass panels from floor to ceiling. They were the source of the blue light and the oppressive heat. Ford assumed they must be tanks full of fish, but when he put his face to the glass he saw there was no water, only a collection of rocks and plants. Just then the head of a snake emerged from the leaves and darted towards the glass. It flicked out its tongue and Ford took a quick step back.

'I hate snakes,' he said.

'Black-headed python,' said Banjo. 'Won't hurt you.' He stood grinning as Ford looked at each enclosure. In most of them the occupant was hidden, but he was sure that each held a snake.

'Any of these poisonous?'

'Nah. I used to keep some venomous ones, but a taipan got out of the vivarium one day and showed up in the kitchen. My old lady went ballistic. Hit the thing over the head with a shovel and then threatened to do the same to me. Only keep the friendly ones now. Carpet pythons, woma, black-heads, plus a few lizards and thorny devils.'

'Why do you keep them down here?'

'Temperature's easier to keep constant, and there are a few that aren't strictly legal. Not endangered or anything, but I'm not exactly a licensed breeder.'

'You breed them?'

'No. You'd be surprised how many bikers find a snake in their swag at night when they're out in the bush.'

'I'm not sure I'm happy down here.'

'Nobody knows about this place besides my old lady and the kids. The bloke that we bought the house off built it, but he's been dead a while. Mad Croatian bastard, he was. Blasted this hole in the ground himself on the quiet. Used to work up at Mount Charlotte as a driller. Every week he'd pocket a few blasting caps from the mine and mix up a bit of ANFO at home. He used to set off the charges at the same time as the main pit, so nobody would hear it. Next-door neighbours even complained to the mine because the vibration was knocking the crockery off the shelf. Old Phil used to grow his mull plants down here and had a nice little collection of antique firearms.'

'Couldn't I stay in the house? At least there'd be more than one exit. I feel cornered down here.'

'Not a good idea. If my old lady sees you, she'll come after you with a shovel, same as that snake. She doesn't appreciate my friends dropping in. If you should happen to meet her, you'll understand why I gave up the club for love.'

'So, what's the bed for?'

'Sometimes, if I find I've outstayed my welcome in my own bed, I creep down here and keep the snakes company. If I have to explain it, you wouldn't understand.'

Ford emptied his pockets onto the bed, and picked up his cigarettes and lighter.

'Don't do that down here,' said Banjo. 'There's not a lot of air circulating and the smoke sends the snakes crazy.' He shuffled past Ford. The basement was hardly big enough for him to pass. Watching him going up the ladder, Ford was surprised at how agile he was.

Following him, Ford stuck his head out of the trapdoor. 'How long are you going to be gone?'

'No idea.'

'What am I supposed to do down here?'

Banjo pulled a six-pack from the fridge and handed it down to him.

'How do I know you won't bring them back with you?'

'You drink my beer and scrounge my bourbon and neck my pills, and then ask if you can trust me. Some strange Pommy manners you've got there, mate. I should've left you in the street. Now, put your head down, you daft bastard.'

'So, why are you helping me?' Ford asked.

Banjo bent down and spoke quietly into his ear.

He bore him in and fixed him right
(Helped by the local drunk),
And wined and oiled him well all night,
And thought beside his bunk.
And on the morrow ere he went
He left a quid and spoke
Unto the host in terms which meant
'Look after that poor bloke.'

Banjo smiled and closed the trapdoor, and Ford had to duck his head. He heard the sheet of plywood scraping into place, then listened for the bike being rolled back, but couldn't hear it. Trapped and alone, he didn't like the idea one bit.

He twisted one of the beers open. With the heat from the ultraviolet lights they wouldn't stay cold for long. He took off the coat and pulled the shirt over his head, kicked off his boots and pants and lay on the camp bed in his jocks, sipping the beer and thinking. He could make his own way from here but he would be in no better position than he had been at the beginning of the day. He had no alternative than to stay where he was and see how it played out.

Lying on the bed, he tried to imagine where Grace was, and wondered whether she was thinking of him. His hand strayed to the nugget around his neck. In the quiet of the basement he became aware of the noise in his ears, a distant echo of the explosion in the armoured van. Now, though, it wasn't a ringing, more of a hissing.

ELEVEN

Ford was disturbed by the sound of the plywood sheet being dragged away from over the trapdoor. He wasn't sure if he'd slept, but he remembered a dream of snakes in trees. It may have been a waking dream born of fever, and it seemed to be continuing when he saw the python looking at him through the glass. He stood up and pressed himself against the wall on the far side from the ladder.

'Banjo?'

'Yeah. Relax, mate.'

'You on your own?'

'Yes. Come on up.'

The trapdoor opened and Ford climbed up the ladder. As he came out into the shed still only wearing his jocks he felt the cool breeze.

When he was clear of the trapdoor he turned in time to see Banjo bringing the shotgun from behind his back. He levelled it at Ford and smiled. 'You could have put your pants on, mate. This is embarrassing enough without you standing there in your grundies.'

Ford shrugged. He looked at the shotgun in Banjo's hand. It was a double-barrelled vintage piece with twin triggers and curled hammers. The barrels had been sawn short and were resting in the crook of his arm. The stock had also been removed and filed into a pistol grip wrapped in layers of gaffer tape blackened with a patina of dirt. Banjo's finger wasn't on the triggers, but both hammers were cocked.

Banjo went on, 'Sorry to do this to you, mate, but you've not been straight with me, have you?'

Ford walked towards the wood stove and put his back to it, feeling the warmth in his kidneys. The dog in the basket stirred.

'Max, come out of there,' Banjo growled. The dog skulked across the floor and lay down behind Banjo's legs. 'The cops have had a tip that the Vipers were involved in something out at the Gwardar mine and now they're coming down hard on them. You came in here wearing pants with the Gwardar logo. You want to tell me about it?'

Ford shook his head. He wasn't ready yet.

'Alright. The cops have been ringing up every club member on their list, asking who's hiding you. They're threatening, unless the guys involved in what happened are turned over to them, to bust down the door of every member, and their families, till they find them. The guys I spoke with don't know what's gone down and they're spooked. If any of the club were involved the club will look after them, whatever they done, there's no way they're going to give up their own brothers. But here's the thing: nobody seems to give a shit about you. If the boys find out I'm hiding you, then I'm in as much shit as you. You've put me in a right bloody corner, between the club and the cops. I was just doing a little favour for Shirley and look where it's landed me. So tell me what the fuck's going on.'

'Who was it looking for me at Shirley's?'

'Don't know yet. Not Kalgoorlie boys. Must have come up from Perth.'

'Wouldn't your mates know if club members from Perth were here?'

'You'd think that, wouldn't you? But they don't. That's why everyone is twitchy.'

Ford looked to the door. Banjo was again between him and the only way out.

'You need to understand your situation,' said Banjo. 'The Perth chapter has put people in town without telling the local boys. Don't know why that is. The clubhouse has already had a visit from the cops, and two blokes are in the lockup after they found them in possession. I think the only reason the cops haven't picked them all up is that they don't have the manpower. Busiest Friday night of the year.' Banjo lifted the shotgun. 'Right now, you seem best placed to shed some light on this.'

Ford looked at the muzzle of the gun, like two black eyes staring at him. 'There was a robbery at Gwardar. This morning. Four men hit the gold room. I was there when they came in.'

'But you're not there now.'

'They drove out of there in the armoured van and took me with them. Out in the desert they blew the van to get to some of the gold. The guard was killed.'

'But you're still with us.'

'I got lucky.'

'Didn't you just. Why'd they take you along?'

'I don't know.'

'I think you do.' Banjo dropped the shotgun to his side and reached for the bottle of Jim Beam on the bench. He lined up the two shot glasses and poured a measure into each. Ford watched him. 'You look like you need a shot of this.' Ford took a step forward, but Banjo stopped him by bringing up the gun. 'First do one thing for me. Go back down that ladder and put your shirt and pants on. I've had enough of looking at your battered carcass.'

Ford edged down the ladder, keeping his eyes fixed on Banjo. He found his clothes on the bed and put them on. As he pulled on his boots, he spotted an unopened bottle of beer on the floor. He picked it up, but it was warm, so he left it on the floor and scrambled back up the ladder.

As his head came through the hole he saw Banjo crouching down to meet him but couldn't move quick enough to avoid the swinging right hook that caught him across the cheekbone. His head snapped sideways and his foot slipped on the ladder. He grabbed at the rungs as his chin hit the edge of the trapdoor and his front teeth sank into his bottom lip. Finding his footing on the next rung down he pulled himself up out of the hole, spitting blood on the floor. He got into a crouch, ready to spring, but when he looked up, Banjo was standing over him smiling.

Ford ran his tongue around his mouth and found a loose tooth. He looked for the gun and saw it lying on the bench.

'Sorry, mate,' said Banjo. 'That was a bit low, I'll admit, but you were taking my easygoing manner for granted. I thought the gun might make you a bit more talkative, but you're a stubborn bastard. Get up.'

'I've had people pointing guns at me all day. I'm over it.'

Banjo held out his hand to help him up. Ford took it and pulled himself to his feet. As he straightened, Banjo drove his fist into his gut. The air burst from Ford's lips and he went down again. He lay curled on the floor, clutching his belly and sucking air.

By the time Ford was back on his feet, Banjo was leaning calmly against the bench, cradling the shotgun. He picked up a rag from the bench and threw it to him. Ford caught it and dabbed at the blood on his lip.

'I'm about ready for that drink now,' he said, walking towards the bench. Banjo took a step back to give him room, and Ford drank both glasses and filled them again from the bottle.

'You thought about why they took you with them in the van?' said Banjo.

Ford raised the glass and held it up to the flickering light from the stove, watching how the flames made the bourbon glow. There was a drop of blood suspended in it. 'They were setting me up to look like their inside man,' he said. 'They were going to leave me there, dead in the van.'

'Why didn't they?'

'I locked myself in the van. They tried burning me out. I was lucky.' He drained the glass and refilled it.

'What happened to your shoulder?' asked Banjo.

'A bullet clipped me.'

'You'd better give me a closer look. That'll probably need something.'

Ford slipped the shirt off his shoulder and Banjo inhaled sharply through his teeth. He took the iodine from the bench and poured it over the black blood, wiping it clean with a wad of gauze from the first aid kit. Ford flinched as the scab broke away and fresh blood began to ooze into the gauze. Banjo took a few adhesive butterfly stitches from the first aid kit and pulled the strips from the backing. He pinched together the sides of the wound and pressed the stitches onto the skin either side. By the time he had finished, Ford had tears in his eyes.

'That should just about see you through. Take a drink, mate.'

'I need to use your phone,' said Ford.

'Who d'you want to call?'

'My wife. I haven't spoken to her since this happened. I want to know where my daughter is.'

'What are you telling me?'

'I'm telling you I'm worried about her.'

'You think they'll go after your family.'

'That's what they said.'

'Who?'

Ford sighed. He picked up the bottle and a glass, and sat down on the battered plastic chair by the fridge. 'Two men paid me a visit in Perth. Wanted the entry code for the gold room at Gwardar.'

'So you gave it to them?'

'No. Somebody else must have. They gave me a phone, though, a prepaid burner. They wanted me to text them the access code as soon as I knew it.'

'D'you still have the phone?'

'No, I destroyed it at the mine.'

Banjo was silent until Ford raised his head and looked him in the eye.

'What did they have on you?'

'What makes you think they had something on me?'

'You've got patsy written all over you,' said Banjo.

Ford slumped. 'Gambling debt. I wasn't lying to you. Bad run on the horses. It got out of hand.'

'And they threatened your wife and kid?'

'They'd been watching them. We don't live together. They'd been following my girl to school.'

'Who was the other man? You only told me about the big guy.'

'A little weasel. Called himself Jimmy.'

'Little Jimmy?'

Ford nodded.

Banjo lowered the hammers on the shotgun and broke it, shaking his head as he laid it on the workbench. 'Why the fuck didn't you say that in the first place? You've taken two sucker punches and half a bottle of my bourbon, you bastard.'

'Who is he?'

'He's a weasel, alright. You picked about the nicest word for him. He's Perth chapter. Heard some talk about him wanting to become president, but that'll never happen. How much gold they take?'

97

'Eight twenty-kilo bars. Maybe eight million.'

Banjo whistled. 'Give me some of that bourbon.'

Ford showed him the empty bottle. Banjo reached under the bench and pulled out a new one from inside a toolbox. He filled both their glasses.

'I need to try and phone my wife,' said Ford. 'I tried a couple of times earlier today and she didn't answer.'

Banjo shook his head. 'The cops'll be monitoring her calls. You call from here and they'll be all over us. How old's your daughter?'

'Five. She'll be six next July.'

'Year older than my girl.' Banjo looked out of the door towards the house. 'She and her mother will both be asleep by now, unless the old lady's sitting up in bed with a frying pan, wondering what I'm up to.'

'So how do I find out if they're safe?'

'You said you wanted to turn yourself in. That would be your best bet. If this turns into something between the Perth and Kalgoorlie chapters of the club, then I can't protect you. Get the cops to track down your family.'

Ford thought about that while he drained his glass. 'Can you drive me to the station?'

'I told you, I don't want to be seen by the Vipers or the cops.'

'Then how?'

'Let me think.' Banjo emptied the glass, and squatted down to stroke the dog at his feet. 'How many men you say did the robbery?'

'Four.'

'Get a good look at any of them?'

Ford shook his head. 'They all had respirator masks, goggles, hard hats. One of them was short, could've been Jimmy, but he didn't speak.'

'You know where the gold is?'

'No. They switched from the van to a plane, it could be anywhere.'

'You don't want anyone thinking you know where the gold is, okay? So who d'you reckon is their inside man?'

'Only a few people would have known the code and when the time lock on the safe would open. Not many would have known there was that much gold there. What I don't understand is why Jimmy would show his face to me before the robbery.'

'Because he's a big-noting wank stain with some sort of short-arse Napoleon complex. He's just playing the big man in front of the other guys, showing them he's the man with the plan. He was telling you that he doesn't give a fuck and that you can't touch him.'

'The robbery looked well planned.' Ford was thinking out loud. 'Little Jimmy doesn't strike me as the mastermind type.'

'Don't underestimate him. He's a hard, sly, vicious little cunt. He's quite capable of pulling off something like that, but he can be an unpredictable bastard, especially when he's tweaking. He showed his face to you thinking that you would be dead at the end of it.'

Ford lifted his arm above his head, stretching his shoulder, testing the stitches. 'So who tipped off the police to the Vipers?'

'Who knows? With Jimmy's big mouth, there could be any number of people heard about it. Plenty of faces around Perth who wouldn't mind seeing Jimmy knocked off his perch. Might not be someone dropping a dime, might be something the cops picked up from phone taps. They got wires on some of the home phones.'

'Any ideas how I hand myself in?'

'You got a lawyer?'

'Do I need one?'

'My experience, you always need a lawyer if you talk to the cops. Specially the ones round here.'

'You know one?'

Banjo started packing away the first-aid kit. 'The club had a good brief. Smart man. You'd need a lot of cash, though. And he's probably not the man you want if you're trying to distance yourself from the club.'

Ford thought about that. 'I don't know a lawyer, but I know a man who does,' he said. 'Alan McCann. Owns the Gwardar mine.'

'Friend of yours?'

'Met him a couple of times. Every now and again he visits the mine. Flies in on his corporate jet. Likes to watch them pour the gold.'

'I know him. Well, I seen him in the paper. Knew his daughter. She used to hang around the club. Nice-looking thing.'

'She hung out with the Vipers? Would she have known enough about the mine operations to tip them off?'

'I doubt it. She was off her tits most of the times I saw her. Became a bit of a liability. McCann sent some guys to get her one day. Dragged her off to some fancy rehab over east. Nasty business. I hear she's clean now. McCann never lets her out of his sight.' Banjo looked at Ford doubtfully. 'He's not the sort of man you can call up on the telephone.'

'I won't have to. He'll be at the races tomorrow and he'll have his lawyer near him. They own horses together.'

Banjo continued to look sceptical. 'He's the sort that looks out for himself first.'

'He'll be surrounded by an entourage of investors, lackeys, arse-kissers and flunkeys, C-list celebrities and sportsmen. That might make him play nice.' For the first time Ford thought he might have found a way out.

Banjo made a face. 'Better than anything I can come up with.'

He disappeared into the office and came back carrying a bucket, which he handed to Ford. Inside was a roll of toilet paper. From the fridge he pulled out a bottle of mineral water and two parcels of newspaper tied up with string. He dropped the parcels and the bottle into the bucket, and put the bourbon beside it, then fetched the bottle of pills from the bench and threw it in. Ford took a step forward and looked into the bucket.

'What's that for?'

'You're back down the hole for the rest of the night. There's some cold sausages in there left over from last night's barbie,' he explained. 'I was going to give them to the dog. Eat the sausages, drink the bourbon, and crap in the bucket if you need to. Don't make any noise. Stay down there until midday tomorrow, then I'll take you to the track.'

Ford backed down the ladder carrying the bucket. The dog was eyeing him as he disappeared with the sausages. Ford looked up as Banjo reached for the trapdoor.

'You're still thinking, aren't you,' said Banjo, grinning through his beard. 'Still wondering what's going to be waiting for you the next time this flap opens.'

'It feels like whack-a-mole.'

'I hung out with the Vipers for fifteen years. Did a lot of riding, rooting and fighting. But there came a time when they told me I had to either shit or get off the pot. Know what I mean?'

Ford nodded.

'My old lady was pregnant with our girl at the time. I was so happy when she was born, it was like I'd been smacked on the arse with a rainbow. I couldn't do what the club was asking. It wasn't me, so I got out for her sake. Didn't want her to be caught up in that. There was suddenly more than just myself to consider when I threw my leg over the bike. Now, put your fucking head down.'

The trapdoor closed and Ford heard the plywood being dragged over it, and the creak of the trapdoor as the bike was wheeled into place.

TWELVE

Ford lay back down on the bed. The bourbon helped him drift off, but the painkillers and the heat in the basement brought on more strange dreams. Grace visited him in his sleep: he saw her sitting on the beach, in the distance. She was waving to him, but his feet were sunk deep into the wet sand at the edge of the waves and he couldn't move.

He woke several times before he finally dragged himself into full consciousness. His body clock was knocked out of sync by the artificial light and claustrophobia, but hunger kicked in, which told him it was past breakfast and likely mid-morning. Hung-over, and dehydrated from the dry reptilian heat, he took a long pull from the water bottle and unwrapped one of the newspaper parcels. It took him a few moments to register what was inside.

Instead of cold sausages, he found a dozen dead mice knotted together with their tails intertwined. Most of them had broken necks or crushed heads, or stripes across their bellies from traps. Looking up, he saw two snakes watching him through the glass and shuddered. As he wrapped the mice back up he thought about opening the other parcel, but his appetite had disappeared.

He stood up, turned his body to the light and examined the bruising to his ribs and back. The scratches on his shoulders, stained yellow with iodine, were starting to scab over. His cheek was sore from Banjo's fist. He bent close to the nearest tank and tried to see his reflection in the glass. There was a dark shadow round his eye socket, which was puffy. His bottom lip was also swollen and a scab had formed over the split. He ran his tongue over his teeth.

Lying back down on the bed he tried to keep his mind clear, but instead drifted in and out of sleep.

He was woken again by footsteps overhead, and was up and dressed before he heard the handle being lifted on the trapdoor.

Climbing the ladder he raised his head hesitantly through the trapdoor to eye level. To his relief, Banjo was on the far side of the shed, squatting down with a wrench beside the bike. Ford pulled himself out and closed the flap, then went to look out the door of the shed. The sky was a clear blue, but there was a cool wind.

Banjo stood up and joined him, looking up at the sky, then turned to face him. He leaned in close and looked at Ford's swollen eye. 'You should have put some ice on that,' he said. 'Be a nice shiner tomorrow. You ready?'

'I don't really feel dressed for the races.' Ford looked down at the worn coat, his pants still creased with dust, and his scuffed site boots.

'It's Kalgoorlie. There'll be all sorts. Just act like you've blown in off the desert.'

'I have.'

Banjo disappeared into his office and returned with a broad-brimmed felt hat. 'Try my old Akubra for size, mate. She'll just about complete the outfit.'

Ford took the hat and turned it around in his hands. He put his finger through a hole in the crown.

'Mice,' said Banjo.

'Get a lot round here?'

'All over the place, the little bastards.'

'Good for the snakes, eh?'

Banjo grinned. 'Opened the wrong parcel, did you?'

Ford nodded. 'Haven't eaten since yesterday breakfast.'

'You'll be alright. Plenty of decent tucker in the corporate marquee.'

'I've been trying to work out a way to get in there, to get to McCann,' said Ford. He tried on the hat. It was a little loose. He pulled it down and levelled the brim, looking for his reflection in the window.

'I've seen better scarecrows.' Banjo reached into his pocket and brought out a laminated ticket attached to a bright green lanyard. 'Pass to the corporate area. Should get you into any marquee you like. Mate I used to ride with is working security, gave me this a couple of days ago. You best take it. I'll go up the TAB and put my bets on there.'

Ford took it and read the print on the front. 'You got a horse for the Cup?'

Banjo shook his head and smiled. 'Never put money on the nose. Worked out a nice quinella for the Cup, and a couple of parlays for the day.'

They walked outside and Banjo slid open the side of the van. Ford got in and sat down on the floor, away from the window. As Banjo started the van and drove out of the yard, Ford tried to think about how he might play the day. He had met McCann twice before, once when the boss was touring the mine with his entourage, slapping guys on the back and telling them what a great job they were doing. The second time he wasn't so chummy. The bearings had failed on the mill and stripped the gears off the pinion, and they had lost five days' production while they put it right. Ford thought management had acted quickly, with people pulling double shifts during the shutdown, but McCann came in on his private jet, still wearing his city suit, and made all the site management and engineers wait for him in the mess hall. He then stood in front of them and gave them thirty minutes of his opinions, punctuated by thumps of his fist on the table in front of him. The talk in the wet mess later was that McCann wasn't a mining man.

After about ten minutes, Banjo stopped the van and spoke without turning around. 'This is as close as I can get to the track with all this traffic. You'd best walk from here.'

Ford opened the side door and stepped out onto a pavement crowded with people. Couples arm in arm, men looking uncomfortable in their best shirts, groups of overdressed women in hats, all walking in the same direction along a street choked with buses and taxis. He turned and stuck his head back into the side door of the van. 'I guess I've got a lot to thank you for.' He traced his fingers over his black eye. 'Is there any way I can pay you back?'

'Don't mention my name. Don't come near me ever again.'

Ford met Banjo's eyes in the rear-view mirror. The smile had gone out of them. He nodded, then closed the door and merged with the crowd. He lit his first smoke of the day and savoured it as he walked. His swollen lip hurt, so he let the cigarette hang out of the side of his mouth.

As he approached the racetrack he saw people standing in line outside the gate, queuing at the ticket booth. Ford found the laminated pass in his pocket and put the lanyard round his neck. He walked past the queues and joined the crowd pushing their way through the front gate. There were stewards checking tickets, searching bags and asking the youngsters for proof of age. They saw Ford's pass and waved him through.

Once through the gate, he found himself looking at a group of police. They were standing outside a mobile incident room parked up behind the entrance. There were five of them, drinking coffee and laughing with each other. Ford put his head down so the brim of his hat hid his eyes and kept walking.

He went with the flow of the crowd towards the track, and found himself on the large patch of grass next to the finish post. The parade ring was to his right, and behind him the old grandstand with its red iron roof. Bookies had taken up positions in front of the stand, and the grass was crowded with people sitting around tables cluttered with champagne bottles and crushed beer cans.

He took a walk up the stairs to the grandstand to get a better view through the wall of glass looking onto the track. Half of it fronted the members' area. This held an older crowd, some in morning dress. Two old men had grey top hats on the table in front of them. The champagne they were drinking was French, not the cheap local fizz from out on the lawn.

Ford took a seat at the top of the grandstand, behind a couple of teenagers in short dresses with feathers in their hair. They sounded as though they had been at the wine for a while. The corporate tents were stretched out along the home straight, he saw now, and flags on the third tent had the Gwardar Gold Mine logo. McCann would likely be there all afternoon and Ford felt he needed a drink before confronting him.

He found a small bar at the top of the grandstand, and stood with a group of men drinking with their heads down, reading the form guide. Realising he had no money, he climbed back down and walked through the bookies' ring under the grandstand to find the tote. The area was packed. Screens covered the wall, showing live races from track meetings over east and their odds. The place smelled of fried food and spilled beer. There was a large bar along the far side, and a cash machine in the corner. He figured the police would know soon enough where he was, so he put his card into the machine and took out a hundred.

After buying a newspaper and race guide he elbowed a space for himself at the bar. He bought a beer and a whisky and drank both before opening the paper.

There was nothing in the paper about the robbery. He spent several minutes thinking about why that might be, then turned to the back pages and the tipsters.

He felt adrift without his notes. Before he went to the track in Perth he liked to sit in the café opposite Cottesloe Beach with the newspaper, his journal and his laptop. He would look for vulnerable favourites, pick horses to beat them, find some outsiders, a few roughies to maybe make his heart race, and look for any obvious quinellas. On his laptop he had spreadsheets and pivot tables, with notes on horses, jockeys and trainers. He had written his own software for calculating the odds, and he liked to check the online message boards for tips and gossip. He disliked country racing: it was too random. The day's feature race had a few names that could be relied on, but the rest of the card was full of horses with no class and little talent from second-rate stables. It was a lottery, held purely to give the locals a good day out at the track. He would have to wing it. He told himself he should just enjoy the day while he could, and tried not to let his mind wander away from the horses.

After another couple of drinks he started to feel better about himself. He wandered out to the track and stood at the rail of the parade ring as they brought out the horses for the next race. The third horse to pass him was a tall grey. He had a soft spot for greys, and this one looked lively and in good shape. On the tote board he saw it was paying ten dollars, which made him curious. He checked the book: the trainer was a name he knew and its recent form made him think they had been avoiding races where it might attract too much weight. They'd put a novice jockey on board to get the weight concession. There were three shorter choices that showed better times but no winning ability, and a soft favourite that hadn't performed at this distance. He thought the grey looked like a closer if it could stay on the pace.

He watched until the horse came round again. The strapper was a handsome girl with sturdy thighs. As the horse passed he smiled at her. 'What do you reckon?' he asked. She smiled back and gave him a wink.

Ford went over to the bookies and checked the odds. The horse had already shortened to below the tote price. Its odds started to shorten further as the jockeys mounted up. He picked his moment and got his bet on before the odds shortened too far, and then returned to his spot high in the stand to watch the race.

The ground inside the track was red dirt and dry yellow grass, but the course itself was green. The video screen above his head showed the horses being put into the starting stalls on the far side of the track and brought to order. As they went off the noise from the crowd rose.

He watched the screen as they came around the turn. The grey was up with the pace but was boxed on the rail. The favourite was well behind and failed to make up any ground at the turn. Into the straight the grey got a split and kicked away. Ford turned his attention to the track. The grey had gone too early, and the field closed in the last furlong. The second favourite got up on the line and there was a photo called for the places. Ford cursed himself for not betting the grey each way. He threw his betting slip on the floor and opened the race guide again.

The next race didn't have a clear play and the favourite was a class ahead of the rest of the field, but Ford didn't have the resistance to sit it out. He stared at the form guide, feeling for a winner. Then he went over to the parade ring; this time none of the horses spoke to him. He spotted a quinella with the favourite that could have made decent odds, but he didn't want to walk over to the tote. He didn't mind laying his multiples there for the full card at the start of the day, but hated lining up at the window before a race. It felt like signing on at the dole office.

He finally went with the jockey who had brought home the winner in the previous race and was up on a decent outsider. He knew he was making a bet for the sake of it, but he was enjoying the day out and it was a way of delaying what he had come here to do.

Standing close to the rail he watched the favourite come home by five lengths. His horse had pulled wide and lost ground, and finished outside the places. Two races and the makings of a bad streak.

He decided to look for McCann in the corporate tents. The area was fenced off, and the big man on the gate looked like he normally worked nightclubs. His shirt could barely contain his chest. Ford waved his pass at him and made to walk through, but found his way blocked by a large arm. The man took hold of the pass and squinted at it, then at Ford's face. He looked him up and down and took in the dusty boots, the badly fitting coat and the old hat. He leaned in close to look at the black eye and split lip.

'Which tent?' he asked.

'Gwardar,' said Ford.

'Been working today?'

'What do you reckon?' said Ford, forcing a smile. He was waved through.

There were fewer people this side of the barrier, and they were better dressed. The men were in suits, and the women in the sort of clothes they wouldn't often get the chance to wear in Kalgoorlie. A few had gone the distance and wore broad-brimmed hats. Ford felt more aware than ever of his own shabby clothes. Every one of the people he saw had a drink in one hand and a race guide in the other. They all had their backs to the track.

He walked past the first two tents and stood for a second outside the Gwardar marquee. Promotions girls stood either side of the entrance in matching white dresses. They each wore an orange diagonal sash with the company logo on it. Ford stepped up and they gave him the same blank mechanical smiles they had no doubt given everyone that day. If his clothes bothered them, they hid it well. Saying nothing, one of them handed him a brochure for the company as he passed. He left it on the first table he saw.

A bored waitress came past carrying a tray of champagne flutes. Ford took a glass in each hand. He drank the first one and put the empty back on the tray before she had time to move on. He sipped the second glass as he walked.

A second waitress went past with a tray of canapés. Realising he hadn't eaten since he'd left the mine, Ford put a hand on her arm to stop her. He put a couple of pieces of salmon in his mouth, and snatched up a handful more. The waitress furrowed her brow at him, and he smiled at her through a mouthful of fish.

He walked around the tent. There was no sign of McCann, but he found himself among the finest Kalgoorlie and Perth had to offer: rich people, clever people, talented people, untalented people, freeloaders, retired footballers, TV weather girls, trophy wives, ladies who lunch, high rollers and chancers, facelifts, drunken eyes and coked-up smiles. He was disappointed that there was nobody so famous that they didn't want to be recognised.

A pretty girl in a flouncy dress looked familiar. She was showing a lot of leg and, as Ford watched her, a breeze rippled through the tent and lifted the hem of her dress. He saw a flash of white panties, and recognised her as one of the skimpies from the Exchange the evening before.

He put his empty glass on a passing tray and grabbed another full one. He was walking back towards the track when he saw Marco Mariotti standing on the edge of a circle of people and staring into his glass. The look on his face suggested that he didn't know the people he was with. Looking up, he caught Ford's eye and raised an eyebrow in surprise. Mariotti was wearing a suit that looked like it had seen quite a few Cups since it was in fashion. It had probably fitted him then, but middle age spread had caught up with him. His hair and his moustache had greyed, and his jowls had stretched to meet his collar. He pulled at the collar nervously, as though it was choking him. Ford walked towards him.

Mariotti took a moment to take in Ford's clothes and bruises before he spoke. 'Please tell me someone beat the shit out of you.'

Ford held out his arms and did a stage bow. 'I know I'm quite a sight, but could you do your staring later?'

'What the fuck are you doing here?'

'Enjoying the big man's hospitality, same as you.'

'Does he know you're here? I heard stories.'

'So tell me.'

'They said you were taken in the van. They reckon you were the inside man.'

'Who's saying that?'

'The guys on site. Werran rang me.'

'Did he tell you he pissed his pants?'

'He told me you were top of the cops' list.'

'You spoken with the police?'

'Not yet. They rang me to find out where I was. I'm going in to talk to them tomorrow.'

Ford thought he saw the beginnings of a smug smile creep across Mariotti's plump face. 'Tell me you're not glad it didn't happen when you were in charge,' he said.

'Werran spent nine hours with the cops yesterday. I'm happy I missed that. I think he's been wetting himself at hourly intervals since it happened, wondering what McCann and his man will do to him.'

'I'm here to hand myself in.'

'You look more like you're having a drink and a punt.'

Ford looked at the glass in his hand and the form guide sticking out of his pocket and shrugged.

'Gambling's a disease,' said Mariotti. 'You need to give it away.'

'We all have a cross to bear. What's your weakness?'

Mariotti ignored the question. 'You pick any winners?'

'No. But I made a bookie smile.'

'I thought you were smart with the horses? The guys in the camp were always talking about the tips you gave them.'

'A man can never know enough about horseracing, or anything else. The moment he thinks he knows it all, he's just beginning.'

'You'll find the cops out by the gate when you're finished here.'

'Came in looking for McCann. I need his lawyer.'

'Too right. Won't find him down here. The gold was supposed to be in here, along with the van.' Mariotti glanced scornfully around at the throng. 'Look at all these pricks, standing around like they're owed all this. They were promised they'd get a look at the gold. It's been stolen, but that doesn't stop them drinking him dry.' He looked back at Ford, his expression sceptical. 'You made him look a right twat. You might want to keep your distance.'

'Where is he?'

'Skulking in the members' bar with his mates. I think his lawyer's with him.'

Ford put his hand to the brim of his hat and bowed again. He headed for the exit and refreshed his glass on the way. When he looked back at Mariotti he saw he was on the phone.

As soon as he was out of the tent, Ford lit a cigarette. As he walked he took deep drags between sips of champagne. Over the loudspeaker he heard the race caller start the commentary for the next race, but he didn't want to watch. He walked through the bookies' circle and along the bottom of the grandstand to the door marked MEMBERS ONLY. There was nobody to check his pass, so he pushed the glass door open and climbed the steps up through the seating to the bar at the top.

A line of people sat along the railing on the top tier facing towards him, watching the race. Front and centre was McCann. He had his binoculars to his eyes, following the race, but Ford had no trouble recognising him. His face was always on the company newsletter, and there was a framed photo of him in the foyer of the mine office, standing in front of an ore truck draped with a company banner and the Australian flag. The strong nose, receding hairline and goatee were distinctive, even with the binoculars obscuring his face. Ford tried to guess his age. There couldn't have been more than five years between them, but McCann was carrying too much weight under his linen suit, and the thinning grey hair made him look much older.

The tall girl standing next to him looked as though she would rather have been somewhere else. Her skin was pale, and contrasted with her long black hair, which hung limply over one eye. She wore a black dress that flowed all the way to the floor. It had a high collar and long lace sleeves, and with her skin and hair it gave her a funereal appearance. Through the lace Ford could see the shadows of tattoos up her arms, and when she raised a hand to sweep back her hair, he saw a row of studs in her ear. He remembered what Banjo had told him about McCann's daughter, and wondered what else the sleeves might hide.

As the horses came down the straight, McCann let the glasses hang round his neck and his eyes followed the leading horse. He drew back his lips in a snarl and Ford could see his teeth were gritted. The well-dressed people around him were shouting, but McCann was silently clenching his fists and pounding the rail in front of him, flexing his knees as if urging the horse forward. The horse crossed the line and McCann blew out his cheeks and his lips relaxed into a smile, but then his eyes met Ford's and the joy left his face.

The people with him were jumping and cheering, and reaching across to slap him on the back, but McCann was perfectly still, his eyes fixed on Ford. When they saw his expression, McCann's companions fell silent and followed his gaze. They were soon all looking at Ford.

He took off his hat and ran a hand through his hair. 'My name is Gareth Ford.'

'I know who you are, mate,' said McCann. 'That's twice you've ruined my day.' Ford lowered his eyes. 'That was my horse, two lengths clear. I should be smiling, but I'm looking at you. I should be in my tent with my gold, but I'm looking at you.'

Ford turned the hat around in his hand, reading the label inside. 'I need your help. I want to turn myself in to the police.'

'Look at me,' said McCann. 'Do you know where my gold is?'

Ford raised his eyes and shook his head.

'Did you have anything to do with it?' The folds of skin beneath McCann's deep-set eyes were flushed red, but his irises were a cool grey. Ford tried to hold his gaze.

McCann turned and nodded to someone behind him, and then looked again at Ford. 'We can't talk here. Come out the back.'

He pushed through the crowd to the back of the bar, and Ford went up the last flight of steps to follow him. McCann opened a wood-panelled door in the back wall and disappeared inside. Ford followed him, stepping into a small function room. He turned to close the door, but a man in a black suit stepped in behind him, filling the doorway. He was a couple of inches taller than Ford, broader in the shoulders, and his neck was as wide as his head. His hair was cropped short in a buzz cut, with a sharp line around the ears, as if it had been clipped that day. He had thin lips, clamped tight, and a nose that looked as if it had been broken and reset more than once. Ford found himself looking at his own reflection in the man's sunglasses.

'Please move inside,' the man said. Ford thought he heard an accent, but couldn't place it. The man closed the door, standing in front of it with his arms folded. Ford noticed the neat creases pressed into the front of the man's trousers, and the deep shine on his dress shoes. He was getting sick of doormen.

McCann stood at the head of the dining table, his hands on the back of a chair. On his fingers were several heavy gold rings. His mouth was curled into a politician's smile, but his grey eyes were the colour of lead. 'You've got about two minutes before I have to go down to the parade ring to collect my trophy.'

Ford stepped up to the opposite end of the table. 'I want to go to the police. I need a lawyer. I thought you might know a good one.'

McCann's expression didn't change. 'They tell me you went in the van.'

'The men took me with them. I didn't have a choice.'

'Did you let them in?'

'No.'

McCann started playing with his rings, pulling them and twisting them around his fingers. 'Where's my fucking gold?'

'I don't know,' said Ford. 'They left in a plane. They could be anywhere.'

'Were you part of this?'

'No.'

'Did they do that to your face?' said McCann, pointing.

'They kicked me round, shot at me.'

'Why'd they let you go?'

'They didn't. I got away.'

'Out there?' said McCann. 'And you made it all the way here. No wonder you look like shit.'

Ford nodded.

McCann took a mobile out of his pocket and selected a number, then spoke into the phone. 'Michael, we're in the club room at the back, could you join us?' After hanging up, he looked Ford up and down again, and then puffed out his chest. 'I pride myself on being a good judge of character, Ford, and not many men could get all the way here in your condition and then have the brass neck to just stand there drinking my champagne.' Ford looked at the glass in his hand. 'And what kind of boss doesn't stand behind his employees? I want this cleared up before it does any more damage to my business.'

There was a knock on the door and the man in black opened it. A thin, pale man in a pinstriped suit came in. He looked at Ford and frowned, but corrected himself and forced a narrow smile before turning to McCann.

'Ford, this is my lawyer, Michael Grimes,' said McCann. 'Michael, this is Gareth Ford, who's been missing since yesterday's trouble.'

The lawyer offered Ford his hand. His grip was unexpectedly firm.

'You going to introduce me to the big fella?' Ford nodded towards the man at the door.

'This is Henk Roth, my head of security,' said McCann.

Ford held out his hand, but got no response. 'I hope you didn't organise the security out at the mine,' he said.

Roth shook his head. 'I can see why people beat you up.' This time Ford picked the clipped accent as South African.

McCann turned to the lawyer. 'Ford wants to help the police with their enquiries, and I'd be grateful if you could offer him any assistance he might require.'

'The police are outside now, looking for Mr Ford,' said Grimes. 'Two plainclothes officers. Very low-key, didn't want to upset the members. Would you like me to talk to them first?'

Ford wondered how the police had already known he was there, then remembered Mariotti's phone call.

The loudspeaker outside announced that correct weight had been declared on the race, and McCann smiled. 'Sounds like I'm needed in the ring. Excuse me, gents.'

As he passed Ford, he held out his hand. Ford shook it and felt McCann's gold rings bite into his fingers. Grimes followed McCann out of the room. Roth closed the door behind them and folded his arms again. He didn't look like a man for conversation. There was nothing for it but to wait. Ford went over to the window, opened it, and lit a cigarette.

THIRTEEN

Ford was on his third cigarette, listening to the loudspeaker and the noise from the crowd, when the door opened again. He'd smoked the last one too quickly and it had burned unevenly down one side. He flicked it out of the window before it got down to the filter.

Grimes gave him a weak smile as he entered. He sat at the table and gestured for Ford to sit opposite him. He then looked over his shoulder at Roth and nodded. Roth slipped out of the door.

The lawyer put his hands on the table and spread his fingers. He spent a few moments examining his nails before lifting his eyes and staring at Ford. His narrow face and prominent nose reminded Ford of a hawk, and the watchfulness of his eyes suggested he was searching for prey. 'There are two plainclothes officers outside the door. They're giving us a few minutes alone before you go with them.'

'Will I be under arrest?'

'No. I persuaded them that it would be best to escort you discreetly from the members' stand and take you to the station.'

'I need to contact my wife.'

'You'll have to ask them if you can make a phone call.'

'That's not what I meant. I can't get hold of her.'

The lawyer looked at his hands again. Through the window the loudspeaker started to announce the runners for the next race, and Grimes checked his watch.

'Not keeping you, am I?' asked Ford.

The lawyer jutted out his chin and his eyes locked on Ford's. 'Normally I would advise anyone in your situation to keep quiet and decline to answer any questions, but you're in a tricky spot. The police have agreed not to arrest you because I've assured them that you wish to cooperate. If you choose not to answer their questions, or if you display any of the attitude I see here, they may decide to arrest you and lay charges. They tell me they have evidence that links you to the robbery.'

'Bollocks.'

'I see you're not going to follow my advice. Alright: if you assist the police in recovering the gold, Mr McCann will throw all his weight behind having any charges against you dropped, or any sentence suspended.'

'I told McCann I had nothing to do with the robbery. He said he believed me.'

'Mr McCann has an optimistic outlook. He likes to display a sunny disposition in matters of business, he thinks it inspires confidence. He's lucky that he has me standing behind him. I don't share his faith in human nature.'

'I'd hoped you'd be on my side.'

'I am, but our first priority is the return of the gold. You offer us the best route to achieving that.'

'Why chase the gold? Why not claim the insurance?'

Grimes didn't answer. He stood up and walked to the door, opened it and left. While he reached into his pocket for his cigarettes Ford thought about his last question. Before he could open the packet the door opened again and Grimes walked in, followed by two men in poorly fitting nylon suits. One was a head taller than the other.

The bigger man was the muscle type, with the build of a rugby player gone to fat. Ford checked his ears, and sure enough they were misshapen. The other man was small and lean, with wavy brown hair that looked too long for a cop. He bounced on the balls of his feet like a welterweight. Both men looked quickly around the room before their eyes fell on Ford.

'Detective Constable Butcher and Detective Constable Morton,' said Grimes.

Unsure of who was who, Ford rose out of his chair and offered his hand. They both looked at his hand for a second, then returned their attention to his face. Neither spoke, but the smaller one made a nod towards the door and they each took a step sideways to allow Ford to pass between them.

Ford put on his hat and made for the door. As he passed between them the smaller one spoke quietly. 'The car is by the police incident van outside the front gate. Walk slowly through the crowd. We'll be behind you.'

'Which one are you?' asked Ford.

He didn't get a reply, so he continued walking out through the door. A cheer went up as he emerged into the bar at the back of the members' stand. For a moment Ford thought it was for his benefit, but when he looked around he saw McCann leaning against the bar pouring champagne into a silver trophy.

'Drinks all round, my shout!' McCann bellowed, raising the trophy and taking a swig. The crowd offered another cheer and started pressing towards the bar. McCann handed the trophy to his daughter and moved through the crowd, allowing them to shake his hand and slap him on the back. He caught Ford's eye, and although the smile didn't leave his face, his eyes slowly tracked Ford as he elbowed his way past with the policemen close behind him.

Ford pushed down the stairs and through the glass doors at the bottom of the stand and walked out onto the grass by the finishing post. The crowd was still thick against the rail. Spotting an empty table with an abandoned bottle of champagne that was still a third full, he swerved to pick it up. He raised it to his lips and took a long pull. It was warm and flat, but he was past caring. He felt a hand on his arm; when he turned, he found himself face to face with the larger cop.

'Butcher?'

'I'm Morton. Keep moving.'

Ford went to walk on, but Morton kept hold of his arm. The burly policeman took the bottle from Ford's hand and put it back on the table, then took Ford by the elbow and pushed him through the crowd.

As they came around the back of the grandstand, Ford had to sidestep a girl in a pink cocktail dress who was on her hands and knees throwing up into a hedge. Her friend, who was kneeling beside her, holding the girl's hair away from her face, saw Ford looking and gave him a little smile and a shrug. Ford pushed on through the crowd.

As they came towards the gate, a knot of people stood watching a band on a scaffold stage belting out some country standards. Ford found himself facing a man leaning against a ticket booth by the gate. The man held an open form guide in his hands but was staring at Ford. He was tall, well built and clean-shaven, with dark hair slicked back and gelled. He wore a green silk shirt open at the neck, the pattern something oriental, and Ford could see scars down his arm as he casually raised a hand to his neck and drew his thumb across it, all the while maintaining his stare.

Ford glanced back to see if Morton and Butcher had seen it, but they were a few paces behind him, their view obscured by the crowd.

When Ford looked back the man in the silk shirt was gone. As they passed out of the gate he scanned the parked cars, searching for that distinctive green silk. Then he saw a flash of green out of the corner of his eye and turned his head. The man was walking towards a car that Ford recognised. It was the green Falcon with the air scoop on the hood.

Ford looked around again for Morton and Butcher, but they had stopped to talk to the uniformed cops drinking coffee by the incident truck. Butcher gestured at Ford to stay where he was, and then continued his conversation. Morton pointed at Ford, and all the cops turned towards him and laughed. Ford looked back in the direction of the Falcon. The man had disappeared again but the car hadn't moved.

Morton stepped inside the incident truck then reappeared a minute later with two steaming styrofoam cups. He and Butcher ambled up beside Ford, and Butcher pointed to a plain white Commodore parked beside the truck.

'I could use a coffee too,' said Ford hopefully.

'Get in the back,' said Butcher.

While Morton fumbled in his pocket for the key and triggered the locks, Ford walked around to the passenger side. He took off his hat and got into the back seat. The car smelled of instant coffee and sickly sweet air-freshener. Butcher sat next to him and Morton sat behind the wheel. Ford heard the locks click.

They moved off slowly through the car park. People were still walking into the races. Ford checked his watch: he reckoned the late arrivals would make the start of the main race. The Commodore crawled between the taxis and buses crowding the road. Ford looked over his shoulder and saw the green Falcon pulling out four cars behind them.

When they reached Hannan Street, Morton turned left and gunned the engine. Ford was still looking over his shoulder and didn't notice the turn until they were past the houses and into the light industrial buildings on the edge of town.

'We're heading out of town,' he said.

Ignoring him, Butcher took a slurp of his coffee. He pulled a pair of sunglasses out of his pocket and put them on.

'The station is the other way,' said Ford, waving his finger over his shoulder. He looked behind him, but the Falcon was no longer following. He looked at Butcher and then at Morton. Both were motionless behind sunglasses.

'So where are we going, fellas?' he asked.

FOURTEEN

The two-lane highway ran straight as a ruler through the workshops and warehouses on the edge of Kalgoorlie, past yards full of mining equipment and ore trucks. The edge of town was marked by a pair of steel towers built to resemble minehead winding gear. Still looking for the Falcon, Ford turned his head as they passed, and read the sign saying WELCOME TO KALGOORLIE.

A distance marker announced six hundred kilometres to Perth, and Ford considered the possibility that they were taking him all the way. There wasn't a lot else along the highway: three hundred klicks of featureless bush, then a couple of hundred more across the great expanse of the Wheatbelt, and finally the climb over the Darling Scarp to Perth.

As soon as the town finished, the red dirt of the bush began. Tall salmon gums crowded the road, their bark starting to glow pink in the late afternoon sun. The car was heading west, and the sun was shining directly into Ford's eyes. He could feel its heat on his skin, a contrast to the chill breeze from the car's air conditioner.

Morton kept the car at a steady hundred. In the rear-view mirror Ford could see his sunglasses and knew that Morton was watching him, not the road behind. Butcher was slumped in the seat beside Ford, but it was difficult to tell if he was asleep behind his glasses.

After fifteen minutes the car slowed as they came up behind a ute with flashing lights. A sign across the tailgate identified it as a pilot vehicle, and another on the top of its cab advised that there was a wide load ahead. Ford could see the slow-moving low-loader a hundred metres further up the road, a dismantled ore truck stacked on the trailer, blocking the entire outgoing lane and half of the other lane as well. Oncoming traffic was passing the loader slowly, edging out onto the red gravel of the soft shoulder, their wheels flicking up stones.

As Morton pulled out to try to see past the loader, the car was overtaken by a pair of motorcycles. They were travelling so fast that Ford hadn't heard them approach, despite the roar from their exhausts. The noise made Morton sit upright and his head spun to the side. The deep note of the engines was unmistakably Harley. They were past before Ford had time to turn his head, and he only saw their backs as they overtook the pilot ute in front. They were clearly bikers, but their leather jackets had no patches and their helmets were plain black.

Butcher leaned forward and spoke into Morton's ear, and the big cop nodded. He turned the wheel and pulled out clear of the ute just in time to see the bikes slice through the gap between the low-loader and an oncoming truck. The truck blew its horn and flashed its headlights. Morton flicked the steering wheel and the car ducked back behind the pilot vehicle.

Once the oncoming truck had passed, the driver of the ute put his arm out of his window and waved them on. Morton pulled out again and the engine roared. They accelerated past the ute, and Ford saw its driver grinning and shaking his head. They were still gaining speed as they passed the low-loader, dropping one wheel onto the shoulder, the gravel rattling against the underside of the car. Once he was past the big rig, Morton tucked in again and maintained his speed to overtake the second pilot vehicle running ahead of the loader.

At last Morton dropped down to a hundred. By now the bikes were out of sight over a rise in the road. Butcher slumped back in his seat, rested his chin on his chest, and let out a sigh like a dog settling. The road stretched out empty in front of them.

Ford leaned forward. 'You going to keep me guessing?' he asked Morton. 'Going to give me the silent treatment all the way to Perth?'

'Not Perth, Coolgardie. Be there in ten. Sit back. Shut the fuck up.'

As Ford slunk back into his seat he saw a road sign announcing that Coolgardie was twenty kilometres ahead. He had stopped there for fuel once on the way to Kalgoorlie, but could think of no other reason to get out of the car. At the turn of the twentieth century Coolgardie had been the third-largest town in the state, centre of the goldfields, but the gold ran out and the miners moved on to the thriving mines further east. Now it was virtually a ghost town, just several hundred people who would rather live there than in Kalgoorlie.

The salmon gums stopped as the road entered a graceful bend at the edge of town. The outskirts were bare red dirt, with a single row of telephone poles next to the road, following the curve. A sign announced they were entering a Historic Town, and beneath it someone had added a hand-painted board: SLOW DOWN. LOOK OUT FOR BLOODY EMUS.

They crawled up the main street, keeping to the speed limit. The road was wide and desolate. The few grand buildings that faced the street were widely spaced, like the remaining teeth in a rotten mouth. He looked at the wide, empty streets and the dusty houses, their tin roofs ablaze with the sun's reflected light, and wondered what it would take to feel at home in a place like this.

There were a few cars pulled up to the wide verandah of the pub, and next to them were parked the two Harleys. Two figures leaned against the posts under the shade of the verandah. They still wore their helmets, as well as red bandanas around their mouth and nose, and wraparound glasses. As Ford watched, their heads turned to follow the progress of the unmarked police car down the street. The only other traffic was a road train rolling towards them down the centre of the highway, its diesel blowing smoke.

The Commodore slowed in the centre of town, Morton waiting for the road train to pass so they could make a right turn, away from the bikes. They stopped directly in front of the town hall, a huge pink-stone building with muscular arches supporting an imposing Greek pediment. It sat marooned in the main street, as if marking the furthest point inland that the tide of civilisation had reached before falling back, leaving it beached there.

They made the turn and doubled back behind the town hall, pulling into an empty red-dirt lot adjacent to a featureless single-storey building. It was a drab concrete-block structure with a flat green roof and wired glass windows mounted high in its walls. A blue sign on a pole by the street announced it as the police station. Theirs was the only car in the street.

Butcher and Morton threw open the doors and got out. Morton came around to Ford's side, opened his door and stepped back, gesturing to him to step out. The big cop then led him by the elbow around the front of the building and through the entrance.

The front office was small and bare, with a plain wooden counter mounted in a hatch in the far wall. A small office was visible through the hatch. It was unattended. Morton pushed

Ford up to the counter and rapped his knuckles on the wood. Butcher sat down on the single steel chair in the corner, took out his mobile phone and thumbed the keypad.

A uniformed officer came through the back office and stood behind the counter. He looked at the two plainclothes men and then gave Ford a once-over, taking in the coat, the hat and the injuries to his face. He looked back at Morton and raised an eyebrow.

The big cop pulled his ID from his pocket and showed it. 'You get a call from Kalgoorlie?' he asked.

'About an hour ago. Can't process him though, nobody else here. Our mob are all up in Kal, working the race round, and they're sending youse blokes over here? A right clusterfuck.'

'Which room?'

'There's only one. It's ready. I'll show you.'

The uniform disappeared into the back office and the door beside the hatch opened. Morton took Ford's elbow again and pushed him through the door and down a short corridor. The uniformed officer stood next to an open steel door. Morton steered Ford through it and into a bare interview room. The walls were concrete blocks painted white, and up high was a single window of wired, frosted glass. A wooden table sat in the centre of the room, surrounded by four moulded plastic chairs.

Morton pointed to a chair on the far side. Ford took off his coat and hung it on the back of the chair, put his hat on the table and sat down. Morton stepped out of the room and had a mumbled conversation with Butcher in the hallway, then ducked his head back round the door. 'Wait here.'

'When's my lawyer getting here?' asked Ford.

'Fuck knows. Said he had a runner in the seventh race.' Morton closed the door.

Ford sat alone in the room, staring at the bare wall in front of him and thinking about what was to come. The room felt hot and stale, as though the trapped heat had spent its force outside and left its radiance in the concrete blocks. Damp air blew from a rattling air conditioner fixed in the window, but Ford guessed that it had been turned on just before he entered the room. He spread his hands out on the table and examined where the skin had been stripped from his knuckles. He pulled his cigarettes out of his pocket and lit one.

The door soon opened and Morton stuck his head around it. 'You can't smoke in here,' he said.

'Can I go outside for one?'

'Just sit and wait.'

'What am I waiting for?'

'For a senior officer to interview you.'

'Where's he coming from?'

'He just got on a plane in Perth. He'll be a while.'

'Reckon he'll get here before my lawyer?'

Morton took off his sunglasses and stared. Despite his size, the look came across as petulant rather than threatening, as Ford suspected he intended.

'Can I make a phone call?' asked Ford.

'Not now.'

'I need to contact my wife.'

Morton made to close the door.

'Can I get some water?' Ford called.

Morton closed the door and soon returned with a black plastic water bottle that he put on the table in front of Ford. Printed on it was the Western Australian police badge, the inverted star with a black swan at its centre.

'What a delightful souvenir,' said Ford, then raised it to his lips and took a long pull of the cold water.

As he folded his arms on the table and put his head down on the crook of his elbow he felt a stabbing pain in his bruised arm. He turned his head to try to get comfortable and became aware of the ache in his shoulder. It had been there as a constant throughout the day, but only now, in the quiet of the interview room, had it fully asserted itself. He mentally made a tour of his body, cataloguing the injuries and assessing the pain.

He remembered the pink pills Banjo had given him. Sitting up, he thrust his hands behind him into the pockets of his coat and found two of the pills buried in the lining. After knocking them back with a swig from the bottle, he put his head back down on the table. He was trying to piece together the order of events since he had woken up on Friday morning when sleep overtook him.

FIFTEEN

Ford was woken by the sound of the door opening. By the time he had raised his head off the table three people had entered the room. He instinctively looked at his wrist to check the time, but it was bare. There was no longer any sunlight coming through the window, and the lights were on in the room. The temperature had dropped and he wrapped the threadbare coat around his shoulders.

The shorter cop, Butcher, had placed a manila file open on the table and was looking through some paperwork. Leaning on the back of the chair opposite Ford was an older man in a crumpled grey suit. His tie was askew and the top two buttons of his shirt were open. He leaned forward to bring his face closer to Ford, and his belly hung over the back of the chair. His eyes were small and rheumy and stared at Ford out of deep folds of skin beneath bushy grey eyebrows.

The man sniffed and wiped a hand across his fleshy jowls. His fingers pinched his lips into a pout and he let out a slow hiss. The only part of him that didn't look dishevelled was his hair: a thick silver mane, parted on one side, combed back behind his ears and sculpted up into a high graceful wave over his forehead. It was held in place by a hair product from a different era.

'You're not what I expected at all,' he said.

'I aim to surprise rather than disappoint,' said Ford.

'I'm Detective Inspector William Chadwick. I was at home, having a nice quiet weekend, when I got a call that you had shown up. I got on a plane right way. I've missed my dinner.'

Chadwick was close enough for Ford to be able to smell his breath. Ford thought he should try to maintain eye contact, but his attention was drawn to the woman in the corner of the room.

She was leaning against the wall, her hands in the pockets of her jacket. She looked to be a head taller than either Chadwick or Butcher, and was slim with it. He glanced down and saw she had tooled black boots with Cuban heels. Her hair was bleached white-blonde and she wore it short, parted at the side and slicked back. Ford wondered whether she had been using Chadwick's hair cream. She had a slender neck that seemed long because of the way her hair was brushed back behind her ears. She was dressed in a white blouse and a tan pant suit of the sort worn by bank tellers and plainclothes police. That, along with the mannish haircut, lack of make-up and bored expression, left Ford in little doubt she was a cop.

She was watching her colleagues closely, with a fixed smile that appeared strangely detached. She was saved from being pretty by the intelligence of her eyes. There was a disdain in them. She probably thought her expression was blank, but Ford could read it plainly enough. He saw something similar in the mirror every morning.

'I'm told you want to tell us about your involvement in this incident,' said Chadwick.

'I need to make a phone call.'

'All in good time.' Chadwick pulled out the chair and sat down opposite Ford. Butcher took the chair next to him, drew a pen out of his jacket pocket and started writing on a notepad.

Chadwick went on, 'You've met Detective Constable Butcher. This is Detective Constable Kavanagh of the Gold Stealing Detection Unit, who'll be assisting us.'

Ford waited for Kavanagh to acknowledge him, but she was looking over Butcher's shoulder, reading something in the file. He turned back to Chadwick. 'Why have you brought me to Coolgardie?'

'Kalgoorlie station is chockers,' said Chadwick. 'They've got fifty additional officers drafted in from all over the state for the race round, and those fifty have been justifying their overtime by nicking every drunk and pub brawler in town. On top of all that, some bastard took a few potshots at the station with a handgun last night, so the street is a crime scene. I thought we'd find somewhere quiet for a chat.'

'Am I under arrest?'

'No.'

'Then I'll wait until my lawyer gets here.'

'That may be some time,' said Chadwick. 'He's a busy man. I heard his horse won. We may as well start without him.'

'I'd rather wait.'

'Mr Ford, you've come in here of your own free will, and that will go in your favour when you're formally charged. But if you wish to remain silent, it won't look so good.'

'You're going to charge me?'

'You were an accomplice. Not just the robbery, but the murder of the guard. Our investigation will prove it. Those four men got into the gold room using the security code that you gave them. You told them when the time lock on the vault would be open and the schedule of the armoured van.'

Ford continued to peel the scab off his knuckles. 'I didn't know there was a van,' he said. 'The gold normally goes out on the plane. They only told me on the day.'

'Your involvement in this crime isn't in question here. You were part of it. You shouldn't waste any more time denying it. What you need to think about is what you can do to help yourself. Give us the names of the four men, help us recover the gold, and we might take that into consideration.'

'If you have the evidence, arrest me.'

'You came to us. We're trying to help you here. I'd like to think someone put you up to this. That it wasn't your idea. You were desperate or threatened.'

Ford looked at Butcher, who was taking notes. 'You going to record this?' he asked.

'This is just a community station,' said Chadwick. 'Unfortunately there's no equipment here to tape an interview. Any arrests made in Coolgardie are transferred to Kalgoorlie for processing and questioning. DC Butcher will write down your statement.'

'He can start by writing that I had nothing to do with the robbery.'

Chadwick shook his head and smiled. 'Can you see why we might suspect you of being an accomplice to this?'

'I can see what it looks like. I can see what you're supposed to think. I was set up.'

'If you got involved for selfish reasons, like gambling or drugs, I wouldn't think much about it. But if you did it because you or your loved ones were threatened, I can understand.'

'You'll have to show that I was involved,' said Ford.

'We will.'

'You'll have to get some evidence.'

'We'll get it.'

'You don't seem to want to listen to my side of it.'

Chadwick stood up and took off his jacket, and hung it on the back of his chair. There were sweat stains under the arms of his shirt. 'There are two types of people that get themselves in this sort of situation,' he said. 'One is the person who makes a mistake in judgment due to some unfortunate circumstances. The other type simply wakes up in the morning and pretty much does whatever they want without concern for others. Which one are you?'

'Neither.'

'You've only been working at that mine six months. That's something to take into consideration. When you're working with this amount of money, it can be a big temptation. Being a new employee makes it all the more important to explain the circumstances. For all we know, you only took this job to get near the gold.'

'I was background-checked by the Gold Squad before I was allowed on site,' said Ford.

'With all respect to my colleague, the Gold Squad don't know shit. They just pull up your police file and see if you have any prior convictions or outstanding warrants. They don't look into your past, see if you have any debts, or a history of gambling, or a drinking habit.'

Ford looked at Kavanagh, but she was still leaning against the wall, flicking through some papers she had lifted from the file, and didn't react to the detective inspector's statement.

Chadwick took some more papers from the file in front of Butcher and examined them. 'We've spoken to the other men present in the gold room yesterday,' he said. 'They're all pointing the finger at you. You seem to be the key. Can you explain why you were taken away in the van?'

'To cast suspicion on me.'

'Why?'

'To deflect attention away from the guilty party.'

'Do you suspect anyone else? On the other hand, can you vouch for anyone else?'

'I don't know anyone on the mine well enough to vouch for them. As for whether any of them could have done this, well, none of them are angels. The guys that end up on remote sites like Gwardar are usually either grasping types, after the money, or dead wood who can't get a job anywhere else. Some of the guys are running away from something: they're divorcees, reformed junkies, recovering alcoholics, ex-cons.'

'Which are you?'

'Why don't you take a guess?'

'Why do you think they would try to kill you?'

'Difficult for me to deny being the bunny if I'm dead.'

Butcher leaned over and spoke in Chadwick's ear, bringing his attention to something in the file. Chadwick nodded, then turned back to Ford. 'Who were you phoning at first light?' he asked, smiling.

'I don't know what you mean,' Ford replied.

Chadwick's eyes flashed. 'You were seen up on the plant, smoking, making a phone call.'

Ford thought back to Friday morning. He'd been standing with his back to the offices, looking towards the sunrise. He'd only used the keypad to text, and hadn't held the phone to his ear. Nobody had seen the phone. 'Bullshit,' he said.

Chadwick smiled again and ran his hand through his hair, pushing the quiff back into position. 'What would you think if you were in my position? Your colleagues don't have a very high opinion of you.'

'That's never been a concern of mine.'

'You have a history of disrespect for authority.'

'I'm a professional cynic, but my heart's not in it.'

'You think you're funny?'

'I was once. Probably not anymore. Maybe I left my sense of humour in that tatty coat.'

'They say you're not very personable. You act like you want to be left alone, think you're too good to mingle with the guys.'

'I think what you're trying to say, in the happy-clappy language of corporate bollocks, is that I'm not a team player. I've heard that before.'

'I imagine you get it a lot.'

'Yeah, from people who prefer to be part of a team so they don't have to think for themselves. Men who like to wear a uniform because it's the only way they can get respect.'

'They say you're up yourself.'

'I have a laissez-faire attitude to the mechanics of career advancement.'

'You're a lazy bastard.'

'No. I'm not. Just because I don't have much time for the pricks I work with doesn't mean I'm shit at my job. You won't hear them saying I wasn't doing my job properly. I just wasn't into the arse-kissing and empire building.'

'They say you drink.'

'Not on site.'

'But you have a reputation as a soak.'

'An intelligent man is sometimes forced to be drunk, to spend time with fools,' said Ford.

'You look like you could use a drink now,' said Butcher, raising his head from the notepad.

'Butcher's right,' said Chadwick. 'You look a little nervous.'

'I'd like to talk to my wife.'

'Why? Did someone threaten you? Your family? Was someone putting you under pressure?'

'I'm worried about my family. I was trying to get to Perth to find them. When they had us in the gold room, the men told us they knew where our families lived. They told us what might happen if we didn't cooperate. I haven't been able to contact my wife. I'm worried, and that's why I'm here.'

'Did they threaten your family before Friday?'

Ford looked at Chadwick and remembered what he'd said about the phone. He made a decision. 'No.'

'We checked your address and there was nobody home.'

'We don't live together. She's at our house. Her house.'

Butcher made a note. Chadwick read what he'd written and looked back at Ford. 'Did you ever think about taking gold from the mine?'

'Who doesn't? There isn't a bloke on that mine who hasn't thought about it. I've been in the gold industry for the last five years. Anyone who spends all his time with gold spends a lot of time wondering whether he can get some of it. I've seen all the angles, all the petty frauds, seen guys try to walk off the mine with flakes of gold stuck in the folds of their pants. I've lain awake in my donga, imagining crazy schemes to get gold out of that room, but I couldn't earn enough doing that to offset the risk of losing my job. They pay us well there, because the work is hard and the hours are long and you're a long way from nowhere. They pay you well to remove the temptation. And then we've got you bastards in the Gold Squad breathing down our necks.'

Kavanagh looked up from what she was reading and fixed Ford with a stare. It was the first time she'd looked him in the eye and it unsettled him. Her blue eyes were so pale he wondered if they'd been bleached by the sun.

He spoke to her over Chadwick's head. 'The Gold Squad came out to the mine two months back. You did a security check and we were given a ten-page report outlining security risks in the gold room. You know what that place is like. Until last year it was a busted-arse mine, shut down in care and maintenance. Only got restarted when the gold price hit a thousand bucks an ounce, and it's working even harder now it's nearer two thousand. The owner wanted to minimise capital expenditure on the place, and security is the first thing to get a red line through it. Big mines have card swipes, biometric security, video surveillance. Gwardar has one camera outside the gold-room door, and one inside. The one outside is only to see who's at the door, and doesn't record, and the one inside is linked to a crappy old tape recorder. The tape is only replaced if they think the staff are pilfering. They rely on their isolation, and the fact that nobody knows how crap the security is. They also know there's never enough gold on site to make it worth stealing.'

'So why was there so much gold in the safe?' Chadwick asked.

'You'd better ask McCann. I heard he was going to big-note himself, showing it off to investors at the races.'

'Did you give the thieves information about the amount of gold in the vault?'

'I already told you, I didn't know there was that much in the vault. I didn't even know it was going out by truck.'

'Why not?'

'Because I've never been in the gold room during a transfer before. Not my job. I got drafted in because every other bugger was at the races. Normally the gold goes out on the plane. There are only a couple of bars, once or twice a week. The time lock on the safe is scheduled first thing in the morning, to meet the dawn plane up from Perth. It's difficult to get a van out there at short notice to meet the time lock.'

'Why were you given the second key to the safe on Friday?'

'You'd have to ask Werran. He's head of security. It was a surprise to me.'

Chadwick checked his notes. 'Why stockpile the gold at the mine? Why not at a bank?'

'Either you tell me or I guess. I don't know the answer. Mariotti is head of production. He knows how much gold is going through the plant. I'm engineering manager. I make sure the plant's running smoothly. Maybe you can tell me why the van didn't have a police escort.'

Butcher looked up. 'All resources were tied up in Kalgoorlie for the race round,' he said. Chadwick turned his head and gave the constable a look.

'But there were cops at Leonora,' said Ford. 'They came past me in the desert.'

'There were only two officers on duty at Leonora,' Butcher replied. 'Not enough for an escort.'

'Sounds to me like you didn't know there was that much gold there either. Did McCann tell you the gold was going to be at the races?'

'He did, but he'd arranged private security,' said Butcher.

'Was that the South African I met? Shouldn't you be asking him these questions?'

'Roth? He's a bodyguard,' said Butcher.

'Why would McCann need personal protection?'

It was Chadwick's turn to answer. He shrugged. 'He thinks he has enemies.'

'Was the gold insured?' asked Ford.

'Let's get back to me asking the questions,' said Chadwick. 'What did they offer you? Are you going to see some of that gold?'

'Is this just going to be you asking me the same questions and me reminding you that I had nothing to do with it?'

Chadwick leaned forward until his face was close enough for Ford to smell his breath. 'Maybe you thought just giving information to these men wasn't much of a crime. Did you think nobody would link it to you? Did it all get out of hand? You wouldn't have expected anyone to get killed. Why did you leave with them in the van?'

Ford leaned back. 'They took me at gunpoint. Everyone would have seen that.'

'The others didn't see anything like that. They were locked in the vault.'

'Then they can't contradict me.'

'The smart money is on you being part of this. They said they saw the leader talking to you up close. Whispering in your ear.'

'I was face down on the floor. He wanted my phone.'

'What for?'

'He took everyone's phones.'

'Including yours?'

'No, I didn't have one. He didn't believe me, so he kicked me.' Ford lifted his shirt to show the bruising across his ribs.

'Did he give you the black eye too?'

'Yeah, and the bullet wound.'

'Why didn't you have a phone?'

'I leave it on my desk when I'm walking the plant.'

'You don't carry it with you?'

'I don't like phones. They let people talk to you without buying you a drink.'

'I need a real reason,' said Chadwick.

'Most of the time when I'm out in the plant I can't hear a damn thing anyway,' said Ford. 'They can leave a message.'

'Is it still there? On your desk?'

Ford nodded. Butcher made a note, then got up and left the room.

Chadwick held Ford's gaze for several seconds, then stood up and stretched, his arms in the air, his mouth yawning wide. Ford found himself looking at the stains under the older man's armpits until the door opened and Butcher came back in.

'Suspicion hangs around you like flies around a dog turd,' said Chadwick. 'When you weren't found with the van, it was assumed you'd left with the others. That is, until your credit card popped up at the Leonora roadhouse. By the time we got officers to the gas station you were long gone. We saw the CCTV of you leaving in that ute, but it's unlicensed and we can't trace the owner. Before we got a message to the roadblock at Kalgoorlie you'd passed through. We're trying to find the driver.'

'I doubt he could tell you much. I was just a hitchhiker he picked up.'

'So what happened after the van left the mine?'

'They stopped out on the highway. Blew the door to the strongbox. Loaded the gold onto a plane.'

'What sort of plane?'

'Small twin-engine thing. Old four-seater. Piper Aztec, maybe, or something like it.'

'You seem pretty sure.'

'I've flown in and out of mine sites on those sorts of planes before. They'd painted over the rego.'

'Did they all leave in the plane?'

'Two of them did. Two were left behind and went out on dirt bikes.'

'And they just left you behind?'

'When they'd loaded the gold I jumped into the van and locked myself in.'

'Was the guard in there with you?'

'Yeah, he was already dead. They shot up the van, then pushed it off the road and set fire to it. Then they left on the bikes.'

'But you got out?'

'I used a jack from the toolbox to pry open a split in the side of the van. You'll have seen that.'

Chadwick took something out of the file and put it on the table in front of Ford. It was his mine security card. 'We found this beside the van.'

Chadwick put another security card next to it. It was warped and burnt. Ford didn't recognise the photograph.

'Who's this?' he said.

'Duncan Toomey, the guard. You never asked about him. He had a family, if you care.'

Ford put his head in his hands. 'I feel bad enough about him already,' he said. 'There's not much you can do to make it any worse.'

'Why did you run from the van? Why didn't you wait for the police?'

'The guys on the bikes came back, they were shooting at me. I ran. I kept running.'

'They could've chased you down. Wouldn't have taken them long on the bikes.'

'I can only think that they were on a tight schedule. They knew how long the police would take to get there. They had a spotter outside Leonora station. There was a truck driver who would've seen the bikes and heard the gunfire.'

'We've already got his statement,' said Chadwick. 'Why didn't you hand yourself in at the Leonora station?'

'I knew I was being set up. I knew you would think I was the inside man. I wanted to speak to my daughter first. I was worried about her.'

'Was she threatened?'

'In the gold room, they said they knew where our families lived. I told you.'

Chadwick stood up and leaned over the table. 'We can offer you protection.'

Ford raised his head and looked at him. 'I don't care about me. Protect my daughter.'

'We can put you in witness protection if you give us the gang.'

'I don't know anything about that. Right now I want to get back to my daughter.'

'Have you spoken with her?'

'No. I've told you all this. I can't get hold of my daughter or my wife. She's not answering her home phone and her mobile goes to voicemail. I was trying to get to Perth.'

'Why didn't you hand yourself in when you got to Kalgoorlie?'

'I tried. I got within twenty metres of the front door and then someone started shooting at me.'

Chadwick sat down and smiled. 'That was you? Who shot at you?'

'Didn't see him. He was in shadow.'

'And where were you between the shooting last night and the races today?'

'Hiding.'

'Where?'

'In a hedge.'

'You look like it. Where did you get the tatty coat and the cowboy hat?'

'From the bloke in the ute.'

Chadwick muttered in Butcher's ear, and the younger cop made a note. Chadwick turned back to Ford. 'So let's talk for a while as if you're just a regular witness. Let's talk about the guns. How many did you see in the gold room?'

'Four men, four guns. The leader had a handgun. Small, stubby automatic. When he was handling it in the van, I saw it had a star embossed on the grip. Two guys had submachine guns. Looked like an AK-47, but shorter, with a stubby barrel and no stock. The fourth guy had a shotgun.'

'You seem to know a lot about guns.'

'I watch TV,' said Ford. 'I know a lot about Ferraris, but I've never driven one.'

Butcher took a couple of photocopied pages out of the file and put them in front of Ford. 'These the guns?'

Ford looked. The first was the chopped-down submachine gun, labelled AKS-74U. The second was the handgun with the star embossed on the grip, tagged as a Makarov. 'Yeah, that's them.'

'Russian guns,' said Butcher. 'Russian ammunition, very distinctive. Shell casings found all around the van.'

'Shells from the same type of handgun were also found outside Kalgoorlie police station,' said Chadwick. 'We're waiting for ballistics to confirm whether it's the same gun. These guns have been popping up all over the place. A similar handgun was recovered during a raid on a bikie house in Perth last week. Ammunition from an AK was found at a drive-by shooting of a tattoo parlour in Rockingham.'

'You seem very sure of the handgun,' said Butcher.

'It tends to focus your attention, having it shoved in your face.'

'But you saw the star on the grip.'

'When we were driving in the van, the guy with the stop-watch had it resting in his lap.'

'Did you speak with him?' said Chadwick.

'He spoke to me in the gold room, and I heard him talking in the van, on the radio and the phone.'

'Did you hear any other members of the gang speak?'

'No, only the leader. The guy with the red hat and the stopwatch.'

'Anything distinctive about his voice?'

'Australian accent. Calm, clear voice, like he was used to people doing what he told them.'

'Like a gang leader?'

'Yeah,' said Ford, 'or a cop.'

Chadwick didn't flinch. 'These are the sort of guns used by terrorists,' he said. 'What kind of people are you mixed up with?'

'I think you might be clutching at straws with that one.'

'These weapons have come out of Afghanistan. They might be in the hands of bikies now, but how long before terrorists get hold of them? We've checked your record. You've got form for this sort of thing. You might think you're some kind of freedom fighter, but to me you're just a mouthy little cunt who thinks he looks good in a beret.'

'So you've seen the photos of my arrest?'

Chadwick put a photo in front of Ford. He barely recognised himself. It was his face, but from twenty-five years ago. In the photograph he was sitting on a bench in a corrugated-iron hut, second from the end of a line-up of ten lank-haired students.

'Pathetic spotty little Che Guevara with bumfluff for a beard,' said Chadwick. 'I bet you reckon all cops are corrupt fascist puppets.'

'Are you trying to change my mind?' Ford looked at the photo of his younger self and was embarrassed by the beret with the black star. It was from a time when he'd believed in things. At least he wasn't wearing an army-surplus combat jacket like most of the others on the bench.

'You hate the police?' asked Chadwick.

'I mistrust anyone who has a powerful impulse to punish people, and right now you're giving me a fine demonstration of what happens to a man when he's given a tin badge.'

'You broke into an airforce base,' said Chadwick.

'I was a student, hardly a terrorist,' Ford said. 'It was the eighties. Greenham Common, cruise missiles, American bombers loaded with nuclear weapons flying from British airfields. The protest we made was non-violent. We wanted to paint graffiti and peace symbols on the runway, so we cut the wires on the perimeter of the base. We were carrying buckets of paint and rollers. We never got more than a hundred yards inside the fence before we were swept up by Americans with big dogs. Sat in that shed for five hours with the Yanks pointing guns at us before the bobbies showed up to formally arrest us. We were never charged.'

'You're a man who thinks the law doesn't apply to him,' said Chadwick.

'I used to care, but things have changed.'

'Not looking for a cause any more?'

'I'm the only cause I'm interested in these days.'

'But if you see a law you disagree with, you just ignore it. Are you that cynical?'

'Inside every cynical person is a disappointed idealist.'

'You realise if we think there's a link with terrorism here, we can hold you indefinitely. We can hand you over to the intelligence boys and put you under a control order. We can make you disappear.'

'I don't think you have those kinds of connections.'

'The bikie we picked up with the gun—you want to know what else we found on him? Explosives. Ten sticks of Powergel and fifteen detonators.'

'Powergel? That's a mining explosive. Someone pinched it from a goldmine. It's not terrorism. Sounds more like a bikie turf war.'

Chadwick stood up and walked around the table towards Ford. 'When we charged the mongrel, he threatened to plant a bomb under a police car in retaliation. They opened fire on a police station last night. What's the difference between him and a terrorist?'

'You're not going to use anti-terror laws against bikies. They'll laugh you out of court.'

'Don't ever challenge me to do something, because I'll fucking well do it. Alright? You can rest assured about that.'

'I don't doubt it.'

'You get one of the bikies, you get them all. Their time is up.'

'You're not making it clear what your little vendetta against the bikies has to do with me.'

Chadwick took another sheet of paper from the file and put it in front of Ford. 'We accessed your bank records when we were trying to track you. We can see how worried you must be about your family. After you claim you escaped from the van, you used your bank and credit cards at the gas station, a brothel on Hay Street, and at the racetrack.'

'I can see how that might be interpreted in a way that doesn't make me look good,' said Ford.

'Let's just say it goes to character. Then, at midnight last night, your account was credited with fifteen thousand dollars. Can you explain where it came from?'

Ford took a moment to look at Chadwick, trying not to show any expression, trying to ignore the sinking feeling in his chest. 'No.'

'Let me tell you what we know. We traced the money to an account we've seen before. It was used to pay the deposit on a rural property in the Swan Valley. Nice little place, nestled among the vineyards. Little old lady next door used to keep donkeys, rescued them from nasty farmers. She complained about the smell coming from the new neighbours and when we paid a visit we found a meth lab in the stables. We busted three blokes. One was a patched member of the Desert Vipers Motorcycle Club, and the other two were known hang-arounds. So tell me who you know in the Vipers.'

Ford felt as though his internal organs were being sucked into a hole in his chest. 'I don't know them.'

'Then we've got another little conundrum for you. We checked with the gatehouse. The four men came on site in two low-loaders without cargo. They had security swipe cards that they used at the gate. Two of the cards were from a haulage firm, and the other two were from an electrical contractor doing maintenance on the substation. Guess whose name is on the paperwork granting them access to the site?'

Ford put his forehead on the table. He felt as if gravity had snatched at him and he was in freefall. He was afraid to open his mouth in case a groan escaped.

'I had a feeling about this job as soon as I heard about it,' said Chadwick. 'I thought it was a bikie operation, and now I know it is.'

'You would've doorknocked the names they used on the gate by now,' said Ford. 'The cards must've been cloned.'

'You know what?' said Chadwick. 'I don't really give a rat's arse whether they were cloned. I've got enough right here to link you and the bikies to the robbery. This is where it ends. Give us the names.'

'I think I need to wait for my lawyer,' said Ford.

'Your lawyer isn't coming,' said Chadwick.

'I have the right to a lawyer.'

'Like fuck you do. Not in this state. The right to a lawyer is a convention, not a right, and you were allowed to consult with a brief before you handed yourself in. Let me remind you that you came here voluntarily.'

Suddenly, Kavanagh leaned over Chadwick's shoulder and slapped her hand on the table. The sound echoed off the bare concrete walls, and Chadwick's head spun around. Kavanagh mumbled something in his ear and he frowned.

'We'll be back in a minute,' he said to Ford, then stood quickly and went to the door. He flung it open and disappeared into the corridor. Kavanagh followed. Butcher gathered up his papers from the desk. Ford caught his eye before the policeman looked away and followed the other two out the door.

SIXTEEN

Ford sat alone in the room, trying to hear the conversation in the corridor outside. The voices were a low murmur, though several times Chadwick's rose angrily. Ford strained to listen, but another, more distant noise grabbed his attention. It was the deep growl of a motorcycle somewhere outside. He listened. It seemed to be circling the station, and when the rumble grew to its loudest he could discern that there were two bikes.

As the noise from the bikes faded again the door opened and Chadwick came in, followed by Butcher and Morton. Ford looked for Kavanagh, but she didn't return. Chadwick took the chair opposite, and the other two came around the table and stood behind Ford. A hard, merciless contempt had settled on Chadwick's face.

'Now that the lady isn't present, we can dispense with the touchy-feely stuff,' he said. 'I'll ask you again: where's the gold?'

'I really don't know.' Ford sighed. 'Are we just going to sit here pushing bullshit around the room like dung beetles?'

'You're a half-smart bastard, Ford. When you leave here, you're not going to be anywhere near as smart as before. Strip him.'

Morton grabbed Ford's arms and pulled them down and around the back of the chair, dragging him across the floor away from the table. Butcher leaned across and put an elbow into Ford's groin and with his free arm undid his boots. Ford kicked out, but Morton pulled down on his arms, pinning him to the chair, and pain shot through his arm sockets to the wound on his shoulder. He stopped struggling. Butcher undid Ford's belt and tugged at his pants, pulling him up off the chair as he did so.

Ford winked at him. 'Is this where I'm supposed to ask, "What's this all about?" and he says, "Shut up, I ask the questions?" '

Butcher put more weight on his elbow and Ford yelled out in pain. He gasped, 'Jesus, just let me go and I'll take my own bloody clothes off.'

Morton released his arms and Ford stood up and undressed. Morton collected the clothes and left the room with them. Ford sat down naked on the chair. He leaned forward, putting his elbows on his knees, and looked at Chadwick.

'We'll be keeping your boots and pants for forensics,' said Chadwick. 'We already found your shirt in the garbage at the roadhouse.'

'Then you'll give me back my new shirt and the coat? I'm getting fond of the coat.'

'We'll find you some shoes and pants out of lost property.'

'Can I get my lawyer now?' said Ford.

Chadwick put his hands flat on the table, and slowly balled them into fists. 'Nobody knows you're here. As far as they're concerned, you could be dead.'

'Then I guess I'll take my lawyer's advice and decline to answer any more questions.'

Chadwick looked at the bruising on Ford's ribs, and the scratches on his arms. He paid closer attention to the butterfly stitches closing the bullet wound on his shoulder. 'Someone patched you up. They didn't do that while you were hiding in a hedge. That's not the first lie you've told us. Hit him, Butch.'

Butcher stepped around in front of Ford and drove his fist into his solar plexus. Ford felt the breath knocked out of him and bent double, gulping air. Butcher moved to the side and jabbed low into Ford's ribs, knocking him off the chair. Ford lay on his side and spat a long string of saliva onto the concrete. He grabbed his knees and curled up into a ball. He tried to get his wind back, but breathing hard only amplified the pain in his ribs.

Butcher leaned over him and hissed in his ear, 'This is where you die, you fucker.'

Ford stayed down until he felt the pain ebb, then pulled himself back onto the chair with difficulty.

'Why are you making it tough for us?' asked Chadwick.

'Your job is meant to be tough. A cop's job is only easy in a police state.'

'Cuff him,' said Chadwick. Butcher pulled Ford's arms back behind the chair and snapped the cuffs on his wrists. Ford winced.

'Bit tight?' said Butcher in his ear. He put a finger through the gold chain around Ford's neck and pulled it up so he could see the nugget. He snorted and let it drop.

'You can't do this,' said Ford.

'Oh yes I can,' said Chadwick. 'I have the authority to tread on serpents and scorpions and over all the power of the enemy. You're going to help me get them. You're going to give up the Vipers.'

'If you want them, there's two of them outside right now. They're doing laps. Go get them.'

'One day soon we'll pass a law making membership of any of those gangs illegal, and we'll sweep them up off the streets. This business is just the sort of thing we need to put a rocket up those piss-weak politicians in Perth.'

'I don't have any issue with the bikies, so please don't create a police state on my account.'

'I'm getting tired of your guttersnipe sneering, Ford.' Chadwick nodded to Butcher, who took off his jacket. His face was damp with sweat, his shirt clinging to his chest. He was breathing heavily as he stepped around and smashed his forearm into Ford's cheekbone beneath his black eye. Ford hung his head and fought back tears.

'I'm not a mean person,' said Chadwick, 'but I'll tell you what: I've done things in my life that you never did, and harder things, worse things, and if I've got to do them again, well, I'll do them.'

Butcher bent low and swung a short uppercut into Ford's ribs.

'There's a sucker at every poker table, Ford,' Chadwick said. 'If you can't spot one, it's you.'

Butcher raised his hand and chopped down on the bullet wound in Ford's shoulder. Ford clenched his teeth and growled through the pain. He looked at his shoulder and saw fresh blood soaking through the fabric stitches.

'We might not be doing the right thing,' said Chadwick, 'but you can be sure we're doing it to the right people.'

Butcher slapped Ford across the mouth, and the split in his lip opened up. Ford tasted blood.

'You have to decide now,' said Chadwick, 'whether you want to stay in here with us and tell us what you know or take your chance out there on the street. We can just turn you loose in the middle of the night and see if the smell attracts any flies.'

Ford held up his head and looked Chadwick in the eye. 'We started out here with you thinking I knew something I didn't. If you're still under that impression, then I'm sorry, I can't help you.'

Chadwick looked at Butcher and nodded towards the door. Both policemen left the room.

Alone in the room again, Ford tried to stand but couldn't get his cuffed hands over the back of the chair, so he slumped back down. The room was getting colder and he could see goosebumps across his naked body.

After what felt like half an hour, they came back in again. Butcher walked up to him and hit him with a combination of open-handed blows to the ribs and slaps to the face. Chadwick ran through his questions again and Ford decided not to reply.

'We're going to keep at you until you roll over,' rasped Chadwick. 'If you show me it's worth my while, I can take care of you, but you better do as you're told. If you go back out there on the street, you won't last long. I've got just a little bit of respect for you for making it this far. If you're smart, like people tell me you are, you might make it through this, but if you keep bullshitting me I'll throw you out there and watch you die.'

They went out and came back in twice more, and each time Ford stayed quiet until they left again. When they left the third time, he moved his shoulder an inch at a time to measure the pain. Closing his eyes, he turned his face up to the caged lightbulb in the ceiling. The light soaked through his eyelids and he tried to picture it as the sun, tried to imagine he was on the beach, feeling the warmth on his skin and the ocean breeze in his face. The circle of light behind his lids wavered and he forced it to take the form of his daughter's face, tried to see her smiling, willed himself to feel her warmth. He lost track of time.

The sound of the door opening brought him back to his senses. He wasn't sure if he'd slept or passed out. He opened his eyes.

Chadwick came in and sat down again in the chair opposite Ford, followed by Butcher, who was carrying Ford's clothes. He put them on the table and said, 'There's a new pair of pants here and some thongs. You can keep the roadhouse shirt and the ratty coat.'

'And my hat?' asked Ford.

'Fuck the hat,' said Butcher.

Chadwick put his hands on the table and stared at them. 'We offered to help you get out of the jam you've put yourself in, but you seem to have made your choice,' he said. 'You can take your chances.' He stood up and took his jacket off the back of the chair, then put it on. From his top pocket he took a comb. He ran it through his hair a few times until he was satisfied that the silver wave was back in place, then put the comb in his pocket and walked out of the door.

'Can I go?' said Ford.

'You're free to go,' said Butcher, releasing the cuffs.

'I was free when I came in here.'

Butcher left and closed the door behind him. Ford untangled his own clothes from the pile on the table. He used his shirt to dab the blood from his shoulder and his lip. His eye had started to close. He got dressed and pulled on the trousers. They were loose cotton work pants. They fitted around the waist but were too short in the leg. He hated the cheap plastic thongs instantly, but had no choice. He put on the threadbare coat, then sat back down on the chair and waited.

There were voices in the corridor, and doors closing, the sound of a car starting outside, and then another; both moved off down the street, and there was silence. He waited five more minutes but there were no more sounds outside. Reaching into the pocket of his coat he found his cigarettes and lighter. He went to the door and discovered it was unlocked. He stuck his head out into the corridor but saw no one. Walking to the end and stepping behind the counter, he saw that the front office was empty. He walked back down the corridor and tried all the doors, but they were locked. He was alone in the station. He returned to the counter, then went through the side door into the front office, and tried the front door. It opened and he walked out into the street. The door closed behind him and he heard it click. He tried the handle but it had locked behind him.

He lit a cigarette and inhaled deeply, feeling the bruises on his chest as it expanded. Stepping to the edge of the pavement, he looked up and down the street as he tried to guess the time. The street was wide, and the light poles were placed far apart and gave little light. Most of the light in the street came from the moon, which hung above the buildings in the east and was a couple of days from full. There were no cars moving and all the houses were dark.

Ford reckoned it was only a block to the pub, and guessed it wasn't late enough for it to be closed. He felt in his pocket for his wallet, relieved to find it still there. He was about to turn and start walking when he heard the motorcycle.

SEVENTEEN

He could hear the bike but couldn't see it. It sounded like it was on the highway close to the pub. The roar was that of a Harley with the exhaust bored out. It slowed down, accelerated as if turning, and then got louder. He saw the wash of the headlight spilling out across the road from a side street a few seconds before he saw the bike. It emerged and turned towards the police station: when the rider saw Ford, he stopped a block away in the middle of the street, facing him.

Ford stepped back into the shadows and waited. The glowing tip of his cigarette floated in the dark. The rider turned his handlebars so that the headlight picked Ford out against the bare wall of the station, dazzling him.

He heard a second bike come around the corner further down the street and accelerate towards him. He looked around for escape routes, but the only options were to run down the street or across the empty lot next to the station, and he didn't think he would get far in either direction running in thongs. As the second bike got closer, the engine note rose. In contrast to the low rumble of the Harley, this was a high-pitched whine; turning, he saw that it had two headlights and the rider was low to the bike.

Ford backed further into the doorway of the police station as the second bike screamed up to the kerb and squealed to a halt directly in front of him. It was a sleek road bike, and the rider was in tight racing leathers. Ford's eyes were still tracking over the graceful shape in front of him when the rider yelled, 'Get on!'

He didn't recognise the voice. The rider raised a hand and lifted the helmet's visor. It was Kavanagh. 'For fuck's sake, get on,' she said.

It was the first time he had heard her voice, he realised. It was deeper than he'd expected.

The Harley rider further up the street had woken up to what was happening and gunned the engine. It lurched towards them with a screech of rubber, the rider fighting the sliding back wheel. Ford ran from the shadows and threw his leg over the back of Kavanagh's bike. He put his arms around her and she opened the throttle. The tyres chirped once as they set off. Ford felt the front of the bike go light and tried to lean forward to compensate. The pinion seat was higher than the rider's, perched over the rising exhaust with the footpegs way up over the rear wheel, and Ford could feel the heat of the exhaust on his bare foot. His knees were bunched up like a jockey's either side of Kavanagh's hips. She was lying low over the tank, so he wrapped himself over her.

He looked over his shoulder at the road behind them. They had about fifty metres on the Harley. The rider was steering with one hand: the other was pointed towards them. Ford saw the muzzle flash, but didn't hear the shot above the scream of Kavanagh's bike.

She ran five blocks dead straight without looking back, and Ford didn't know whether she knew they were being shot at. By the time she eased off the throttle and started dropping through the gears to make the turn back onto the highway, she had increased their lead to a hundred metres. He felt her shift her weight on the bike, her hips almost off the edge of the seat, pushing against his knee, her own knee hung out wide as she threw the bike over and took the corner. They shot out onto the wide highway at speed, Kavanagh not bothering to check for traffic. She pulled the bike around in a tight turn into the centre of the lane and opened it up.

As the bike surged forward, Ford felt himself slide backwards on the seat, his long coat tails flapping behind him. He glanced around again and watched the Harley come out onto the highway, making a much wider arc than Kavanagh had and crossing onto the opposite lane, the rider fighting the weight of the bike.

Turning forward, Ford ducked his head to the side of Kavanagh's helmet to get a look at the speedo. Still within the town limits, they were already past one fifty. Kavanagh didn't let off the throttle through the long curve out of town, and by the time they hit the long straight road to Kalgoorlie it was reading two hundred and the Harley was out of sight behind them. The headwind made Ford's eyes stream, so he buried his face in Kavanagh's back and inhaled the smell of her leathers.

They ran for five minutes at a steady two hundred, the headlights throwing shadows among the gum trees lining the road. Eventually they crested a rise and ahead of them were the lights of Kalgoorlie. Kavanagh throttled back and then braked, bringing the bike to a stop at the side of the road. Planting her feet firmly either side of the bike she cut the engine. The road was clear in both directions. She lifted the visor of her helmet and turned to face Ford.

'We've got about a minute on the guy behind us,' she said.

'There were two of them in Coolgardie watching the station when I was brought in.'

She nodded. 'The other one will be waiting at the Kalgoorlie end to box us in on this stretch of highway. The bloke behind will have phoned ahead.'

'Where can we turn off?'

'There's a mine access road, and a couple of bush tracks, all gravel leading nowhere. I brought the wrong bike for that. The Ducati stays on the bitumen.'

'Any ideas?'

'The second guy will be waiting at the edge of town, where the streetlights begin. When we get there, I'll be going fast and might need to duck and weave. Don't try to lean into the corners. It'll be hard enough turning with two up without trying to second-guess where your arse is going to be. And try not to hang on so tight. Back there you were clinging to me like a koala with vertigo.'

She slapped down the visor and restarted the bike. They accelerated away as briskly as before and the lights of the town came rushing towards them. Looking back, Ford saw a single headlight come over the rise behind them. He tried to streamline himself behind Kavanagh as they screamed down the centre of the highway.

As they came closer to the streetlights, Ford lifted his head and looked for the painted steel winding gear marking the edge of town. Silhouetted against an advertising billboard was a man on a motorcycle. The bike moved slowly onto the road ahead of them, turning towards them with its lights off. It stopped in the centre of the road, directly under the streetlight. The rider put down the kickstand and took both hands off the handlebars. Kavanagh feathered the throttle and moved to the edge of the blacktop, then put her head low behind the windshield.

As they got closer the waiting rider raised a gun in both hands, the streetlight shining off the short barrel, and Ford ducked his head behind Kavanagh as the muzzle flashed. Something bit into his thigh and he felt a punch in his shoulder. If Kavanagh was hit she didn't show it: she kept the bike fast and straight through the traffic lights and down the highway. Ford looked over his shoulder and saw the gunman swing his bike around and set off after them. The second rider pulled level with him and they gave chase side by side.

Kavanagh slowed as she came up on traffic heading into town. There were two lanes in each direction and she weaved in and out of the cars, switching lanes and then surging ahead. The road curved gently past some motels, and when it straightened out again she looked over her shoulder for the first time before standing hard on the brakes and banking the bike tight left into a side street. She cut her lights and ran to the next intersection, then did a series of right and left turns through the gridiron network of residential streets until she pulled up at a small roundabout bordered by white-painted iron railings. A single spotlight lit up a statue of a soldier with his rifle levelled for a bayonet charge. The statue stood lonely in a vast empty car park in front of a low sandstone building with a sign announcing itself as the railway station.

Kavanagh took off her helmet. 'Get off,' she said, without looking round.

Ford swung his leg over the bike and dismounted. He staggered, and took a moment to find his balance. At first he thought his leg had cramped from the high footpegs, but when he rubbed his thigh it stung and his hand came away wet with blood. He remembered the shotgun, and his hand went to his shoulder. It was sore but there was no blood. He dug his fingers into the shoulder flap of his coat and found the pellet buried in three layers of heavy oiled canvas.

'You alright?' asked Kavanagh, looking at a crack in her helmet.

'I'm not sure,' said Ford.

Kavanagh walked around the bike, ran her fingers over the chipped windshield, and knelt down to examine the fairing. Then she picked idly at the padded shoulders of her jacket and prised loose a pellet embedded in the leather. She flicked the pellet towards the statue and it pinged off the bronze. 'Bloody idiot,' she said. 'Shooting at us with rabbit shot.'

Ford was leaning over, dabbing at the blood seeping through his trousers. 'It hurts plenty enough,' he said.

'Don't know what he expected to hit. Moving target and a sawn-off? He shot too early and with too big a spread. Bastard was lucky he hit us at all.' She pulled another pellet from her jacket. 'Look at this shit. What's that, number six shot? You couldn't bring down a duck with that.'

Ford looked at the bike, trying to see if there was any damage. 'Anything serious?'

'Was running a bit hot just then, so I pulled over. I think they clipped the radiator or one of the lines.'

'Will she run?'

'She'll get us where we're going.'

'Where's that?' asked Ford. She didn't answer, turning back to the bike and kneeling down beside the fairing. 'You going to tell me why you rescued me back there?'

'Wasn't a rescue.'

'So what was it?'

'Chadwick wanted you swinging in the breeze, to see if you could draw them out.'

'I kept telling him I didn't know anything.'

'He doesn't give a toss. Butcher was writing up some bullshit notes tying you to the Vipers and the robbery. That's how Chadwick works. Stitching you up with an old-school verballing. He's counting on you not seeing out the weekend, so he can present Butcher's notes as evidence of your interview. De facto confession. No tape or video, and you won't be around to contradict him.'

'I was being set up?'

'You're everyone's favourite patsy.'

'What's it to you?'

'I've been in that interview room before. It had a tape machine, and a little Handycam on a tripod. They stripped the room and made sure there were no other officers around.'

'But you were there.'

'Yeah, I managed to put a bit of pressure on him to get in the room, but he soon kicked me out. He's trying to get it all sorted this weekend. On Monday he'll have the Major Crime Squad and the Gang Squad crowding him out. He wants to have a go at the bikies before he loses control of the investigation.'

'He seems to have a hard-on for the Vipers.'

'Them and all the rest. Goes back way before my time. Last year he put one of them away on drugs charges. Then someone put a bomb under his house. Timer didn't work properly and it went off after he'd left for work. Chadwick reckons it was the Vipers. It was certainly half-arsed enough to be them. Know anything about bikes?' She had her hand inside the front air scoop, feeling around the radiator. There was coolant dripping onto the bitumen.

'I ride them. I can't fix them,' said Ford.

'I thought you were an engineer?'

'I am, but in all the years of university we only did one day of motorcycle maintenance, and I was sick that day.'

'I thought you lot spent your spare time tinkering with steam engines and all that shit.'

'There are a few old nuff-nuffs still do that. You can spot them by the beards and the halitosis.'

'So what sort of engineer are you?'

'The kind with a laptop and a master's degree. Asking me if I dismantle machines in my spare time is like asking a surgeon if he relaxes by doing embroidery.'

Kavanagh's eyes flared. 'Not much of a bloke, are you?'

'Probably not by your measure.' He took a couple of steps away from the bike to test his leg. The pain was manageable. 'Thanks again,' he said, turning away and limping across the car park.

'Where do you think you're going?'

'Perth,' said Ford without stopping.

He heard her footsteps behind him, and in a few long strides she was level with him. Putting a firm hand on his shoulder she pulled him to a stop. 'It wasn't a rescue back there. I'm keeping you alive until Major Crime show up on Monday. Homicide might be joining the party as well. I don't want Chadwick or the bikies making a mess of you before they get here.'

'They already made a mess of me,' said Ford. 'I need to get to Perth.'

'How do you intend doing that this time of night?'

Ford looked around the station. The goods yard was lit up with floodlights, but the station itself was dark and there was no sign of movement.

'No trains till tomorrow, and by then the station will be chockers with the crowd from the race round and crawling with uniform,' she said. 'The airport will be the same, and I don't imagine you could walk too far with that leg.'

Ford turned to face her and leaned in so she could see his eyes. 'I'm going to Perth,' he said.

'You're staying with me,' she said. 'I'll arrest you if I have to.'

'You going to take me in?'

'Probably best if we keep you away from any of Chadwick's mob, don't you think?'

Ford looked at the clock over the entrance to the station. It was later than he'd thought. If Diane was at home, or at Walsh's house, then it would be a good time to find her.

'I need a phone,' he said. 'Give me your mobile.'

She shook her head. 'Chadwick's been monitoring all phone traffic since the robbery. He might be monitoring calls to your wife and any other known associates. I don't want my number showing up.'

'Then I need to get to a public phone, or get access to a computer. I want to check if there's any contact from her on any of my email accounts.'

Kavanagh turned and walked back towards her bike. 'I know somewhere you can get online,' she said after a moment. She threw one leg over the bike and waved for him to get on.

He limped after her and slowly took his place on the pinion. 'You have to know that I am innocent in this.'

'Innocence is relative,' she said, pulling on her helmet. She hit the ignition and let it idle, her head tilted to one side listening to the motor. Then she pulled away carefully and headed back through the residential streets.

They rode slowly, turning so many times through the side streets that Ford lost track of where they were. He noticed when they crossed over Hannan Street because it was the only time Kavanagh gunned it, but he lost his bearings again soon after, though he figured they were heading southeast towards Boulder.

They pulled up at last in front of a small weatherboard cottage with a galvanised iron roof, sitting behind a wooden picket fence. It was old but neat. Kavanagh killed the motor and kicked down the stand.

'Where's this?' he asked as she pulled off her helmet.

'Friend's place,' she said. 'I need a coffee.'

EIGHTEEN

Kavanagh rang the doorbell and Ford stood behind her, try-ing to blend into the shadows. He heard footsteps in the hallway and a silhouette appeared behind the coloured leadlight window in the centre of the front door.

'Who is it?' called a woman's voice, confident, with a musical quality.

Kavanagh leaned close to the glass. 'It's me.'

Ford heard the bolt being drawn back and a chain being released, and the door swung open. The woman smiled at Kavanagh, but her face clouded when she saw Ford. She was a head shorter than both of them, and peered up at him over the top of half-round reading glasses, which had a chain that went around her neck. Ford thought it must be a considered choice, because she was younger than him by at least ten years. Her brown clothes also looked like they belonged to an older woman. Her eyes were pretty and betrayed a sharp intelligence, and he started thinking about what she would look like if she cut her hair and wore something better. Maybe that was what she was trying to avoid.

Kavanagh stepped inside and turned to let Ford past her into the narrow hallway. 'Alannah Doyle, this is Gareth Ford,' she said. Ford held out his hand.

Doyle paused a moment, studying his face, then shook the offered hand. 'You look pale,' she said. 'Like you've had the life drained out of you.'

'Beaten out of me, more like,' said Ford, and returned her smile.

'You're white as a sheet.' Doyle looked at Kavanagh and raised an eyebrow.

'Why don't you take him into the kitchen and make some coffee,' said Kavanagh. 'I'm going to move the bike round the back.'

'Coffee's always on,' said Doyle.

Ford limped after her down the hallway and into a kitchen that took up the back half of the cottage. A wood-burning stove filled one wall of the kitchen, and an enamelled coffee percolator bubbled on the hob. The room was warm and stuffy. The smell of fresh coffee and wood smoke made Ford realise how tired he was. He yawned, then winced at the pain in his lip.

'You want some ice for that eye?' asked Doyle.

'I think it's beyond that.' He lifted his shirt to show his blackened ribs. The bruises were tinged with yellow at the edges. Now that he was in the light, he bent over and took a look at the pellet wound in his leg. It was still bleeding. With the adrenaline of the chase subsiding, he was beginning to feel the pain. Thinking back, he realised he'd been in pain ever since the first kick in the gold room. It had been so constant that at times he'd forgotten it was there, like a distant background noise.

'We'll have some coffee and then see about cleaning you up,' said Doyle.

'Got anything stronger?'

She shook her head and laughed, then pointed to the kitchen table for him to sit down. The table was piled high with books, magazines and newspapers. There was a laptop next to a stack of looseleaf handwritten notes. He sat down in front of the computer and started reading the screen. Doyle walked over to him with a mug of coffee, made some room on the table and set it down. She reached across Ford and closed the laptop.

Ford switched his attention back to his leg. The pellet had made a ragged hole in his pants and some of the threads had been dragged into the wound. He started plucking at the material and pulling it clear of the neat circular hole. The wound wasn't deep, and when he moved his head in the light he could see the pellet shining just below the level of his skin. The flesh around the wound was starting to swell.

Kavanagh strode into the kitchen, her boots thumping on the hardwood floorboards. She took off her leather jacket and held it up to the light to look at the rips in the shoulder, then hung it on the back of the chair. Ford looked at the way she filled her leather trousers. Her white T-shirt was a similar snug fit. She ran a hand through her hair, messing it up where it had been pressed flat by her helmet, then pulled up the sleeve of her shirt and looked at her shoulder, rotating and flexing it. A small mark was the only evidence of where the pellet had hit her, but Ford was looking at the muscle definition in her slender arm and the length of her fingers. She had the body of a gymnast and the hands of a musician.

She caught him looking, turned away and went to the stove. When she turned, he saw the gun tucked into the back of her leather pants. Her T-shirt had ridden up around it and he saw that the skin across the small of her back was tattooed. He couldn't make out the design.

'Nice tatts,' he said.

She put her hand on her back and pulled down her T-shirt, touching the gun as she did so. He saw her jaw tighten as she realised he had seen it.

'That's a lot of ink,' he said. 'Did it hurt?'

'Just enough,' she said.

She found herself a mug and filled it from the pot in a way that suggested she knew her way around the kitchen. She then stood next to Doyle, both of them leaning against the counter, cradling their coffee mugs in their hands and looking at Ford. He stared back, trying to read the look in Doyle's eyes.

When nobody said anything, Ford reached into the pocket of his coat and felt around for any of Banjo's pills that might still be there. There were no pills and he remembered the police taking his clothes out of the interview room. He pulled out his wallet, flipped it open and checked the credit cards and what little cash he had. Then he caught Kavanagh's eye and nodded towards the computer.

'Don't you want to get that wound sorted first?' she asked.

Ford looked at his leg. The blood was turning black and the bleeding had stopped. He shook his head. 'It can wait. I need to get online.'

Doyle looked at Kavanagh. 'I was about to go to bed when you two walked in here with all this heavy drama.'

'We need your help,' said Kavanagh. 'We need your computer.'

Doyle frowned and gestured towards the hallway. Kavanagh followed her out of the kitchen. Ford listened to them whispering. He couldn't make out what they were saying, so he looked over the laptop. It was newer and more powerful than his computer at work. There were no cables: it was running on batteries and the light on the front told him it was connected wirelessly to the net. He looked around until he saw a black box on the shelf next to the telephone, blue lights winking at him.

The women came back into the kitchen. Doyle reached across him and opened the laptop, then closed the text document on the screen. Ford managed to read another couple of lines before the window vanished, a report on local identities seen at the races. With the newspapers and books piled on the table, and the report he'd just seen, he picked her as a journalist, and he began to think about how she might help him.

She continued to lean across him as she typed, and he could smell her perfume. He looked down at his grubby feet in thongs, the stained shirt and pants, the tattered coat, and wondered what he might smell like to her.

'I've logged you in as an anonymous identity I sometimes use, and routed you through a proxy server in Indonesia,' she said. 'You should be pretty much invisible.'

'Thanks,' he said, eager for her to step away from the keyboard. 'I need to go through my own proxy, but I'll piggyback through your server.'

She stepped back, looked at him over her glasses, and gave him a smile with more respect in it than before.

Ford cracked his knuckles, placed his fingers on the keys and began to type. He found his proxy and then checked his home email, which had no new mail since Friday. His work mail was routine traffic until Friday morning, when there was a company-wide announcement that the email system would be going down for a period of routine maintenance. Service had been restored on Saturday.

Ford imagined the arguments between Gwardar management and the police about any loss of production, and made a bet with himself that the plant would be up and running within forty-eight hours of the robbery, which would be Sunday morning. The clock in the corner of the screen told him it was already Sunday. He decided to log into the Gwardar control systems later, to see if the plant was back in production.

He checked several of his private email accounts that Diane might have addresses for, but there was no contact from her. He went to her email accounts, personal and business, but there had been no activity in any of them since Friday. When he heard a cough behind him he turned to see both women reading over his shoulder.

'You access your ex-wife's email?' asked Kavanagh.

'She's still my wife.'

'I'm not sure that makes much difference.'

'She's used the same password for the last eight years, her date of birth. She asked me once whether she should put the day before the month, or use the American format. She's not very security conscious.'

'Well, that's alright then,' said Doyle.

'I'm not sure you're so clean that you can lecture me,' said Ford. 'It's your proxy I'm hiding behind. What do you use this set-up for?'

She smiled and returned to the stove.

'So how often do you read her mail?' asked Kavanagh.

'Fairly regularly since last year.'

Kavanagh folded her arms, and Ford turned back to the screen. He opened an old video-conferencing account he'd set up under a pseudonym and tried ringing her home phone number, her mobile and her voicemail accounts, but all of them rang out.

'I need to tell her a phone number where she can reach me,' he said.

Doyle shrugged. 'Not this house.'

Kavanagh pulled a business card from her wallet and put it on the table next to the laptop. 'Use this mobile number.'

Ford picked up the card. 'Detective Constable Rose Kavanagh,' he read aloud. 'I never pictured you as a Rose.'

'By any other name would smell as sweet,' said Doyle, putting her arm across Kavanagh's shoulders.

Ford raised an eyebrow at Kavanagh. She narrowed her eyes at him. 'You're not the only one who prefers to use their last name,' she said, and shook off Doyle's arm.

Ford wrote emails to each of Diane's addresses, saying he was worried about her and asking her to phone Kavanagh's number. He signed each of them 'Lambchop'.

'You need to be careful passing judgment on names,' said Kavanagh.

'It's an old nickname that would mean something only to her.' Ford stood up and turned to face Kavanagh. 'I need your help. I need to know where my wife is, I need to know if my daughter's safe. You said Chadwick might be monitoring her phone—maybe he's set up surveillance on the house too? You could find out if she's been home since Friday. I'm all out of options.'

Kavanagh let out a hiss of breath and turned away. She walked over to the stove and refilled her mug from the coffee pot.

Ford followed her. 'You know something's not right here,' he said. 'You already took the first step out of line when you picked me up in Coolgardie.' Kavanagh kept her back to him, staring at the wall. 'You could send a patrol car past her house.'

Kavanagh turned slowly to face him. She leaned back against the counter and her shoulders slumped. 'I can't do that,' she said. 'But I can make a phone call.' She pulled her phone out of her pocket, thumbed the keypad and put it to her ear, striding across the floor. In a few steps she opened the back door and walked out into the darkness of the yard and out of earshot.

Ford turned to Doyle, who had sat down at the computer and was tapping at the keyboard. 'Are journalists in league with the police now?' he asked.

She looked up at him and frowned. 'You make out like it's a new thing.'

'She seems to know her way around the kitchen,' he said.

'I've known her a long time.' She resumed typing.

'Professional or personal?' said Ford.

She took off her glasses and looked up at him. Her eyes narrowed. 'We met ten years ago in a club in Perth. It was two weeks before she told me she was a cop. Since then it's been all about the work.'

'Still sounds like consorting with the enemy.'

'That's your view. When I started as a cadet it was much simpler. Journos and cops used to drink together and trade stories. It's changed since then. The Royal Commission killed the love. These days the paper doesn't have enough journos to chase the stories, and the cops don't trust us to spin the story their way. So now the police give us a press release and we print it. Their media office has more staff than our paper.'

'But you and Kavanagh are doing it old school?'

'Everything about the Gold Squad is old school. A handful of officers in that shabby office, no resources: they rely on rumour and gossip. It's a small town—nobody can fiddle gold from the mines without somebody hearing about it. There'd be pub talk, someone flashing the cash, a bloke with a new boat, a shiny new ute. Kavanagh relies on tip-offs and so do I.'

'Which paper?'

'There's only one. *Goldfields Courier.*'

'You run the Gwardar story yet?' said Ford.

'It used be the rule that if it bleeds, it leads. We wanted to run it Saturday morning. We heard gossip from the mine and had a few phone calls from people who'd seen the wreck in the ditch and been held up in roadblocks, but the cops refused to release anything. Then we got pressure from management to hold off.'

'Why?'

'Some horseshit about jeopardising an ongoing police enquiry, but my guess is that it came from Alan McCann. He owns a fair chunk of the paper, and he owns horses with most of the other shareholders. He was embarrassed enough at the races yesterday without having it splashed around the paper.'

'Yeah, I saw that story on your laptop. You were there?'

Doyle nodded. 'I'd arranged an interview about his big investment drive, and then I heard about the robbery and wanted his comment on that. But he was sulking in the members' bar all day and that South African bastard wouldn't let anyone near him.'

'What about the Perth papers and TV: did they run it?'

'They didn't hear about it till Saturday morning, and they were holding fire, waiting for the police to say something. Then they fell into line with the bullshit about ongoing investigations. It's all over the internet anyway. These days it's irrelevant if the paper prints it or not, the news gets out.'

'Are you going to run the story?'

She smiled. 'Without fear or favour. The only good story is one that someone, somewhere, doesn't want you to print. The rest is just advertising.'

'So how come you know so much about it?'

She raised her eyebrows. 'What d'you reckon?'

Ford looked out towards the backyard. He could see Kavanagh's outline, her face lit a ghostly blue by her phone.

'What's her game?' he asked.

'She's trying to get to the truth.'

'I meant, why has she left me alone with a journalist?'

Before Doyle could answer, Kavanagh came back through the kitchen door and stood fidgeting with her phone. 'Chadwick stopped monitoring calls to your wife's address when he heard you handed yourself in,' she said. 'No calls from any of her numbers since Thursday. Uniform did a doorknock at her address on Friday afternoon and Saturday morning, but there was no answer. No signs of life, no lights, no cars in the driveway, mail still in the letterbox. They also went to her office on Friday and were told she wasn't at work that day and they hadn't heard from her.'

'No sign of her at all?'

'No, sorry.' Kavanagh bowed her head.

Ford tapped Doyle on the shoulder. 'Can I get back online?'

She got up, and he sat down and started tapping feverishly. Kavanagh stepped up behind him as he brought up a schematic of the gold plant at Gwardar. The screen flickered, numbers scrolled, and graphs showed ore flow and power use from the machinery.

'Looks like the plant never stopped production over the weekend,' he said.

Kavanagh leaned in closer. 'You're in the mine system? How did you hack that?'

'It's no hack. I've got remote administrator access for the whole of Gwardar's systems. The privileges of being engineering manager. I wanted to be able to see how it was running when I was on leave back in Perth, make sure nobody was fucking things up while I was gone.'

'Doesn't sound legit to me.'

'Possibly not, but I arranged with the network manager to leave a few back doors open in the system for me. You can get anything done up there for a carton of beer and a few tips on the horses.'

Kavanagh pulled up a chair and sat down next to Ford. 'So what can you get access to?'

Ford looked at her. 'Haven't your lot been through the system yet?'

'They tried on Friday, but the management refused to let us. Made us get a warrant. There'll be people there bright and early Monday morning with the paperwork.'

'So where do you want to go?' asked Ford.

'Can you get access to email accounts and staff hard drives?' Kavanagh's eyes were bright.

'I can get you anywhere.'

'How can you do that?'

'You asked me about beardy engineers messing with steam engines: my generation stayed indoors and spent their spare time tinkering with computers. Those were the days when, if you wanted a personal computer, you built your own and wrote your own code. I spend my nights on the mine streamlining some of the control systems. Easier to hack them and do it quietly myself than to wait for some spotty geek in Perth to raise a purchase order and then piss away forty hours fixing a simple glitch.'

'Can you access the security department?'

'What's it worth?'

Kavanagh leaned back on the chair, folded her arms and sighed.

'You're already out on a limb with this,' Ford pointed out. 'You may as well tell me why you dragged me out with you.'

Kavanagh got up and walked over to the fridge. She pulled a bottle of vodka out of the freezer compartment and set it down on the counter. Ford looked at Doyle, who shrugged. 'May as well pour us all one,' she said.

Kavanagh opened a cupboard above her head and took down three glass tumblers. She splashed a shot of vodka in one and drank it, then poured a measure into each glass. She handed them around. Ford knocked his back and waved the empty glass at Kavanagh. She poured him another measure, and he drank it and waved the glass again. She half-filled his glass and then put the bottle down in front of him, leaning her hip against the table.

'I don't think you were the inside man,' she said. 'I told Chadwick that in Coolgardie and he shut me out of the interview.'

'Why'd he do that?' asked Ford. As he drank, he looked at the bottle. It was cheap vodka and there wasn't much of it left.

'Because he was already in the process of verballing you. He wanted a quick link to the bikies, so he could pull them in on the weekend and have his face on the front page before the Gang

Squad and the Major Crime heavies come over the horizon on Monday and start strutting around scratching their balls.'

'If it wasn't me, who was it?'

'We'd heard background static about Gwardar for the last few weeks. There were a couple of known faces out there, guys whose names had cropped up in previous investigations, but nothing more than pub talk. I thought we should be looking at those guys first. You were too much of a cleanskin. And you'd been offered up to us on a plate.'

'Who were you looking at?'

She shook her head. 'That's already too much. Get me into the staff email.'

Rather than turning back to the computer, Ford poured himself another shot.

'You going to leave any of that?' said Doyle.

'In certain situations the only thing to do is get juiced up to the back of the head on plain-label vodka,' he said.

He slumped in his chair, watching the light reflect off the surface of the liquid. As he tilted his wrist the greasy trails of alcohol slid back down the inside of the glass. He thought for a moment. 'The only people who knew the key code to the gold room on Friday were me, Werran, Petkovic and Mariotti. Normally there would be three or four operators authorised to work in the gold room, but they did the last pour on Thursday and most of the crew were in Kalgoorlie for the race round. The code would have been changed and they may not have been told the new number. Wouldn't take long to check up on that small group. Doesn't take much deduction to pick Mariotti as the likely candidate.'

'What about the other two?' said Doyle.

'Could be Petkovic, I guess. I doubt it was Werran: he pissed himself when they put the gun in his face. But somebody should ask why Mariotti made sure he was off site on Friday.'

'If you could hack into the computer system, what's to stop someone else?' asked Doyle.

'I'd still look at Mariotti first. I saw him at the races, said he hadn't been interviewed yet.'

'They were due to talk to him later in the afternoon,' said Kavanagh, 'but they were more interested in you by that stage, after your grand entrance.'

'They never interviewed him?' Ford was surprised.

She shook her head. 'Chadwick had you. They were looking at you from the moment you went missing. Then they had the link through the bank and the security cards, and finally you came walking in. Chadwick didn't give a shit if you were a patsy or not: the Vipers had coughed you up and he was going to use you against them.'

'So what do you reckon about Mariotti?' asked Ford.

'It's a fair call. There were a few instances of gold concentrate going missing from some of the smaller mines around town. There was also a rumour that the bikers had their own mill hidden somewhere in Williamstown, but we never knew for sure. They would have needed someone with processing smarts to help them set it up. Mariotti was one of several faces we were looking at.'

'Even if Chadwick isn't interested, why haven't the Gold Squad pulled him in?'

'Because he vanished after the races. My guess is you put the wind up him by showing up like you did. He'd have known that, with you alive, the spotlight would soon fall on him, and then the Vipers would be looking to dust him. He's taken off.'

'So what are we looking for on the Gwardar computer?'

'Anything linked to the gold shipment and the security arrangements.'

'You think he'd be dumb enough to use the company email?' asked Doyle.

Kavanagh sat back down next to Ford and refilled her glass. She looked at the screen. 'I don't know what we're looking for,' she said. 'But we might get lucky.'

'I can check his internet history, see if he used any remote mail accounts,' said Ford.

'We'll flag his phone account on Monday, but I'll bet he's already dumped it if he's trying to get lost.'

Ford turned his attention to the laptop and opened up Mariotti's email account, then scrolled through it. 'There's a whole load of crap in here. Most of it's humdrum management stuff, correspondence with subcontractors.'

'Who would have known how much gold was in the safe?' Kavanagh asked.

'I didn't, but Werran and Petkovic did, and so did the guys in the van who had the docket. McCann would have known, and probably his security guy, Roth, and any number of security people at the track.'

'Check the correspondence between McCann and Mariotti. Maybe that could point to some information only Mariotti knew.'

'Someone else knew how much gold was in that transfer,' said Ford.

'Who?'

'The police.'

Kavanagh looked at him but said nothing.

NINETEEN

Ford spent an hour going through Mariotti's email with Kavanagh watching on. He looked at Werran and Petkovic's mail as well but found nothing that wasn't routine. He finished the rest of the vodka and waved the empty bottle at Doyle, but she shook her head and started grinding more coffee. When the pot boiled she took it out onto the back verandah and Kavanagh followed her.

When Ford next looked up from the screen, Kavanagh was walking towards him carrying a small green plastic box. She put it on the table and Ford saw the first aid sticker on the lid. She opened the box, took out some small scissors and a pair of tweezers, and then sat on the edge of the table and looked him in the eye. 'I'm starting to wonder whether you know what's best for you,' she said. 'I don't know if you're stubborn or just plain stupid.'

Ford looked at her, shrugged, and turned his attention back to the computer.

Kavanagh sighed. 'If I can't drag you away from this screen, at least move back a bit so I can get at your leg.'

Ford pushed the chair backwards until his arms were fully extended, his fingers still on the keyboard. She knelt down, grabbed his leg and pulled it sideways beyond the end of the table. Pain shot up his leg and he yelped.

'I'm just trying to get you into the light so I can see what I'm doing.' Kavanagh leaned in close to the leg, used the scissors to cut a hole in his pants and peeled the fabric away from the wound. Ford winced as the material tore away from the dried blood. Kavanagh was so close he could smell her. Petrol and leather mixed with her perfume, an old-fashioned cologne heavy with bergamot. There was another note in it, something dark. It smelled familiar, but he couldn't place it.

'This would be a lot easier if you took your pants off,' she said.

'In your dreams.'

She used the tweezers to briskly remove a few stray threads that had been dragged into the wound by the pellet and he flinched. 'Find anything on Mariotti's computer?' she asked.

'Nope. I doubt he'd be clueless enough to send anything from his work address. I'm just running a search now for stray email addresses in his outbox. He's probably got a few anonymous mail accounts somewhere. If we're lucky, he might have forwarded routine mail to them without thinking. There's a lot of harmless stuff he thought he'd deleted but is still on the server. You still think he's the link to the Vipers?'

'I'm not convinced the Vipers are behind this.'

'Well then, who just shot me?' Ford looked down at Kavanagh. She was dabbing at the wound with a gauze pad dipped in iodine and the blood was smeared in a brown stain up his thigh. He felt the sting as the liquid pooled in the neat circular hole around the pellet. 'You going to share your thoughts with me, detective?'

She looked up from her work and shook her head. 'We haven't reached that place yet.'

'Then why don't I just let your forensics boys do their own sweep of the mine's computers?'

She jabbed the tweezers into Ford's thigh. He yelled out and tried to jerk his leg away but only succeeded in driving the tweezers deeper into the wound and pulling them out of Kavanagh's hand. He looked down at the silver shaft sticking out of his leg, fresh red blood welling around the base of it and running in a thin rivulet across his skin to where it soaked into his trouser leg.

'Keep still, you bastard,' she hissed, punching the top of his good leg. 'I nearly had it.'

'You got any anaesthetic in that kit, or at least some more vodka?'

'Shut up,' she said, snatching the tweezers out of his leg. Ford clenched his teeth to keep from yelling out again.

She put the flat of her hand on the top of Ford's thigh and pushed it hard onto the chair, digging her nails into the muscle and forcing all her weight down onto it to keep it still. With her face inches from the wound, she inserted the tweezers into the hole again. Ford's lips curled back and sweat beaded on his forehead as she fished around for the shotgun pellet. He let out a long groan as she pulled the tweezers free and raised them to the light, holding the bloodied pellet aloft in triumph.

'That's one way of getting out of answering his question,' said an amused voice.

Ford opened his eyes and saw Doyle standing in the back doorway holding the empty coffee pot. Her eyes took in Ford stretched out on the chair, catching his breath, with Kavanagh kneeling between his legs.

Kavanagh stood up and showed her the tweezers, then dropped the pellet in Ford's shot glass. The blood mingled with the dregs of vodka in the bottom. Kavanagh lifted it to eye level, rattling the pellet around to wash the blood off it. 'Puny little thing,' she said. 'Don't know what you were screaming about.'

Doyle stepped further into the kitchen and put the coffee pot down on the counter. 'The door was open. I heard the conversation. Answer the question,' she said, leaning against the bench and folding her arms. 'Why have you gone cold on the Vipers?'

Kavanagh sat down at the table and sighed. 'Just seems a bit too slick for the bikies,' she said. 'They never pulled off anything like this before. We've had them for cooking meth, dealing drugs in the pubs, a bit of protection, and trying to muscle in on the security business. They pinched the odd bit of gold from the mines, but only small stuff: flakes pilfered from a refinery, an old tobacco tin of nuggets swiped from a prospector, a few barrowloads of concentrate walked out the back of the mine. Two guys once walked into a gold room in Coolgardie with a couple of shotguns and bailed up the crew. Didn't bother to cover their tatts. Took us two days to find them and to identify the guy who opened the door for them. This job used shaped charges: the only history the bikies have with explosives is some ANFO and Powergel stolen from the mines. Crude pipe bombs lobbed into each other's clubhouses, nothing like this.'

'There are plenty of ex-military blokes in the bikies,' said Ford. The pain had subsided a little and he managed to look down at the blood pooling around his wound. 'You going to bandage this?'

Kavanagh took a flat packet from the kit, ripped it open with her teeth and pulled out the gauze dressing. 'The vets in the bikies are either stoners from Vietnam or fucked units from Iraq and Afghanistan. Not the sort of guys that have access to a plane.'

'Where do you think they flew to?' asked Ford.

'Anywhere they liked. There are hundreds of airstrips out there. Every town has a strip, in case they need the Flying Doctor. Then there are mine sites, sheep stations and cattle ranches, and thousands of kilometres of open highway that a small plane could drop on.'

'Couldn't air traffic control track it?' said Doyle.

'No chance. Pilots only need a flight plan if they're near the commercial air corridor, so at least we know they didn't fly into Perth or Kal. Outside that, if they kept low and turned off their transponder, they'd be invisible. Two and a half million square kilometres of bugger-all is an easy place to lose yourself.'

'So where's the gold?' asked Doyle.

'Why do you think I would have a clue?' said Kavanagh. 'When the plane landed it, they probably moved it by road, and then there's twenty thousand kilometres of unguarded coastline where they can put it on a boat and get it out of the country.'

'Why take it overseas?'

Kavanagh frowned. 'You going to get out your notebook and start taking shorthand?'

Doyle looked unconcerned. 'You're playing an angle here, so stop pretending you don't want this story out. There's other places you could have gone tonight.'

Kavanagh sighed. 'Go get another bottle,' she said.

Doyle went out into the hallway and came back with a second bottle of vodka. 'It's warm,' she said.

'We'll manage,' said Ford quickly.

Doyle collected the three shot glasses together on the table and filled them up. Ford's had a pink blush from his own blood. He lifted it and looked at the shotgun pellet. He knocked back the vodka and then spat the pellet across the room. It bounced across the floorboards and rolled under the sink. Doyle frowned at him.

'So where's the gold going?' she asked.

'Chadwick's hoping the bikies will try and sell it in Australia, or try to get it refined here,' said Kavanagh.

'Refined?' asked Doyle.

'It's not pure,' said Ford. 'The gold from the mine refinery is doré, rough-cast gold straight from the processing plant, only about ninety-five percent, with five percent impurities, mostly silver and copper at Gwardar. Normally we ship it straight to the mint in Perth, where they purify it and frank it and make it into those shiny bullion bars you're thinking of.'

Kavanagh rolled her eyes. 'There's no way they could dump over a hundred kilos onto the local market without the Gold Squad getting a sniff of it. Same if they tried to get someone to refine it. They could try and sell it as scrap gold to jewellers and dodgy traders, but it would take them forever. Chadwick's dreaming if he thinks a bikie's going to show up trying to fence a twenty-kilo bar.' She knelt down next to Ford and peered at his wound. 'My bet is that it'll be melted down locally into something smaller, maybe pellets or ingots that can be handled more easily, and then shipped overseas. India, most likely. Lots of new money over there and the wives like to wear their wealth around their neck.'

She wiped the blood off Ford's thigh and laid the dressing over the wound. 'Press down on that,' she told him, then cut strips of tape off a roll and stretched them over the dressing. 'You're done,' she said, and slapped his thigh. 'It could really do with a couple of stitches, but it should heal, although it might give you a scar to brag about.'

Ford pulled down the collar of his shirt and dipped his shoulder towards her. 'How's this one travelling?' he asked.

She looked at the bloodied gauze, then peeled back the tape and fingered the butterfly stitches underneath. 'It's holding. Wish we'd had some of those for your leg. Who did that for you?'

Ford pulled his shirt back up over the dressing and poured himself another shot of vodka. He pulled the chair back up to the table and looked at the computer screen.

'Nobody here too flash hot on answering a direct question,' said Doyle, looking over Ford's shoulder at the screen. 'If this is going to take all night I'm going to bed.'

The computer chimed, and Ford tapped at the keyboard. 'It's finished the search for email addresses,' he said. 'A few possibles here that look like personal accounts. I'll go back through his browsing history and see if he's logged into any of them recently.'

Kavanagh and Doyle exchanged glances, picked up the coffee pot and mugs, and went into the backyard. Ford could hear them talking and laughing on the back verandah as he typed.

They came back in thirty minutes later, giggling together. Ford looked up from the screen and watched Kavanagh come through the door. It was the first time he'd seen her smiling. He felt disappointed that he hadn't been the one to crack her cold expression, but then thought that they might have been talking about him outside.

She saw him looking and dropped the smile. 'Found anything yet?'

'Yes, but not what I was looking for. I had to wade through a lot of stuff that didn't mean anything before I found something that did.'

The women sat down either side of him at the kitchen table. They leaned close to see the screen and he could smell their perfume mingling over the ripe smell of his own shirt.

'I found four private email addresses where Mariotti forwarded copies of correspondence,' he said. 'I got access to three of them.'

'You hacked them?' asked Kavanagh.

'I'd like to play the hacker, but truth is Mariotti uses the same password for these accounts as he uses at work, and I've got admin privileges for the mine. He uses one of the accounts for correspondence with Alan McCann. The second he uses to write to a stockbroker and a real estate agent who's buying up property for him in Perth, and the third one's for cruising a series of adult dating websites.'

'What about the fourth one?'

'That one must be really important to him, because he uses a different password, but the address is ozsubguy67, so I'm guessing it's more personal stuff.'

'Did you access the photos on his dating profile?' asked Kavanagh.

'You don't want to look. A few years working long hours on a remote mine can warp a guy.'

'So what did you find out?'

'That he has a preference for leather and he's still looking for a lady who will strap one on.'

Kavanagh slapped his thigh and his vision momentarily clouded with pain. 'I was hoping for some loose talk about the gold,' she said.

'Sorry to disappoint. I'm working backwards through the mail. Most of the chatter with McCann has been about the recent shipment and the need to keep quiet about the quantity of gold in transit. McCann brags about his plans to park the van in his marquee at the races, and talks about the players he wants to invite. There's a lot of background noise about McCann's big announcement at the races and the need to keep a lid on it.'

'Well, that's bullshit,' said Doyle, slamming her coffee mug down on the table.

Ford and Kavanagh both turned to her. Doyle polished her glasses and put them back on.

'McCann's full of shit,' she said. 'He's been choreographing this big announcement for the last two weeks, crapping on about how secret it is, then putting out stage whispers about how important it is. Came into the *Courier* two weeks ago, telling us that it's all hush-hush and that we'll get the story as soon as it breaks.'

'And you listened to him?' said Ford.

'Have to, he's a major shareholder. Supposed to be a silent partner, but he makes sure the paper gives him plenty of coverage when he needs it. Wanted us to do a big feature on him at the race round: the gold, the horses, the B-list micro-celebs he was flying in. He seemed pretty sure his horse was going to win.'

Kavanagh was nodding. 'We've been hearing gossip about the exploration drilling going on out at Gwardar. What do you know, Ford?'

The two women looked at him and he felt hemmed in. 'Not much,' he said. 'They were drilling out there for a few months, but I never met the exploration crews. They had their own camp about ten klicks north of Gwardar.'

'McCann was keeping them quarantined?' said Kavanagh.

'Don't know about that. Not unusual for the company to want the drillers kept away from the rest of the mine. They were all South Africans. McCann has some contacts out there. Rumour was he thought they talked less than Aussies.'

'But you must have heard something,' said Kavanagh.

'Nothing more than the usual bullshit in the wet mess. A few guys reckoned they heard they were getting good results. A couple of powder monkeys from the mine tried going over to the exploration camp to take a look, but the drill cores were all locked up in a container. Some of the drillers caught them and bashed the shit out of them, then handed them back to mine security. They were sacked and flown out the next day. It was all whispers until this week, when the share price started going up and blokes started talking about McCann laying on the champagne for the race round. Everyone was trying to wangle an invitation to the marquee.'

'And how much did Mariotti know?'

'From the mail to his stockbroker, it seems he started buying up shares last week. Looks like some of it was hidden behind trusts. They've been going up sharply all week.'

'And you didn't buy any?' asked Doyle.

'No, I didn't. Firstly, I don't see why I should put money into the company's shares just so McCann can buy himself another racehorse, and secondly because I have no money.'

'We know that,' said Kavanagh. 'You've found nothing that might link Mariotti to the robbery?'

'Not where I'm looking.'

'And the Vipers?'

'No mention of them either. Maybe they're not the sort of guys to use email.'

Kavanagh looked at Doyle. 'If Mariotti was buying shares, it's a safe bet that McCann was too,' she said.

'I looked for that already,' said Ford. 'Gwardar is wholly owned by Glycon Holdings, which also owns most of McCann's other interests. He floated ten years ago, but maintained a majority shareholding and ensured he was CEO and chairman of the board. There's a lot of movement, but nothing that looks obviously like McCann. Lots of funds and offshore companies, though, and he could be hiding behind any one of them.'

Doyle shook her head. 'You'll never find that out and you know it. I tried last year and got nowhere. The paper trail leads offshore, to Labuan, the Cook Islands, Macau. Companies within companies, like Russian dolls.' Grabbing the bottle of vodka, she got up from the table, then strode over to the kitchen counter and poured herself a measure. She knocked it back and glared at Kavanagh. 'Time to drop the damsel-in-distress routine, Rosie. Doesn't suit you. You rock up on my doorstep dragging a witness behind you, trying to pull me into something with McCann. You're taking the piss.'

Kavanagh looked at her hands and then at Ford. Finally she turned to Doyle. 'They're going to come to you,' she said.

'Who?' asked Doyle.

'McCann will come first, and then Chadwick.'

Doyle watched her and let her talk.

'McCann knows he has to do something before the stock market opens on Monday morning. His share price is high on rumours of the gold exploration at Gwardar, but before he could release the information to the market his mine's been turned over. He'll be working the phones all day Sunday with his PR people, making sure there's a positive spin on things, and he'll want it in the papers.'

'There are other journos. He could ring my editor direct, push him to run a leader.'

'Maybe, but I'm betting he'll call you. Nobody else on your paper has any pull. You're the only one who strings for the *Gazette* and the papers over east.'

'McCann won't talk to me. He blanked me at the race round yesterday. He hasn't changed.'

'Which is why he'll come to you now.'

Ford looked from one to the other. 'You've got form with McCann?' he asked.

'Ancient history,' said Doyle, reaching for the bottle. 'I wrote a few pieces on him when I was on the *Perth Gazette*, back when he was just a cocky property developer, before he started selling himself as the last of the four-on-the-floor Perth entrepreneurs. Back then he was residential and commercial property, and racehorses were his only indulgence. That was before he bought the mine, the Margaret River vineyards, the restaurant, the big boat and the private jet. Before he started pretending he was the king of the bare-knuckle tycoons.'

'I detect a note of bitterness,' said Ford.

Doyle scowled at him. 'McCann is the unacceptable and unpleasant face of capitalism.'

'I'm guessing there's more to this than just a dislike of his gauche taste.'

'How long've you been out in the desert?' asked Kavanagh. 'She broke the Risely story.' There was the hint of a smile in her eyes as she looked at Doyle, something like pride, but it vanished when Doyle glared back at her.

'Heard of it, but it was before my time,' said Ford. 'I was in London back then.'

Doyle sighed. 'I'd been following the story of one of McCann's property deals in Perth. Nice big high-rise on the Terrace. Planning permission was stalled. Risely was a new member of the Legislative Assembly, painted as a bit of a boy wonder. Starts asking questions in state parliament, heckling the planning minister from the backbenches, lobbying on McCann's behalf. There were reports of him having lunch with McCann at his restaurant. Bit too much cash in his pocket for a first-term member of the lower house. I start digging into it, and get warned off. I hear that Risely is under investigation by the Corruption and Crime Commission. I run the story in the *Gazette* anyway and Risely resigns before the commission can put together any sort of case.

'The next weekend I'm visited by the cops, wanting to know who my source was. They think it's either from inside parliament, or one of their own. I tell them to get fucked. Sunday morning they show up with a warrant and toss the place. More cops are at the newspaper going through my desk and computer. I'm called up in front of the commission and ordered to reveal my source. I respectfully tell them to get fucked as well. The union stands behind me but my newspaper's nowhere to be seen. My limp-wristed gimp of an editor's getting it in both ears from the government and the commission. Bastard hangs me out to dry.

'I get put on the stand again. Seems there's no right to silence in that kangaroo court. I get done for contempt. They give me seven days. While I'm away, soon as the news cycle's moved on, the *Gazette* declines to renew my contract.' She looked at Kavanagh. 'And now you think McCann will come crawling to me to spin his story?'

'You know he'll come to you,' said Kavanagh. 'You know he'll call it in.'

'Call what in?' said Ford.

Doyle shook her head but Kavanagh smiled at her. 'McCann stepped in and saved her job,' she said. 'The paper wanted rid, but McCann played the white knight. Leaned on the newspaper until they agreed to offer her a place here on the *Courier*. The *Gazette* owns the *Courier*. He came out as a champion of free speech, said he had no grudge against Alannah. Claimed he hadn't bribed anyone but that Risely had come to him offering his services. Claimed he thought it was all above board. Risely took most of the blame, but he was already on a plane to Bali for an extended holiday. No comment from him. Alannah came out of Wooroloo Prison Farm as a bit of a legend, and McCann got to play the victim.'

'He's that sort of bastard,' said Doyle. 'Shows me he's my buddy by getting me a gig in this shithole of a town working for this pissant parochial rag.'

'That's what money gets you in Perth,' said Kavanagh.

'The only thing McCann's gained from his wealth is the fear of losing it,' said Doyle. 'He doesn't make friends, he buys them. If you're not his friend, you're his enemy, and he's always on the lookout for enemies.' She looked at Kavanagh, who was still sitting at the table massaging her knuckles. 'What if McCann doesn't come to me?'

'Then you go to him,' said Kavanagh. 'He'll talk to you. You've got the clean image. Anything he wants to spin will have a veneer of authenticity if it comes from you.'

'And why would I be doing this?'

'Because I need to know what he knows about Mariotti, and anything Chadwick might have let slip about the investigation.'

'You didn't answer the question. Why would I want to put myself in the middle of this?'

'Because you want it. I can see it in your eye. You haven't had a sniff of a story like this since you left Perth. When did you hear about the robbery? And what have you been doing since then? You've been trying to get an angle on the story that will get you back in the game.'

'There's no story here. You've given me nothing.'

'Not yet, but you know it's there. I'll bet you've been digging already.'

Doyle smiled and Ford felt the tension in the kitchen subside. 'I spent most of yesterday afternoon during the races trying to get an interview with McCann,' she admitted. 'At the time I just wanted to ask him why he'd bolted from his marquee when he was about to make his speech, and why the champagne had run out. Most of his guests had wandered off into other corporate marquees to get their glasses filled. By the time I heard about the robbery, McCann had gone back to his hotel. I went over there and doorstopped for a while, saw some uniformed and plainclothes going in, then headed to the newsroom and started researching my piece for Monday's paper. I tried reaching out to the cops but got told there would be no police statement this weekend. I was just writing up my notes when you rang my doorbell.'

'And you thought Kavanagh was being evasive,' said Ford, shaking his head. He looked through the recent history on the laptop and opened up the files that Doyle had been working on. 'What did you find?' He peered at the screen.

'Stay out of my work,' said Doyle, slamming the screen down on Ford's fingers. 'Why do you give a shit about McCann?' she asked Kavanagh.

'I don't,' said Kavanagh. 'The bastard can crash and burn for all I care, I just need you and McCann to knock Chadwick off balance.'

'Sounds like you've both got an axe to grind,' said Ford.

Both women glared at him. 'Every arsehole in this town's got an axe to grind,' said Doyle. 'What's yours?'

Ford ignored her and turned to Kavanagh. 'There was a while there I thought you were interested in clearing me, but it seems you're after Chadwick. Me and her, we're just means to an end for you. What's your problem with Chadwick?'

'He knows. You don't have to.'

'So I just get dragged along, do I?'

'What this is, if you really want to know, is me trying to recover the gold. This is me taking some professional pride in uncovering the truth. You two are the only route available to me just now. Until the big hitters arrive from Perth I'll have to play it alone, and thankfully the Gold Squad sits outside Chadwick's chain of command. He's using the robbery as a way to destroy the Vipers. I need to take the momentum off Chadwick until I can get you into the custody of the Serious Crime Squad.'

'I'm not going back to the station,' said Ford. 'I need to get to Perth.'

'You said that like I'd just given you a choice,' said Kavanagh.

'My daughter's still missing. If I go back into custody I'm no use to her. You take me back in there and I may as well sign the confession.'

Kavanagh stood up. Balancing her weight on the balls of her feet, she reached behind her back.

'You think a gun will change my mind?' Ford said. 'Not the first I've seen lately. If you want me to go back to the station, then arrest me and take me there in cuffs, but my cooperation ends there. I doubt it'll do you much good. Chadwick will've moved against the Vipers already and the whole thing will be way beyond you. The gold will be out of reach by now, and Chadwick will have created so much white noise that nobody will be able to make any sense of it. I don't know what you think you can achieve, but I'm a long way past caring.'

She stood looking at him, her hand still at her back, and he held her gaze. After a few seconds she dropped her head and released her breath, and sat back down. She lifted her empty glass and held it out towards Doyle.

'So tell us what you've got on McCann, Alannah,' she said as the other woman filled her glass.

After putting down the bottle, Doyle looked from Ford to Kavanagh as if gauging the mood. Kavanagh was staring at the contents of her glass, Ford had turned his attention back to the screen. She let the silence settle for a while before speaking.

'The bastard's having a rollercoaster of a year,' said Doyle. 'Bit of a poster boy for the West Australian economy. The global financial crisis dumped him in the shit but he still came out smelling of roses. The crunch came with his latest office tower—his biggest development yet, Mounts Bay Road, river views. Had cash-flow problems, then a dispute with his main contractor. He'd brought in a firm from over east, claimed all the local builders were rorting him, trying to write their own ticket. This eastern mob underestimated doing business here, the transport costs, skills shortage, material supply, and they were on the outer with the unions. They were losing money and wanted to jump ship. McCann gave them an out when he missed a milestone payment, and they grabbed the opportunity and downed tools. The program went to shit and then the prospective major tenant threatened to cancel. Building's been standing half-built for the last three months.

'McCann would have been sunk if it wasn't for the gold-mine. When the rest of the world economy tanked, the gold price soared. McCann's been keeping the rest of his businesses ticking over on the income from the mine, and his share price has performed better than most through the crisis. Since the price has been going up in the last week he's been beating his chest, threatening to drag his contractor through the courts. He said he had another builder ready to start and reckoned he'd be pumping concrete by the end of the month. He was bragging about raising capital to expand the mine, upgrade the processing plant.'

'That ring true to you, Ford?' said Kavanagh.

'Not his style,' Ford said. 'He's spent fuck-all on the plant in the last few years. I don't think the guys snapping up his shares are letting the glitter of gold cloud their vision. You don't buy into a busted-arse mine like Gwardar looking for a dividend. If the grades are good and the reserves are big everyone hopes one of the big miners will come sniffing around and push the price up further. If they're really lucky, one of the big Canadian players will try a takeover and offer a share swap and they can exchange their Glycon script for blue-chip stock.'

'How's your own portfolio?' Kavanagh asked.

Ford threw his head back and looked at the ceiling. 'I don't have money to play the markets, that's why I back the horses. The nags are more predictable, and the racing game has fewer crooks.'

'And they've got a bar at the track,' said Kavanagh.

Ford looked at the screen and scowled. He grabbed the mouse again and started clicking. 'I'd like to have a look at what the geo found. If McCann was going to go public at the races it shouldn't be hard to find.'

Doyle laughed. 'I'm surprised he hasn't leaked parts of it already.'

'How much more of Mariotti's mail have you got to look through?' asked Kavanagh.

'There's still plenty, and I haven't even started trawling through his cache and recovered stuff deleted off his hard drive.'

'You can get that?' said Kavanagh. 'Our forensics guys can usually get old stuff if the disk isn't too full, but they can't often get it remotely.'

'Watch and learn,' said Ford. 'Most of it will have been backed up to the server.'

Kavanagh and Doyle sat down again on either side of him. He could feel the warmth of Kavanagh's thigh through the fabric of his trousers. The other thigh was still burning from the iodine on his wound.

'Here we go,' he said. 'Didn't take long. Mail from McCann dated two weeks ago. Just a few comments on the report. Says they struck fair grades of gold. Strike lengths of nine hundred metres, based on interpolation of inferred geology. Sample numbers indicate the intersections are quite close. Some of the drill cores finished in ore. Estimated reserves of eight million tons grading at 0.14 ounces per ton, giving a million ounces of contained gold. The bastard's hit paydirt sure enough.'

Kavanagh shook her head. 'This is just fluff from McCann. Where's the geologist's report? We need to see the test results.'

'There's a document referenced here. I'll see if I can find it.' He keyed in a search of the mine's main server and sat back, folded his arms and tried to concentrate on the screen rather than Kavanagh's leg. He glanced sideways at her face. She was biting her bottom lip and her eyes were blank, flitting from side to side tracking the flickering data. It was the first time he had seen anything like anxiety on her face. Perhaps it was merely excitement. She was drumming her fingers on her leg and tapping her foot. He could feel the vibration through his thigh.

'Here it is,' he said, and heard her sharp intake of breath. 'Not very well hidden. He'd partitioned his hard drive and snuck it away behind a password. I guess he thought it would be invisible. Maybe he was hiding it to outside eyes, not mine.'

'Open the fucking thing,' said Kavanagh. Her fingers were at her mouth, worrying her bottom lip.

Ford clicked to open the document, and page after page of data scrolled across the screen. Columns of numbers, photographs of drill samples, bore-hole logs, test data, coloured maps, and three-dimensional computer renderings of the ore body, the gold-bearing rocks shining like a bulbous nugget buried beneath the landscape.

'It's all there,' said Ford. 'Want to read it?'

'Just tell me who wrote it.'

Ford scrolled through to the last page and the signature block at the bottom. Beneath the gaudy logo of Gwardar Gold Mine was a smaller one in a simple sans-serif font: Bonner Walsh and Associates. He looked for the author's signature, his head spinning. When he saw Matthew Walsh's name, he paused and tried to decide whether he felt relief or anxiety. He stared at the signature, small and cramped, scratched beneath the typed name, and his mind reeled as he tried to link cause with effect, tried to make a connection between his wife and Walsh. He couldn't fix on anything, except a feeling of vertigo, and a greater fear for his daughter.

He tried to control his breathing, and exhaled slowly. It came out as a groan.

'What?' asked Kavanagh and Doyle together.

'The geologist is my wife's partner.'

Kavanagh raised an eyebrow.

'Business partner,' he said.

'And you didn't know that he was working for McCann?'

'There's a lot I don't know about Matthew Walsh,' said Ford. 'There's correspondence here saying he'll be granted share options now that he's on the board of the mine.'

'He's on the board?' said Doyle. 'Bit of a conflict of interest there.'

'Sure it is, but common enough with junior mining companies. They normally have a geologist on the board, helps them answer technical questions from investors.'

'And talk up their reserves,' said Kavanagh.

'That's why they have to get the exploration work independently audited,' Ford explained. 'The Joint Ore Reserves Committee requires that they get third-party verification before they announce any new find to the market. It doesn't look like McCann's got his JORC compliance yet, so the jump in his share price is certain to raise a few eyebrows in the stock exchange. The smart players always get in there at the first rumour of a new find and take a punt before any formal announcement. Buy the rumour, sell the fact, as they say.'

A loud slam made them jump and turn towards the doorway. They had all been so intent on the document they hadn't heard the back door open. It banged shut and they all sat up straight.

A man stood with his back to the door, leaning against the door frame. He was tall and lean and seemed to fill the doorway. One hand stroked the long moustache that drooped past his chin, the other reached inside the top pocket of his sleeveless leather jacket and pulled out a packet of cigarettes. Ford read the patches sewn on the front of the jacket and sat frozen as the man flicked open a lighter and lit the cigarette. He blew out the smoke, coughed and then smiled, showing a row of yellow teeth, his eyes moving between Ford and the two women.

'Nice little sandwich you've got going there, mate,' he said.

TWENTY

Kavanagh was the first to react. She rose out of her chair and in a single smooth movement pulled the gun from behind her and levelled it. The man in the doorway slowly turned his palms outwards, the cigarette still burning between his fingers. Ford and Doyle shifted nervously in their chairs.

'Step into the room, buddy,' said Kavanagh. 'Slowly.'

He took two steps away from the door and stood looking at her, his moustache parting either side of a wide grin. Ford's gaze was drawn to his eyes. The irises were pale brown, the whites flecked with red. Set within deep folds of skin pulled taut by his smile, they were framed above by a thick line of deep red eyebrows. His moustache merged with a set of mutton-chop whiskers. He was at least sixty, Ford estimated, his red hair wiry and peppered with grey and white, pulled back into a loose ponytail. Combined with the leathery skin of his face, tanned by sun and wind, it gave him the appearance of a rusted piece of mine machinery abandoned to the desert.

'Open your jacket,' ordered Kavanagh, waving the barrel of the gun.

He transferred the cigarette to his mouth and opened up his palms again, hooking his thumbs under the seams of the jacket and opening it. Underneath he wore a black T-shirt printed with BAD SAMARITAN in small white text. His arms were sleeved in tattoos down to the wrists; Ford made out the now-familiar words DON'T TREAD ON ME swamped in a sea of faded blue ink.

'Now turn around,' said Kavanagh.

He did a slow twirl, swaying gently from side to side and waggling his fingers in a jazz dance. He stopped when he was facing away from them, and Ford saw the patches sewn across his back. A snake writhed across the jacket, its fangs bared, ready to strike. The rocker above it read DESERT VIPERS.

'Lift your jacket.' Kavanagh sidestepped around the table and moved into the centre of the kitchen, stopping a few feet away from the biker, who lifted the back of his jacket and his shirt to show the waistband of his jeans. A tattoo of a snake crawled up his back from out of his pants, its head partially hidden by his shirt. A silver chain was hooked onto the belt loop and disappeared into the back pocket.

'Show me what's on the chain,' said Kavanagh.

He hooked his thumb through the chain, pulling out a wallet.

'Now roll up the legs of your pants.'

The man bent slowly and pulled up a leg of his jeans. Kavanagh tensed when she saw the sheathed knife strapped to the outside of his calf.

'Lose the knife,' she said, and he ripped open the Velcro straps. 'Toss it.' The man flicked his wrist and the knife skittered across the floorboards. Kavanagh picked it up and tucked it into the back of her trousers. The man straightened slowly, his palms still held out, and turned to face her. Among the dozen patches on the front of his jacket, Ford now noticed a small rectangle with the word PRESIDENT.

'There's something about a chick with a gun that does something powerful to me,' the man said. 'How've you been doing, Rosie?' His voice was husky and cigarette-raw. When she didn't speak he went on, 'That your Italian crotch-rocket parked outside? Never knew you rode. Can't see the appeal of those bikes myself. I prefer to ride with my head higher than my arse. You see those guys squatting up there like a jockey, hugging the tank, their ring high in the air like they're biting the pillow and waiting for a friend. It's not dignified, is it? Although I can see that in your case it might be a beautiful thing.' His lips didn't move when he spoke; only the occasional movement of the cigarette in the corner of his mouth disturbed his moustache.

Kavanagh steadied herself with both hands on the gun, her feet braced wide. Her eyes were cold and fixed. 'What're you doing here, Doc?'

'Is this the way it is now, with the gun? First response is the last resort? No middle ground, just straight out with the Glock? I thought youse all had tasers now?'

'How did you find us?'

'You know how the Vipers roll, baby. Fast and right at you.' He started laughing, a smoker's ragged laugh that slid into a cough, smoke billowing out around the cigarette. He dropped his hands and plucked it from his mouth, then squinted at Kavanagh as he threw it on the floor and ground it under his boot heel. 'I've been trying to avoid the jacks all night,' he said, 'and here I go walking right into one.'

'Why are you here?' she said.

'I just want a quiet word with our Mr Ford here.' He turned to face Ford, who rose out of his chair and backed up against the wall.

They heard footsteps in the hallway, the heavy tread of boots on floorboards, and Ford turned towards the door behind Kavanagh. Banjo stepped into the kitchen and nodded sheepishly to Ford. He had a dark bruise across his cheek, swollen around a trail of cuts that looked like a cat scratch. He held the sawn-off shotgun braced against his hip, levelled at Kavanagh.

She glanced over her shoulder at Banjo, and Ford was surprised at the speed with which Doc moved. He stepped sideways out of the line of her gun and made two long strides across the kitchen towards her. He grabbed the gun by the barrel in one hand and pushed it down and into her body, twisting it against her thumb and wrenching it from her grip. At the same time he drove the heel of his other palm into her throat. She let out a choked gasp and stepped backwards, fighting for breath and clutching at her neck.

Still holding the gun by the barrel, Doc turned to Ford, his smile strengthening for a second. He transferred the gun to his right hand and pointed it at Ford. Ford scrambled from his chair and flattened himself against the wall and waited. He looked for Kavanagh, but she was on her knees, breathing hard. Doyle still sat at the table, watching the events in her kitchen with a detachment that puzzled him. He looked at Banjo pleadingly, but when their eyes met, Banjo looked away.

Doc winked at Ford, then thumbed the release on the side of the gun and let the clip drop into the palm of his left hand. He put it in his pocket and Ford saw that he was missing the middle two fingers on his left hand.

'Relax, dude. If I'd wanted to clip you, you wouldn't have heard me coming.' He racked the slide to eject the round in the chamber, then flipped the gun in his hand, stripped the slide off the receiver, pulled out the barrel and the spring, and laid the parts on the table in front of Doyle. He turned back to Kavanagh, frowning when he saw her still on her knees. 'Sorry, darl, but I don't want you with a gun, and you certainly don't want me with a gun. Now, if you'd all just put your phones on the table, we can talk.'

Doyle reached into the pocket of her cardigan and put her phone on the table. Doc looked at Ford.

'My phone's still at work.'

'You look like you've only got the clothes you're standing in,' said Doc.

'True. Most of them aren't even mine.'

Kavanagh stood up and stretched her neck, swivelling her head from side to side as if checking nothing was broken. She walked to the table and reached inside her leather jacket. She put her phone on the table, and stacked the battery on top of it. When she spoke, her voice was raspy. 'My phone's been off and the battery out since I returned to Coolgardie. I didn't want anyone tracking me.' She looked at Doc, her eyes narrowed. 'That's assaulting an officer right there for a start. Probably theft as well if you keep the magazine.'

'I can wear that. You going to arrest me, detective?'

'Sometime soon,' she said.

'You and the rest of them.' He picked up the phones and walked over to the microwave oven on the counter. He put them inside and punched the start button. The oven sparked and popped for a few seconds before beeping. Doc reached into his pocket and brought out his own phone, then thumbed the screen. 'They took down the door on my house about five hours ago.' He turned the screen towards Ford. It showed a blurred photo of a pair of policemen in body armour in the hallway of a house, guns drawn. The leading officer was in plain clothes and, squinting at the screen, Ford thought he recognised Butcher.

'Security camera,' said Doc with pride. 'They triggered it when they busted the door. Takes a picture and mails it to my phone. Miracle of the digital age.' He turned to Kavanagh. 'Why don't you sit down at the table, Rosie? I don't want you behind me. Feels like any minute you're going to lay me out with a frying pan.' He looked at Doyle. 'Where d'you keep the kitchen knives, love?'

Doyle blew out her cheeks and waved a hand towards the kitchen cabinets. 'Top drawer.'

'Banjo, mate, keep an eye on the cutlery,' said Doc.

Banjo stayed by the door. He let the shotgun hang loosely by his side. Kavanagh sat down at the table, and Ford joined her. His leg was aching and he tried not to limp.

'Where's the rest of your crew?' Doyle asked, still looking bored.

'Do I know you, darling?' said Doc.

'Alannah Doyle,' she said. 'I tried to interview you last year after your trial.'

'After my acquittal, you mean. My mistrial. I remember you did that piece for the *Courier*. Bit of a hatchet job.' He looked at Doyle then Kavanagh, and nodded and smiled. 'A copper and a journo in the same room? Explains a lot. Cooking up something nice, are we? Getting the citizens all worked up at the rising crime rate? Well, I'm your bogieman. The walking embodiment of the climate of fear. Right here in your fucking kitchen.'

He walked around the table looking at each of them in turn. Ford caught the smell of petrol, tobacco and leather as he passed. Doc stopped behind Kavanagh and leaned in close to her ear. 'And I know you too, don't I, Rosie? We go back a ways. Nicked my mate Possum for receiving that gold from the refinery at Norseman. He's still in Casuarina. You collared him, but you never got the bastard that was thieving the stuff.'

Kavanagh turned her head and spoke softly into his face. 'We never found him. Came across his boat, though. Drifting in deep water off Esperance with nobody on board.'

'He must still be a fugitive from justice, then,' said Doc.

'Like you?' said Doyle.

He leaned across the table towards her. She recoiled. 'Just because the cops have paper on me doesn't mean I've committed an offence. After last year I thought you would have understood that.' He spat out the words and his whiskers moved with the force of his breath. 'If they can't get criminal charges to stick they try other means to harass me. Can't drink in any pubs in town now. I've been banned, have to do my drinking at the clubhouse. They put that on me in a closed session of the licensing board. Secret police intelligence, for the board's ears only. Never got to challenge it. Never got to say my piece.'

'You intent on saying it now?' asked Kavanagh.

'Like I said, I came here to meet the famous Mr Ford,' he said. 'Find out what he's been telling you lot. Find out why the cops have been landing on the Vipers like a flock of seagulls on a bag of hot chips.'

'I haven't told them anything,' said Ford.

Doc leaned in close behind Kavanagh and put his hand on her shoulder. He slid his other hand down her back and pulled his knife from the waistband of her pants. He unsheathed it, and held it up to the light. It was a skinning knife with a narrow blade that ended in an ugly curved point. The varnish had been rubbed off the wooden handle and the edge was worn from repeated sharpening.

'Nearly forgot about this,' he said. 'Wouldn't have been a good look, getting stuck with my own blade.' He looked at Ford and twirled the knife, reflected light dancing across his face. 'They had warrants on me and half the club. If the security system hadn't tipped me off, I'd be sitting in the lockup with my brothers.'

'How many they pick up?' asked Kavanagh.

'They keeping you out of the loop, sweetheart?'

'They raid the clubhouse?'

'They hit it at the same time as my crib, about ten. Way too early for our boys. Most of them were still in town after the races and the two-up. Ten tactical guys went in there with guns drawn and only found two blokes using the quiet time to give an old mama a spit roast. They searched the place top to bottom and the most dangerous thing they found was a redback spider. Kiddies have Christmas, but the adults have the race round, and the cops've fucking ruined it for me.'

'So where are your buddies now?' asked Doyle.

'My sergeant-at-arms is in the lockup. They knocked down his front door and he gave the first one through the door a slap for barging in without being invited. The rest of the boys are either with him in the lockup or have gone to ground, keeping off the phones. When I couldn't get hold of anyone, I got on my bike, put my face to the wind, and went to look for my old mate Banjo.'

They all looked at Banjo. It was the first time Ford could remember him without a grin on his face.

'Boof here isn't so flash at covering his tracks,' said Doc. 'Nobody in the club hears a peep from the fat fucker in months. He's stopped hanging round the clubhouse, started turning down free beer and pussy since his old lady's put the hard word on him. Only stuck his head up when he needed some meds from the Doctor's black bag. Suddenly last night he's ringing up everyone like he's their brother again, wants to know about Mr Ford here. Wasn't hard to work out who knew most about what's going down.' He pointed the knife at Ford and spun it in his fingers. Ford leaned away. 'You scared of me?' said Doc. 'That can't be good. You stay that way.'

Ford watched the knife as it moved in front of him, and read the words DUTY FIRST tattooed across the back of Doc's hand. Around his finger was a ring fashioned like a snake; Ford noted that the pattern of coils matched the scratches across Banjo's cheek.

'There's a gun on the table,' said Ford. 'Why are you waving a knife at me?'

Doc smiled, and slipped the blade back into the sheath. He put his foot on the table and strapped the knife back into place on his calf. 'Well then, let's do this all friendly like,' he said. 'I need to know what you told Chadwick in that room.'

'I didn't tell him anything.'

'But there's a statement with your name on it.'

Ford looked at Kavanagh. She was still massaging her throat, her eyes cast down, looking at the parts of her gun laid out on the table.

'Not my statement,' said Ford. 'Just another loop in the noose that you and the police are putting round my neck.'

Kavanagh raised her head. 'He's telling the truth,' she said. 'Whoever told you there was a statement was right, but it won't hold water. He never signed it. He was verballed. He never grassed up the Vipers.'

'You keep out of it, Rosie,' said Doc. 'I hate coppers more than I hate informants. If I want any shit out of you, I'll squeeze your head.'

'I was there,' she said.

'All the time?' Doc asked.

Kavanagh swivelled in her chair to face him. He held her gaze for a few seconds and then smiled wide enough to show her his crooked teeth.

'You know, we all love Banjo here,' he said, tipping his head towards the door, 'but the cunt's got such a big mouth he was a liability when he was patched, and there was a limit to how much of his bullshit bush poetry we could stand.' Banjo forced a smile and shuffled his feet. 'Mr Ford might have been able to keep his mouth shut, but Banjo here can't keep a secret for long. He was just telling me all about Little Jimmy and his meeting with Ford.'

Ford glanced at Kavanagh and waited for a reaction, but she was smiling. She looked at him and the expression on her face was something approaching admiration. 'You're not much of a liar,' she said. 'I've been in enough interview rooms to know that. Shifty eyes, no control over your body language. You should stick to the horses—you'd be no good at poker. Pretty clear you were holding something back, that's why I stuck close.'

'Looks like we're all wondering why you didn't give up Jimmy in your statement,' said Doc.

'How would you know that?' said Kavanagh, her eyes flicking back to Doc.

Doc ignored her. He turned his chin a fraction of an inch towards Ford and spoke quietly. 'I need to know everything you know about Little Jimmy.'

Ford looked at his hands and tried to hold them steady. 'I didn't say anything to Chadwick about the Vipers or Jimmy,' he said.

Doc nodded. 'Just for a little while, I'm going to believe you, but you need to tell me what the stunted bastard has done. What's Jimmy got on you?'

Ford felt their eyes on him. He squirmed in his chair and started plucking at the loose threads around the hole in his trouser leg, picking off specks of dried black blood. 'He took over my debts. Wanted me to text him the access code to the gold room.'

'Did you?'

'No, I didn't.'

'Why not?'

'Do you do what people tell you to do?'

'No, but I'm not you,' said Doc.

'I thought I might be able to stop it happening, but he didn't actually need the code. He'd already got an inside man. I was just a red herring to wrong-side the police.'

'You said he threatened your family,' put in Kavanagh.

'I said that the guys in the gold room told us they knew where our families lived,' he corrected her. 'Little Jimmy had been watching my daughter walk to school, said he'd been round to my wife's house.'

'That's Jimmy all over,' said Doc. 'No respect for things. It's out of order him going after family. Kids is worse.'

'So why do you let him?'

'Jimmy doesn't answer to me, he's Perth chapter.'

'I need to get to Perth,' said Ford. 'I need to find my daughter.'

Doc's eyes softened. 'Little Jimmy is seventy kilos of tweaker that can't stand still and can't shut up. He talks faster than his brain can function. More balls than sense. He wants to be an outlaw, doesn't care about honour and respect, for himself or any other bastard. Looks like we're going to have to school him. He wants to play the big man, wants to raise hell. He was just getting a kick out of scaring you.'

'He did a fairly good job,' said Ford. 'If you don't pull Jimmy's strings, who does?'

'Not the president of the Perth chapter,' said Kavanagh. 'Jimmy's master of his own domain.'

'And the riders who chased us?'

Doc let that hang for a minute. 'Not Kalgoorlie boys, not without my order. Must have been Perth boys up for the races. Who did Jimmy have with him when he bailed you up?'

'There was a huge guy. Shaved head, beard, broken nose. Had a flat face like a frying pan.'

'You're not exactly being specific here.'

'There was a third guy, chased after me in a green Falcon,' said Ford. 'I saw him at the races too. Clean-shaven, slicked-back hair, looked too smooth to be a biker. He was the one fired the shots at the police station. Then there were two guys on Harleys in Coolgardie. One looked like he could have been the big guy I met with Jimmy, but the other one was too tall to be Jimmy.'

'Any of these guys wearing colours?' said Doc.

'No.'

'Jimmy's been patching a lot of new members, guys who haven't done their time as nominees, guys I haven't met. It's been too long since the Perth chapter invited us to party with them.'

'Sounds like you don't have much of an idea what's going on in your club these days,' said Kavanagh. 'You know who the robbery crew was? Were they Vipers from Perth too? Ford's seen four guys—are they the same four that hit the gold?'

'You think four of my brothers hit that mine? I think we've reached the limit of how much of this I want to discuss with a cop.'

'Ford, you reckon those four guys you've seen were the crew?' she asked.

'I can't be sure,' said Ford. 'They all had their faces covered at the mine. Only one of them spoke. There was one man short enough to be Jimmy, but nobody big enough to be the bald bloke.'

Kavanagh stood up and turned to face Doc. He took a couple of steps backwards until he was blocking the back door again, and watched her carefully as she spoke. 'What we know is that they had Russian guns, and a plane, and used shaped charges. The Vipers don't have that kind of hardware. My bet is that forensics are going to show that the explosives were a bit more sophisticated than the mining gel the bikies have been caught with in the past.'

'They got forensics up there yet?' asked Doyle. She sat upright, her hands in her lap, and Ford thought she must be taking mental notes. There was a notebook and pen on the table but she resisted the urge to write.

'They're travelling up from Perth,' said Kavanagh. 'The van was being towed into Kal. Probably won't get results for a while. Post-mortem on the guard could take a while, there wasn't much left of him.'

'They won't find anything,' said Ford. 'They wore gloves, masks, had their hair covered. Then they burned the van, with me in it.'

'They would have torched the van whether you were in it or not,' said Kavanagh.

'That would be the triple F principle,' said Doc. 'Fire fucks forensics.'

'I don't think Jimmy's got it in him, and I'm not sure you do either,' Kavanagh said to Doc.

'You seem intent on getting a rise out of me, Rosie.'

'You don't seem to be so happy to shoot your mouth off now,' said Kavanagh, taking another step towards him. 'I'm just trying to see how off balance you are with this. You've got Harleys from another chapter riding through your turf and you know nothing about it. You've got a robbery pulled off right under your nose. You've got half your club in the lockup and the other half in hiding. People out there are going to think you're getting weak.'

'Oh, baby,' he said, 'you're just winging it. You got no idea what's going down here.'

'Nice try, Doc, but I can see you're starting to look over your shoulder. We've been getting all sorts of background noise about American gangs looking to get a foothold on the west coast. The Organised Crime Squad sent up a flare last month, telling us to be on the lookout for this sort of operation, and now we're seeing Makarovs and AKs and high-grade Afghan heroin being picked up on the streets.'

'Nothing to do with my club,' said Doc. 'We don't do needles and powders.'

'You sure about that? You think you know what Jimmy's doing? You're going to lose your club. Before you know it, the Perth chapter will be patched over and they'll be looking at you. Small clubs like the Vipers are going to get swallowed up by the big clubs.' Kavanagh took another step forward until she was close to his face. She looked like she was starting to enjoy herself.

'One of the reasons I don't allow needles and powders is that it divides the club against itself,' said Doc. 'Some guys want to make and sell, but there are others with families to support and jobs to hold down: if they don't want to get involved with anything that might get them sent down, it drives a wedge between them. And what's a brotherhood for if not mateship?'

'Jimmy's into doing business,' said Kavanagh. 'It's not even about the bikes for him anymore. When was the last time you saw him on a Harley? Dude drives around in a custom '57 Chevy, wearing all those rockabilly shirts of his. Times are changing, Doc, and your code of honour is starting to look as slow and obsolete as that old Shovelhead you ride.' She walked to the kitchen counter and pulled open the top drawer, taking out a small kitchen knife before Doc and Banjo had time to react.

Doc looked at her hand and smiled. 'That's not much of a blade,' he said. Banjo raised the shotgun but Doc shook his head.

Kavanagh looked from one to the other and laughed. 'You worried about me bringing a cheese knife to a gun party?' She walked over to Ford, who flinched away from the knife. 'You're as jumpy as those two,' she said, shaking her head. She kept talking to Doc as she lifted Ford's coat off the back of his chair and ran her hand down the seams. 'Something's not seemed right to me for a while now. You know about the interview, you've seen the statement: someone's feeding you information. But how did you find us here? I didn't tell anyone where I was going, and my phone's been off for the last few hours.'

She continued patting down the coat until she paused and her eyes lit up. 'Here we go.' She forced the tip of the blade under the seam and sliced up the lining, then put her hand inside the coat and pulled. Ford heard the stitches rip. She raised her hand; between her thumb and forefinger she held a small silver box. Ford thought for a moment it was his old Zippo lighter, but then remembered the coat wasn't his.

Kavanagh tossed it onto the kitchen table and it clattered across the wood. She threw the knife after it. 'GPS tracker. Chadwick must have had it sewn in there during the interview. Explains how you found us, but not why.'

Doc stepped up to the table and calmly palmed the kitchen knife. He picked up the tracker and dropped it in Ford's glass, then poured a measure of vodka on top of it.

'There were only five people in that interview room,' said Kavanagh, 'plus the uniform on the front desk. You want me to start making guesses?'

Doc walked back to the doorway, turned, and started cleaning his fingernails with the kitchen knife.

'When did Morton get the chance to show you the statement?' she asked.

Doc took the phone out of his pocket and waved it at her. 'How did we survive before camera phones and email?' he said.

'Did you take any time to think why he would tell you where to find Ford? Did you wonder how he knew?'

Doc shrugged and looked at Banjo.

'Chadwick wants Ford's statement as evidence to sweep up the Vipers,' Kavanagh said. 'The statement won't last long in court if Ford's around to dispute it. He let him loose to draw you out, in the hope that you'd make him disappear. He hopes maybe you'll be in such a hurry that you'll get sloppy and he'll have another murder to pin on you too.'

Doc raised his chin towards Banjo. 'Take a look outside, compadre.' Banjo nodded and disappeared down the hallway.

Kavanagh went on, 'Chadwick will have put out the word that the Vipers have the gold, whether he believes it or not. He's going to make sure every other bike club knows that you're weak and up for the taking. There'll be Slavs and the Italians too, plus the Asian Sword Boys. Every standover man and toecutter in the state's going to be looking for the Vipers. And he'll just sit back with a big shit-eating grin on his face watching you all carve each other up, then he'll scrape up whatever's left.'

Banjo came back through the door, breathless. 'Took a peek through the picket fence. There's an unmarked white Commodore across the street with a pair of cop aerials on it. No lights, but I could see a cigarette. Checked the laneway out the back, and it's clear. Don't think anyone's clocked my ute.'

'Probably Morton and Butcher,' said Kavanagh.

Doc slapped the knife on the palm of his hand. He thought for a minute, and then walked to the table and started reassembling Kavanagh's gun. 'Only two cops? Where are the rest of them?' he asked.

Kavanagh smiled. 'They didn't know where we were heading so they won't have a warrant. Probably didn't have authorisation for the tracker either. They're waiting for probable cause: you fire that gun, they'll be in here soon enough, and if they see you leaving with Ford, they'll pick you up.'

'And what about you, detective?' said Doc. 'Won't look good if you get swept up with me and him. They could fit you up as the rat at the station.'

'You want to play that angle? Maybe I was here chasing you. I could arrest you and take you in.'

Doc pulled the clip from his pocket, slid it back in the Glock and racked the slide. 'You got some balls, girl, I'll give you that,' he said. 'Crazy fierce.'

'You have to understand that I'm compensating for my feelings of inadequacy as a woman in a male-dominated environment by over-asserting myself,' she said.

Letting the sarcasm hang, Doc flipped the switch by the door to kill the lights in the kitchen.

Ford could still make him out by the orange glow from the wood stove. 'Where you going?' he asked.

'None of your fucking business, loser.' Doc pointed the gun at Ford.

'Going to Perth to find Jimmy?' Ford asked, trying to ignore the gun.

Doc didn't answer. Turning away, he opened the door and looked out into the garden.

'I'm coming with you,' said Ford. He rose out of the chair and picked up the ripped coat from the table.

'Like fuck you are.'

'I need to find my daughter. I've been calling for two days. Jimmy's got to know. I've got nothing left here. I'm asking you to take me with you.'

'We don't carry passengers.'

'If you leave me here, I'll either get knocked over by Jimmy's boys, or the cops'll pick me up again. Either way works bad for you.'

'You've got Kavanagh here to protect you.'

'She might not be enough,' said Ford. 'You need me alive. You need me to dispute the statement, otherwise Chadwick will keep coming at you. I can identify the other three guys as well.'

Doc lowered the gun. He thought for a moment then looked at Banjo, who nodded. 'What a shitstorm,' Doc said. 'Guess you're with us.'

Kavanagh stepped across beside Ford. She looked at him with an expression of bland, fathomless contempt. 'Wherever he goes, I go,' she said.

Doc laughed and it quickly changed to a cough. 'You got some brass neck. I might be starting to like you.'

'When we get to Perth, I'm taking Ford in,' she said.

'To do what? You think you're going to get Jimmy? He's a Viper. The burden falls on the club. We don't need a cop to take care of our business.'

'You don't see that this is what both Jimmy and Chadwick want? They want you to stick your head out so they can knock it off. You need to go at this sideways.'

'No, we go straight at them. Never been any other way.'

'And how far do you think you'll get if you leave me here?'

'Probably a lot further than if we give them the excuse of looking like we've taken a cop hostage.'

'You've got my gun. I can't let you leave with it. Might as well take me along with it.'

'So many reasons, none of them really closing the deal with me.'

Ford pulled on the coat and examined the ripped lining.

Doc laughed. 'You look like that coat, coming apart at the seams. What you got, it's called bad luck, and you got so much of it you're a mug to play the horses. Don't let that jinx rub off on us or I may regret taking you.'

'My hex would feel a lot better if you guys had some more of those big pink happy pills,' said Ford, looking at Banjo.

Banjo put a hand in his jeans pocket and rummaged. He stepped forward and slapped his hand on the table, pulling it back to reveal half a dozen white pills. 'These should put a smile on your dial, soldier.'

Ford picked them up and swallowed two dry, squirrelling the rest in a pocket.

'Right, we're leaving,' said Doc. 'Banjo, mate, check out the front.'

Banjo stepped out into the corridor. Doc was watching Doyle, who hadn't moved from the table. 'What about you, sweetheart? You got a burning ambition to be a biker chick? Is a wild girl lurking behind that whole librarian vibe you're giving out? Want to stop writing about life and start living it?'

'As tempting as that sounds, I'll stay here,' she said. 'If they get any ideas about walking into my house without a warrant I can probably stall them.'

'You going to be writing all this down? Cobbling together a story for Monday?'

'There's no story here. Not one my paper would run, unless you'd care to make a statement before you leave?'

'Fat chance, love. The club has a policy of not making any comment to the press. You only twist whatever we say.'

'You say that, but you haven't shut up since you've been here.'

'Strictly off the record. You know that. But you can find the story on your own, if you're the kind of journo that digs for the story rather than the type that tries to bury it.'

Banjo came back into the kitchen. 'There's another car showed up, and there's two plain-clothes standing in the street. Looks like they're about ready to come in.'

'No,' said Doc. 'If they've got more bodies they'll cover the back exit before coming to the door. Time to go.' He opened the door and waved Banjo through. Kavanagh picked up her leather jacket and made to follow him. Doc raised the gun and put it to her temple. 'I'm getting tired of saying no to you.'

'And I'm getting sick of your bullshit macho swagger,' she said. 'You go ahead and pull the trigger and bring them in here.'

He lowered the gun. 'I don't need the gun, sweetheart. All of you cops together wouldn't add up to one half of a good fight, and I'd end up looking like a bully.'

'You weren't so fussy consorting with cops when you had Morton on the payroll. What did you have on him? Was it a bloke thing? Beer and bourbon and strippers down the clubhouse? Free blow and get blown for free? I can see why you'd have no use for a female copper. Forget Morton. He's burned you. Who you got now? Who's going to tap you into what Chadwick's doing? You going to try and second-guess the cops all the way to Perth? I stay close to Ford and maybe I'll help you. Help you all the way till I find the gold.'

Doc hesitated, scratched his head with the end of the gun barrel, and then nodded and waved her through the door.

As she passed him, Kavanagh leaned in close. 'When we get out of here, I want my Glock back.'

'Don't push it, sister. Just get in the bloody ute.'

Ford and Doc followed Kavanagh out the door, and the four of them stood on the verandah. Ford glanced back through the window at Doyle sitting at the table, her head in her hands, staring at the glass of vodka with the tracker in it. She suddenly looked exhausted.

They walked in single file across the yard with Doc leading the way. Ford winced in pain as he stumbled on the patchy grass and loose sand. He looked round to see Banjo bringing up the rear, the shotgun held loosely by his side, the muzzle pointing at the ground.

The sun was still below the horizon, casting a pink glow behind the gum trees, but there was enough light now to see to the end of the yard. Ford shivered in his coat. The dawn air was crisp and clean, his breath fogging in front of him.

The yard ended in a corrugated asbestos fence, cracked and stained and listing, with a battered steel gate on rusty hinges. Doc swung the gate and grimaced as the hinges squeaked. He ducked his head out into the laneway, then motioned them through.

They walked down the laneway in the shadow of the fence. At the end of the lane, Ford saw a white ute parked in the street. Banjo's blue heeler stood on the tailgate with its ears pricked, tail wagging, watching them creep along the fence.

'You brought your fucking dog?' hissed Kavanagh.

'He goes where the ute goes,' whispered Banjo. 'Who else was going to warn us if the cops spotted it?'

TWENTY-ONE

Ford stood in the middle of the road, looking at the dawn light in the east silhouetting the gum trees along the road. When they had still been a family, Sunday was his day with Grace. In the morning Diane would go to the gym and he would make pancakes for the two of them. They would pick blueberries from the straggly plant that withered in the sunny spot by the back fence and squash them into the pancakes with the back of a spoon. In summer they would go to the beach, and in winter he rode his bike in Kings Park with her on the back. Once they had cycled the length of the Swan Valley. They had seen a pair of horses hanging their heads over the fence of a vineyard, and had stopped to feed them the crusts from Grace's cheese sandwiches. He'd promised her riding lessons. It was the first of several promises he'd broken.

He realised he'd been daydreaming when Kavanagh slapped him across the back of the head and shoved him towards the ute. It was an old Hilux dual cab, sitting high on its suspension. There was a heavy bull bar across the front, and a steel rollover bar fitted with a yellow hazard light and a bank of spotlights. Ford recognised it as an old company vehicle kitted out to a mining

220

specification. The hood was painted red, and a snorkel snaked up from the battered side wing. The heavy off-road tyres were red with dirt, and mud was splattered high up the sides. The driver's door had an uneven grey rectangle where Banjo must have painted over the mining company logo, and on the rear door a large Eureka flag had been painted by hand. The aluminium tray on the back was packed with gear rolled in a tarpaulin, along with a pair of oxy tanks and two stacked toolboxes. There was a rack standing up from the tailgate, linked with struts to a similar rack on the roof of the cab. It was empty, but Ford guessed it was normally used for carrying lengths of plumbing material. There was just enough room on the back of the tray for the dog. It paced in circles as they approached and then curled up with a groan on a ragged pile of blankets.

Banjo opened the driver's door, slipped the shotgun under the seat, and pulled himself up behind the wheel. Doc opened the rear door for Ford and Kavanagh. There was dust ground into the upholstery, grease stains on the seat pads and oily thumb prints on the door handles. Ford grabbed the overhead grip, put a foot on the dented aluminium running board and hauled himself into the cab. He slid across the bench seat to make room for Kavanagh, who pulled herself up, crinkling her nose when she saw the mess. She swept a collection of empty beer cans and iced-coffee cartons off the bench into the footwell, climbed into the seat, and then squashed them flat under her boot.

Doc sat up front in the passenger seat. Cradling Kavanagh's Glock in his lap, he leaned forward to scan the street. Banjo turned the ignition and the rattling throb of the diesel kicked in. They moved off slowly, no one speaking. The brightening sky in the east still wasn't light enough to drive by, but Banjo left his headlights off. They rolled slowly around the corner, and it wasn't until they had made two more turns and were heading south along Federal Road that Banjo turned on the lights and accelerated.

There were a handful of other vehicles on the road, all utes and four-wheel drives like theirs. Men stood on street corners in yellow high-viz jackets, their hands thrust deep in their pockets, black beanies pulled down over their ears, waiting for their ride to work for the Sunday shift. The ute turned into Burt Street and crawled past the old Federation facades of Boulder. After passing under the railway, Banjo took a sharp right, pulling into a side street of dilapidated weatherboard houses standing between vacant lots choked with weeds. He cut the engine and leaned back, stretching and yawning.

'Now what?' he said, looking at Doc.

'Are you guys just winging this?' said Kavanagh.

Doc slapped the dashboard and they waited for him to speak. 'We're going to find a route to Perth,' he said.

'Just us? No motorcycle escort?' said Ford.

'For the moment.' Doc turned to Banjo, and Ford tried to read the look between them.

'What's your plan?' said Kavanagh. 'Every cop along six hundred kilometres of that highway is going to be watching the road. There'll be hundreds of punters driving home from the races, so there'll be speed traps and random breath tests. Gives the country cops a reason to justify their existence. If they put out a bulletin on us we'll never get through.'

Doc's expression didn't change. 'There's more than one road out of here.'

'You want to go south to Esperance or north to Leonora? Either way it's a hell of a long way round. You think they won't have cars on those roads as well?'

'You're thinking too linear, Rosie. Don't they teach you lateral thinking at detective school?' Doc leaned over to Banjo and whispered in his ear. Banjo laughed silently, his shoulders moving. He started the engine and pulled away quickly, turning south onto the Goldfields Highway, and then left onto a side road heading out towards the shadows of the spoil heaps. Ford could see the lights of ore trucks high above them, running along the flat top of the man-made hills, tipping waste rock from the Super Pit down the slopes of the dumps. Banjo swung the wheel hard and bumped down the gravel shoulder and onto a dirt road stretching out across a salt pan. Ahead of them Ford could see the smoke stack of the nickel smelter standing tall against the tree line, its plume of white smoke caught in the first orange light of the rising sun.

As they crossed the salt pan the sun appeared over the horizon and a golden light filled the cab. Ford glanced at Kavanagh, her face suddenly illuminated. She stared at the road ahead without expression, and he noticed she looked tired.

Leaning forward, she put her hand on Banjo's shoulder.

'We're a bit exposed out here on this lake.'

'Only for a few minutes,' said Banjo. 'Once we're beyond the smelter we'll get among the trees.'

Ford watched as the smelter got closer. They crossed a highway and continued along the gravel road until they passed along the fence to the north of the chimney, where they looped around the back of the rail yards and headed south. The track became wider and better graded, cutting a straight line through the mallee scrub alongside the freight railway. On the wide road Banjo increased his speed, gravel spitting from under the tyres and red dust boiling behind them.

'Is now the time you tell me which way we're going?' said Ford.

'We'll loop south around Karramindie,' said Banjo, 'then cross below Coolgardie through some of the old mining leases. Join up with the Holland Track at Victoria Rock.'

'The Holland Track?' said Kavanagh. 'That's three hundred kilometres of bush bashing, then another three hundred of back roads through the Wheatbelt. It'll take us all day, even assuming the track is passable and not overgrown or washed out. You sure this rust bucket is up to it?'

'This thing'll take you anywhere,' said Banjo. 'New donk last year. She ain't pretty, but she's solid.'

He spun the wheel and slewed them west onto a rutted track. The ute started to buck fiercely, and the gear in the back clattered. The dog was on its feet, swaying easily with the rolling of the tray, but Ford winced with every jolt, the seatbelt cutting into his shoulder and ribs.

Doc looked over his shoulder at the oxy tanks swaying on the back tray. 'You sure that welding gear's secure?'

'Never had a problem with it yet,' said Banjo.

'Was it a good idea to leave the tanks there when there's a chance someone might shoot at us?' Doc went on.

Banjo smiled. 'You didn't give me much time to set up the truck, and nobody mentioned a cross-country getaway. You're lucky it's the weekend and I had the swags and the eskies all set up to take the dirt bikes to the bush.'

'You got food and water?' asked Kavanagh.

Banjo nodded. 'And beer.'

'Is it a safe road?'

'A lot safer than the highway.'

'No GPS?' she noted.

'Don't need it,' said Banjo. 'We just keep heading southwest, and I can judge that by the sun. I know most of the landmarks. There aren't many.'

'You know the tracks?'

'Been down some of them last summer on the dirt bikes. There are stretches further west that I drove down a few years back.'

'You think they'll be passable?'

'Guess we'll find out. If we're lucky they won't have seen much rain this winter.'

They drove in silence for an hour, the landscape unchanging, the steady rattle of the diesel and the thumping of the suspension the only noise. Banjo stared straight ahead, his big hands resting easy on the top arc of the steering wheel. The ute was skittish on the loose gravel, but he worked the wheel from side to side in a relaxed way, letting the back end fishtail. Doc had one foot on the dashboard, one hand gripping the handle above the door, swaying with the ease of a sailor on a rough sea. Kavanagh was looking out of the window at the passing bush with the thousand-yard stare Ford had seen in the interview room.

They crossed the Esperance Highway and plunged back into the bush on the far side. The trees grew taller and crowded in on the track, the mallee scrub giving way to salmon gums, the track snaking between their pink trunks.

The ute hit a deep pothole and Ford groaned. He doubled up in his seat, skewed sideways, drawing his knees to his chest and hugging them. He rested his head on the back of his seat and screwed his eyes shut.

'We walk on unfrequented paths,' he said.

'You still with us, Ford?' said Kavanagh.

He groaned again. 'Slow down,' he whispered.

'How much pain you got?' she asked.

'Enough to go round if you feel like sharing.'

Doc tapped Banjo on the shoulder and waved to him to pull over. The ute broke out of the trees into a clearing. They pulled up in the shadow of a disused timber mine headframe, the winding gear gone, the top of the shaft filled with rubble. The clearing was ringed by the remains of mine buildings, the roof sheeting long since scavenged, leaving timber skeletons.

Doc stepped down from the ute and opened the back door. 'Get out, stretch your legs,' he said to Ford. 'Bit of fresh air might help.'

Ford pushed out his legs and climbed down slowly, his eyes closed against the bright sunlight.

'You're pale,' said Doc. 'You look like some kind of ghost. I never saw skin so white.' He put his hand to Ford's forehead, then a couple of fingers to his neck, checking his pulse. 'You'll live.'

Ford forced open his eyes. 'You some kind of real doctor, Doc?'

'Not any kind of doctor. Had a mate in the army who was a medic. Used to help him out when things got hot. Taught me a few tricks. Been patching up the Vipers ever since. Your temperature's up, and your pulse is weak, but nothing to worry about.' Doc reached into his pocket and brought out a ziplock bag of pills. He shook them out into his palm, chose a couple and handed them to Ford. Then he pulled a water bottle from the recess in the door and handed it to him.

As they set off again, Ford curled up in his seat, his head lying sideways against the headrest and his eyes closed. He tried to think back to the last time he'd slept. He'd snatched a few hours in Banjo's cellar and in the police interview room, but that seemed longer ago than yesterday. He tried to drift off but the jolting of the truck kept the pain alive in spite of the pills, and he eventually gave up.

'You got any music?' he asked. 'Anything that'll take my mind off it.'

Banjo flicked on the radio in the dash and the cab filled with static. He punched a few buttons, then turned the dial, but all that came through was a faint AM country station. Doc slapped Banjo's hand away from the radio and took a short cable from the glove box. He slotted one end into the radio, and the other into his phone. A guitar riff kicked in, followed by thunderous drums. Banjo smiled, nodded his head to the beat and sped up.

Ford groaned. 'That's not helping, fellas,' he croaked.

Kavanagh leaned forward between the front seats and jabbed Doc in the shoulder; when he turned to her, she ran her finger across her throat to tell him to cut the music. He lowered the volume, but let it play.

'Is that phone getting a signal?' Kavanagh asked.

Doc checked the screen. 'Only just. Fades in and out.'

'Why the fuck have you left your phone on?'

'Relax, darling, it's a burner. Prepay. Cash only. Not linked to me.'

'How many Vipers in Perth know that number?' she asked. Doc looked at her and then at the phone, turning it over in his hand. 'Give it to me.' She held out her hand.

He made to put it back in his pocket and she punched him again in the shoulder. 'You've done enough damage. I may as well use it to see what's happening before we ditch it. Give me the bloody phone.'

Doc pulled out the cable and the music died. Ford exhaled in relief. Doc held up the phone and Kavanagh snatched it from his hand. She leaned back and thumbed the screen.

'I'm not getting a signal,' she said.

'Who d'you want to call?' he asked.

'Alannah. See what happened after we left. How long before we're at the rock?'

'Ten minutes, maybe,' said Banjo.

'Stop there. Maybe I can get a signal from the top.'

They drove in silence until the trees thinned out and they emerged onto the Victoria Rock. The smooth red monolith sloped gently in front of them, rising above the trees, the size of a hill. As soon as the ute rolled to a stop, Kavanagh jumped down, and Doc and Banjo followed her. Ford climbed down and limped slowly after them. He stumbled on the uneven surface, the plastic thongs flapping uselessly on his feet. He kicked them off, picked them up, and continued barefoot.

By the time he caught up with her, Kavanagh was standing by a cairn of loose rocks that marked the summit. They weren't much higher than the trees that ringed it, but the rock was the highest point in the landscape. The trees spread to the horizon in every direction, a solid carpet fading from green to a blue haze in the distance. Ford turned around slowly, trying to work out where they had come from, and where they might be going, but the bush looked the same in every direction.

Kavanagh held the phone at arm's length and took a few steps back and forth, looking for reception. Then she broke into a smile. 'Two bars,' she said. 'Should be enough.' She tapped a number into the screen and held the phone to her ear. She turned her back to them when she started talking, and walked slowly out of earshot. Doc made to follow her, but she raised her hand to stop him and carried on walking away.

Banjo strode over to a large round boulder, hopped up onto it and gazed out. He threw his hands out wide and declaimed:

Desolation where the crow is! Desert where the eagle flies,
Paddocks where the luny bullock starts and stares with reddened
 eyes . . .
Bush! where there is no horizon! where the buried bushman sees
Nothing—nothing! but the sameness of the ragged stunted trees.

Ford squinted in the direction Banjo was facing and caught sight of a small dark shape approaching from the north. At first he thought it was a crow, but as his eyes followed it he decided it was moving too slowly. It was something bigger, further away, and it flew straight.

Doc turned around when he heard the plane's engines, and Ford pointed to it. Banjo looked too. They stood watching for a minute, until it was clear that the plane was travelling towards them. Kavanagh was still talking with her back to them. Doc walked up to her and snatched the phone from her hand. When she turned to him with a scowl, he pointed to the plane.

She stared at it for a moment, then looked for the ute. It was two hundred metres away and in plain view out on the lower slope of the rock. The plane would be on them before they could find cover: there was nothing to do but stand and watch. It passed low over them, then banked left and made another pass. There was no doubt the pilot had seen them.

'That your plane, Ford?' asked Kavanagh.

He watched it turn and head away west. 'Looks the same,' he said. 'Twin engines, plain white, four-seater, registration covered.'

'It's not one of ours,' she said.

Doc started walking back to the ute, ripping the battery and the chip out of the phone as he went. Banjo jumped down from the rock and hurried after him. Kavanagh broke into a jog. Ford stumbled behind, looking up every few steps to see if the plane had disappeared. By the time he got back to the truck, Banjo had folded down the side panel of the tray and was stripping the tarpaulin and opening the toolboxes. He lifted a long nar-row nylon bag out of the toolbox, unzipped it and pulled out a hunting rifle. He laid it on top of the toolbox and adjusted the telescopic sights.

'If they decide to come after us, and they're starting from Kalgoorlie, we've got about a hundred-kilometre head start on them,' he said.

Doc had the Glock in his hand. While Kavanagh watched him, he pulled out the clip and began counting the rounds.

'Still the full fifteen,' she said. 'I'd say now's about the time you give it back to me.'

Doc looked at her, reloaded the clip, and stuck it down the waistband of his jeans. He walked to the ute and leaned over into the toolbox. She stepped up next to him and put a hand on his shoulder.

'If someone's coming after us, I think we'd be better off if I was armed,' she said. 'It would also give me a degree of confidence that you're not going to leave me and Ford in a shallow grave out there.'

Doc grabbed her wrist and twisted it off his shoulder. She took a step backwards and tried to pull away, but he kept hold and twisted it down, forcing her to drop to one knee. 'You seem to have got the wrong idea about me, detective,' he said. 'You think I'd kill a cop? You think, with all the heat coming on my club, that I'd give them an excuse like that? I'm still a cleanskin. Six times you lot have had me up on bullshit charges, and six times I walked.'

She gritted her teeth, wrenched her wrist from his grasp and jumped to her feet. Stepping in close to his face, she said, 'Just because the charges didn't stick doesn't mean you were innocent. I've seen your file.'

'That's how you lot work, isn't it? Just because I wear these colours and ride a motorcycle, you think that gives you a free kick. The legal system's just a hindrance to you. This state hasn't changed since the time of the convicts. You lot are descended from the prison warders, and you still think you're here to watch over us. Don't think I'm going to forget what you are, copper. One of the hard and ready minions of the Establishment, and I don't agree with a single thing you stand for.'

Doc went back to digging around in the toolbox. He pulled out a folded bundle of oilcloth and put it on the lid of the box, unwrapping an enormous pistol. When he raised it and pointed the barrel to the sky it looked as long as his forearm. The sun reflected off the nickel plating.

Kavanagh sniggered. 'Why are you carrying a Dirty Harry gun like that?' she said.

'This, my darling, is a Colt Python .357 magnum with an eight-inch barrel,' said Doc. 'I wanted a gun that was as big as my dick. If I ever have to pull this on a guy, I want to see the same wide-eyed expression of shock and awe that I saw on my old lady's face the first time she unzipped my pants.'

'It'll take your thumb off.'

'You don't understand. A magnum is like a big Harley, so powerful that it challenges your ability to control it.'

Kavanagh shook her head.

Ford limped up to the ute and climbed back into his seat. 'What did you learn from Alannah?' he asked.

'She said that the four cops who came to her house think the four of us are now travelling together. I was going to phone Perth and talk to a mate in the Gang Squad, see if he would take us in.'

'I'd rather have a gun in my hand than a cop on the phone,' said Doc, flipping open the cylinder of the revolver and feeding rounds into it. He snapped it shut and spun it, then laid it on top of the toolbox. He started filling his pockets with loose rounds.

'Are you still trying to plead innocence, even after hearing Ford tell you that Jimmy is involved?' said Kavanagh.

'Involved how? One minute you're telling me the Vipers are too dumb to do this. Next you're telling me we're part of it. What the fuck would our club want with gold? Our currency is cash, booze and drugs. Occasionally we'll accept motorcycles or pussy in part payment. We've got no way to move gold bars.'

'Maybe Jimmy's got bigger ideas. Maybe Jimmy's outgrown you, moved on from standing over nightclubs and getting bouncers to push speed, and got into heroin and running guns.'

Doc took off his leather cut, held it up and shook out the creases. He placed it flat on the tray of the ute and stared at the snake patch sewn on the back. His fingers traced the stitching along its curve. He folded the vest carefully, and then laid it in the toolbox and shut the lid. He pulled the Glock from the waistband of his jeans, spun it in his hand, and held it out to Kavanagh butt-first. She looked at it and then at him, raising an eyebrow.

'Take it,' he said. 'I want to be sure that if I have to shoot someone in self-defence you're going to be next to me firing at the same time. Otherwise your lot will try and stick me for murder.'

'Are we starting to establish some sort of trust here?' she said. 'I'm quite moved.'

'Not trust. I can never trust a cop. Let's just call it an interest in mutual safety. As long as you understand that you're not my hostage, and I'm not your prisoner.'

'What do I get?' said Ford. They turned to look at him. He pointed to Banjo's rifle. 'It's me that's in the most danger. I need a gun too.'

'You ever fired one?' asked Doc.

'Went clay shooting once with a twelve-gauge. I was pretty good.'

'Every man thinks he's a good shot,' said Kavanagh. 'Like they all think they're good drivers and considerate lovers.'

'Some of us are, darling,' said Banjo. 'My Remington can put a group of three through a playing card at one hundred metres. This rifle isn't a fuck-around thing.'

'One out of three isn't bad,' she said. 'I've seen your driving. I hope you're better in bed than you are behind the wheel.'

Banjo put his hand over his mouth and poked his tongue through the V of his fingers. Kavanagh turned away to hide her smile. She racked the Glock, flipped the safety and put it down the back of her pants.

'Shall we get driving, boys?' she said 'Maybe make the most of this head start?'

TWENTY-TWO

Ford had lost track of time. They had been driving for hours, and the sun had passed over the ute and was now ahead of them in the west, so he figured it was well into the afternoon. For long sections of the drive the bush had changed so little there was nothing to indicate that they had travelled any distance at all. The same eucalypt scrub, the same flat landscape with the dirt road scratched out ahead of them. The temperature had risen outside, and the ute's air conditioner was struggling to cope. Ford ran a hand across his forehead and felt the film of dust and sweat. He still felt feverish, sweating but with a chill at his core. He reached into his pocket for the pills and swallowed another two dry.

The road had deteriorated since they left the rock, reduced to a pair of sandy wheel ruts snaking between the trunks of the salmon gums and gimlet. At one point Banjo had stopped to lock the wheel diffs, and then swapped seats with Doc. Doc was driving in low range, working the steering wheel to keep a straight line as the ute weaved in the loose sand. Banjo was now slumped asleep in the passenger seat, his head wedged into his coat, which was balled up against the window. Doc had taken off his shirt and was down to a stained blue singlet. The smell in the cab was ripe and unpleasant. Ford had opened a window an hour back, but flies had blown in along with the dust, so he'd closed it and settled for the smell. Sleep eluded him, and the rocking of the cab kept the pain of his wounds alive. He had lost count of the number of pills he had swallowed, but he was sure he was well beyond the recommended dose.

He looked at Kavanagh, who was dozing next to him, her chin on her chest. Her hair had slipped out from behind her ear and swung in front of her face as the ute swayed. Doc looked hot and sweaty in the driver's seat, his skin flushed pink, but Kavanagh's was as pale as milk. He wondered how she could sleep with the seat bucking as it did, and envied her for it.

He leaned forward between the front seats to look at the speedo. They were doing seventy. He did the arithmetic in his head and realised they would not get to Perth in daylight. Doc's eyes met his in the rear-view mirror, and Ford moved his head to catch his own reflection. His eyes were ringed with dark shadow, his cheeks hollow, and his chin peppered with grey stubble. The bruising round his eye had turned a sickly shade of yellow. As he studied his reflection he thought that maybe his whole face had the yellow tinge of jaundice. He pulled down an eyelid and moved further forward to check the colour. Doc looked at him sideways.

'Am I yellow?' said Ford.

'Yeah, now you mention it. Must be your liver packing up after all the abuse you given it.'

'I'm not that much of a drinker.'

'You tell yourself that if it helps.'

'I don't drink in the morning,' said Ford, 'or at lunch, and I don't drink when I'm working. I blow zero every day. It doesn't affect my work. I don't have a problem. Other people like to think I do. They like to rationalise my life for me, link cause and effect: he's a fuck-up because he drinks and, guess what, he likes a punt as well.'

'If that's not the cause, why are you such a fuck-up?'

'You as well?'

'I can smell it on you,' said Doc. 'You smell like a fuck-up and a loser. It comes off you in a cloud along with the booze and the sweat. I reckon anyone can smell it. That's how they make you as a mark. You're like a man with a spoon in a world of forks.'

'But we're cool?' said Ford.

'You never know why people are the way they are, but I've found that if you go with your gut feeling you're usually right on the nuts. I could tell by your body language that you weren't bullshitting me about what you said in that interview room.'

'I'm beyond the point where I have any cards left to play. Honesty is all I've got left. I feel like the last ball on the pool table, between two players too pissed to see straight, bouncing from side to side waiting for someone to sink me in the corner pocket.'

'But you kept it together with the cops. You know when to talk and when to shut the fuck up. You may be a loser, but you're not a rat. I might be starting to like you.' Doc smiled as Ford sat back in his seat and looked out of the window at the bush passing. 'How you doing?' said Doc. 'You look tense. Need a little something to take the edge off?'

'I've been taking the painkillers but they don't seem to be helping.' He looked at Doc in the mirror, trying to read his eyes. 'I keep thinking you and Banjo are up to something. Using me to get to Jimmy, or keeping me between you and Chadwick. I'm waiting for the other shoe to drop.'

'That's your nerves. They make you keep looking over your shoulder, imagining things creeping up on you. We're cool, you and me. Jimmy's the only one needs to be looking over his shoulder.'

'What have you got planned for him?'

'Like I'd tell you. You don't need to think about that. Whoever's backing Jimmy better be hardcore, because they're going to have the Kalgoorlie Vipers coming at them.'

'I see only one Viper.'

'There are enough guys still free that are blood true. They'll be out on the road, keeping the cops busy. We've got twelve patched members in Kal, and last I heard there were six in the lockup. As far as I know, the Perth chapter has sixteen patches, but Jimmy might have given a few more their top rocker. I reckon I can count on at least six who'll look to the club rather than to Jimmy. I won't be on my own.'

'For individualists, you guys never seem to like being alone,' said Ford.

'Who the fuck you got? No job, no old lady, half the state wanting to knock you on sight. No mates to turn to. Me and Boof and the cop are all you've got. The four of us, following the yellow brick road, although you seem to be the one with no heart, no courage and no fucking brains, Dorothy.'

'That's not what I'm saying,' said Ford. 'No disrespect, but I just don't get it, the whole club thing. You guys stress the importance of individuality, and then demand that anyone who wants to express it submit themselves to your creed. Sometimes it looks like some sort of cult.'

'When people are free to do as they please, they usually end up imitating each other,' said Kavanagh.

Ford turned to look at her. She was smiling. 'How long've you been awake?' he asked.

'Long enough to hear most of this bullshit,' she said.

'You mean you don't agree with me?' said Doc, with mock disbelief.

'It's my job not to agree with people like you. You and your mates think you live outside the law.'

'And you and the Big Blue Gang reckon you're above it,' said Doc.

'Both of you defined by your uniform,' said Ford.

'And you're not?' Doc said. 'I've seen those cosy little middle-class university signals you give out. You hide behind it like all the others. Like the cops, the lawyers, and those stockbrokers in their suits. Western suburbs tossers down the golf club in their daft trousers and their stupid fucking shoes, identical German cars in the car park. They got a uniform too. They think they've expressed their individuality by buying an Audi instead of a fucking BMW.'

'Yeah, now you mention it, I can see how the bikies are like a golf club,' said Ford.

'Just because we ride motorcycles, the police give us trouble, and the citizens like to watch. They're fascinated because we're sex, violence, craziness and filth all in one package, and the cops hate us for it. What they're trying to do to us is just history repeating. If they can't get us with the laws they have, they just create new laws. That's what they did to Ned Kelly and Ben Hall. They passed that Felons Apprehension Act and then sent an army of blokes into the bush to shoot them down. It won't be long before they try the same stunt with us.'

Kavanagh snorted. 'Is this where you try to paint yourselves as the guardians of civil liberties?'

Doc turned to face her, one hand on the headrest, the other loosely on the steering wheel, and opened his mouth to speak.

'Watch the bloody road, you fool,' said Kavanagh, and slapped the seat hard. Doc jerked around at the same time as a pair of kangaroos jumped onto the road ahead of him, leaping from the bush in a single hop. All Ford saw was the flash of white fur beneath their tails as they rose up in front of the hood of the truck before he felt the thump as the bull bar hit one. He was thrown forward as Doc stamped on the brakes. The ute's back end bucked as the rear wheels jumped out of the ruts in the road and the vehicle slewed, Doc fighting the wheel, gravel spitting from the tyres. Then the front wheel hit a log at the side of the track and jolted sideways, and Ford was flung the other way. Finally the front wing hit the trunk of a salmon gum and they lurched to a stop.

'Shit,' said Doc, banging the steering wheel. Ford found himself on top of Kavanagh, crushing her into the door. She put both hands on his shoulders and pushed him off, and he was surprised by her strength. Scowling, she sat upright, straightening her T-shirt and sweeping back her hair.

Banjo had rolled forward off the front bench and woke up wedged in the footwell. 'Thumped my fucking head,' he moaned. 'What the hell happened?'

'Hit a roo,' said Doc.

'Like fuck we did.' Banjo grabbed the handle over the door and groaned as he pulled himself back onto the seat. 'It's broad daylight. Too early for roos to be on the move.'

'Maybe they didn't get your memo.'

'How fast were you going?'

'Seventy,' said Ford. 'I was watching the speedo.'

Banjo looked at Doc. 'You hit a roo in daylight travelling at seventy? You put us into a fucking tree? Hang your head in shame.'

'Fuck off, all of you,' said Doc, pulling on the door handle. The ute was listing to the left and he had to put his knee to the door to get it open. Dust streamed into the cab. Banjo climbed out on his side, but when Kavanagh tried her door it was jammed. She looked at Ford and he opened his door and climbed out, holding it open while she slid across the seat and stepped down.

They gathered by the front of the ute and stood in a line looking at the damage. The bull bar had taken most of the impact, and the heavy fender had cut through the bark and embedded in the trunk of the tree. The driver's side front wheel had been pushed up and over a pile of sawn logs from a tree that must have fallen across the road some time past. The wheel was askew and jammed against the bodywork.

'Looks like you've knackered the steering on this side,' said Banjo.

Doc nodded, walked around and squatted next to the wheel. He ran a hand over the tyre and under the panel.

'Where's that kangaroo?' said Banjo. 'I don't see any blood, and I sure as hell don't see any fucking kangaroo. Sure it's not a figment of your imagination? You been tweaking a little whizz to keep you sharp on the road? Because I've got to tell you, it didn't work.'

'There were two of them,' said Doc. 'Big reds. I hit one and it went under. I must've just winged it. Can't have got far. Must have a busted leg at least.'

'Which way'd it go?'

'I didn't see the one we hit. The other one went that way.' Doc waved casually towards the right of the track. The dog barked from the back of the ute, standing with its front legs on the toolbox, puffing out its chest and looking north, its ears erect.

'You got him, boy?' said Banjo. The dog barked again. Banjo reached inside the cab and picked up his rifle. 'You see if you can get my ute back on the road, and I'll see about dinner. You know the rules in my truck: you dirty it, you wash it. You break it, you fix it. You fuck up, you walk.' He slung the rifle over his shoulder and strode off through the bush. The dog leapt over the tailgate and bounded after him.

Doc watched him go and wiped his brow, then looked at Kavanagh and Ford. 'Don't just stand there. You push, I'll reverse.' He sat behind the wheel and turned over the engine, then leaned out of the open door.

Kavanagh grabbed the bull bar with both hands, bent over, stretched a leg back and braced against the front of the ute. Ford was looking at the line her thigh made in her leather pants when she turned to him and slapped the hood. 'When you're ready,' she said.

Ford grabbed the bar, braced his legs and felt a jab of pain run from his shoulder down his spine to the wound in his thigh. He closed his eyes and bit down and waited for it to pass. When he opened them, the bush around him looked washed out. Kavanagh was looking at him, and her eyes had softened.

'Push when I gun it,' shouted Doc. The engine note rose and Ford felt the truck jolt as Doc let out the clutch. Kavanagh grunted next to him as she pushed. He tried to put pressure on the bull bar, but the pain intensified and his bare feet slid in the sand. The ute rocked on the logs and then, with a burst of revs, rolled backwards onto the track. Ford watched Doc bounce in the driver's seat as the truck went back over the wheel ruts, its doors swinging open.

Doc straightened the wheel and killed the engine. The truck was sitting low on his side, the front tyre in contact with the wheel well. Ford looked at the other front wheel, which was pointing in a different direction. He fumbled in his pocket for a cigarette and put it in his mouth. As he raised his lighter, a rifle cracked behind him, and the sound was followed by the sharp bark of the dog. He flinched and the cigarette fell from his lips.

'Sounds like Banjo caught up with that roo,' said Doc. He had climbed out and was lying on his back in the dirt with his head under the front of the ute.

'How's she look?' asked Kavanagh. She was sitting on the log, rubbing gum leaves between her palms. She brought her hands to her face and inhaled.

Doc pulled himself upright and clapped the dust from his hands. 'Looks like I've buggered the wishbones. Put a crack in the top one and bent the bottom.'

Ford heard a branch snap behind him and whirled around.

'Still jumpy, mate?' said Banjo, walking out of the bush. The kangaroo was draped across his shoulders, its head lolling and dripping blood down the side of his shirt, the tail swinging down the other side, the dog snapping at it. 'Didn't get far. Broken leg. I thought you said it was a big red? This is a little grey. Hardly worth the bullet.'

He heaved it over his head and thumped it down on the hood of the truck, smearing blood across the paintwork. The bullet had gone through the eye and taken off most of the back of the skull. Ford backed away from it and turned his head.

'You squeamish, Dorothy?' said Doc. 'The thing was on its last legs. Banjo did it a favour.' The dog sat in front of the radiator grille looking hard at the kangaroo, its tongue hanging out.

Banjo leaned over to look at the tyre. 'What the fuck did you do to my ute, chief?'

'Busted wishbone.'

'At seventy? That little grey?'

'The bloody thing was rusted through. I thought you kept a clean vehicle?'

'It is what it is, I guess.' Banjo put his head inside the truck and looked at the mileage, then stared west down the track, shielding his eyes against the dipping sun.

'You know where we are?' asked Ford, trying to follow his gaze.

'Reckon we're not far from Sandalwood Rocks,' said Banjo. 'Be better to fix things up there. You reckon we'll get there without the wheel falling off?'

Doc considered that for a moment. 'If we take it slow. How long before that roo starts to stink? Hopefully we can drive fast enough to keep the flies off it. Couldn't you have butchered it where it fell?'

'Prefer to do it on the hood, and I'll need to pack it in the esky. Best wait until we're stopped and can unload.' Banjo grabbed the dog by the collar and dragged it around the back. It jumped onto the tray and Banjo slipped a chain on its collar. He slid his rifle behind the seat and climbed behind the steering wheel. 'No offence, boss, but I think it would be better for the wildlife if I drive.'

They all returned to their seats and he started the engine, his head cocked to one side, listening. When he was satisfied it was running smoothly, they moved off. The front end started to judder immediately, and at any bump in the road they heard the tyre grind against the wheel arch. Banjo scowled and dropped his speed until they were at walking pace.

'How long to the rocks?' asked Ford.

'Fuck knows at this rate.'

'And how long before whoever's following us catches up?'

'If there's anyone behind us, you can be sure they'll have someone ahead of us as well, so it won't do much good to worry about it.'

Ford thought about that for a while, then reached under the seat in front of him and put his hand around the shotgun Banjo had stashed. He dragged it out and sat cradling it in his lap. He turned his head and saw Kavanagh looking at him. 'Don't try and take this off me,' he said.

TWENTY-THREE

Ford peered into the cast-iron pot over the camp stove. It was suspended from a long steel rod spanning an old fire pit, resting on a pair of steel poles pushed into the ground on either side. The rig looked like it had been knocked together from pieces of reinforcing bar. The stove was an ancient primus. Banjo had collected firewood, but Doc didn't want smoke attracting attention and had insisted on the stove.

Beside the pot was a small pile of empty tin cans with their lids hanging off. None had labels. The stove sat under the overhang of a boulder larger than the Toyota. It was one of several round rocks scattered across an expanse of stony ground that formed a clearing rising gently out of the surrounding bush. The high point was marked by a tall cairn of loose rocks that offered views across the trees.

As they were unloading the camping gear and toolboxes, Ford had caught a familiar whiff on the breeze coming from the tree line and remembered that Banjo had called the place Sandalwood Rocks. The smell had made him turn and look at Kavanagh, but he hadn't known why. Now, as he stood watching her crouched over a map spread out on the ground, running her finger along the single dotted line that indicated the Holland Track, he caught the same smell again and realised that sandalwood was the dark note in Kavanagh's perfume that he hadn't been able to identify before. She took a long pull from her beer, her head thrown back, her neck arched, and Ford watched her throat move as she swallowed.

He drank from his own beer and wiped the back of his hand across his lips. He was trying to remember the other fragrance in her perfume when the smell from the cooking pot filled his nostrils. He looked into the pot again. The dark brown slurry was bubbling like volcanic mud.

'That smells rank,' he said.

Banjo was sitting on the far side of the fire with his back against a boulder. His hunting rifle lay across his knees and he was fiddling with the scope. He looked up at Ford and raised an eyebrow. 'If you don't like what I cook, feel free to call room service.'

'The cans aren't even labelled,' said Ford. 'You could have thrown any old shit in that stew. Sure you didn't get some of Max's dog food mixed in there?'

As if he'd heard his name, the dog came trotting out of the bush, his head held high. Ford watched as he bounded over the flat rock towards them with something clamped between his teeth. The dog ignored Banjo and came to a stop at Ford's feet, sat down and raised his head to look at him.

At first Ford thought the dog had its dirty tennis ball in its mouth, but when Max dropped it at his feet, he saw that it was trailing two strands of fur. He bent to take a closer look and saw that they were ears. It was a rabbit's head, bloody and caked in red dirt. He recoiled.

'It's a gift,' said Banjo, laughing. 'I think he likes you.'

Ford kicked it away and the dog went chasing after it, scuttling across the rock and snatching it up again in his jaws. He padded over to the ute and leapt up onto the empty tray, dropped the head there and lay down with a sigh. He hung his head over the open tailgate, his tongue hanging from his mouth, looking at the bubbling pot.

'That mongrel is the only one drooling at the prospect of your cooking,' said Ford. 'What does that tell you?'

'Don't go calling Max a mongrel, he's pure-bred Australian cattle dog,' said Banjo. 'I bought him from the best breeder in Australia, had to fly him over from Queensland. He's one of the best-looking blue heelers in the state.'

'But he's got a bloody great scar across his nose and his ear's torn.'

'Well, he's a working dog. He's not one of your poofy show dogs.'

Doc was still under the ute, his feet sticking out. His hand appeared and walked crab-like across the fallen gum leaves until it found the wrench he needed. His disembodied voice came muffled from beneath the engine. 'I've been eating Banjo's nameless brown slop for the best part of twenty years. I think those tins are still from a palletload of army rations he flogged off a truck in Albany. That stew is as fucking awful now as it was the first time, but it's nothing that a few beers and a shitload of barbecue sauce won't fix.'

'How's she looking?' asked Banjo.

'If we can get the wishbone straightened before dark, we'll have done some good today.'

The hood of the ute was still smeared with blood where Banjo had butchered the kangaroo. With Ford watching, he'd cut its throat and hung its head over the front fender till it bled out; then he'd taken the hindquarters and the tail, skinned them, filleted them and stacked the steaks in the coolbox. He'd left the carcass hanging in a tree for the crows. The first bird that arrived sat on the branch and looked at them before tearing at the meat, and Ford had the feeling that he and the crow had met before.

Banjo had made a poor job of cleaning the ute when he'd finished, and the ground in front of the fender was still dark with blood and clouded with flies. Ford slapped at mosquitoes around his ankles.

'Bastards like your Pommy blood,' said Banjo.

'I say we let the dog eat your stew first,' said Ford. 'If he lives, I might try it.'

The dog jumped to its feet, tail stiff and ears pricked. It had turned away from the campfire and was looking towards a tall tree. A salmon gum, taller than everything around it, its trunk straight and featureless and glowing pink in the late afternoon light that hung in the sky as if trapped by the heat. A flock of black cockatoos was in the top branches, picking at the gumnuts. Ford could hear the steady patter of the empty husks falling through the leaves as the birds discarded them. Suddenly the birds all took off as one, squawking and squabbling as they wheeled and dived in a huge black cloud.

Ford stood up to watch them pass overhead. 'Black cockatoos on the wing are supposed to mean rain is coming, isn't that what they say?'

The dog gave three sharp barks and stopped. Banjo sat upright and looked at the tree line where the dog's head was pointing. The birds had gone and the bush was silent. Ford looked at Kavanagh and saw the warning in her eyes, but it was too late.

The first burst of gunfire cut across the ute. Ford heard the rounds clatter into the metal and the dog yelp. He turned to look at the trees and saw the muzzle flash from the shadows and heard Kavanagh shouting and he started to run. The second burst careened off the rocks around him and something heavy hit him in the shoulder. It spun him around and knocked him face down in the dust. He felt the burn in his shoulder but no pain, and lifted his head to look at Kavanagh. She was squatting on her haunches with her back against the boulder, her gun in one hand and the other held level, the fingers splayed, signalling for him to stay down.

'You hit?' she hissed.

'Shoulder.'

'Can you use your other arm?'

He waved his right hand at her and she scooted towards the stove and picked up the shotgun from the pile of camping gear. A third burst of automatic fire knocked the billy can off the stove and sprayed Kavanagh with stew as she threw herself back against the rock. She tossed the sawn-off to Ford and he stretched out his arm to grab it.

Banjo was motionless against his boulder, looking towards the ute, where his dog lay lifeless on the tray. Ford's eye was drawn to a sudden movement and he saw Doc dart away from the Toyota in a running crouch to find cover, the big revolver in his hand. He paused behind a rock and lifted his head quickly to look for the shooter. Another burst came from the trees, this time passing over their heads.

Doc turned back to Ford. 'Might be a while before we can get to you, buddy. You going to hang in?'

'Left shoulder,' said Ford, his voice quiet. 'Hurts now.'

Doc, Banjo and Kavanagh fanned out between him and the tree line a hundred metres away, staying low behind the rocks. 'Keep your fucking head down, Dorothy,' Doc yelled back. 'Sounds like an AK on auto. He won't be able to hit much at that distance, but don't give him anything to aim at. We'll take care of business.'

Ford looked around and saw a low ripple of rock ahead to his right, not much taller than his prone body but offering a degree of cover. He tried to crawl forward but as soon as he put strain on his left arm the pain shot through his shoulder and his vision clouded. Rolling onto his back, he laid the gun across his chest, and with his good hand unbuttoned his shirt, which was wet with blood. He pulled it open and turned his head to look at the wound. It was just within his field of vision, but his eyesight was blurred and all he could see was a dark circle ringed with red.

He took hold of the gun and lifted it up so he could see it. He thumbed the release: the gun broke and he saw that it was loaded. He hoped Banjo hadn't loaded rabbit shot. His left hand was numb and it was a two-handed job to close the barrel again. He braced the barrel against his knee and pushed down on it until he heard it click home; then he cocked both hammers with his thumb and let it drop by his side, lying still while he tried to catch his breath. He became aware of the gunfire again and tried to focus on the voices ahead of him.

He made out Doc's voice first. 'Banjo, mate, are you there? I need you with us, buddy.'

Banjo was further away. 'He killed my bloody dog.' His voice was steady, and his tone sounded more like anger than grief.

'Can you see where he is?' said Doc.

'I've got him.'

'I'll give him two and then you wait for the flash, mate.'

Ford heard Doc's magnum boom twice, answered by a crackle of fire from the tree line. Then there was the sharp report of Banjo's rifle echoing off the rocks.

Ford stared upwards. His breath was shallow and the sky seemed faded. He made himself look for stars, birds, anything to take his mind off the hole in his shoulder. As his eyes wandered, the pain subsided and the colour returned to the sky, the deep blue of the late afternoon, pure and cloudless. He looked west, away from the fight, looking for the first tinges of orange sunset.

The gunfire was intermittent behind his head and he lost interest in it. Bursts of automatic fire were accompanied by the random thump of Doc's Colt and the steady crack of Banjo's rifle, slow and regular as a metronome. He could hear voices, but they slipped in and out and were beyond understanding.

A shiver ran through him, and sweat beaded on his forehead. He fought back tears. His eyes felt heavy, but a flicker of movement made him turn his head. Initially he could see nothing but boulders, their shadows lengthening in the dipping sun. One shadow changed shape: he forced his eyes to follow it until it resolved into an outline, the silhouette of a man moving slowly between the rocks, a blurred dark form wobbling in the heat haze. It merged with the shadow of a boulder and Ford lost it again.

He waited for it to reappear and fought the urge to close his eyes. The sound of gunfire receded and he became aware of the sound of wind in the trees. He gave in, closed his eyes and imagined he could feel a cool ocean breeze passing over his face. The wind rushing through the trees became the sound of waves breaking, and the light burning his eyelids was from a different sun, the one that warmed the beach. His bare feet felt cold, as if he'd been wading through surf.

He opened his eyes and through a veil of sweat and tears saw the shadow move again and thought it might be his daughter. He tried to focus his eyes, and when the figure became distinct he remembered where he was. The shadow didn't seem that far away now. It struck him that all he had to do was raise the gun and fire. He lifted the shotgun in one hand and tried to hold it steady. The shadow stopped moving, now aware of him, and turned swiftly.

Ford saw the outline of a gun and a shaft of sunlight reflecting off it streaking upwards from the steel. He squeezed his hand around the shotgun and a column of flame burst from the barrel, the butt jogging his palm and jarring his wrist. A great noise surrounded him, a crash of rock roaring and echoing, pulsing into a deep ringing in his ears. He saw the shadow stagger, one hand clutching at its neck, then drop. All that was left before him was the clear blue sky, and in it he thought he saw the first bright star before everything turned black.

TWENTY-FOUR

Ford woke to bright light in his face. He felt heat in his shoulder and a warm glow in his chest. He closed his eyes again and tried to turn his face away from the light. There was no warmth to it, and the place where he lay felt cold against his bare skin. He opened his eyes again and waited until they adjusted.

Doc and Banjo were leaning over him. Banjo held a white electric spotlight, while Doc had his hands on the wound in his shoulder. He could feel the slight tugging of Doc's fingers moving there, but no pain.

Noticing he was awake, Doc leaned back and wiped the blood from his hands with a rag. 'There you go,' he said. 'I told them you'd come round before we were done. Shock wasn't that bad.'

Ford went to sit up, but his elbow was numb and collapsed under him.

'You stay where you are, mate,' said Doc. 'We're not done yet. You're all sewn up but you still need that dressed.'

'How bad is it?' he said, the words coming out slurred.

'Too lucky, that's what you are. Went straight through your shoulder. Missed the clavicle. Not too much blood about the place. Small calibre, military metal jacket, no fragmentation. For a puny cunt, you're difficult to kill. You'll be walking soon enough.'

Ford looked around. He was lying on a plastic sheet on the ground in front of the ute. The headlights were on and his shirt was off. The sky above the ute was dark, but there was still an orange glow behind the boulders. Doc was pressing a gauze pad onto the wound.

'Did I get him?' said Ford.

'You let loose both barrels at once. You tore his throat out. That double-ought shot Banjo put in there made a right mess of him.'

'Where is he?'

'Still lying where you dropped him. We'll get to them when we're finished with you.'

'Who was it in the trees?'

'Fuck knows. Kavanagh flanked him and put him down. Was a pleasure to watch her work. We'll drag him out of the bush later and have a look at him.'

'She's alright?'

'Alright? She's magnificent.'

'What about you two?'

Doc looked him in the eye. 'Lo, though I walk through the valley of the shadow of death I fear no evil, because I am the most evil motherfucker in the whole fucking valley.'

Ford managed a smile. 'How long have I been out?'

'Bit over an hour. You came round a little while after you caught that bullet. You were screaming like a bitch. Gave you a shot to knock you out while I stitched you up.'

'You know what you're doing?'

'What's my name again?'

'You said you weren't a trained medic.'

'As I said, my best mate was company medic and I ran with him.'

'You don't strike me as a soldier type.'

'Vietnam. Two tours. First Royal Australian Regiment. B Company.'

'That where you lost your fingers?'

Doc lifted his left hand and looked at the gap where the middle fingers were missing. He stuck out his thumb and waggled his hand in the devil's horns gesture. 'I left those fingers up the cunt of a fifteen-year-old whore in Saigon,' he said. 'I swear she had teeth up there. You ever hear stories about Vietnamese pussy vampires? She bit three inches off the end of my dick as well, so now I'm only two inches bigger than the Australian average.'

'Even without the fingers he's a wizard with a darning needle,' said Banjo. He pulled up his shirt to show a long red scar across his shining belly. 'A big Maori with a boning knife tried to fillet me one night in the York Hotel.'

'I hope he did that in a cleaner place than this,' said Ford.

'This is a combat-acceptable sterile surgical environment,' said Doc. 'There's nothing much I can't do with a razor blade, a sharp knife, a bottle of peroxide, penicillin powder, a needle and a few grams of heroin.'

'You gave me heroin?'

'Gave you some of my own true medicine. Are you in pain?'

'I'm kind of numb,' said Ford. 'Feels like I'm floating.'

'Then shut the fuck up.'

'I thought you had a no-needles policy?'

'There's a difference between what junkies do and what I do with my black bag. Just don't tell the copper. Pretend you've just been biting down on your belt.' Doc grinned.

He taped down the gauze pad, then he and Banjo lifted Ford into a sitting position and wound a bandage around his shoulder. Doc fixed the arm in a high sling strapped across Ford's chest.

'Reckon you can stand?' he asked. 'Best to get you warm under blankets by the fire.'

They got on either side of Ford and pulled him up, pausing for a moment to let him find his balance, then walked him to the rocks. The face of the largest boulder glowed orange with reflected light from the campfire burning in the pit under the overhang. Kavanagh was crouched beside it, breaking branches and feeding them into the flames.

'I thought we were avoiding fires?' said Ford.

'Bit late for that. They found us anyway.'

'Looks cosy,' said Ford.

'*The campfire's "cheery blazes" are a trifle overdone,*' said Banjo.

'And yet whenever he sees a fire Banjo gets the overwhelming urge to spout his bush poetry,' said Doc.

'You going to give me some Paterson at last, mate?' said Ford.

'Fuck off,' said Banjo. 'Paterson was a class tourist.' He went on:

It was pleasant up the country, City Bushman, where you went,
For you sought the greener patches and you travelled like a gent.

Doc punched his arm.

They helped Ford sit, propping him against the boulder. Kavanagh pulled him into a checked flannel shirt that smelled of wood smoke and was several sizes too large. She straightened the collar and fussed with the buttons while Ford watched her slender fingers work.

When she had finished he said, 'I could use a drink,' loud enough for everyone to hear.

Doc looked up. 'You're medicated enough already.'

'Humour me.'

'I have a bottle of whisky stashed in the Hilux,' said Banjo. 'I keep it with me in case of snakebite.'

'I was bit by a snake once,' said Doc, 'but it was the snake that died, not me.'

Banjo disappeared towards the ute and returned with the bottle and a stack of enamel cups. He poured a measure into each and passed them around. They drank without speaking, their attention drawn to the flames. Ford felt the heat of the whisky in his stomach, and a deeper inner glow from the medication.

Banjo pulled a long joint from his top pocket, carefully straightening it and smoothing out the wrinkles in the paper. He pulled a burning stick from the fire and held it to the twisted paper at the tip, sucking on it until it was alight. He inhaled deeply and held the smoke until he started snorting through his nose, a strange strangled choking sound that reminded Ford of a duck, and then coughed out the smoke.

Holding the joint out to Ford, he said, 'Just when you thought you couldn't get any more mellow.'

Ford accepted it and took a deep toke, then passed it to Doc, who gave him a smile so broad his teeth flashed in the firelight. Doc inhaled and then reclined against the rock, one hand behind his head, his eyes raised to the stars overhead.

'It doesn't get much better than this,' he said.

'Getting shot is not my idea of a relaxing day.'

'I meant the campfire, a few cold beers and a smoke with your mates, way out in the bush.'

'Two hundred kilometres from medical attention.'

'This is the life, man. The last place of true freedom. Out here is the last place the wowsers can't spoil your fun. You can smoke, hunt, drink, roll a spliff, drive crazy and jump the old lady under the stars without some cop lurking behind a tree with a radar gun and a breathalyser.'

Kavanagh coughed. 'Am I invisible or what?'

'Hey,' said Doc. 'I saw you take out that ninja in the bush. I've seen that Ducati of yours. You're practically one of us.'

'Ninja?' asked Ford.

'The dude in the trees was all dressed in black. Combat fatigues and body armour, some kind of Batman utility belt round his waist full of all kinds of deadly shit. His vest wasn't good enough to stop Banjo's rifle, though. Boof hit him in the chest and Kavanagh sneaked round his blind side and put one behind his ear. Stone cold.'

'Where is he?'

'Still where he fell. Didn't want to move him until he'd stopped bleeding. Now that you're up and about, I guess we'd better go bring him into the light and see who the bastard is.' Doc sat quietly for a moment longer, smoking and staring into the fire. Then he passed the remnants of the joint to Ford and stood up. 'Come on, Banjo, mate. Stop mourning your dog and help me with these dead bastards.'

They stumbled away into the bush. Branches cracked and their flashlights flickered among the trees. With no other light beyond the glow of the fire, the stars filled the sky, and for a moment Ford thought he was back at the mine. He looked for Orion and the Dog Star, but they had yet to rise.

He turned to Kavanagh. She was staring into the flames, nursing her cup of whisky. 'You ever done that before?' he asked.

'Done what?'

'Killed someone.'

'Once, back when I was in uniform.'

'I'm not sure what to feel. How did you deal with it?'

'I got out of uniform.'

'Did they offer you counselling?'

'If you think I'm going to get all touchy-feely with you, Dorothy, then you're reading me wrong.' She looked at him and her eyes held that distant look. They were wet with tears, reflecting the flames like the glass eyes of a doll. 'Shut up and give me that thing,' she said.

He passed it to her and she looked at what was left of it. It was mostly roach, and she put it in her mouth and squinted into the fire as she sucked a cough out of it, then tossed it in the flames. She looked up at the sky. 'You need chaos in your soul to give birth to a dancing star,' she said, almost under her breath.

He followed her gaze upwards and saw the Southern Cross embedded in the Milky Way, which stretched clear and wide across the sky.

The sound of footsteps and cursing brought them back to earth, and they watched as Banjo and Doc shuffled out from the trees, carrying the dark shape of the body between them, Doc holding the flashlight in his mouth. They grunted as they dropped the body onto the flat rock. Then they stumbled off around the back of the Toyota to fetch the other body, looking like a pair of removal men forced to work through their lunch break. They dropped the second man next to the first and stood over them, playing their torches up and down the bodies.

Kavanagh got to her feet. 'Let's look at who we've been arguing with,' she said, and held out her hand for Ford. He grasped it with his right hand and she pulled him up, then turned her back to him and walked towards the others.

The two bodies lay on their backs, their blank eyes staring at the stars. Both were younger than Ford, slim, clean-shaven with close-cropped hair. Ford thought one of them looked shorter than the other, but it was difficult to tell with them laid out. The one Ford had shot was in green camouflage fatigues. He had a webbing belt fitted with mesh pouches bulging with equipment. His shirt was heavy with blood across the chest from where his neck had bled out. His throat was mostly gone, ripped out, as if an animal had pawed at it. There were holes in his chest and face where stray pellets had hit him, and one eye was an empty black hole.

Ford studied his face. He thought it should trigger some emotion, some sense of guilt or even of responsibility for the man's death, but he could dredge up nothing.

The second man was dressed in black. He wore a padded vest, which Ford assumed was the armour Doc had spoken of, and the same webbing belt loaded with pouches. The vest had a single hole in the chest. The hole was ringed with blood. His head was turned to one side and there was another neat hole just above the ear, where Kavanagh's bullet had found him. At his side lay two guns, the same stubby AKs with folding stocks that Ford had seen in the gold room.

'Are you going to bury them?' asked Ford.

'Let the bastards rot,' said Banjo. He kicked the body in black, burying the toe of his boot in the man's ribs. The head rolled so that Ford could see the other side, where the bullet had exited and taken parts of the skull with it. 'I'm going to bury my dog.' Banjo turned towards the ute.

Doc knelt on one knee over the bodies and started emptying the pouches on their belts, pulling out ammunition, knives, phones and chocolate bars. Ford noticed the butt of a pistol poking from a nylon holster strapped beneath the shoulder of the man in green. He leaned over and pulled it out. It was an automatic, small but heavy. He hefted it in his palm and saw the star embossed on the plastic grip.

Beneath the holster was another pouch. He tried to open it but struggled with only his right hand. He put the gun on the man's chest, popped open the pouch and pulled out a spare clip for the pistol. As it came free from the pouch, two loose bullets spilled out, skittering across the rock. He picked them up and looked at the cross filed into the tip of each. He pushed them into his hip pocket and then picked up the gun and the clip. Looking up, he caught Kavanagh watching him.

'Careful with that,' she said.

'It's the same type of gun that was shoved in my face during the robbery.'

Doc stood up and held out his hand. 'Give it here,' he said. 'I still don't trust you with a gun.'

'I did alright with the shotgun. Told you I was a good shot.'

'You're just fucking lucky. Leading a charmed life. The spread from that sawn-off was wide enough to clip anything in front of you, especially with you snatching both triggers at once.' He took the pistol and examined it. 'The safety is off on this. You could have discharged the bloody thing. Let's see if you can avoid shooting anyone else today.' He laid the gun flat in his palm and showed it to Ford. 'Russian Makarov. Everything is arse-about on this thing, see? The safety is engaged in the up position.' He dropped the clip out of the pistol and laid it on the ground next to the other guns. 'You seen these AKs before as well?'

'Two of the guys on the robbery had them,' said Ford, rolling his left shoulder and feeling the pinch from the latest wound.

'AKS-74U. Nice little carbine chopped down from the big assault rifle. When I was over in the States, all the brothers were trying to get hold of these. Not seen them in Australia before. These and the Makarov, they're all Russian. Built for close combat. Not so accurate at the range that guy was shooting from.'

'He was close enough,' said Kavanagh. 'How did they get so close without us hearing them? I didn't hear any engines.'

Doc nudged the pile of equipment with his boot and shone his torch on it. 'This gear might explain that,' he said. 'Satellite phones and handheld GPS units. If they saw us from the spotter plane they knew we had nowhere to turn off this road, and it was easy for them to do a squeeze play: one guy follows behind from Kalgoorlie, the other races ahead on the highway and comes back towards us from the far end of the track. They keep in contact and tell each other their position from the GPS. If they get within ten kilometres of each other without making contact with us, they leave their vehicles and walk towards us. They probably knew they were outnumbered, but didn't know what guns we had. The first guy opens up with suppressing fire from the trees, to see how we reply, and that fucker in the green sneaks up from behind. Kavanagh was smart enough not to fire, so they never knew she was there. The guy in green must have been heading towards our firing positions and missed Ford lying on the ground until he was right on top of you.'

'If they've got phones, how long before someone works out they're missing?'

'Not long, I reckon,' said Kavanagh, 'but probably long enough for us to get off this road. On the other hand, they might not have a second team ready to go. Four guys in the robbery, two of them lying here. There might only be two more to come at us.'

'Still, with Ford's luck he's likely to collect some more lead,' said Doc. He undid the straps from the dead man's chest and pulled the vest over his head, then held it up for Ford. 'When we get moving again tomorrow, you're going to wear this, Dorothy. There might be more people shooting at you.'

'It didn't seem to do the owner much good,' said Ford, pointing to the hole in the padding and the bloodstain.

'It's the old type of Kevlar. It'll stop a handgun and small-calibre stuff, but it wasn't going to stop a high-velocity round from Banjo's rifle.'

'Or a shot to the head,' said Kavanagh. She turned to Doc. 'You know these men? They Vipers?'

'Do they look like bikers?' Doc shone his torch on their faces. 'I don't know them. Could've been brought in from inter-state. The local cops don't communicate very well with plod over east and get very territorial if the federal cops put their noses in. Using someone from out of state usually slows things right down.' He leaned over the body and opened the shirt, then rolled the guy over with the toe of his boot and stripped the shirt off his back.

'See,' said Kavanagh, 'there's the exit wound from Banjo.'

'I'm not looking at his wounds, I'm looking for ink. If these guys are from a club, they'll have some tattoos.' He ran the torch over the torso and arms, then leaned in closer. 'Fuck,' he said, under his breath. Across the man's back was a large tattoo of an eagle, its wings spread wide across his shoulders. It perched on a globe of the world with a large anchor behind it. The eagle had a pennant in its beak bearing the words SEMPER FIDELIS.

Kavanagh grabbed Doc's wrist to keep the torch steady. 'You know this?' she said.

'Yeah, I seen it before. Not for a while, though.'

'Doesn't look like a biker thing.'

'It's not.' He lifted the dead man's arm and twisted it to show another design tattooed into the bicep, a bulldog baring its teeth above the letters USMC. 'United States Marine Corps,' said Doc. '*Always Loyal*. Spent a few nights drinking with them in Saigon on rotation.'

'Plenty of veterans hook up with biker clubs when they get out,' said Ford. 'You did.'

'Sure I did, but I've got twice as much Viper ink as I've got regimentals. There's nothing on this guy except Marine Corps. Let's see what the other guy can tell us.' Doc pulled the knife out of his boot and opened up the seams of the second man's shirt, grabbing the material and ripping it off. Kneeling beside the body, he used the shirt as a rag to wipe away the blood from a tattoo of a red lion, rampant on its hind legs, with the initials RFC beneath it. 'I don't recognise that one,' he said. 'Doesn't look military or biker.'

'It's not,' said Ford. 'It's Rangers Football Club. Soccer to you. From Glasgow.'

Doc pulled at the dead man's arms, rolling the body forward and back, looking for more. There was a large thistle on one bicep, and the right arm was almost a full sleeve of intricate Celtic knotwork. In among this, running the length of his forearm, was some writing in Celtic script. 'Who the fuck is Nemo?' he asked.

Ford looked where he was pointing and read it aloud. '*Nemo me impune lacessit.*'

'I'm still none the wiser.'

'More Latin,' said Ford. '"Nobody provokes me with impunity." It's an older version of "Don't tread on me".' Kavanagh raised an eyebrow at him and Ford shrugged. 'Benefit of a classical education. You never know when it'll come in handy.'

'So who is this guy?' Kavanagh asked.

'Definitely Scottish,' said Ford. 'There's something else in the middle of all this stuff on his arm.' He pointed to a patch on the bicep, a list of names in smaller script, and squinted to read them: '"Jonesy, Mutton, Wee Billy, Tavish." Can't make out the fifth name. Then it says: "Not forgotten, Basra 2004". Another soldier, then. Maybe the thistle is regimental, the motto too.'

Doc got up and threw the shirt over the dead man's face. 'So are these the guys that jacked the gold?' he said.

Ford shook his head. 'I really don't know. They had hats on, dust masks, glasses, gloves. The guns are the same, sure, but I never saw their faces or heard them speak—I guess they didn't want anyone to hear their accents. There was one guy who was shorter. I thought maybe it was Jimmy, but now it looks like it was this guy in black. The leader spoke—he was Australian, but too tall to be Jimmy.'

'If they're ex-military, it explains the guns,' said Doc. 'There's plenty of Russian stuff lying around in Iraq. Bit tricky to get it into Australia, though.'

'Explains the precise use of explosives, too,' said Kavanagh. 'That always struck me as a bit too savvy for the bikies.'

'But what's Jimmy doing hooked up with these guys?'

'What about Afghanistan?' said Ford. 'Didn't you say Jimmy was getting into heroin?'

Kavanagh turned to him. He couldn't see her face in the shadow but felt the pressure of her eyes.

'What did I say?' he asked.

She didn't reply, seeming lost in thought.

Banjo walked up to them, carrying a folded trenching spade in one hand and a torch in the other. His face looked crumpled. 'If you'd like to join me over in the trees, I found a bit of ground soft enough to bury Max. Thought you might like to raise a beer with me to send him off.'

They followed him across the rock, his torch sweeping the bare ground ahead of him until they reached the scrub and found a small square hole in the dirt. Banjo shone his torch down into it and they saw a bundle of black plastic at the bottom, bound with twine. There was a small esky beside the hole and Banjo took long-necked beers from it and passed them around. He stood over the hole, his head bowed, his hands clasped in front of him holding the beer.

'That there dog has been a better mate to me than I was to any man, or any man to me. He's watched over me, fought for me, saved my life and took drunken kicks and curses for thanks, and forgiven me. He's been a true, straight, honest and faithful mate to me.'

He paused a moment, then raised his beer to his lips, flung his head back, and finished it in three long pulls. He threw the empty bottle in the hole with the dog and recited solemnly:

I has me smoke, he has his rest, when sunset's gettin' dim;
An' if I do get drunk at times, it's all the same to him.

So long's he's got me swag to mind, he thinks that times is good;
He can do anything but talk, an' he wouldn't if he could.

Ford looked at the other two and Doc nodded, so they all downed their beer and pitched their bottles after Banjo's. Ford's landed last and smashed against the others. Banjo picked up the shovel and filled in the hole, then planted on it a crude cross whittled from two sticks and lashed with twine. He stared at it for a minute, then turned away.

'How much of that plastic sheeting have you got?' asked Kavanagh.

'There's a roll of it over there on the ground with all the other kit we pulled off the back of the ute.'

'Then help me get those two stiffs wrapped up,' she said. 'We need some way of keeping the crows off them till we can send someone to get them. You guys don't seem to want to offer them a Christian burial, but we can at least keep the flies out and the stink in.'

Banjo and Doc looked at each other. 'Lead the way, officer,' Doc said.

Ford nodded towards his sling. 'I'm not sure I'd be much help.'

'Go convalesce by the fire, Dorothy,' said Kavanagh. 'We'll clean up.'

Ford walked back to the camp and groaned as he lowered himself down by the fire. It was burning low and he reached out to the stack of firewood and tossed more branches into the embers. He saw Banjo's bottle of whisky lying beside the fire pit with the stack of enamel cups, and felt a need. He looked over to where the other three were working, and decided they would be some time.

Gripping the cork with his teeth, he pulled the bottle with his good hand, then steadied the cup between his knees while he poured himself a generous measure. He leaned back against the boulder and inhaled the fumes of the whisky. It was a better malt than he had any right to expect so far from the city. He found some pills in his pocket and chased them down with the whisky, closing his eyes and waiting for the pain to subside.

He drank and tried to decide what his next move would be. He wondered whether he was free to act when travelling with Doc and Kavanagh, or whether he was only baggage on their journey. He had trouble imagining what the next day would bring. So far he had been simply avoiding the people behind him as he travelled west towards his daughter. He tried to picture her face but couldn't fix it in his mind until he remembered her smile framed by the halo of blonde hair lit by the sun.

He was pulled out of his memory by the sound of voices. Doc and Banjo were walking towards him, Doc's arm across his friend's shoulder, both bellowing in a loose baritone, *'Brave Ned Kelly muttered sadly as he loaded up his gun, "Oh, what a bloody pity that the bastards tried to run."'*

They sat down heavily by the fire, collapsing against the rock face. Their eyes looked wet in the light from the flames. Banjo snatched the bottle from Ford's lap, found a couple of cups and splashed whisky into each.

The three men sat staring into the fire, Doc and Banjo leaning against each other, until their attention was drawn to Kavanagh, who was standing in front of the ute, washing her hands in a bucket and holding them up to the headlights to see if they were clean.

'You fellas going to clean yourselves up?' said Ford.

'Maybe later, buddy,' said Banjo. 'We've still got to fix my fucking ute. We'll wash up later. Though I'm in such a stink that maybe I'll stay as I am, curl up in my swag and do the black snake.'

Kavanagh was squatting down in the headlights, examining her clothes, which were splashed with blood. She sat on the fender and pulled off her motorcycle boots. The men watched as she stood up, unzipped her pants and pushed them down. She hung them over the bull bar of the ute in the light of the headlights. She pulled her T-shirt over her head and used it to wipe down the leathers, then dumped it in the bucket and poured in clean water after it. Leaning over the bucket in her bra and panties, her pale skin glowing in the harsh white light, she kneaded the T-shirt, lifted it out, balled it in her hand, and used it to sponge herself down.

Ford looked at Banjo and Doc. Both had their mouths open but weren't making a sound. Banjo caught his eye and grinned. 'You been there yet, mate?'

Ford laughed and shook his head. 'When would I have got the chance? I've known you longer than I've known her, and I didn't know either of you before this weekend.'

'The first time I met you was in Shirley's place. You were being chased by half of Kalgoorlie, yet you stepped inside a knocking shop for a quick one. I figured you for a fast worker.' Banjo watched Kavanagh run the wet T-shirt over her belly and sighed. 'I'd go through her like lightning through a wet dog.'

She put one foot up on the truck's fender and started to wipe down her leg. Ford watched the long muscle in her thigh ripple as it flexed.

'She looks durable,' said Doc. 'She's got a face, a body and a brain all working together. I didn't realise they still made them like that. A great little fighter for her weight.'

She turned away from them and began to wash under her arms.

'Would you give that a crack, mate?' said Doc. 'You'd get your gold wings for nailing a D.'

'Not me, chief,' said Banjo. 'I gave up that life when I handed back my patch and put on a wedding ring.'

'Bollocks. I've seen you at the clubhouse, sniffing round the strippers. You're still a dog.'

'I look but I don't touch, and I'll tell you something: one day my old lady was rummaging in the shed and she found an old pair of crutching shears from when I was a sheep shearer, before my back gave out. Rusty they were, forgotten I had them. Well, soon enough she worked out what they're for, and now she keeps them in the bedside drawer. Any time she thinks I might have a wandering eye she takes them out and shows them to me.'

Kavanagh dunked the T-shirt back in the bucket. She pounded it some more, squeezed out the water, and then held it up to the light, shaking her head at the stains that hadn't shifted. After hanging it across the bull bar of the ute, she grabbed an army blanket and wrapped it around her shoulders.

'Would you like something clean to wear, officer?' said Banjo.

She looked over at them, scowled, and pulled the blanket tighter around herself. 'You took your bloody time waiting before you asked.'

'Just waiting to see if your underwear needed a rinse.'

'Quick as you like,' she said. 'The temperature drops sharply out here at night.'

'We could see that by the headlights.'

She opened the blanket and looked down at herself, then frowned and folded her arms across her chest.

'I keep a spare set of my old lady's clothes in the Hilux. Sometimes she helps me out on weekend plumbing jobs and needs a change. They might be a bit baggy in the arse for you, though.' As Banjo got up he turned to Ford and spoke under his breath. 'With this girl, her legs go all the way up to her arse. With my missus, her arse sags all the way down to her knees.' He walked over to the ute, and he and Kavanagh disappeared around the dark side of the Toyota.

'Turn off the lights on the ute,' Doc called after them. 'It'll be hard enough getting the bastard back on the road without having to deal with a flat battery.'

TWENTY-FIVE

Two hours later, Doc and Banjo were still under the Toyota. They had rigged up a ramp with some branches propped on the nearest boulder, then driven the ute up the ramp and raised the front differential on a toolbox. They worked by a spotlight running off a small diesel generator Banjo had found among his camping gear, and a soft blue light came from under the ute where he was welding the cracked wishbone with the gas torch.

Ford hadn't moved from his position near the fire. Wrapped in blankets, he sat on the ground with his back against a boulder; in spite of the warmth of the fire a chill cut into his bones. Kavanagh sat opposite him. She wore her biker jacket over a faded rugby shirt several sizes too large for her, and a baggy pair of denim dungarees. She sat cross-legged, a blanket over her knees, cradling her gun in her lap.

Beside Ford were the whisky bottle and the shotgun, and the cup rested on a flat rock within reach of his right hand. He and Kavanagh sat in silence watching the moon come up over the eucalypts. Veiled by the dust in the air, it was an ugly yellow. It was past full now, a quarter gone. Ford looked up, craning his neck to find Orion, which had drifted slowly west.

'The powdery course of the Milky Way is like a giant rift across the heavens that lets the faint white light through,' he said. His voice was quiet and the words were slurred.

He looked down in time to catch Kavanagh's raised eyebrow. 'You should sleep,' she said. 'The sooner you feel well enough to travel, the sooner we can get on our way.'

'My head's too restless. I thought the pills and the Scotch might help, but my brain seems to be fighting against them. What about you? Why aren't you asleep?'

'I'm on some of Doc's little wide-awake pills,' she said. 'I've no intention of sleeping with those two around.' Her hands tightened on the gun.

'You seem tense,' Ford said. 'Perhaps you need a settling drink.' He passed her the whisky and she took a slug from the bottle. He took it back and splashed a measure into his cup.

'I thought you were trying to quit?'

'Under the circumstances, I'm not sure there's any point,' he said.

'Isn't that why you went out to Gwardar? Go out to the desert to get back on the wagon?'

'Too many potholes in the gravel roads out there. I fell off.'

'It looks like you hit the ground running,' she said.

'That's the thing with drinking,' he said. 'You pick it up right where you left off. One drink's too many, fifty isn't enough.'

'So why were you running away?'

'I didn't run, I was flying.'

'It's odd, but you're a lot easier to get along with when you're drunk. There aren't many men I can say that about. Most of them are ugly drunks.'

'Yes, well, I'm one of the lovable ones. Gets me past my English reserve.'

'Marooning yourself in the desert was a bit extreme. You could have joined a program in the city.'

Ford drank from the cup and let the whisky numb his tongue. 'I went out to that mine because it seemed a good place to convalesce from the disappointment of middle age. It was self-exile after my wife kicked me out. Somewhere to contemplate the wreckage of my life. I went someplace remote in the hope that I might be able to hear my own thoughts, but the only thing I heard was the sound of my own liver rotting.'

He caught her smile, her teeth flashing in the firelight. 'Did you get in touch with your feelings?' she said.

'My feelings? I wasn't looking for them. I hid my feelings somewhere, and now I don't remember where.'

'Is that what you were digging for out at that mine?'

'I thought I could change. I thought I could shed my skin, but when I tried to move on I tripped over the old bits of my life that I had cast off.'

Kavanagh looked at him, her eyes narrowed, and he thought she might have got the measure of him. 'Wasn't there anyone you could turn to?'

'I didn't have anyone here. I'd met Diane in London and fol- lowed her across a lot of time zones. I've got friends—well, I've got colleagues and drinking buddies, but nobody who could catch me when I fell. Diane and Grace were all I had, and they were enough for me, but we weren't enough for Diane.'

'Don't you get lonely?'

'Only around people,' he said.

Her smile was gone as quickly as it had arrived. 'There you are,' she said. 'You pretend to regret your cynicism but you cling to it. It's your life raft.'

'I don't know. That stuff seems so very far away now. It seems very small and selfish from both Diane and me, when we should have been thinking about our daughter. I just want to get back to Grace.'

'If your daughter was so important to you, why did you go so far away?' Kavanagh asked.

'At the time, it seemed the best of both worlds. Fly in, fly out to the mine. Three weeks on site, on the wagon, decent money, keep paying the mortgage on the house I didn't live in anymore, then one week in Perth close to Grace. It seemed to be working.'

Kavanagh picked up a stick from the pile of firewood and poked the logs at the centre of the fire, rolling them together. 'What went wrong with your marriage?' she said. 'What did you do?'

Ford lit a cigarette and inhaled, then blew his smoke towards the fire and let it mingle with the column rising off the logs. 'You assume I was to blame?' he said. 'I did nothing. That was the problem. I took up space but left no trace. Just your average midlife crisis. We grew apart. Fill in the blanks yourself. Diane had six months of counselling after we broke up, but in the end her therapist told her it wasn't her, it was me.'

'You don't seem the type to go in for that head-shrinking shit.'

'You're right. Not my thing. I didn't need a therapist to tell me my issues, I had my wife pointing out my character flaws on a daily basis.'

'You make marriage sound so appealing,' she said.

'You've never come close?'

She gave him a look. 'Not my thing.'

'Fair enough. It's harder than it looks. By the time I realised what it takes to be a husband and father rather than a friend and lover, it was too late: Diane had reached the conclusion I was beyond salvation. She'd quickly adapted to the whole mother-hood thing and grown up in a hurry, and then she looked at me and saw that I was just the same as before. When we first met she used to say I was dark and mysterious, but after a while she started telling me I was just plain cold.'

'You certainly seem plenty chatty now. Maybe she just needed to shoot you and pump you full of pills and booze to get you to open up.'

'I'm surprised she didn't just gun me down. I gave her plenty of ammunition, tried and true deal-breakers like drinking and gambling.'

'Did you cheat?'

Ford shook his head. 'She used to say she never worried about that. She reckoned I could never summon up the emotional energy required to show interest in somebody long enough to get them into bed.'

'Sounds like you couldn't summon up the energy to save your marriage either.'

He looked up at the stars and took another drag on his cigarette. 'I guess you're right,' he said. 'I'm one of those people who, if there's the slightest hint that the person I'm with doesn't want to be with me, I think, well, that's it. So I've never fought for love. Does that sound cold? I never thought it was, I thought that was the way it should be. Grace changed that. She never had that choice, and neither did I with her. I loved her whether or not she loved me. I'm only just beginning to realise that. '

'So this is your shot at redemption?'

He paused. 'On the days Grace and I spent together, we often went to the beach. The beach became our special little thing, Grace's and mine. We went up and down the whole coast. I remember chasing crabs through the tide pools, watching her climb the pylon for the first time, ice cream and hot chips and chasing away the seagulls, her hair smelling of sunshine. She would fall asleep in the car home and I'd put her to bed in sandy sheets.

'I used to take her to Mettam's Pool to teach her how to swim. It's sheltered there behind the reef. We'd go early on Sunday mornings when all the old folks were doing their sidestroke. I'd hold on to her as she floated, practising her strokes. Sometimes a wave would break over the reef and lift her up out of my hands or splash her face. She used to squeal at me not to let her go. She made me promise never to let her go. At some point I forgot.'

Kavanagh tried several expressions before settling on one of patient concern. 'We'll find her,' she said.

'I know we will,' he said. 'I hadn't realised how much of my world revolved around her, and now I can feel her pulling me towards her. She's like my sun.'

Kavanagh toyed with a strand of hair that had fallen across her face, then tucked it behind her ear. Her pale hair seemed to shine in the moonlight, as if it was glowing from within. Ford watched her for a moment, waiting for her to look at him, but she was staring into the fire.

'I'm having a lot of fun trying to guess what your motives might be,' he said.

She looked up at last, and shook her head. 'I don't have motives, I'm just doing my duty.'

'But you don't have to be here. This isn't your gig. You could have left all this to the Serious Crime Squad. Aren't they the ones to deal with armed robbery and gangs?'

'There's a Gang Squad now. They got the job of stepping on the bikies.'

'So leave it to them.'

'By the time they get to Kalgoorlie and play "highest up the wall" with Chadwick to decide who's primary on the case, then sit there polishing their guns while they wait for forensics, the gold will be out of the country. A kidnap only adds another complication to what will become, without doubt, a complete train wreck.'

He saw the campfire reflected in her eyes. The coldness had gone. 'You remind me a bit of my wife,' he said. 'Same temperament. Same anger.'

'That's me. All sound and fury signifying loathing.'

'You and Doyle seem an interesting match. Both of Irish heritage, strong opinions, short tempers.'

'I prefer the word "fiery".'

'How did that work out? There must have been sparks.'

She sighed. 'It doesn't work. It didn't work. Not like that.'

'You don't give out a lot of sugar, do you?' said Ford, smiling. 'It's all vinegar with you.'

'Yeah, well, my dad was an old-school copper. He thought showing affection was a weakness. Different generation, I guess. That was women's business, and my mother wasn't around.'

'Surely every little girl can get her own way by climbing into her daddy's lap?'

'Not this one. I won his approval by putting on the uniform. It sounds like you have a different sort of relationship with your daughter. You shouldn't beat yourself up about it.'

'So you're just following in his footsteps?'

'I'm not sure becoming a cop was ever a conscious decision. It just seemed the only job for me. I was so used to being the copper's daughter, used to the respect it brought, it never occurred to me to be anything else.'

'Country girl, huh. No urge to move to the city?'

She shook her head. 'I was born in Perth. My father took a country posting after my mother died, moved us out to the Wheatbelt. Wanted somewhere quiet. Spent fifteen years as sergeant at the station. He was of that breed of coppers who were at the heart of the community. Nowadays the guys want to do their two years' country service then get back to the city quick smart, but my dad knew everybody in the town and helped out every one of them at some time or other. Once, I remember, the town footy club won the grand final. Thirty blokes drank the clubhouse dry and then staggered down to the pub, shit-faced, stayed there drinking until the small hours. My dad gets a complaint about the noise so he drives down in his slippers, tells them he'll arrest anyone who tries to get behind the wheel. Then he drives them all home. Some of them lived way out of town. A couple of guys didn't want to have to come back into town to collect their cars, so they slept it off in the cells. Another one stayed in our spare bedroom. That's the sort of bloke my dad was. Khaki uniform, Akubra, six-shooter on his hip. It's not the same these days. The prick of a sergeant who's there now sits on the edge of town in his patrol car all afternoon handing out tickets. He drew his gun in the pub once to break up a bar fight.'

'That why you left uniform?'

'One of several reasons. I got offered the Gold Squad. Bit of a backwater but seemed like a good job. Nice and simple, old-fashioned cops and robbers. Get away from all the politics and bullshit. Get away from arseholes like Chadwick, the old boys' network, the lads' club.'

'And now you hang out with outlaw motorcycle clubs, the last bastion of equal opportunities.'

'At least the bikies broadcast their sexism openly, unlike the police force.'

Ford laughed and felt a twinge of pain in his shoulder. He sat up straighter and thought about looking for some more pills. The fingers of his left hand were numb. He lifted his elbow in the sling and tried to flex his arm, but his joints felt stiff and swollen. He was aware of the wound itself as a dull ache, with the occasional pinch from the stitch sites.

Kavanagh must have seen him wince. 'Starting to bother you again?'

'A little,' he said. 'Can't feel my fingers. Help me get this sling off.' He leaned forward so she could reach behind his neck, and felt her fingers fumbling with the knot.

'You need to turn to the light,' she said. 'I can't see what I'm doing here.'

Ford moved around and soon she'd untied the knot and gently unwrapped the sling from his arm. He sat up, his legs crossed, and stretched his arm out in front of him, pumping it forward and backwards. He clenched his fist and then splayed his fingers, looking at the silhouette of his hand against the flames.

'If it's still painful you should keep it in the sling, keep the weight off your shoulder,' Kavanagh said.

'Not pain,' he said. 'Just pins and needles.' He dropped his hand into his lap, nursing his elbow in his good hand.

She moved around in front of him, pulled her feet up into the lotus position, and sat with her knees in the baggy dungarees touching his. 'Give me your hand.' She took it and laid it in her lap, palm upwards, sandwiched between her own hands. With confident, firm movements she ran her thumbs across his palm and up his forearm, her fingers digging into the muscles and tracing his bones. Ford felt the numbness in his fingers lessen as if the blood were returning to them.

'Your hand's very soft,' she said. 'Give me the other one.' He put his right hand next to his left in her lap and she ran her fingertips over his palms. 'It's like you never did a day's work in your life.'

'I told you, I'm not that sort of engineer. You get calloused hands in your job? Maybe a blister on your trigger finger?'

She touched the wedding ring on his left hand. 'Everything you just told me, and you still wear this?' she said.

'Force of habit. Gold has magical powers.'

She frowned at him. 'Please try not to lay any hippy shit on me.'

'Sorry, it's just something I used to tell my daughter. I told her that gold was magic, and that's why it's so valuable. That's why we all go so far out into the desert to find it, why we dig so far underground. I told her that the magic in this ring formed a link that bound her mother and father together.'

'And the nugget?' She gestured to his neck.

Ford pulled his right hand away and put it to his throat. He tugged the chain free and clasped the nugget in his palm. 'When I told Grace about my wedding ring, she wanted one too,' he said. 'Something to bind us together. I told her rings were for grown-ups, but she wouldn't let up. I had a few nuggets in a matchbox; some mad bloke I used to work with insisted on taking me out fossicking in the bush one time, said he had a secret spot about a hundred klicks east of the mine. We found a few little nuggets, but not enough to cover the cost of the fuel we burned to get out there. I got a couple of the nuggets mounted and gave her one of them. This is the other. I told her that when we were apart, she only needed to hold it in her hand and I would know that she was thinking about me.'

He let his hand drop and Kavanagh took it and laid it in her lap and continued to massage his palm. Ford thought he read something in her eyes, and leaned forward. She turned her head away.

He drew back and tried to read her expression. 'Was I going too fast, officer?'

'Way above the limit.'

'Are you going to give me a ticket?'

She smiled and let go of his hand. 'Maybe I'll let you off with a warning this time.'

TWENTY-SIX

Ford woke with a start. He had sat awake for so long with his mind churning that he was surprised he had slept at all. He found himself still leaning against the boulder, blankets pulled up around his throat, his left arm back in the sling. As he rested there he became aware that he could map the exact dimensions of his liver. It felt as swollen as his tongue. His lips were dry and encrusted. He pushed his tongue through them but winced at the taste. Daylight filtered through the eucalypts from the east, and a magpie was warbling somewhere among them, but the sky was still dark in the west. He looked around for the others, but he was alone.

The fire had gone out, though a few delicate strands of smoke still snaked up from the embers, suspended in the light mist that hung in the hollows of the rock and around the trees. A heavy dew had settled on him; when he noticed it, he shivered and pulled the blankets tighter.

The ute was back on its wheels and parked closer to the fire. All the camping gear and toolboxes had been loaded onto the back tray and secured under the tarp. He heard a branch snap and a pair of honeyeaters came bursting out of the bush, chasing each other through the wattle and then settling on the rock above him, their yellow breasts the same colour as the sun as it appeared between the trunks of the trees.

He heard a crash of timber from the tree line and looked around for the shotgun, but it was gone. His eyes scanned the rocks behind him, looking for somewhere to take cover, and he rolled onto his stomach and made to crawl under the shelter of the overhang, but as soon as he put weight on his elbow his vision clouded with pain. He heard another branch snap and looked up to see Banjo and Doc striding through the trees. Kavanagh followed a dozen paces behind, carrying the trenching spade, her hands red with dirt, her face wearing an expression of disgust. She caught Ford looking at her and rearranged her face hastily.

Banjo smiled at him. *'The sickly daylight breaks over the bush,'* he said. 'You look like shit.'

Doc clapped his hands. 'Sleeping Beauty awakes,' he said. 'Pretends to sleep while we do all the heavy lifting, then conveniently stirs just in time to get under way.'

Ford unravelled himself from the blankets and sat up rubbing his shoulder. He tried to stand but his thigh was stiff around the pellet wound. He put out a hand to brace himself against the boulder and pushed himself upright on his good leg. He plucked at the dressing under the sling.

'Leave that alone,' said Doc. 'We'll clean it and then set off.'

'How safe is the suspension on that Toyota?' asked Ford. From where he stood the front end still looked low on the driver's side.

'That ute is the least of your worries. You're a shit magnet, dude, and I'm dreading what trouble you'll bring down on us before we get to Perth.'

'You think I bring this on myself?' said Ford, fidgeting with the sling.

'I'm beginning to believe you do. You got fingers like Errol Flynn: everything you touch ends up fucked.'

Kavanagh turned away, but not before Ford saw her face crack into a smile. She threw the spade into the back of the ute and slapped her hands against her thighs to shift the dirt.

'Where are the bodies?' said Ford.

Banjo cocked his head towards Kavanagh. 'She insisted we put some dirt over them. Reckons there are feral dogs in these parts that would tear through that plastic and rip them apart.'

'Frankly, I'd be happy to watch those two get torn up by dogs,' said Doc. 'The pair of them came out here with the sole intention of scattering pieces of us across the bush. They deserve the same.'

Doc, Kavanagh and Banjo packed the last of the tools onto the ute. Banjo was wearing a blue singlet and matching stubby shorts that looked as if they'd been bought for a much younger, slimmer man. On his feet were a pair of faded rubber thongs that bore the teeth marks of the dog. His legs were tanned a deep brown, except for his feet, which were pure white up to the line of his work boots.

Doc was wearing the big pistol in a long leather holster fitted to his belt and tied around his thigh like a cowboy. The weight of it dragged down the waistband of his jeans and made him walk with a limp as bad as Ford's.

'Hey, Hopalong,' said Ford, 'you sure you can drive with that thing strapped to your leg? You try to do a quick draw and it'll be Wednesday week before you get the barrel clear of that rig.'

Doc turned swiftly and dropped to one knee, drawing the pistol from the holster. By the time his knee hit the dirt the gun was levelled at Ford and he was waving his hand over the hammer in an exaggerated fanning motion. 'Shut up and get in the truck,' he said.

Ford limped across, rolling up the blankets as he went. He threw them in the back seat. Doc reached for his black bag.

Letting out a long sigh, Ford sat down on the seat with the door open. Doc untied the sling, opened Ford's shirt and peeled back the tape on the dressing. As he exposed the wound he glanced up at Ford's face. 'You look like you regret what you've done,' he said.

'I don't remember much about it.'

'You need to get over whatever guilty shit is clouding your head. If you hadn't slotted that first one, he'd have got behind us and it'd be us lying in a shallow grave right now.'

'Seems strange how easily we got out of this. They were soldiers, trained killers.'

'So am I, mate. But it looks like they were too cocky. Brought the wrong weapons and underestimated how many guns we had. They wouldn't be the first to underestimate the Vipers. You won't find a better shot than Banjo, and Kavanagh surprised me more than she did them with the way she handled herself.'

'But I'm not a killer.'

'You are now, son. Let's have a look at how you're healing.' Doc lifted the dressing. Ford tried turning his head to look, but he was too close to see clearly.

'There's no pus on the bandage and a bit of clotting round the stitch sites,' said Doc. 'Looking good, fella. I'll give you a feed of Keflex, which should keep you free of infection, and just for today I'll put another jab into that shoulder to get you back to Perth.'

'Same stuff you gave me before?'

'Yeah, but maybe lay off the whisky and the OxyContin cocktail with it. How's your shoulder now?'

'Sore as hell.'

Doc put his hand on Ford's ribs and ran his fingers over the bruises. 'Any pain here?'

'Difficult to tell. It seems to surround me like white noise at the moment.'

'Well, you were ghostly white yesterday, but you've turned yellow today. Bit of jaundice creeping in, probably from those first wounds that Banjo and the lady dressed for you. Bloody amateurs.' Doc taped fresh dressings over the stitched bullet wound front and back, then re-dressed the crease in the other shoulder and the pellet wound in Ford's thigh. 'Quite an inventory you've got,' he said. 'I'm only patching you up here. You'll need to get to a hospital soonest and get this gunshot seen to. You might need some internal stitches to hold the muscle together. And you need to stop popping these pills like they're Smarties, or you'll get yourself an expensive habit once my free pharmacy closes.' He snapped shut the black bag.

'You must have seen much worse than this?' said Ford.

'You're not wrong.' Doc ripped the end off a packet containing a fresh needle and fitted it to the top of the syringe. 'Ever seen what a flechette round can do to a squad of infantry out in the open? Chopped liver, man. You're alright. All your limbs still attached.'

'Vietnam?'

Doc was drawing fluid into the syringe from a vial, and paused to look at Ford. 'Six nights in a foxhole, your own artillery dropping danger close, the enemy and your own mates dying screaming.' He jabbed the needle into Ford's shoulder and smiled when Ford flinched. 'The original Vipers were all guys coming back after 'Nam. Good to have a few buddies around you when you get back into civvies. Helps you adjust to the boredom and quiet of normal life after drowning in chaos.' Doc slowly buttoned the front of Ford's shirt over the dressings. 'Try moving your right arm,' he said.

Ford flexed his shoulder and the pain made him suck in his breath.

'Your mobility's coming back,' said Doc. 'I'll leave the sling off unless it gets too sore bouncing around in the back.'

'Many veterans still in the club?' asked Ford.

'Not as many as there used to be,' said Doc. 'Some died, some moved away. Some just got old. They got sick of hearing some of the shit the young guys sling, the guys that get their muscles from standing in front of a mirror at the gym. All pumped up on steroids and meth, their balls shrivelled to peanuts, wanting to go out and take on the world. We went out to fight the world, and then we came home and wanted the world to leave us the fuck alone.'

Doc picked up the body armour from where it lay on the seat. Ford touched the nylon to see if the blood there had dried. His fingers came away clean. He touched the hole in the chest panel where some fibrous stuffing was protruding.

'Careful with that,' said Doc. 'Kevlar threads. Get them under your fingernails and they'll hurt like a bastard.' He lifted the vest and motioned for Ford to put his head through it, then lowered it slowly onto his shoulders. It was heavier than Ford had expected, and the weight of it on the wounds in his shoulders made him wince.

'What about veterans from other wars?' asked Kavanagh. She was standing in front of the ute, one foot up on the bull bar, wiping the dust from her boot with a wet rag. 'Any of them in the club? Any servicemen returning from Afghanistan and Iraq?'

Doc slowly put his equipment away in the bag and closed the lid, then peered at her. 'Every time I start to like you, you do something to remind me you're a pig,' he said.

Kavanagh lifted her other boot and started to wipe it down. 'I know you're trying to make the link yourself. Someone in the Vipers has links to the guys that bushwhacked us. It explains the Russian guns, the military precision of the raid. I don't think you know who it is, or you'd have left me and Ford in the desert long ago. I reckon you're still waiting for things to play out, and I can wait too.'

Doc turned back to Ford. 'Lift your arms,' he said.

Ford tried to bring his hands up over his head, but the effort was excruciating. He laced his fingers behind his head and gritted his teeth while Doc fitted the straps that joined the front and back panels of the vest. When he pulled them tight, Ford felt them cinch against his bruised ribs. Doc held up the coat and Ford slid his arms into it.

'You're done.' Doc helped him swing his legs into the cab. He held his open palm out to Ford to show him the collection of pills before slipping them into the front pocket of the vest. 'Some lollies for the car trip. For when the jab wears off. Go easy on them.'

Kavanagh climbed into the back seat next to Ford and reached across him to pull over his seatbelt, the sandalwood of her perfume mixing with the dark smells of wood smoke and gunpowder coming off the vest. She secured his seatbelt and reached over again to pack blankets between him and the door, then stacked more rolled blankets on the seat between them until Ford was wedged in.

He caught her looking out of the window and turned to see Banjo kicking over the embers of the campfire, high-stepping out of the fire pit when the heat got too much through the thin soles of his thongs. Seeing the two of them laughing, Banjo gave them a grin. He picked up the last of the blankets and brought them over to the ute. After rolling them up he went to pack them in the tray, but paused a moment to look at the space he had left there for the dog. He pursed his lips, blew out his cheeks and dropped the blankets in the gap.

His shoulders slumped, he walked around to the driver's door and climbed in next to Doc. He turned the key and tilted his head to listen to the engine idle, then leaned out to take one last look at the campsite before slamming the door.

They all sat quietly as Banjo drove slowly across the rock to find the gap in the trees that led back to the Holland Track. The sun cast long shadows through the trees, and shafts of sunlight lit the dust kicked up by the tyres. Ford got one last breath of damp eucalypt and sandalwood before the dust swirled in and Banjo wound up his window.

'Did I miss breakfast?' asked Ford.

Doc turned in his seat to look at him, an eyebrow raised. 'Your appetite's back then? Good sign.'

'We'll stop for food when we find a town,' said Banjo. 'A few more hours on the track and we'll be out into the Wheatbelt and it'll be blacktop all the way. Should get to Perth sometime this arvo, if that jury-rigged wishbone holds together.'

The ute jolted over a pothole and there was a solid thump from the front suspension. Banjo screwed up his face in a panto-mime scowl. 'Just bedding in,' he said. 'She's never let me down. Always got me home. Remember that time we blew the head gasket out on that salt lake past Menzies? Cut up a bit of lino as a seal and got home firing on two cylinders, pouring in a pint of oil every half hour.'

Doc looked at him and shrugged. 'I'd rather be on two cylinders than three wheels.'

They joined the track again and swung west with the rising sun behind them. Ford tried to find a comfortable position among the blankets but was wedged in so tightly he had no room to squirm. The balled bedding made him feel as though he was wrapped in cotton wool, but when he closed his eyes he realised that might be the onset of the drugs.

Banjo kept the speed low, using the rear wheels to drive. He leaned forward with his head cocked to one side as if listening for noise from the suspension. After a few more potholes and ruts had tested it, he relaxed back into his seat and turned on the radio. Country music drifted in and out of the background static, and the air conditioner rattled a faint trickle of cool air through the vents.

Ford allowed himself to slip backwards into the warm embrace of the injection, turning his face to the window, feeling the heat of the sun coming off the glass, and trying to drift away. Letting the noise of the ute engulf him, he closed his eyes and sank back into the nest of blankets.

He tried to replay the events of the shooting, searching inside himself for some feeling about what he had done, but found no remorse, no guilt or shame. When he tried to picture the face of the man he had killed, nothing formed in his mind. The bloody face they had shown him was too disfigured to hold any meaning.

Ford's breathing was even, his heartbeat steady, but he felt empty and bankrupt. He wondered if this was the coldness his wife had described in him. 'When I need you, you're not there,' she'd once said, in tears at the kitchen table. 'Even if you're in the same room, sometimes it feels like you're miles away. Present but absent. Where do you go?'

He leaned his head on the window and felt its warmth against his cheek. He listened to the buzz of a fly hitting itself repeatedly against the glass, distinct above the noise of the engine, and let himself drift into a half-sleep.

When he awoke and looked ahead the track was straight, a single red line stretching through the flat bush that shimmered in the heat haze. The road was smoother, with fewer bumps to trouble the suspension, and the vegetation had thinned out, the trees becoming more sparse until they reached a fence line and a gate. Banjo pulled to a halt.

The fence ran dead straight from northwest to southeast. On its eastern side was the wild scrub and bushland they had just crossed, but to the west was a geometric pattern of vast wheat paddocks stretching out like a great quilted bedspread. The spring wheat was shooting up straight and green but wasn't yet high enough to hide the wheel tracks that the tractors had left in the red soil, making huge swirling patterns within the rigid grid defined by the fences. Ford looked at the order the farmers had imposed on the landscape, and after the insanity of the last three days he felt grateful for it. He let out a long sigh. They were still four hundred kilometres from Perth, but the fields felt like a sign that he had stepped back within the borders of civilisation.

Doc jumped down from the cab and opened the gate. Banjo drove through it and waited for him to close it again. As Doc climbed back into his seat a phone began to ring. Banjo turned to look around the cab. The ringing was muffled.

'Don't look at me,' said Kavanagh. 'You put my phone in the microwave.'

Banjo looked at Ford, who shrugged. 'Haven't had a phone since I left the mine.'

'I turned mine off back at Victoria Rock,' said Doc.

'It's in the glove box, Sherlock,' said Kavanagh.

Doc pulled down the flap and the ringing got louder, a shrill piercing trill that made him wince. He sat there watching the screen on one of the satellite phones they had stripped from the dead soldiers flash on and off, lighting up the inside of the glove box. Kavanagh leaned forward and watched it with him.

'Do we answer it?' asked Banjo. He was looking at Doc, but Doc turned and looked at Kavanagh.

'Is there a number showing on the screen?' she said.

Doc picked up the phone and checked the display. 'Says private number.'

Ford leaned forward and nudged Kavanagh aside. 'Don't just stare at it,' he said, 'answer the bloody thing.'

'And say what, exactly?' hissed Kavanagh.

'Whoever it is, they might be the people who've got my daughter.'

'Well, in that case we'll just ask for an address and tell them we'll be right over,' said Doc. 'Ask them if we should bring a bottle.'

'We could pretend to be the soldiers,' said Ford.

'Except that they likely have a code,' said Doc, still looking at the screen.

Ford reached for the phone. 'It's the first real lead I've had on where she might be,' he said. Doc moved the phone away. 'What harm can it do?' asked Ford. He was panting now, his face contorted in pain.

'Just speaking for myself,' said Banjo, 'I'd rather let them think there's some doubt about whether we're alive or not, rather than have them send another couple of heavies out here just to make sure.'

'I can do it,' said Ford. 'One of the squaddies was Scottish. Who can understand a Scotsman, even when he's sober? I can pull off the accent.' He looked at each of them in turn, pleading, but they turned their blank faces away one by one.

The ringing started again. Doc looked at the phone in his hand but it was dark and quiet: the trill was coming from the second phone in the glove box.

'Give it to me,' said Ford. 'Please.'

Doc looked at Kavanagh and she shrugged, sliding backwards into her seat and waving a hand at him in defeat. Doc passed Ford the phone. He sat back in his seat and looked at it in his palm. He took a deep breath, trying to calm his heart.

'Banjo, mate, turn the radio up,' he said. 'Turn it to static, loud as you can.'

Banjo nodded and spun the dials until the cab was full of white noise. Ford bit his lip, pushed the talk button, held the phone to his ear and waited. He heard nothing. He thought the line might be dead, but still he waited. Kavanagh was staring at him, but all he could do was shake his head.

'Status report,' a voice said at last. It was curt and without character, with a distinct pause between each syllable. It took Ford a moment to make sense of the words. 'Status report?' There was a slight rising intonation and Ford realised it was a question. The voice spoke again, more insistently. 'Tango Three, this is Hotel One Nine. Status report, over.'

Ford put his hand over the phone and leaned towards Doc. 'He wants a status report. Sounding military.'

'Tell him: "Engaged and complete".'

Ford nodded. He thought back to a share house in Manchester, and to a red-headed Glaswegian called Roddy who'd had the room by the front door. Roddy's accent was so thick that the Chinese student in the attic couldn't understand a word he said, and they'd developed their own sign language. Ford tried to channel Roddy when he spoke. 'Engaged and complete.'

The line was quiet. Doc raised an eyebrow, and Ford nodded. Finally, the man said, 'How long before you get here?'

Ford was out of ideas but knew he had to keep talking. The man on the other end was beginning to relax and speak naturally. His language wasn't as formal, but still sounded clipped and stilted. Ford improvised. 'Nae fucking idea, laddie,' he shouted, hoping the volume would distort his voice down the line. 'That fucking biker bastard winged me. I'm fucking hurt bad.'

'Why are you on this phone? Repeat, why are you on Tango Three's phone?'

Ford clamped the phone between his knees. 'Fuck,' he spat at Doc, 'I've got the wrong bloody phone. This one's the Yank's.' He took a breath and spoke into the phone. 'My bike's a mess. Tomorrow I'll be back, unless you can send someone to get me.'

'What about Tango Three?'

'He's deed, man. They're all fuckin' deed. Come get me.'

'Negative. Repeat, negative. Go to Protocol Bravo. Out.'

The phone went dead. Ford dropped it in his lap and looked at the others.

Kavanagh was scowling. 'Laddie?' she said. 'Who was that supposed to fool?'

At least Banjo was smiling. He turned off the radio. 'Did they buy it?'

Ford passed the phone back to Doc. 'I can't tell. I think I threw him. He told me to adopt Protocol Bravo and hung up. Sounded like he was leaving me to fend for myself.'

'No surprise there,' said Kavanagh. 'Unlikely he would take the bait and come out here. He might shut up shop and go to ground, though.'

'He would have done that if he hadn't got through. At least this way I got him to break out of his military patter. I heard his normal voice and I recognised the accent. South African. Afrikaaner. I think I've met him already.'

'Roth?' Kavanagh asked.

'I think so.'

She smiled properly for the first time since he'd met her, broad and natural, and he noticed what fine teeth she had. Her eyes joined in as well, creases appearing around them. He couldn't help smiling back.

'Roth,' she said. 'That bastard is so close to McCann we didn't see him.' She punched the headrest in front of her. 'Give me that phone.' She held out her hand to Doc. He looked at her and shook his head, but she fluttered her palm in front of his face. 'This is moving fast now. Either way, he'll be spooked by that phone call, and if I don't get someone after him soon he'll be gone by the time we get to Perth. I could use your phone, or you could give me the one in your hand. But if we don't pull Roth, then Chadwick's going to be quite happy to leave the Vipers in the frame.'

Doc slapped the phone into her open palm. 'Don't fuck it

up. If I find a police roadblock waiting for us up ahead I'll be very disappointed in you.'

'I won't be talking to uniform,' she said. 'I don't know how far Chadwick's reached out.'

'You going to tell me you've got someone in Perth you can trust?' Doc asked.

She looked at him and rolled her eyes, then got out of the ute. She walked off down the road, thumbing the pad on the phone.

Ford, Doc and Banjo sat staring through the windscreen as she walked away. They watched in silence as she turned to face them, the phone to her ear. The only sound in the cab was their breathing. Kavanagh was the tallest thing in the landscape, a solitary figure in the middle of the straight ribbon of bitumen receding in front of them, the fence posts and wheat stalks the only other vertical elements among the flat paddocks.

Doc broke the silence. 'What do you think?'

'I think she's got an arse like an onion,' said Banjo. 'It makes me want to cry.'

'I meant, do you think she'd sell us out?'

'She's had plenty of opportunity to do that already,' said Ford. 'You know that, or you wouldn't have given her the phone.'

'I brought her because at some point we're going to have to face down the cops, and she's the only edge we've got. It can play out several ways, but if she's not with us they'll shoot us down like dogs.'

Kavanagh took the phone from her ear and grinned at them, but this time none of them returned her smile. She jogged back to the Toyota, moving with the grace of a dancer.

'Who'd you talk to?' asked Doc.

'An old buddy in Serious Crime.'

'Someone you can trust?'

'Again with that? This guy, we went through Joondalup Academy together. Made our first arrest together. He stood next to me the first time I discharged my weapon in the line of duty, and then in court throughout the enquiry into the perp's death. He's about as solid as your paranoid little head could imagine.'

'You didn't answer the question. Can you trust him?'

'All that bullshit you spout about brotherhood, how you'll stand by your mates through anything: one in, all in? That's how it is with him and me.'

'The Big Blue Gang, huh?'

'Something like that.'

'You going to give us a name?'

'Not likely.'

'So what did he say?'

Kavanagh climbed into the ute and slammed the door. She sat there looking at the phone in her lap before she spoke. 'Roth isn't on their radar. Not even a suspect. They questioned him at the racetrack on Saturday and were satisfied he could account for himself. They didn't even check his story. Chadwick told them to focus all their resources on the Vipers.'

'Did you find out where Roth is?' asked Ford. She turned to look at him and was surprised by the look of sadness in his eyes.

'My friend will call me back with all known addresses and associates, and trace the number of this phone. He's going to check with Immigration as well. That accent suggests he hasn't been in the country long, so there should be a file on him.'

'I can give you a bit of history on that cunt,' said Doc.

Kavanagh turned quickly to look at him, her eyes wide. 'You've met him?'

'Not personally, but I've heard stories. Last year a few of the brothers had a run-in with him in Perth. They'd gone down from Kal to work on a construction site, one of McCann's high-rise condos. He sells them off the plan to Singaporean gamblers and eastern states speculators and then jerry-builds them to a half-arsed spec and lets the buggers chase him through the courts. The boys were labouring. Used the club to get some more brothers on the site and then shut out the competition. Soon they had control of all the non-union casual labour on the site.

'McCann wasn't happy. He had some deal with the Slavs from Fremantle and wanted the Vipers off his site. McCann sends Roth down there, and that South African bastard tells them they've got twenty-four hours to vacate the site. Next day, two of the boys are in casualty with their kneecaps smashed. Day after that, two Harleys are torched. Then my mate Flymo gets a bullet through the thigh. Told me Roth just walks up to him in the bar at the Rivervale, puts a gun to his leg, squeezes one off and is out the door before anyone works out what happened.'

'So the Vipers backed down?' said Kavanagh.

Doc leaned towards her. 'We came to a negotiated settlement to let the union take over. The Slavs got nothing.'

'Why didn't you tell me this earlier?'

'There's a lot of things I decided were none of your business, officer. I've shared far too much already.'

'But he has a history of violence,' said Kavanagh.

'Look around you, sister: everyone in this vehicle has a history of violence. Even Ford's popped his cherry. Roth's McCann's bodyguard, so he's not exactly hiding his skills.'

'But he would have access to McCann's security information, and now we know he has links to the Vipers in Perth.'

'After what he did to Flymo, he couldn't walk into a room of Vipers without getting payback. He might go all Dirty Harry when it's one on one and he's holding a gun, the other guy's holding a beer, but it'd be different facing up to the whole club.'

'Not the whole club,' said Kavanagh. 'Chadwick's put half of you in the can and scattered the rest to the wind.'

'And we've just buried two of them in the bush, so by my reckoning there's only Roth and one offsider left.'

'And what about my wife and daughter?' asked Ford. They turned to look at him. 'If Roth has them, what'll he do with them once he thinks I'm dead and he has no further use for them? And if he doesn't think I'm dead, if he thinks we're onto him, then what will he do? The police have done nothing to find them.'

'Sorry to be blunt, Ford, but they wouldn't be a priority to the police,' said Kavanagh. 'They've only been missing a couple of days, and nobody has reported them. There's nothing to suggest they're being held against their will.'

'I reported them missing at the station in Coolgardie.'

'While you were being questioned as a person of interest. Not exactly a reliable source, especially since you're the estranged husband. It's not much of a stretch to imagine she might be avoiding you.' Kavanagh looked away. Banjo turned back to the steering wheel and did a poor job of pretending to be interested in the dials on the dashboard.

Only Doc met Ford's gaze. 'Start the fucking engine, Banjo,' he said. 'We need to get to Perth while there's a chance Roth still thinks we're dead.'

Banjo nodded. The engine fired up and they moved away, the smooth gravel road feeling like silk under their wheels after the rutted track. Banjo picked up speed until a cloud of dust marked their wake. Doc punched the radio. The signal was clear now, and he turned the dial until he found a channel playing Creedence. He turned it up loud enough to make conversation impossible, and they tore across the Wheatbelt, each wrapped in their own thoughts.

TWENTY-SEVEN

Two hours' driving hadn't changed the landscape. The same stripe of blacktop stretched ahead of them, parting the chequerboard of wheat paddocks, and the shimmer of heat haze on the road reflected the dome of deep blue sky dusted with horses' tails of high cloud. No one had spoken in that time, each of them apparently content to watch the fields flash by. Each settlement they passed through was the same as the last: a row of flat-fronted facades facing a single main street, a railway siding with a grain tower, and then a petrol station marking the edge of civilisation before the signs started counting down the distance to the next town.

Occasionally a larger sign would show the distance to Perth, and Ford drifted into a litany of numbers: the distances, the needle on the speedo, the fuel left in the tank, the time on his watch. Only these numbers hinted at any progress across a landscape so broad that he felt the curvature of the earth again. He became aware of a strange sense of vertigo that made him distrust the gravity that stopped him from spinning away. Fighting back the nausea, he spread his palms across the seat, clawing his nails into the fabric.

Banjo was absorbed in the music drifting out of the radio, his head cocked to one side. Every now and then he would grunt a snatch of some cowboy melody.

A hand-painted sign announced the distance to the next town, and promised hot food and fuel at the roadhouse. As they passed the sign, Banjo raised a hand and gave it a thumbs-up. Ford took his gesture as a statement of intent and his stomach growled in agreement. His last meal had been a few mouthfuls of Banjo's stew before gunfire had sprayed it across the campsite. He felt queasy from the injuries and the meds, but a craving for fried food was nonetheless nagging at his gut.

They saw another sign, this one welcoming them to Corrigin, and passed a handful of agricultural businesses, a forecourt full of tractors and a dusty cricket oval before Banjo swung off the road and under the shade of the flat roof stretching from the roadhouse over the two bowsers. Theirs was the only vehicle in sight.

Through the tall windows of the roadhouse Ford could see two teenage girls staring back at him from behind the counter. Both had badly bleached hair and poor complexions, and their eyes showed the forlorn resentment common to those left behind in country towns when their friends have gone to the city. Ford saw the doors to the restroom on the back wall next to the counter. The sight cheered him: it would be nice to use a flushing toilet and a basin with hot water. The other three had got out and were stretching their legs by the time he had opened his door and unravelled himself from the nest of blankets.

Stepping down from the cab, the sudden weight on his legs was a surprise but the pain was not. As he leaned over into the cab to retrieve his thongs from the footwell, his head spun and he had to grab the seat to stop himself from pitching head first onto the floor. He reached under the driver's seat for his thongs and found a flat half-bottle of Johnnie Walker wedged there. He pulled it out and stashed it among the blankets. Then he dropped his thongs onto the concrete and slid his feet into them, pausing to look at the red dust caught between his toes. He rested against the ute a moment to find his balance before setting off across the forecourt in a stooping limp.

The girls behind the counter watched him approach with puzzled expressions. He initially thought it might be the bruises on his face, but then he caught his reflection in the glass of the door and realised that his coat was hanging open and the bulletproof vest was showing. He smiled at them and whatever apprehension they'd felt dissolved into blushes and giggles. As he opened the door a bell rang.

He shuffled across the shop and through the swing door to the bathroom, but his hopes of a clean place to freshen up evaporated at the sight of the blocked toilet. Regardless, he relieved himself, fretting at the dehydrated nature of his piss, which was still streaked with blood, and then went to the basin. At least the hot water worked. He splashed his face and thought about washing his feet, but one attempt to lift a foot up to the basin persuaded him the effort was futile.

On his way out he met Doc ordering food at the counter and bummed a cigarette and a light from him. He saw a stack of newspapers, picked one up and tucked it under his arm. The girl behind the till caught his eye and he nodded in Doc's direction. The bell rang again as he left, and he walked over to a bench in the shade. He sat down, lit the cigarette and straightened the newspaper.

The robbery had made page three. There was a photo of the armoured van on the back of a flatbed truck. The article was light on detail. It said that the police wouldn't reveal the value of gold stolen, or the names of any suspects. They named the dead guard but there was no mention of Ford or the Vipers. Police were continuing their enquiries. It ended with a comment regarding the effect the robbery might have on Alan McCann and his mine, referring the reader to an article in the business section.

As he flicked through the paper, looking for the business pages, Ford saw a story about police raids on bikie homes and clubhouses in Kalgoorlie and Perth. Chadwick was quoted as saying that the coordinated raids were an ongoing campaign against the Vipers and other outlawed motorcycle gangs and had been sparked by recent violence. The police minister was also quoted, talking at length about the legislation he would be bringing in to hobble the activities of the gangs. There was a photo of the two men standing side by side on the steps of Parliament House next to a confiscated Harley, and Ford couldn't decide which one looked more smug.

The business article didn't add much to the report on the robbery. It described recent share movements of McCann's holding company, Glycon, based on speculation that he was about to announce the discovery of significant new gold reserves at the Gwardar mine. McCann had refused to answer questions as to whether the lost gold was insured, or whether it would affect his cash flow. Pressure was being brought to bear on him to release any positive geological reports to the stock exchange, together with the appropriate third-party verification.

In the accompanying photo, McCann was shown leaving the races with his daughter, his face like thunder, his hand up to shield them from the camera. The report added that he hadn't been seen since Saturday afternoon, when he had flown back to Perth on his plane, and there were unconfirmed reports that he had put to sea on his yacht. If he didn't present himself to the press, the markets were expected to react badly when they opened on Monday morning. Ford looked at the photograph and the byline at the top of the article, and smiled.

As he got up and walked back to the Toyota he felt weak, and when he put out a hand to open the door he noticed it was shaking. He sat back down in his seat and rearranged the blankets, uncovering the whisky bottle.

Banjo was refuelling the ute, while Kavanagh sat in a small patch of shade thrown by a straggling cocos palm planted in an old tyre. She was perched on the edge of the tyre, staring at the sat phone in her hand as if willing it to ring.

Ford heard the doorbell and watched Doc walk across the forecourt, white plastic carrier bags dangling from his fingers. He dumped the bags on the driver's seat and started rummaging through them. Banjo put the hose back on the bowser and walked off towards the counter, giving the two girls his biggest grin.

Ford looked at the bags of food and licked his cracked lips. 'You never asked me what I wanted,' he said.

'Two reasons for that, buddy. First, you're under doctor's orders, so you eat what you're given. Second, you're at a country roadhouse, so you can imagine the limited range of culinary delights available, especially this late on a Monday morning when the first mob of truckies have been through there like a plague of locusts. A Chiko Roll is about as exotic as you'll get in these parts.'

'Did you bring me a Chiko Roll?' Ford asked hopefully.

'I bought some for Banjo, because he's a bit of a demon for the deep-fried cholesterol bomb, but you need some protein, clean carbs, and a sugar hit.' Doc threw a packet of jelly snakes into Ford's lap and followed it with something wrapped in white paper. 'We don't want anaemia on top of the jaundice. You're pale and yellow, like yesterday's custard. That bit of lean meat might help.'

It smelled good, and Ford ripped off the paper to find a hot beef roll. He felt his mouth water. As he lifted it to his mouth the gravy dripped down the front of his vest and he scooped it off with his finger.

'This is starting to feel like babysitting,' Doc said.

A phone rang and they both looked at Kavanagh. Doc threw the bags back on the seat and took three steps towards her, but she raised her hand and he stopped dead. She stood up and started walking, waving her hands as she spoke into the phone, her face animated. Ford watched her closely.

He heard the doorbell and turned to see Banjo coming out of the roadhouse, rearranging the cash in his wallet. Doc caught his comrade's eye and nodded in Kavanagh's direction. Banjo took in the scene while he picked up the Chiko Rolls from the seat, passed one to Doc and ripped the wrapping off the other with his teeth. They stood side by side, leaning against the Toyota and chewing, watching Kavanagh pace around the palm tree talking into the phone.

They finished the food, opened an iced coffee each and slurped from the open cardboard spout of the carton, Doc with a hand shading his eyes so he could see Kavanagh. When she took the phone from her ear and turned towards them, they straightened up expectantly.

Ford leaned out of the window. 'So, what's your guy have to say for himself?'

'Where's Roth?' asked Doc.

'Nobody knows,' she said. 'They've got a last known address for him and they might send uniform round for a doorknock, but he's still not a high priority. Most of them have been busy raiding the Vipers' Perth clubhouse this morning.'

'They arrest anyone?'

'There were a couple of patch members there, with a cleaner. But they found nothing—the place looked like it had been swept before Chadwick could put the warrant together.'

'So where's Jimmy?'

'Gone to ground. A few Vipers were arrested when uniform took down their doors at home, and three were picked up riding on the street, but it was a thin haul.'

'What about my family?' said Ford.

'I didn't ask,' said Kavanagh. 'Sorry, Ford. Perth police did a history on this satellite phone and the number Roth called from. Both owned by a small holding company, which in turn is owned by an offshore company. No more than that. They'd need some serious paperwork to find out if they were linked to Roth. Basically, all we've got out of this is Roth's life story.'

'His death would excite me more,' said Doc. 'Couldn't they do a cell-site location on the phone?'

'They did,' said Kavanagh. 'He was at Perth airport.'

'So send the blues-and-twos round there and get him.'

'On what evidence? Anyway, all the uniform are tied up chasing Vipers.'

'What did your man find out about Roth?' asked Ford.

'He's former military in South Africa. Served in the Special Forces Brigade, the Recces. No service history, all very secret squirrel, but those boys got up to some nasty shit in Namibia and Angola. After that he was some sort of soldier of misfortune, popping up in places like Bougainville and New Guinea. Seems to like the hot weather. Arrested once in Timor but released without charge. He told Immigration he's been in Iraq for four years as a private security contractor, with some mob called Redstone. After that he showed up in Perth, employed by a number of McCann's companies, all going back to the Glycon Group. McCann's business sponsored his visa and work permit for three years until he got residency.'

'Fine way to repay him,' said Doc, wiping iced coffee from his moustache. 'Explains how he got the personnel and the hardware, but not why he would hook up with Little Jimmy.'

Kavanagh shrugged. 'Guns, drugs, security, extortion, protection: who knows? They seem to like the same things.' She looked at the empty food wrappers. 'Did you buggers buy me any breakfast?'

Doc hooked a plastic bag off the seat with his finger and held it up like a trophy. 'Now, it was difficult to decide what a lady like yourself might like, but seeing as you're watching your figure, I got you a salad roll and an orange juice.' He picked the roll out of the bag and threw it to her like a cricket ball.

She snatched it out of the air and peeled off three layers of clingfilm, then lifted off the top and peered at the contents with her lip curled. 'Beetroot, onion, a bit of limp lettuce, colourless tomato and grated carrot.' She picked out an orange wad and flicked it across the forecourt. 'What's this thing roadhouses have about grated carrot?' She bit hard into the roll like she was eating an apple.

Doc finished his iced coffee and pitched the carton into the forty-four-gallon drum that stood between the bowsers. 'I don't reckon we'll work this all out until we've got Roth or Jimmy pinned to the wall with my magnum shoved up their arse,' he said.

He turned on his heel and walked back into the roadhouse. Ford watched as he walked to the payphone on the far wall and fished in his pocket for coins. The call couldn't have lasted more than thirty seconds before he slammed down the handset, pushed his way out of the roadhouse and strode across the forecourt towards them. He opened his mouth to speak but was interrupted by the roar of a road train rattling past, two double-storey trailers packed with live sheep. It trailed a stink in its wake that made Kavanagh stop eating and look at her roll before wrapping the rest of it in paper and throwing it away.

'If you think that stinks, you should try the restrooms in there,' said Ford. 'It's pretty medieval. I think the truckers are less fussy where they shit than the sheep.'

'Can't get good plumbers out here,' said Banjo. 'We're a rare breed.'

Kavanagh opened her door, lifted the newspaper off the seat and sat down. Ford nodded to it. 'Your friend Alannah's been busy,' he said. 'She's been tailing McCann.'

They pulled out of the roadhouse. As they bumped over the railway crossing, a police car could be seen parked outside the hotel further down the street. There was a silhouette in the passenger seat, though they were too far away to tell if it was looking at them. Banjo's hands tensed on the steering wheel.

'Easy, mate,' said Doc. 'Just the local plod doing his rounds. The driver's probably in the pub, goosing the barmaid.'

They rolled slowly over the tracks and gradually picked up speed. In a hundred metres they were through the town and driving between broad paddocks of bright yellow canola.

Banjo kept his eyes on the rear-view mirror. 'Did your mate on the phone tell you whether we're still on Chadwick's wanted list?' he asked.

'Chadwick's mad as a cut snake,' Kavanagh said. 'Pissed off that they lost surveillance on Ford. There's a warrant out for you, Doc, same as there is for all patched Vipers.'

'But not for Banjo?'

'He's just listed as a known associate wanted for questioning.'

'That's fucking typical,' Banjo said. 'Guilt by association. No proof required. If they want one of us, they'll drag in all of us, with or without evidence.'

'So what was your little phone call about back at the road-house?' Kavanagh asked Doc.

'Secret men's business,' he said.

'Any of the Vipers still at large?'

'Enough.'

Ford took a sly slug from the whisky bottle. 'Is that satellite phone up for grabs now? I'd like to try my wife's home number again.'

Kavanagh scowled at him. 'I thought Doc told you not to drink when you're on the pills and the jabs?'

'This isn't drinking,' he said. 'This is just maintenance. Staying two drinks ahead of reality. Just enough to keep the edge off and keep my mind quiet.'

'With all the pills you've had, I wouldn't have thought you'd have any edges left. Just one long blur.'

'Yeah, well, it's not every weekend you get shot three times. I'm trying to push it to the back of my mind with a bit of help from Banjo's whisky.'

Banjo tilted the mirror so he could see Ford. 'I was saving that bottle for a rainy day.'

'Look ahead of you,' said Ford. 'I see dark clouds.'

They had left the flat country behind and were into rolling pasture ringed with windbreaks of eucalypts and stands of wandoo. The dark line of the Darling Range edged the horizon, and the sky above it was crowded with columns of grey cloud.

'So can I use the phone?' asked Ford.

Kavanagh shrugged and tossed it into his lap. He punched in the number, letting it ring a dozen times with no answer, no machine pick-up. 'Still nobody there,' he said. 'I want to go take a look.'

Banjo and Doc glanced at each other but didn't answer.

'You fellas got other ideas?' asked Kavanagh.

Doc shook his head. 'We need to get to the clubhouse, see if we can round up some brothers and track down Little Jimmy. I'm sure we can persuade someone to fill us in on what we missed. We'll drop you wherever you need to go.'

Kavanagh leaned forward and rested her Glock flat on Doc's shoulder. Her other hand grabbed his ponytail and pulled his head gently back against the headrest. 'Did you think I'd let you get to Jimmy without me being there? That's not going to happen.'

'You think he'd talk to you?' said Doc, through clenched teeth. 'You think he'd give up anyone in the club? Jimmy's a cunt, but he's not a rat. Whatever he's got going with Roth, he's still a Viper, and we'll deal with it inside the club.'

'I reckon Jimmy would be more scared of Roth than he would be of you,' said Kavanagh, twisting her ponytail. 'Do you know what they used to call him in the South African forces? The Roach. They reckoned he'd still be scuttling around after everything else was dead. We get to Roth, then Jimmy is irrelevant. Only Chadwick has any interest in the Vipers. I just want Roth and the gold.'

'Then you can have Roth, and leave Jimmy to us.'

'I'm not sure you want to go to the clubhouse. There's probably still a dozen cops there on their hands and knees looking for gold dust. We may as well try to get a lead on Ford's family.'

'I thought we did all this territorial pissing back at the dyke's house?' said Doc.

'Quite a few things have changed since then,' said Kavanagh, tapping him on the shoulder with the gun. 'I'm just reminding you that we're better off sticking together.'

Doc twisted his head sideways until the cold steel of the gun rested against his cheek. 'You know, sweetheart, I'm sixty-four years old, like the Beatles song. My old lady still needs me and still feeds me, but these days she's trying to feed me those little blue pills. She thinks my friend can't get by without a little help. I haven't got the heart to tell her that it's not me, it's her. Old age does it to us all. Everything gets hairier and closer to the ground. She'd be bloody spewing if she knew that I get wood every time you put a gun on me. You make me feel like a younger man.'

Kavanagh grimaced and sat back in her seat, resting the Glock in her lap, turning her attention to the changing landscape outside her window. They were out of the farmland and into the forested hills, native bush fringing the road, tall ghost gums casting shadows across the highway, the road snaking in broad curves as it climbed. The mileage signs were counting down to Perth.

'Don't hog that whisky bottle,' Doc said to Ford. 'We all need bracing for what's coming.' He held out his hand. Ford slapped the flat bottle into his palm and Doc took a generous slug before passing it to Banjo.

'Only one pull, mate, or you'll be over the limit,' said Kavanagh.

'Go on, officer, tickle me with your gun,' said Banjo. 'I'd like to see if it has the same effect on me.' Doc laughed until he coughed. Ford looked at Kavanagh and rested his hand on her thigh but she swatted it away.

They crested the range and coasted downhill past orchards and horse pasture, the trees parting at turns in the road to reveal views of the coastal plain. Ford caught sight of Perth, the small cluster of high-rise office towers standing lonely among the blanket of suburbs that sprawled uncontrolled across the flats. One long downhill curve brought them off the scarp and out onto the plain, the country highway finishing abruptly at a set of traffic lights, beyond which the red-tiled roofs of suburban bungalows stretched away.

While they waited for the lights to change, Banjo turned to Ford and asked for the address. Ford told him the suburb and the street, and thought of the house he had bought but barely lived in.

Banjo was looking at the traffic lights and shaking his head. 'I can't help thinking we're walking into something. Someone is leaving a berley trail for us to follow.'

TWENTY-EIGHT

The sudden bustle of vehicles and stoplights unnerved Ford after the wide open spaces he had travelled through. They had hit the start of the afternoon rush and were trapped in snaking tails of traffic, looking at the sour faces of commuters, reluctant prisoners in their own cars. They pushed their way westwards towards the city, knowing they had to pass between the office blocks of the business district and through the tightest knots of pedestrians to get to Diane's house in Shenton Park.

They crossed the Swan River over the causeway, then joined the procession of buses, taxis and cars up the Terrace. As they crawled through the canyon formed by the glass-fronted office towers facing the Terrace, its footpath crowded with office workers, Ford stared open-mouthed out of the window of the ute, like an underwater explorer peering from his submersible at the teeming fish of a deep-sea trench.

A stream of pedestrians crossed in front of them at the traffic lights. Watching them, Banjo muttered to himself:

The human river dwindles when 'tis past the hour of eight,
Its waves go flowing faster in the fear of being late;

But slowly drag the moments, whilst beneath the dust and heat
The city grinds the owners of the faces in the street—
Grinding body, grinding soul,
Yielding scarce enough to eat—
Oh! I sorrow for the owners of the faces in the street.

They climbed the hill at the head of the Terrace, skirted the park, and then they were into the tree-lined streets of Diane's neighbourhood. Ford leaned forward between the front seat and quietly directed Banjo. They turned into the street and drove past the house at walking pace. There were no cars in the driveway and the curtains were drawn. They looked up and down, checking the street for anyone watching the house, but the parked cars were empty. Ford told Banjo to turn at the next cross-street and park at the end of the laneway separating the back of Diane's house from those in the next road.

Telling them he'd be fifteen minutes, Ford stepped down from the ute. He caught Kavanagh looking at him with a look in her eyes that he liked. She held up the shotgun, but he shook his head.

He walked into the lane, hugging the fence line. The lowering sun threw long shadows from the European trees in the backyards. He peered over the fences to check the manicured gardens and the squares of tended lawn for signs of life. Squeals of children playing could be heard somewhere nearby, but he saw nobody. Looking down at his torn clothes, worn thongs and filthy feet, red dirt caked under his toenails, he felt like a stranger again.

When he had first arrived in Perth, he'd found the identical streets, the iron roofs and the timber verandahs quaint and foreign, and the attempts to re-create suburban English gardens in the southern sun absurd. The lawns cried out for rain, and the deciduous trees seemed confused by the inverted seasons.

Then he had gone out to work in the desert. Now, whenever he returned he found the suburbs absurd again, but for an entirely different set of reasons. Here was the most isolated city in the world, a small blister of irrigated greenery teetering on the edge of a vast dry continent.

He crept down the lane until he recognised the picket gate that he had painted in bright Indian Red. Sliding a finger through the gap between the gate and the fence, he lifted the latch and pushed the gate open, then walked into the garden. He stood in the shade of the lemon tree for a whole minute, watching the house for movement, before stepping onto the verandah, lifting the third geranium pot by the back door and picking up the key.

He turned it slowly in the lock and pushed the door inward. As he stepped into the kitchen, he held his breath and looked for the movement sensor in the corner of the ceiling, then waved his arm until the red light blinked at him. The alarm stayed mute.

He looked around the house. It was familiar, yet strange. He'd lived here for six years, but it had never quite felt like home. It had been Diane's house then, and it still was, even though he was paying most of the mortgage. It had been her choice, her aspiration, based on her expectations growing up in this part of town. In a thirsty place like Perth, status was conferred by how close you lived to open water, the river or the ocean, and fresh water trumped salt. The upwardly mobile clamoured for a view of the ocean, and developers pandered to them by building new subdivisions stretching up and down the coast, levelling sand dunes to create shadeless suburbs beyond the end of the freeway. Those with real money closed ranks by the Swan River, looking out over the broad stretch of Melville Water, where the river was wide enough to accommodate their yachts and cabin cruisers.

Having grown up under the low grey skies of northern England, Ford had wanted to live near the beach, but Diane had laughed at him. She called him a gauche arriviste and told him he belonged with the other Poms in a salmon-brick McMansion in a sandpit suburb on the northern coast, with a concrete yard and a swimming pool ringed with cocos palms. They didn't have enough money to cosy up to the river, so the next best thing was the wedge of older western suburbs between the river and the railway. He had sat in the back of the real estate agent's car while Diane sat in the front, pointing to the Federation detailing on houses in Claremont, Dalkeith and Nedlands. She eventually chose a tidy bungalow in a quiet street in Shenton Park, and he'd only had the opportunity to walk through it once before she sat him down with the paperwork.

Now he walked through the house to the front door. It was locked and there was no sign of it being forced. He opened the side door to the garage, but it was empty. Going back to the kitchen, he checked the hook by the fridge: her house and car keys were gone.

His attention was caught by the paintings and photographs stuck to the fridge. Grace's artwork had advanced beyond the finger painting displayed on the wall of his apartment. Now, unicorns and ponies seemed to fill her life. He preferred her early, abstract work. There was a photo of her smiling as she sat on a small, bored-looking Shetland pony, her black felt riding hat so large it almost rested on the bridge of her nose. He'd wondered why she'd stopped asking him for lessons, and now he knew. There were photos of her with her mother, hand in hand in the country with vineyards in the background; in another they sat on a beach. The sand was black and there was a large villa behind them, so it wasn't Perth. Ford wondered who was holding the camera, and how long ago his own photos had been taken down.

He opened the fridge. It was empty except for a few jars and packets, as well as two bottles of chardonnay and half a six-pack of beer. She never bought him beer. Towards the end, when she took to making an issue of it, she even stopped buying herself wine and wouldn't allow any alcohol in the house. They had played a game of cat and mouse, where she would hunt for bottles he stashed around the house and pour them down the sink. His final hiding place was the electricity meter by the front door. He fitted a lock to it and told her the power company had put it there.

He looked more closely at the bottles in the fridge and wondered what kind of man drank light beer. Right now, however, they looked cold and inviting, with beaded condensation on the neck, so he put aside his prejudice and twisted the top off one. He finished it in three and took another.

It had been a long time since he'd been in the house. When he first started picking up Grace at the weekends, he'd been invited in for tea and the three of them had sat in the kitchen together. Then, one Saturday morning, Diane had made Ford wait on the doorstep while she packed an overnight bag, and two months later she suggested dropping Grace off at his place.

It was a woman's house now, just mother and daughter together. No sign remained of a man's presence.

The house smelled of rose petals, of cinnamon baking, and of citrus cleaning products. All the surfaces in the kitchen were clean and clear, with no signs of habitation, but that had always been Diane's way; over time, he knew, she had started to find his untidiness trying.

He wandered into Grace's room. There were toys he didn't recognise, a collection of dolls and plush animals arranged in height order along her bed. Halfway down the line was a hand-stitched rag doll he had bought for her.

He remembered the day he had bought it. He had wanted to take Grace for a weekend stay on a farm where she could ride a pony, but Diane had refused to let him take her out of town overnight, so they had made a day trip to Balingup Field Day. As they wandered through the stalls, Grace had picked up the doll from the stand of a wild-looking woman dressed in purple and recking of patchouli and marijuana, her red-dyed hair spilling out of a pink knitted hat. She also sold homemade jam and fruit wines. Hugging the doll to her chest, Grace gave Ford the fierce look that dared him to defy her. The woman smiled at him and her teeth scared him. She must have spent long hours stitching the doll's patchwork dress and twisting the wool strands to make the rainbow-coloured dreadlocks that framed its embroidered face; the price she asked could never have compensated her for the hours she'd invested in it. He bought the doll and a bottle of apricot port. After he'd carried Grace, sleeping, from the car and put her in her own bed, he drove home. Sitting on his balcony he drank the whole bottle alone. It was sweeter than anything he could remember and had a punch like an iron fist inside a velvet glove. When he woke up in the deckchair, it was daylight and a cool morning breeze off the ocean was goosing his skin.

Wherever Grace was, she hadn't taken her toys. Maybe she had outgrown them. He picked up her pillow and put his nose to it, inhaling her scent, then pulled back the doona. When he closed his eyes, the smell of the room was so familiar he felt he might open his eyes and find her standing there. He picked up the doll, clutched it to his chest and breathed deeply.

He went into Diane's bedroom and finished the second beer, staring at the floral pattern on the bedding. He opened her bedside drawer and found only a dog-eared paperback and a blister pack of sleeping pills. The drawer on the side where he used to sleep was empty. The wardrobe was half full of clothes, all hers. In the bathroom, all her toiletries were laid out neatly on the glass shelf. He looked for toothbrushes and there was only one, and it was pink.

He lifted the lid on the laundry basket, tipped the contents onto the floor and picked up a pair of panties that fell out on top of the pile. They were small and lacy, and she had never worn anything like them when they were together. He had once bought her something similar as a gift and she'd asked him whether it was for his benefit rather than hers. She told him she would buy her own underwear in future, on the basis of comfort, and not to facilitate her objectification. He'd told her he preferred her naked anyway, and she'd laughed. As he thought of that, he found himself holding the panties to his nose. The smell was familiar but didn't stir him.

Walking into the study, he saw the light on the telephone blinking at him. Picking it up, he keyed in the number he remembered and sat at the desk leafing through the pile of documents stacked there while he waited for the machine to connect. The code still worked. The machine told him there were messages, and he switched it to speaker and leaned back to listen. The first message was from a man who sounded hesitant and breathless. He had a Manchester accent with slight Australian inflections and wanted Diane to contact him as soon as possible. Only when he heard his name did Ford recognise it as his own voice on the recording; he slammed the phone back onto the cradle before he had to listen to anymore. He did a mental count of how many times he had called the house and figured all the messages were his. He felt the same way about hearing his voice as he did about seeing a photograph of himself or catching his reflection in a mirror: he found the experience unsettling and deeply unnecessary.

It was then that he saw the large gilt-framed mirror over the fireplace and understood why the house looked so unfamiliar: she had put mirrors in every room. He had refused to have more than one small shaving mirror over the sink and a dressing mirror behind the wardrobe door, but now she had them everywhere. He stepped in front of the fireplace and checked his reflection. He was gaunt and unshaven and his hair was greasy and sticking up. His eyes appeared sunken and were still ringed with bruises, while his skin looked pale and clammy. He put out his tongue and it was as yellow as his skin.

He returned to the desk and continued looking through the stacks of files. There was nothing that mentioned Gwardar or Glycon. At the bottom of the pile he found her laptop. He opened it and pushed the power switch but the battery was dead. In the drawer he found a couple of memory sticks that he stuck in his pocket, but no power cable. He would have to power up the computer later. Tucking it under his arm, he headed towards the back door. On his way past the fridge he took the last beer and drank it while he crossed the lawn to the back gate.

TWENTY-NINE

Ford opened the door to the ute and tossed the laptop onto the seat next to Kavanagh. The sun was low now, and a sea breeze was rattling the leaves on the plane trees lining the street. He saw Banjo's eyes watching him in the mirror but felt no need to speak. They pulled away and turned back into Diane's street, making a final pass of the house. Ford picked up the shotgun from under the seat, checked it was loaded, and rested it in the crook of his arm. In his other arm he cradled the rag doll. As they passed the house he looked up the garden path, along the row of white roses, and thought about whether he had changed at all and, if he had, what kind of man he was becoming.

They left the western suburbs and were across the freeway and into a bleak stretch of warehouses before anyone spoke.

Doc turned to Ford. 'Your luck changing?'

'Too soon to tell. I don't really believe in luck.'

'But you play the horses.'

'Exactly. I play the percentages, and only play the odds that I think the bookies have miscalculated. I don't believe in fate, or karma, or any of that. The cruellest thing about life is that it's random. I just try to make my play when the odds are in my favour. Where do we look now?'

'We're going to the Snake Pit, to pay a visit to Little Jimmy and his International Cunt Circus.'

They turned into a dead-end street in an industrial area of low warehouses and blank-faced workshops. The building sitting across the end of the street was partially hidden by a high concrete wall topped with coils of wire. Banjo pointed the Toyota at a gap in the wall; as they passed through, Ford saw that the plated-steel gate was hanging open, buckled and twisted off its hinges. They pulled up in the wide yard in front of a corrugated-steel shed that bore no signage except for a coiled snake painted above a riveted steel entrance door. Two motorcycles stood by the door.

Doc jumped down and walked to the bikes, the big revolver held loosely at his side. He put his hand on the motor of the first bike, an old Harley with flames painted across the tank. He looked at Banjo and shook his head to indicate that it was cold. He walked in a wide arc to the door, flattened himself against the wall beside it and pushed it. It swung open and he craned his neck to look inside. Then he slipped through the door and Ford climbed down and limped across the yard after him.

There wasn't much light inside. A little came through the door, a blue glow came from a jukebox against the side wall, and a pale light shone out of a pair of glass-fronted fridges behind a counter. The only sound was the hum of the fridges and the slow tick of the jukebox as it scrolled through its sequence of blue lights. In the time it took Ford's eyes to adjust to the gloom, Banjo had pushed past him.

Doc was striding between a pair of pool tables towards a scaffold stage at the far end of the large room. The banner on the wall behind the stage displayed the snake patch and the words WELCOME TO THE SNAKE PIT. The top rocker bore the title STREET

VIPERS. Doc stepped up onto the stage and turned to survey the room, then looked at the banner.

'Looks like Jimmy went and renamed the club,' he said. 'I thought this might happen. Should have kept to the country. It was always going to be a mistake opening a chapter in the city, treading on the toes of the big clubs.'

'If he's broken away without telling you, he's only one step away from patching over to the Americans,' said Kavanagh. Ford turned to look at her, silhouetted in the doorway.

'I don't remember inviting you in, copper,' said Doc.

'The door was open.'

'You still need a warrant.'

She walked into the room and leaned against the jukebox, bowing her head and peering through the glass to read the track listings. 'Don't you boys listen to anything other than cock rock?'

'This isn't a place for you,' said Doc.

'As a woman or as a police officer?'

'Oh, women are welcome,' said Doc, rapping his knuckles against the stainless-steel pole in the centre of the stage, his ring clanging on the metal.

Kavanagh pressed the buttons on the machine and tilted her head, waiting for the music, but nothing came. 'Is this jukebox like your motorcycles, all retro styling and rockabilly posing, but basically unreliable window dressing?' She looked around the room. 'Where's the party?'

'It's the Snake Pit, sweetheart,' said Banjo. 'You never have to ask "Where's the party?", because it's always at the clubhouse, and it lasts as long as we do. The Snake Pit's got all the trouble you can handle.'

'Looks like nobody got their invitation.'

'You weren't invited,' said Doc.

Kavanagh walked over to the bar and peered into the fridge. 'About twenty coppers in heavy boots have already come through that gate and served a warrant on that front door. Whatever you think you might have to hide in here has probably already been taken into evidence. Just for the record, though, as a sworn officer of the Gold Squad, I have statutory powers to enter any premises I wish if I have cause to believe there might be stolen gold there. We're like the fisheries department. Those blokes can take your door down if they get a whiff of illegally caught fish. I can do the same looking for gold. I don't need a warrant, even though I thought you and me were well beyond the legal niceties by now.'

'Bollocks to the law, this is the Snake Pit. You only come in here if you're the guest of a patched member.'

'Sorry, are we on foreign soil here?'

'Fuck yeah. You're in the Viper Nation. This is a Temporary Autonomous Zone, a libertarian enclave, a rathole in Babylon. This is the pirate utopia, the home of the last free men.'

'You can't fly like a bird just because it takes your fancy,' she said, taking a Coke from the fridge and twisting the cap. 'You can't get free from your own weight.'

Doc had finished listening. He jumped off the stage and walked towards the booths arranged opposite the bar. Ford turned to see where he was heading and saw the outline of a figure sitting at one of the tables, slumped in the corner of the curved banquette, a vague shape among the shadows. Banjo walked towards the booth from the opposite side, picking up a pool cue as he passed the table. He waved to Kavanagh and pointed at the ceiling, and then to the end of the counter. She found the bank of light switches and flipped them. First a pair of coloured spotlights lit up the stage, then the strip lights hanging low over the pool tables came on, and finally the house lights kicked in.

The sudden brightness made Ford squint and he put his hand over his eyes. When he took it away, Doc and Banjo were standing by the booth looking at the man slumped there, his chin on his chest where the front of his shirt was soaked with blood.

Ford recognised the broad face and broken nose. 'He was in Kalgoorlie, at the Exchange Hotel with Jimmy,' he said, backing away from the body until he was leaning against the bar in front of Kavanagh.

Doc leaned over into the booth to feel the man's neck for a pulse, arching his back to avoid the pool of blood smeared across the white vinyl of the seat. 'He's still warm,' he said. 'We can't be far behind them.'

'Behind who?' asked Ford.

Kavanagh finished the Coke and tossed the empty bottle in the trash. 'This must've happened after the warrant was executed,' she said. 'I'll need to phone it in.'

Doc straightened up and walked towards a small door beside the jukebox. He opened it and looked into the dark corridor beyond. 'That there is Panhead,' he said, without turning to them.

'You know him?' asked Ford, surprised.

'You'd never forget a face like that. Met him a couple of times. He came to Kal once and partied with us.'

'But I gave you and Banjo a full description of him. You said you didn't know him.'

Doc shrugged. 'I knew who you were talking about, I just didn't see a reason for you to know it too. Never know who you'd tell.'

Once he'd found the light switch, Doc put his head through the door again to check the corridor. 'About ten years ago Panhead's old lady comes home and finds him balls deep into this stripper from Broken Hill. She's understandably not best pleased about him doing her in the marital bed. We built a clubhouse so you don't have to get caught doing that sort of thing at home.

She loses the plot about him soiling her best linen, grabs a frying pan from the kitchen and goes berko. He cops it right on the nose and his face gets flattened like in a Tom and Jerry cartoon. He bought that '63 Softail outside and tried telling everyone that he's named after it, but you can't escape a story like that.'

'So you know who he came with?' said Ford. 'Who was on the other bike?'

Doc didn't reply. He raised his gun and stepped through the door and out of sight. Ford and Kavanagh caught up with him in a small office behind the bar. He was leaning against the desk, opening each drawer in turn. Then he started on the battered filing cabinet beside the desk. An old iron safe sat in the corner, its door hanging open, its shelves bare.

Finally he stopped, spread his arms wide and gestured around the room. 'Now this,' he said, 'this is the work of the West Australian Police Force. Whoever did for Panhead didn't give a shit about making a mess, but these bastards have gone through every drawer. They've bagged it, tagged it, and left a fucking receipt.' He picked up the trailing ends of a cluster of electrical cables that snaked across the desk. 'The buggers took the computers, the discs from the security cameras and even the recording machine. They've got the contents of the filing cabinet, the membership records, the club accounts, and all the money.'

'At least they left a few cold ones in the fridge,' said Banjo, appearing in the doorway clutching a fistful of beers between the fingers of each hand. He stood them in a line on the empty desk. Ford reached for one and sucked it down gratefully.

Kavanagh pointed to the security camera hanging from the ceiling. 'That still looks active. The light's on, but nobody's home.'

Doc frowned. 'The disc machine the cops have taken is a dummy,' he said. 'We're not stupid enough to record our own business and leave it in the clubhouse to be confiscated. The machine records to a remote server. We could look at it, if your mates hadn't taken the fucking computer.'

Ford finished his beer and put the empty on the desk. He looked to see if anyone was interested in the remaining bottles and then took one. 'There's that laptop in the truck,' he said. They all stared at him until he turned around and limped out to the Hilux.

He returned and put the computer on the desk next to the hanging wires. When nobody else made a move, he sat on the chair and looked for a power cable. By the time he'd powered up the laptop and patched it into the network he was onto his third beer.

'There's a wireless server somewhere around here, but it's asking for a password,' he said.

'Let the dog see the rabbit,' said Doc, and waved him off the chair. 'Just stand behind me for a second, mate, so the cop can't see what I'm typing.'

Once Doc had typed in the password, there was a pause and then the screen broke into four panels, each showing the view from a different camera. The time signature started at six in the morning and showed people arriving at the club as day broke.

'Movement sensors,' said Doc. 'Recording only kicks in when someone moves past and triggers it.'

'The security in this place is better than at the mine,' said Ford.

'Didn't keep anybody out, though,' said Kavanagh, moving up to stand beside him.

The recording jumped to show three people walking into the bar area. Doc fast-forwarded as two men restocked the bar and a woman in hot pants with thick legs mopped the floor. At six thirty the camera outside the fence showed a large black armoured car crash through the perimeter gate. The vehicle stopped in the yard and out spilled six men in black fatigues, carrying assault rifles.

'Look at the fucking tank they got,' said Doc. 'They bought that thing after the terrorist attacks in the States, bleating about how they needed to be prepared for hostage situations. So far they've only used it to harass us. Would you believe they had the brass balls to paint "Rescue Vehicle" across the front of that thing?'

The men in black took a steel battering ram to the riveted door and ran into the building with guns raised. The two men who'd been restocking the bar were already face down on the floor in the middle of the room before they were inside. The cleaner just leaned on her mop and mouthed obscenities at the police. The men were led away in cuffs.

Doc flicked through the next eight hours of recording, which showed a vanful of uniform arriving and searching the clubhouse. A truck was backed into the yard and the motor-cycles parked out front were loaded up. Cartons of documents were carried out and three bikes were taken in pieces from the workshop at the back.

'You see them take any gold out of here?' asked Doc. Kavanagh ignored him and leaned in closer to the screen. 'You see them find any guns, any drugs? You see anything there that links this club to the robbery?'

'Shut up,' she said. 'We're getting to the good bit.'

Doc tracked forward until the outside camera showed Pan-head ride into the yard. He was followed by the second Harley. The rider took off his helmet and pulled his bandana down off his mouth but it wasn't a face Ford recognised. He was bald, clean-shaven, tall and rangy.

'Who's that?' he said. 'He must be around here somewhere.'

'That would be Crock,' said Doc. 'Him and Panhead are never far from each other. Crock shacked up with Panhead's sister. They're practically family.'

Banjo reappeared in the doorway. 'I've checked the whole building. There's nobody else here.'

They watched the screen as the two men walked into the bar area and surveyed the damage, checking each room in turn until they got to the workshop and disappeared into a corner of the room out of view of the camera. The recording jumped ten minutes before they returned to the bar and tripped the camera again. They helped themselves to beer and were sitting on bar stools talking when they both turned towards the door as if in response to a sound. At the same time, the external camera showed a black van pulling into the yard. Two men in blue boilersuits stepped out of the van and walked to the door, their heads hidden under baseball caps with chequerboard banding. They went through the riveted door and the two bikers got off their stools and turned to face them.

Ford didn't see the first shot, as the shooter's back was still to camera, but Crock fell to the floor clutching his knee. Panhead started to run; when the gunman turned to track him, the gun came into view. It flashed once and Panhead stumbled and fell against the table. Just as he pulled himself upright the gun flashed again, and he sat down heavily in the booth. He raised his head to look at his killers and his mouth moved as if he was shouting. He spat on the table, then his chin dropped to his chest and a dark stain spread across his shirt.

'Do those look like police clothes to you, Kavanagh?' asked Doc.

She shook her head. 'The chequerboard caps mean nothing. You can get them at a costume shop. The overalls have no markings. They're not police.'

On screen, Crock had crawled over to the pool table and pulled himself up. He picked up a pool cue and held it ready behind his head, but the man with the gun blocked the swing with his forearm and swung the heel of the pistol into Crock's face. He caught Crock as he fell and the two men dragged him through the door into the corridor. They appeared on camera again in the workshop, where they carried him into the corner, out of view.

The time code jumped thirty minutes before they reappeared. They stopped in the bar to check Panhead's pulse and, apparently satisfied with their work, left in the van.

'I guess we know where Crock is,' said Ford.

Doc led the way down the passage and the four of them stood together in front of the tool cupboard that filled the corner of the workshop. Doc pulled open the double doors and they stared at the rows of tools that lined the cupboard from floor to ceiling.

'Come on,' said Kavanagh, 'stop pretending you don't know what's there. That act won't wash.'

Doc looked at her and nodded. He reached under the second shelf, pulled the handle and the cupboard swung out. Behind it was a riveted steel door with a recessed handle above a heavy mortice lock. Doc tried the handle and it was unlocked. He leaned back to pull the door open.

The room behind the door was dark, but enough light spilled from the workshop to illuminate the scene that had been prepared for them. Crock sat on an office chair in the middle of the small storeroom. His mouth was covered with silver gaffer tape and his wrists were taped to the arms of the chair. The middle two fingers of his left hand had been severed and the stumps had dripped blood on the floor. A pool had formed beneath his bare feet, where only the stumps of his toes remained. There were dozens of coins scattered across the floor and the blood had spread around them. There was a bullet hole through the knee of his jeans, and another over his heart. A pair of boltcutters lay on the floor next to his motorcycle boots.

Ford looked at Kavanagh, who was leaning against the door frame staring at the wreckage of Crock's body. Her eyes had turned pale and distant. Stepping forward, she stooped to pick up one of the coins that had escaped the widening slick of blood. She turned it towards the light and twirled it in her fingers, then smiled. 'I think we can dismiss any wild ideas about those two being cops,' she said. 'A vanload of uniform went over this place and never found this room.'

'They couldn't find their own arse in the dark using both hands,' said Doc.

'But those two guys came straight to this room. They've been here before. The only mistake they made was not knowing that the security recording was backed up, but they knew where the cameras were and they shielded their faces with the caps.' She flipped the coin and watched it spin high. 'Heads or tails?' she asked as she slapped it onto the back of her wrist.

'I don't bet fifty-fifty,' said Ford. 'There's no margin in it.'

'If you'd played two-up instead of the horses, maybe you'd have broken even.'

'Heads!' called Banjo. 'What do I win?'

'You lose,' said Kavanagh. She uncovered the back of her hand and held up the coin for them to see. It was blank. It wasn't a coin, just a flat disc of metal, the surface pitted and uneven. She twisted her wrist until it caught the light. 'It's gold,' she said. 'Rough cast into these washers.'

'They planted it,' said Doc. 'More bullshit to pin on the Vipers.'

'Why'd they cut his fingers?' Kavanagh asked. 'Is that some sort of warning to you?'

'Some bastard with an AK emptying a clip at me, that was a warning. This is just another frame-up. Make it look like some kind of internal beef within the club, or maybe as if toecutters and standover men have stepped in and ripped us off for the gold. I'll bet they've planted guns and drugs and all kinds of shit in here. They'll have loaded us up with stolen microwaves and kiddie porn and whatever else they can think of to keep the cops busy while they get on with whatever they're doing.'

Ford looked at Crock's motorcycle boots, which had been discarded at the side of the room. He stepped out of his thongs and put his bare feet beside them to check the size.

'You wanting to walk in dead men's shoes?' said Doc.

'I feel like I've been doing that all weekend,' said Ford. 'I doubt he'll mind. Why do they call him Crock? As in crocodile?'

'As in a crock of shit. He was full of it.'

Ford put his feet in the boots and stamped his feet. 'How did you really lose your fingers?'

'I was trying to perfect my leg spin with a grenade,' said Doc.

Kavanagh flipped the coin again and Doc snatched it out of the air. He held it up to the light and squinted at it. 'This could be from anywhere,' he said.

Kavanagh stepped towards him and made to reach for the coin, but then changed her mind and stooped to pick up another one out of the blood. She found a rag on a shelf and wiped the coin clean and slipped it into her pocket. 'We'll get it tested,' she said.

'It was planted here.'

'That's not the point. I need to find out if it's from the robbery.'

'You can do that?'

'We can fingerprint it. Laser ablation inductively coupled plasma mass spectrometry. Trace elements in the gold will identify its origin.' She stepped out of the storeroom and into the bright light of the workshop.

'Sounds like you'll be heading back to the station then,' Doc said.

'We all are.' Kavanagh turned to face them and drew her gun.

Doc looked at her and sighed. He let his hands hang at his sides, then slowly reached around behind his back. Banjo watched him and took a step backwards.

She tutted through pursed lips and shook her head. 'I told you that big revolver was no use,' she said. 'I'll have emptied my clip before you get that thing clear of your holster. Why are you boys so obsessed with size?'

He stopped and held his hands wide, the palms spread. 'You just love being a cop, don't you? I saw it back in Kalgoorlie in that kitchen. Coming at me with the gun and the knife. You play it a little different, a little twist for being a woman. Quieter about it. You don't get that whole testosterone rush of blood to the head, but it's the same shit. As long as you've got that warrant card, you think you've got the right to do anything you want.' Doc took a step forward and spread his arms wider. 'I don't think this is what you want,' he said.

'Just stay where you are, Doc. I need to call this in. This is the first real sniff I've had of the gold. I've been chasing shadows up till now.'

'You tried doing this *High Noon* shit in Kalgoorlie and it didn't work then. Now you're on our turf. How you going to explain this? You've been running with us for two days, and then you decide to take us in? You conspire with us to kill those men, then decide we're enemies. You think this gold puts the club in the frame, but you take us in and you give Chadwick everything he needs to snuff us out. The two boys in blue on the cameras, that's Roth and the fourth guy from the robbery. Right now they're tying up loose ends. Who else have they got to mop up?'

'My wife and daughter,' said Ford. He had been crouched beside the door trying to work out the buckles on the boots. He stood tall now, and turned to Kavanagh. 'I'm sure you think you've got things to do, but I can't be a part of it anymore. I have to keep looking for my family.' He stepped forward between her and Doc and looked her in the eye.

'Step aside, you piece of shit,' she hissed. 'You're in my line of sight.'

'We're all pieces of shit when we're in your way, aren't we? I never asked to be part of this.'

'You were part of it the minute Jimmy roped you. You were in it the moment you thought you were smarter than the book-ies. You had plenty of chances to bail out, but you didn't have the balls. You could have come straight to the police, but you waited till you were all the way in before you found an ounce of guts. Then you get a second chance to side with the law, and you decide you're going to stand up for yourself.

Kavanagh took a step sideways but Ford moved in front of Doc to block her again.

'You're a brainless piece of shit, Ford,' she said. 'You're a gut-less coward when things are heavy, then suddenly a foot soldier for freedom and liberty when nobody gives a shit. You sure pick your moments.'

'Rosie's always moralising when she's got the drop,' said Doc. 'You know, I'm still not sure she's not working an angle on this. Maybe she thought we'd lead her to Jimmy and then she could take us all in. Maybe she's got an eye for the gold herself. I want to believe it's an honour thing. Honour's good, I've done a lot of things in the name of honour. But flying solo, making out it's some beef with Chadwick that's driving her. I don't buy the honest-cop thing. Never met one yet.'

Kavanagh took a deep breath and steadied the gun with both hands. She eyed the roll of gaffer tape on the shelf. 'We're getting to the endgame now,' she said. 'Time to play by the rules.'

Doc snorted. 'There are no rules. The game is rigged. When we do something right, nobody remembers; when we do something wrong, nobody ever forgets. So fuck you, and fuck the world.'

Ford took a step towards her and raised his palm to the gun as if to shield himself. 'I'm out of here,' he said. 'All I can see is the frame. I want to get a look at the picture.'

Doc laughed. 'Sometimes you got to decide whether you want to kiss arse or kick arse, and it looks like this boy's got some new boots.'

Ford stepped around Kavanagh and was halfway across the workshop when he heard her gasp. He turned. Doc had drawn his gun.

'So, Rosie,' he said. 'Are we going to lower our guns and go our separate ways, or is this going to have to go a different way?' He raised his free hand slowly, put his outstretched palm on the barrel of the gun and gently pushed it down.

She dropped her hands and put the gun back in the waistband of her pants. 'Where will you go now?' she asked.

'I think Banjo and me will go find Jimmy,' said Doc as he slipped the big revolver into his holster. 'If he's lucky, we'll find him before Roth does. As long as Jimmy's got enough of his people behind him, he'll act tough. Whenever a fight breaks out, he'll always let his crew take the brunt of it while he walks away without a scratch. Sometimes that doesn't sit well with the other Vipers. Right now he's running out of friends fast, and I reckon most of his crew are ready to come back into the fold and ditch Jimmy and his little adventure. Shouldn't be hard to find him. Come on, Banjo, me old son, time to put on the colours and show some class.'

THIRTY

Ford stepped out into the dark yard with the laptop under his arm. He opened the driver's door of the Toyota and looked for the keys, but the ignition was empty. He didn't fancy his chances of getting them from Banjo, so he took the satellite phone from the dash, and the shotgun and the whisky off the floor, and turned towards the two motorcycles.

The newer one had no keys in the ignition either, but the old Duo-Glide belonging to Panhead didn't seem to need a key. Ford put the laptop and the gun into the tatty leather saddlebag and slipped the whisky and the phone into the long pockets of his coat. After flicking the switch on the tank he checked the fuel tap and located the kick-starter. He flipped it out, opened the throttle and tried to kick it. The engine barely turned over and the starter sprang back and jarred his leg, sending pain shooting up into the shotgun wound.

He gritted his teeth and tried again, this time standing up on the starter, lifting himself off the ground and giving it his full weight. The engine spluttered to life, coughed out a burst of smoke and settled into a low rumble. He lowered himself into the wide-sprung saddle, found the gearshift with his left foot and squeezed the clutch. It felt agricultural after the ease of his Vespa: the clutch was harsh, the gear change heavy. He stamped it into first gear and kicked up the stand, gave it some throttle and fought the clutch for the biting point.

The noise brought Doc out of the clubhouse at a jog. He looked at Ford struggling with the big Harley and smiled. 'We might make a biker out of you yet.' He raised his voice above the growl of the motor. 'You've got a bit more grunt under you than that pissy Vespa. Can you feel your balls swelling as you sit there?'

Ford tucked the tails of his coat under his backside and took the helmet from behind the seat.

Doc stepped in front of the Harley. 'It looks like whatever romantic notion you had about a band of righteous misfits riding together to rescue the princess is over,' he said.

'There's another bike there,' Ford said. 'You can tag along.'

'I've got a club to save, brother.' Doc stepped forward and put a hand on his shoulder. 'Courage is being scared to death and saddling up anyway,' he said. 'You need to decide how far you're prepared to go to protect your family. This here is my family, and I don't fight fair, I fight to win. There's no reverse gear on a motorcycle.'

Ford forced a smile, let out the clutch, and roared out of the gate.

He rode into the city and along the foreshore with no real idea where he was going, but the wind in his face helped to clear his head. Recalling the newspaper article claiming that McCann was on his boat, he continued alongside the river towards the marina. Then he remembered the phone in his pocket.

He pulled up in a parking bay on Mounts Bay Road, the shadow of Mount Eliza behind him, and sat on the bike looking out over the water towards the lights of the yacht club. He called the *Goldfields Courier*, and when the night desk answered he got them to patch him to Alannah Doyle's mobile.

'Doyle, it's Gareth Ford.'

He listened to her breathing before she answered. 'Is Rose with you?' she asked.

'No, I just left her.'

'Then she's safe?'

'I left her at the Vipers' clubhouse. She was going in to the Beaufort Street headquarters. I didn't want to go with her.'

'Still avoiding Chadwick?'

'I'm avoiding everyone, except Alan McCann. I need to find him. That's why I'm calling.'

'They found Mariotti,' she said.

'I thought he'd show up sooner or later. What's he got to say for himself?'

'Not much. They found him in the trunk of his car out at Kalgoorlie airport. Shot through the head.'

'When did this happen?'

'About an hour ago. No medical examination yet, but our bloke got to the scene and said he was stiff when they pulled him out.'

'Was he wearing that God-awful shiny suit he had on at the races?'

'Is that important?'

'Might suggest when he was done. What's the chatter about the Vipers?'

'A lot of nonsense coming out of Chadwick's mouth. He's rounded up a couple of dozen bikies up here and in Perth. He's not come out and linked them to the robbery, just spouted a lot of crap about the spectre of organised crime.'

'So why haven't you broken the story?'

'As if my editor would let me without something attributable. If you want it in print, you could go on the record?'

'We reckon Roth is behind the robbery. I think he's got my wife and daughter. McCann is the person most likely to help me find him. Tell me where I can find McCann and I'll give you an exclusive.'

'I don't want an interview, just an accredited quote.'

Out of the corner of his eye, Ford noticed something white moving fast towards him. He looked up and fought the urge to duck as a pair of pelicans swooped low above him, angling their wings to catch the air currents rising up the scarp. The headlights of the passing cars lit them from below, their feathers pure and white against the night sky.

'Is McCann still on his boat?' he asked.

'He has been since Saturday night. The *Gazette* had a journo looking out for it yesterday and today. Saw him come back into the river at sunset tonight. He's got a berth out in the big pens at the yacht club, but he didn't use it. He's tied up at one of the public moorings out in Matilda Bay.'

Ford watched the pelicans turn and land on the water, where a dozen boats were moored in the approaches to the yacht club. 'What's his boat look like?'

'It's a big Rotto Rooter. Just the sort of flash cabin cruiser you'd expect. Three decks, sixty foot at least. Not the biggest thing on the river, but getting there. Named it *Ellen*, after his daughter.'

Ford looked out across the river and saw the boat bobbing on its mooring.

'Is your man still watching it?'

'No, he's gone home. There was little chance of getting a quote from McCann before they went to press.'

'You running another story on him?'

'I'm stringing for the *Gazette* and for some papers over east who've shown an interest. McCann's office has called a press conference for tomorrow. His company is tanking, the share price is going to shit. He's been riding high on all the gossip about new gold discoveries, but now with the robbery the stock exchange has taken notice and asked him to explain the sudden fluctuations in his share price. It's putting the wind up the market and driving the price down and he needs to front up with that geo report.'

'I showed you the report in your kitchen.'

'Yeah, well, tomorrow everyone else will get to see it. You caught me on the way to the airport. I'm going to take a look at the Mariotti crime scene and then I'm on a plane to Perth to watch McCann do his used-car salesman routine at the press conference. The bastard's got to get off that boat sometime between now and then.'

'I can see his boat from where I'm sitting,' said Ford. 'It's all lit up. Someone's moving about on deck. Has Roth been seen with him?'

'I wouldn't know.'

'He's casting off. Looks like he's moving the boat. Maybe he's coming ashore. I need to go.'

'If you get a quote, let me know. This story could get me back in the game.'

'I'm glad someone's getting something positive out of this.'

Ford rode the Harley around the bay and stopped outside the gates to the yacht club. He took a slug from the Johnnie Walker, then got off the bike and walked through the gates and down past the clubhouse to the jetty, to watch the boat come in.

He could see McCann on the flybridge, his face lit from beneath. Lights glowed in the main cabin and below decks, but Ford couldn't see anybody else moving about. He looked around for cameras and guards, but if there was any security at the marina it was well hidden. His motorcycle boots thumped on the timbers as he walked onto the jetty, the sound mingling with the metallic snap of rigging against the masts and the steady slap of waves against the hulls. He walked out to the big pens at the far end of the jetty, where the cruisers were lined up with their bows pointing towards the city.

Finding a patch of shadow away from the light poles, he watched as McCann swung the boat around and brought the stern towards the jetty, the water roiling over the reversing propellers. McCann climbed down and shimmied along the rail to secure the bowlines, and when he came aft to tie up the stern, Ford stepped aboard holding the shotgun.

At the sound of Ford's boots on the deck McCann looked up, and stumbled backwards when he saw the gun. Ford raised a finger to his lips and waved McCann inside with the shotgun barrel. McCann backed himself into the cabin, Ford following closely, the shotgun pointed at the other man's gut. McCann stepped back towards the cream couch built along one side of the cabin and sat down heavily. Ford perched on the matching couch opposite, resting the gun across his knees, and they sat there looking at each other.

'Is Roth on board?' asked Ford.

'I haven't seen him since I left Kalgoorlie.'

'Where is he?'

'I don't know. I sent him after the Vipers.' McCann shifted in his seat, pulling at the open collar of his blue silk shirt. Ford took in the rope deck shoes and the white canvas pants rolled up above the man's bare ankles and wondered whether he had a peaked captain's hat somewhere. Then he heard the sound of somebody moving around in the cabin beneath him and stood up, clutching the gun. He moved to the front of the cabin, where a spiral stair disappeared below.

'Who's down there?' he said.

'Just my daughter,' said McCann.

'Get her to show herself.'

McCann called her name and a moment later the pale girl appeared on the staircase. Her black hair was pulled back from her face in a ponytail and she wore a tight black singlet that revealed the tattoos and scars down her thin arms. She looked at Ford with her big nervous eyes and then turned and disappeared below.

'If anyone else comes up that stair, I'm going to shoot them,' said Ford.

McCann sat twisting the gold rings on his fingers. 'Just do what you came here to do and leave my daughter out of it.'

Ford looked down at the shotgun and laughed. 'You think I'm here to kill you?'

McCann shrank back into the couch, plucking at the cuffs of the shirt, his eyes darting round the cabin. The second time he caught McCann glancing at the locker above the bar, Ford opened it and found the gun. It was a small .22 automatic, a stainless-steel Beretta not much bigger than Ford's palm. He sighted along the stubby barrel and the weight of it felt like a toy.

'You really need a matching handbag to go with this,' Ford said.

'Three days as an outlaw and you're Lee Marvin.'

'Scared, aren't you?'

'In Kalgoorlie you looked me in the eye and told me you had nothing to do with the robbery. I took you as a man of your word. Now you come here threatening me and my daughter and doing the Vipers' work for them.'

'I'm not doing anything for them or anyone else. I've stopped being everyone's chew toy. I'm trying to find my daughter.' Ford put the Beretta in one pocket and lowered the shotgun, then slid it into the long pocket of his coat. McCann spread his hands out on the table in front of him and Ford saw they were shaking. 'The shotgun was in case your bodyguard decided to play rough. What made you think it was for you?'

'The Vipers have been trying to squeeze me for months. They've threatened me personally and my business as well.'

'This got something to do with your daughter?'

McCann nodded, got up and walked over to the bar. 'You've been drinking already?' he asked.

'I have, as a matter of fact.'

'All day?'

'More like thirty years,' said Ford.

'It looks like I've got some catching up to do. Can I offer you something?' McCann waved his trembling hand in front of the decanters and carafes fixed in a rack on the bar.

'Not if it's that insipid lolly water from your winery down south. That shit is strictly for the tourists and the drive-through bottle-shop market. Whisky, if you have it.'

'I've got a couple of nice Islay malts.'

'I would have expected that. Kind of goes with the boat. Flashy and over the top. All mouth. You wouldn't have anything elegant and refined?'

McCann looked at Ford's biker boots and torn coat and raised an eyebrow. 'You don't like the boat?'

'Never saw the appeal myself. Just like a caravan, really, but with the possibility of drowning.'

McCann reached into the locker and pulled out a bottle of dark whisky. 'Springbank,' he said. 'Twenty-one years old. I laid down a cask in bond in Campbelltown when my daughter was born, and every few years I do my own private bottling.'

Ford smiled. 'Maybe I misjudged you.'

'You'll have to forgive my vulgar ostentation,' said McCann. 'I was born poor and impatient.' He handed Ford a tumbler and splashed a measure into it. Then he sat back down on the couch, swirling the whisky in his own glass and staring into it. 'I blame myself for letting Ellen drift away from me. After her mother died, she closed in on herself. She was in deep with that lowlife before I realised what was happening. You're a father: imagine if your daughter had taken up with a man called Ferret? I watched what she became and did nothing. It had gone too far before I acted.'

'I heard you put her in rehab.'

'I did. And I put the arsehole responsible in jail.'

'You did? Or did you get Chadwick to do it?'

McCann thought about that. 'How did you put that together?'

'When that lawyer didn't show up to the police station in Coolgardie, I figured you were helping Chadwick tie my noose. You were both trying to use me to get to them.'

McCann sighed. 'The Vipers wanted compensation. That guy who calls himself Little Jimmy came to me, talking about blood money for Ferret. He was talking about retribution, revenge, and a whole bunch of other bullshit he didn't understand, except that they all meant I had to give him money. The second time he visited he brought along this huge bastard with an ugly flat face like a cold pizza, told me the guy was a murderer and a psycho. This ape stands in my kitchen with a baseball bat, slapping it into his palm. Jimmy tells me he wants half a million or he'll let the bloke take off my toes with a boltcutter.'

'Did you give him money?'

'No. I don't give in to intimidation.'

'But you thought they'd sent me to kill you?'

'I got death threats on the weekend. They said the robbery showed how much they could hurt me.'

'So where's your bodyguard?'

'You asked me that. Like I said, he went off after Jimmy.'

'Why not get another?'

'No time. I put to sea instead. I've been hiding in deep water on the far side of Rottnest.'

Ford watched McCann for some indication of how much he knew about Roth and Mariotti. 'But now you're back. The newspapers are talking about your press conference tomorrow.'

McCann stood up, refilled his glass and stared out at the lights of the high-rise buildings. 'I've got my ring hanging out trying to keep my business afloat after all the shit that's happened this weekend.'

'And you blame the Vipers?'

McCann turned and looked at Ford. 'The damage goes way beyond the loss of the gold and the threats to my life. That marquee at the races was chock to the gills with top-drawer investors and I was too embarrassed to show my face.' He started fidgeting with the heavy rings on his fingers. 'I was going to show them the gold and then take them up to the mine to watch a gold pour, but now the place is a bloody crime scene.'

Ford frowned at him. 'People are casting doubt on the extent of your new discovery.'

'Just that bitch Alannah Doyle. The questions she asks, the story she's trying to write, it's a fucking outrage: heavy-handed and unnecessary. She's part of a well-oiled disinformation campaign, proliferating bare-faced lies based on unsubstantiated allegations from unnamed sources.' He filled Ford's glass, then drained his own and splashed more into it. 'We've had positive reports from mining and investment analysts. We gave them to her but she wouldn't publish them. All the rumours they've been spreading is just them trying to trash the share price so they can mop us up.'

'Who's they?'

'The silent voyeurs, the lurkers in the shadows. The bastards who're trying to short my stock, either for their own profit or for my rivals and enemies.' McCann looked out of the window at the black water of the Swan River. 'Beneath that glittering surface is a universe of gliding monsters,' he said, as if to himself.

'So why have you waited so long to release the geo report and get it independently verified?' asked Ford.

McCann turned and smiled. 'A touch of mystery is key to the show, mate. The big players buy the rumour and sell the fact.

You've got to tease them a bit, give them a bit of foreplay, and it's all the more pleasurable for them when they finally get you into bed. But now I've got a fucking speeding ticket from the stock exchange and they're making me go public.'

Ford toyed with the little automatic in his pocket. 'I've seen Walsh's report,' he said.

McCann hesitated, a flicker of surprise passing over his face before he controlled it. 'It's big, it's real and it's there,' he said, 'and now big money, smart money, is in the market, making a play for my company.'

'What'll you do?'

'I'm going to fend them off and then I'm going to burn the bastards.'

'Is Walsh going to be at the press conference?'

'He's in Indonesia, on one of those little islands you've never heard of.'

'So will Diane Bonner be attending in his place?'

McCann put down his glass and started twisting his wedding ring around his finger. 'The company never did any work with your ex-wife.'

'She's still my wife. It would be normal for her, as his partner, to peer-review his work.'

'You'll have to ask her.'

'I plan to, when I find her.'

'Walsh told me she was joining him up in the jungle. They were getting prospecting work from one of the big Canadian mobs.'

Ford thought about the laptop in the saddlebag and decided he needed to get home. 'So where are the core samples? Half would have been assayed by Walsh and the other half will be waiting for independent analysis, so you can do a full compliance for the stock market.'

'We'll get that sorted tomorrow. I've got my speech all written and the press release ready to go.' McCann stood tall, his eyes brightening. His back stiffened and he lifted his chin as if addressing a crowd. 'Gwardar is poised to make a rapid transition to being a significant gold producer. Exploration has upgraded the viability of the deposit and more mineralisation is awaiting confirmation. Naturally we have experienced the effects of the credit squeeze and the downturn of the property market. We have the confidence of our financiers and, once through this difficult period, we see a sound long-term future. The sensational reportage accorded in recent days to our company has created a lack of confidence. Traditionally, property companies are highly geared. Our company is more fortunate than some, in having a majority of long-term arrangements backed by sound investments. The value of the company does not properly reflect the market. We will be pursuing a sound strategy to develop the company into a middle-tier natural resource company as expeditiously as possible. We're looking at increased production on our own, rather than seeking a senior partner or allowing a takeover.'

'You can sit down,' said Ford, reaching for the bottle. 'You don't need to give me the sales patter, I'm not buying.'

'You're an employee. Your own shares stand to benefit from this.'

'I don't have any shares,' said Ford.

'Why not? I offered options to my staff.'

'I'm not your staff, I'm an independent contractor. Self-employed, and I never felt like contributing to the upkeep of this boat.'

'The company doesn't own this. It's owned by a trust in my daughter's name. It's not just named after her.'

'Whatever. I don't play the market. It's snakes and ladders.'

McCann finished his drink. 'But you play the horses?'

'At the track I only stand to lose what's in my pocket,' said Ford. 'If you don't stop this slide, you'll be bankrupt by the end of the week.'

'Failure is a function of risk,' said McCann. 'The higher you fly, the further you fall. But that will never happen. Too many banks have too much invested in me to let me go under. In the end, nobody fights profit. That's your problem, you play with your own money.'

'Or sometimes my bookie's money. I guess it's the same game, just a different scale.'

'The difference is that I generate wealth and create jobs. You should know—I paid your wages so you could sit on your bony arse out in the desert on a six-figure income. I'm one of the risk-takers in the engine room of this state's economy. You're just sitting on the upper deck catching a ride and enjoying the view.'

'That's another thing about boats,' said Ford 'You can't get off when you're bored, which is usually about ten minutes after casting off.'

But McCann seemed to have hit his stride. 'If it wasn't for the gold industry this state would barely exist. The big mining companies control this state, like the railway companies and the cattle barons used to bully the settlers in old Gary Cooper movies.'

'Didn't Gary Cooper wear a white hat? I don't see any good guys, just black hats all round. This place has got so twisted that the bikies are setting themselves up as the guardians of civil liberties.'

'You've been riding with them?' asked McCann, looking at Ford's boots. 'You've run all this way and now your back's to the ocean. You've run out of continent. I can call Chadwick and you can hand yourself in. I have some influence with him.'

'You said that in Kalgoorlie,' said Ford, picking up the whisky bottle and putting it in his pocket, the coat now hanging heavy on his shoulders. 'You'll forgive me if I don't take you up on that offer twice.' He walked to the end of the boat and made to step onto the jetty.

'You're taking my gun and my whisky?' said McCann.

'Consider it my severance package. I regret to say I will not be available for work tomorrow.'

'As soon as you step off this boat I'll be on the phone to Chadwick. You're playing for bigger stakes than you know. How long do you think you can keep running away?'

Ford stepped off the boat onto the jetty and pulled the coat around him against the sea breeze. 'I'm not running away from anything,' he said. 'I'm running towards something.'

THIRTY-ONE

The climb up the stairs left Ford breathless, and he rested against the door frame, panting, waiting for the thumping in his head to recede. He winced as he stretched his arm above the door, ran his hand along the ledge and found the spare key. His apartment was on the upper floor of a small two-storey block on the top of the ridge at Scarborough. He was three blocks back from the ocean, but high enough that in daylight he could see a stretch of blue ocean through a gap in the buildings on the other side of the street. The apartment block was a tired seventies development of salmon-pink brick and terracotta tiles. The streets around it were slowly being filled with modern condo blocks that Ford detested. His tatty block had so far resisted the tide of new money, and the rent was within his reach. There were no lights showing in the other apartments, and the street was deserted of traffic. He figured it was close to midnight.

He stabbed the key into the lock but it resisted going in. When he stooped to see what the problem was, he saw that the wood around the lock and down the frame was split. Kavanagh had told him that the police had been through his apartment, but he'd presumed they would have brought a locksmith.

Perhaps they'd been in a hurry. He pushed at the door but it was locked.

With some jiggling the key pushed home, and he turned it. His shoulder to the door, the laptop under his arm, he pushed it open, wondering if there was anything cold in the fridge. He didn't bother to turn on the lights, just made the familiar right turn into the kitchenette and three steps to the fridge. He opened the door and light spilled out.

The smell that escaped with it wasn't encouraging. He tried to remember how long it had been since he'd been home. He was usually smart enough to ditch the milk and toss anything green before leaving for his roster on site.

When he saw two beers lurking at the back of the shelf he smiled and clapped his hands. He grabbed them both and opened one on the edge of the door. He took a long pull. The only other item in the fridge was a cloudy plastic container, probably containing leftover takeaway. He thought it likely to be Chinese. Whatever it was, it was the source of the smell and he didn't feel like tackling it.

He left the fridge door open and turned around to check the apartment in the faint light. He didn't own much, but what he did was scattered around the floor, tossed among the stuffing from the couch. He was thinking about whether the police were really that careless, or whether this was just a little fuck-you from them, when he saw the silhouettes of the two men reclining casually on the ripped sofa. They both stood up.

'Sorry, fellas, there's only one beer left,' said Ford. 'You'll have to fight over it.'

He swung the fridge door shut and took two steps in the darkness towards the door before the main light in the room came on. As he turned to face the two men he saw they both had guns. He thought about McCann's automatic in the bottom of his pocket and regretted leaving the shotgun in the saddlebag.

'Hello, Jimmy,' he said.

He didn't know the other man's name but recognised him as the man driving the green Falcon. He wondered if the gun in the guy's hand was the same one he'd used outside Kalgoorlie police station. His hair was the same, slicked back in some rockabilly quiff, and for the first time Ford noticed thick black sideburns. He was wearing the blue boilersuit Ford recalled from the security video at the club but the chequer-board baseball cap had gone.

The man smiled, and Ford saw the glint of a gold tooth. 'Mr Ford, you keep bobbing up like a turd that won't flush,' he said.

Ford recognised the voice now, remembered the Australian accent, less broad than he was used to hearing in Kalgoorlie. He wondered if he was military too, maybe an officer. He tried to recall him in the gold room, in the red hard hat and with the stopwatch, barking orders into the radio, and remembered the man's breath in his ear, his gun to Ford's head while his face was against the cold concrete. This was the fourth man.

Ford finished the beer, watching both men over the top of the bottle. 'Where's Roth?' he asked, wiping his mouth on the back of his sleeve. Neither of them answered. 'Do you have a name I can use?' he said to the man in blue. 'It's the fourth time we've met, but you've never introduced yourself.'

'His name is Carlson,' said Jimmy, grinning. The man looked at him sideways in disbelief. 'Chill out, mate, it's not like it's your real name, I know that.' Carlson turned back to Ford and shrugged.

'You seen Roth today, Jimmy?' asked Ford. He let his hand drop off the counter and reached into his pocket. Carlson watched Ford's hand move, shook his head and smiled, and Ford brought the hand out again, showing him the pack of cigarettes. He tapped one out and went back to the pocket for his lighter. Holding it to the cigarette, he flicked it once, calm, showing that he had it all together. He took the smoke deep and held it until his lungs strained, then put the lighter back into his pocket and let his hand rest on the Beretta.

Ford looked at the guns facing him. Carlson had the Makarov he'd seen the wrong end of already. Jimmy had an untidy old police revolver, a .38 Smith & Wesson with the wooden grip long gone and wrapped in duct tape. The sights had been filed off, no doubt the serial number too. Ford pointed to it with his cigarette. 'Didn't they give you one of their nice Russian guns, Jimmy?'

Jimmy didn't reply. He stood there pointing the gun as though he wasn't sure what to do next; he was clearly waiting for Carlson to take the lead.

Ford tried again. 'What about your mates Crock and Pan-head, you seen them today?' That got Carlson's attention. He was staring at Ford, unsmiling. 'What did they promise you, Jimmy?' said Ford, warming to it now. 'Guns and drugs and gold? Is that what you sold your club out for?'

Jimmy shook his head and laughed, but it sounded forced. 'You think you got it worked out, dude? You're so blind to what's happening, it's fun to watch you stumbling along.'

Carlson exhaled and dropped his gun. 'Put your gun down, Jimmy,' he said. 'Let's have a drink.' He unzipped his boilersuit and slipped his gun into a shoulder holster, leaving the zip undone. Jimmy stuck his revolver into the back of his pants, try-ing to look relaxed. Carlson walked around the counter into the kitchen, and Ford tensed as he walked behind him and picked up the second beer.

Carlson opened it on the fridge door and took a swig. 'I think he's trying to rile you, Jimmy,' he said. 'Play you off against me. Trying to drag this out a bit. It's a lame move.'

Jimmy grinned, putting a hand inside his shirt to scratch at the tattoo across his chest. 'Yeah, well, if I wanted to get filthy with you, I'd be getting pissed off that you just swiped the last beer.'

'Too slow, mate. It's the quick or the dead,' said Carlson, between swigs.

Without turning around, Ford listened to the man breathing behind him, watched Jimmy's eyes following him. When he knew Carlson was behind him again, he said, 'I saw Crock just a few hours ago. Tied to a chair in your clubhouse. Tortured and shot. I watched security video of Roth and Carlson in the clubhouse. They left gold there. They're setting you up for a fall, just like they did to me. We're part of a long conga line of patsies, Jimmy.'

Ford heard Carlson's breathing change behind him. He tried to keep his eyes focused on Jimmy's face, watching his expression slowly change as he put things together.

Jimmy's eyes narrowed and he went into a crouch, his arm reaching behind him, but Carlson's arm was already up and over Ford's shoulder, and his gun roared twice close to Ford's ear. The little man fell spinning, his arm still twisted, slumping backwards into the couch with two holes in his chest.

Ford's ears were ringing as Carlson walked around the counter and over to where Jimmy lay. He saw Carlson's lips move, but whatever he said was lost to Ford because of the din in his head. Carlson leaned over Jimmy, looked into his face and nodded. Ford took a step towards the door, but Carlson casually raised his gun and waved him back into the kitchen. The ringing in Ford's head decreased, and was replaced by the rasp of his own breathing.

When Carlson stood upright he was holding Jimmy's Smith & Wesson, his finger through the trigger guard, swinging it upside down in front of his face. 'What a piece of shit,' Ford heard him say, and wasn't sure if it was for his benefit. Carlson twirled the gun around his finger, caught the handle and cocked the hammer, and in one smooth movement extended his arm and shot Ford once in the chest.

The impact knocked the breath out of him. He tried to take a step back but his leg gave way and he stumbled and fell, hitting his head on the edge of the sink as he went down.

His breath came back to him as he was lying on his side on the narrow strip of lino behind the counter. His chest felt like it was full of broken glass, but he knew that the vest had stopped the bullet. There was a sharp pain below his heart where a rib must have been broken. His hand was still on the automatic. He wrenched it out of his pocket, his thumb finding the safety, and sighted along the barrel, waiting for Carlson's face to show above the counter. Nothing happened. Forcing himself to stay still and make no sound, he fought the pain and held his breath and listened.

He heard the electronic tones as Carlson used his phone, and the apartment was quiet enough for him to hear the purr of the ringing at the other end. It stopped ringing and Carlson spoke. 'Complete . . . Yes . . . Sixty minutes? Roger that.' The call ended with a beep and Ford held his arm level, tried to keep his breathing shallow and steady.

Carlson stepped around the edge of the counter. As Ford pulled the trigger he watched the man's eyes widen in surprise above the sights of the Beretta. The shot caught Carlson in the temple and knocked his head back. His eyes rolled but then focused back on Ford, and he lifted his hand to reach inside his overalls.

Ford fired again, and the second shot went through Carlson's left eye. He fell backwards, his free arm flailing. He hit the wall and slid down it, coming to rest in a seated position, one hand still on the holster.

THIRTY-TWO

Ford lay on his back on the kitchen floor, his cheek resting against the cold lino, trying to keep his breathing shallow until the pain in his chest subsided. He was alone, abandoned, lost and cold; especially cold. It was a glacial deadness that seemed to lie at his very core. He clung to it. He had built himself around it.

He unbuttoned the coat, snaked a hand up under the vest and ran his fingers over his ribs, yelling out when he located the broken rib. He could feel the lump of the bullet embedded in the vest. Running a finger over the outside of the vest, he found the hole in the fabric and winced as loose Kevlar fibres pierced his fingertips. His mind turned to the sound of the gunshots, and how long it might take the police to respond. He reached up, took hold of the edge of the sink and pulled himself upright, struggling to find his balance.

He looked at Carlson. A trail of blood ran from the man's left eye, soaking into the collar of his overalls. His right eye was still open and staring straight at Ford. There was a smaller trickle of blood running down from the hole in his temple. Ford looked around the back of his head but neither bullet had passed through and the wall behind was unmarked. Carlson still held the phone in his hand. Ford took it and checked the screen, scrolling to find the last number dialled, then put it in his pocket.

Ford looked at Jimmy slumped sideways on the couch and thought he might be able to complete the scene that Carlson had presumably been intending to create. Pushing Carlson forward, he got his hands under his armpits and lifted him, gritting his teeth against the pain in his rib and shoulder, his head spinning. He moved the body a few steps and dumped it on the floor, facing the couch. He got the Makarov from the holster and put it in Carlson's hand, the fingers still pliant. The Beretta he wiped down and placed in Jimmy's hand. To make the scene more convincing he'd have to ensure there was gunshot residue, but for that he'd have to make Jimmy fire the gun, and he didn't want to risk more noise.

He picked up the old black revolver and broke the cylinder. There were only two bullets in it besides the spent casing. He thought about looking for more ammunition in Jimmy's pockets and taking the gun with him, but he doubted it was very accurate or reliable. He wiped the handle and stuck it down the back of Jimmy's pants again. Stopping to gaze at the tableau he'd created, he knew it was unlikely to fool anyone.

In the bedroom, he picked up the backpack that held his laptop. He stuffed Diane's laptop in next to it and slung it over his shoulder. He considered his fingerprints, but it was his flat and only his prints on the beer bottles needed to be removed. Back in the kitchen, he picked up the bottle that Carlson had opened. It was half full, so he reached into his pocket and felt around in the lining for some of Doc's pills. He unearthed a few white tablets, the bullet he'd taken from the soldier, and the memory stick from Diane's laptop.

He swallowed all of the pills and washed them down with the rest of Carlson's beer, then put the empties in the backpack.

For a whole minute he stood at the counter, looking at the two bodies. Finally he turned and went to the door. After checking that the landing was clear, he limped down the stairs to where he had left the Harley.

He transferred the shotgun and the whisky from the saddlebags to the backpack and was about to get on the Harley when it occurred to him that anyone in the building would have heard the bike arrive; if they had since heard the shots they would certainly notice it leaving. He left it and headed around the back of the block. The green Falcon was parked opposite under the shadow of a tree and he cursed himself for not seeing it when he arrived. He crossed the small parking area to the low roof beneath the peppermint tree. There was a rack of bicycles, and his Vespa. He rocked it off its stand and pushed it out into the car park. The key was where he always left it, in the ignition under the seat: he never worried about it being taken as he'd never met anyone else who could start it.

Ford turned on the fuel tap under the seat, pulled out the choke, and rocked it off its stand. He walked it out into the street, keeping under the trees and away from the streetlights. He gave it a push and stepped on, freewheeling down the hill towards the beach until he was far enough away not to be heard, then he put it in gear and let out the clutch. He heard a telltale rattle in the motor, then it caught, turned over a few times, and started to die. He feathered the throttle till it caught again, and then opened it right up, smiling as it rasped into life and blew a cloud of smoke. His Super Sport was as old as him, but better for being run regularly since he'd got rid of the car. He waited till it stopped blowing smoke, then pushed in the choke, turned on the lights, and twisted the throttle as far as it would go. As the motor started to purr smoothly he felt himself slipping the bonds of normal life, experiencing the same rush he'd had when he was a teenager on his first ride.

Down at Scarborough Beach he parked the Vespa outside a late-night café on the beach-front. He walked inside and chose a table in good light. As he sat down with the backpack he tried to attract the attention of the skinny girl behind the counter, but she gave him a look that told him it was counter service only and then went back to finding the split ends in her streaked hair. Realising he had no money anyway, Ford turned his attention to the computers. He opened both laptops and stitched them together with a blue network cable, and while they booted up he drew out Carlson's phone and wrote down the last number dialled. He rang directory enquiries and got put through to the night desk at police headquarters in Beaufort Street, where he was patched through to Kavanagh.

'Ford,' she said, sounding weary, 'where are you?'

He was surprised by how pleased he was to hear her voice. 'I'm in Scarborough. I have a phone number that I think belongs to Roth, a different phone from the one he used before. It was called from this phone maybe twenty minutes ago.'

'What happened to you?'

'Long story. I need you to locate the number. Can you do that? Some sort of cell-site location?'

'I can. Might take a little while. Are you at your apartment?'

'No, I'm in a coffee shop.'

'You got anything else you want to tell me?'

'No, not now.'

She went quiet for a moment, then said, 'Give me the number.'

He read it out to her. 'I think this is my last chance. I think they're cleaning shop and then moving out.'

'I got the lab results from that gold,' she said. 'It's from the mine.'

'I didn't expect anything different. It's not important now. Please hurry with that number.'

He ended the call and turned to the computer screens. He opened up a routine on his own machine and used that to break the security on Diane's. Once he was in, he found that her hard drive had been partitioned into several blocks, each with its own encryption. He wondered when Diane had got so picky about security. He broke each in turn, but the drive was empty. The whole hard drive had been wiped. He then plugged in the memory stick, but that was blank too.

He was thinking about that when the phone rang. It was Kavanagh.

'Where is he?' said Ford.

'The call was to a prepaid mobile phone, no owner, located on a street behind Perth domestic airport, out at the north end of the runway.'

'What's there?'

'All those charter airlines are based out there,' she said. 'Those little outfits that fly to the remote mines.'

'Quit stalling. McCann parks his plane out there, doesn't he?'

'He's got his own hangar.'

'Is that where Roth is?'

'The cell site wasn't accurate enough.'

'The plane they used in the robbery, maybe that's where it went? Give me the address.'

Kavanagh paused. He could hear muffled voices in the background. 'You can't go out there, Ford,' she said.

'Then try and get there before me.'

'Listen, I can't send back-up. I don't have that authority and Chadwick is insisting everything goes through him.'

'Where is he?'

'I don't know, but he's got his sidekick, Butcher, keeping a close eye on me.'

'If you can't send back-up, can you at least stop any planes taking off from McCann's hangar?'

'Unlikely.'

'If the police won't act, then I will,' said Ford. 'I've checked Diane's computer. It's been wiped. I'm beginning to think this is more about her than it is about me. McCann seems very jumpy about releasing the geo report on his mine. I think Diane might have found something. I'm going to find her.'

'Let me handle it,' said Kavanagh. 'Your luck's just about run out.'

Ford looked across to see if the waitress was watching, then tucked the phone under his chin and took the shotgun out of the backpack and broke it open. He checked the cartridges and snapped the gun shut. 'I think I left some part of me behind in the bush,' he said. 'Something that got burned in that van. If I'd died today, nobody would've ever known if I was just a fuckup or whether I still had a chance of salvation.'

Kavanagh began to speak, but Ford ended the connection and turned off the phone.

THIRTY-THREE

He enjoyed the wind in his face as he rode, squeezing tears from his eyes, ruffling his hair, dragging the long coat tails out behind him. He had left the helmet behind on the Harley and he felt good about that. The roads were quiet, just him on his Vespa under the yellow sodium lights, weaving through the few cars on the highway. He joined the freeway and jammed the throttle wide open through the tunnel, listening to the rasp of the engine echo off the walls. For a few moments he forgot where he was going and enjoyed the feeling of being alone and free. He sat as far back as he could, dropped his chin low behind the handlebars and pulled out to overtake a truck.

Great Eastern Highway was deserted and he was soon on the dark slip road that skirted the northern end of the airport, passing the long-stay car parks and the small hangar terminals of the charter airlines. Most of the buildings were dark, the runway apron full of small jets and turboprops parked up for the night. He followed the road around to the last hangar, the orange Gwardar and Glycon logos lit up on the side. From the street he could see light spilling onto the runway from the open aircraft doors on the far side, moths floating in the glow, the air full of the whine of jet engines.

There was a glass doorway at the front of the building, and outside it four cars were parked in a row under a single street-light. He stood the Vespa beside them and looked them over, wondering how many people would be inside the hangar, and wishing he had brought the revolver. He took the shotgun from the bag and checked again that it was loaded. The spare shells he put in the left pocket of the coat. Then he ripped the seams of the right pocket and put his hand through it, holding the shotgun vertically along his leg under the coat. He left the coat unbuttoned and the vest visible.

There was light showing in the east now, Venus hanging bright above the silhouette of the hills beyond the airport, and he thought back to when he'd last watched the dawn over the desert from the mine. He fought to stop his mind from wandering, forced himself back to the moment, and was angry with himself for losing the straight line, even for a moment.

He walked to the door and took a deep breath. Closing his eyes, he focused on the pain in his chest, the throb of the bullet wound in his shoulder, the sting of the pellet hole in his leg, and tried to summon up whatever strength he had left. He became aware of something else deep within him alongside the pain, as if he had swallowed something hard. It was rage. He felt it glowing inside him, shining like a nugget. The anger was all that was keeping him going: without that, his body was dull with fear and pain and fatigue.

His hand clenched around the shotgun, and he pulled back both hammers with his thumb and pushed open the door. He found himself in a small reception room, the desk in front of the company logo empty, with no sign that it had ever been occupied. In the far wall was a second door. As he reached for the handle his hand was shaking. He didn't think it was nerves, just fatigue combined with the anger working its way to the surface. He paused with his hand on the door, thinking about the last conversation he'd had with Kavanagh, and hoping she would come; then the pitch of the jet engines changed and he opened the door.

The smell of jet fuel hit him as he stepped out into the empty, brightly lit hangar. The far side was open to the runway, the tall doors pulled back flush against the side walls, the Learjet parked out on the apron in a pool of light.

The hangar echoed with the whine of idling engines, and the small group of people standing by the plane's wing tip hadn't noticed Ford come in, but Grace turned to look at him and smiled as if she'd known all along that he would be there. She tugged at her mother's hand and Diane looked down at her, then followed her gaze to where Ford was limping towards them. He saw McCann and Ellen, but Roth wasn't with them. Looking around, trying to spot the bodyguard, he saw the pilot in the cockpit, his face lit from beneath, his head tilted upwards to the banks of switches. Ford wondered whether it was the same pilot who had flown the gold out. Beside the cockpit the door to the plane gaped open, split in two like jaws, the bottom half lowered to form steps.

Grace was still smiling. She wore a cotton summer dress with a blue cornflower pattern, her blonde hair loose. She brushed it away from her face and gave Ford the smallest of waves with her fingers. Her mother tightened her grip on her other hand. Diane wasn't smiling. She wore a tailored pinstriped blazer, a navy-blue pencil skirt and tall black boots. Her hair was pulled back in a ponytail and shone like burnished copper. Her make-up looked smart and fresh. The effect was of an efficient professional. She didn't look like a hostage.

Ford looked down at his own clothing, thick with dust and dirt, torn, stained with blood, and realised he'd been the hostage all along. He'd thought he was free, but he'd simply been running from one open cage to another.

McCann now noticed him and soon all four had turned to face him. Ford walked to where he thought he would be heard above the engines and then stopped. 'All this time I've been looking for you,' he said to Diane, 'and you didn't want to be found.'

Her face was blank. Ford caught her looking to his right and turned to see Roth and Chadwick step through a side door into the hangar. Roth quickly started walking towards Ford, his hand going to unzip his blue boilersuit.

Ford put up a palm to stop him and was surprised when Roth hesitated. He looked back at Diane. 'Were you on the boat last night? Was I ten feet from my daughter and you kept her from me?'

Diane stepped in front of Grace, shielding her. 'You amaze me, Gareth,' she said, 'the lengths you will go to in order to accomplish your own destruction.'

'Where's Walsh?'

She shook her head. 'In Indonesia.'

'You wrote that report,' he said. She didn't say anything. 'Where are the drill samples? Did you salt them? What happens when they get independently assayed? Will Walsh take the fall for that? Is he another patsy in your long daisy chain?'

Diane glanced at McCann before she answered. She looked down at the floor when she spoke. 'You shouldn't have come here.'

'Is anyone going to be able to find Walsh?'

'I told you, he's in Indonesia, prospecting.'

'Is that where you're going?'

Roth took a step closer to Ford. 'You need to move away from them,' he said, his hand reaching inside the boilersuit.

'And you need to keep your hands where I can see them,' said Ford. He noticed that Chadwick was edging sideways, away from

Roth. The policeman was wearing the same old grey suit as in Coolgardie, his tie loosened at the neck, his shirt collar undone, his hair untidy. Ford knew what they were doing, spreading out as they came for him, making it difficult for him to cover them both, hoping to catch him in a crossfire. They were about thirty metres away to his right, and Grace was twenty metres in front of him by the plane. The pilot was looking out of the cockpit now, watching what was happening.

Ford turned his body towards Roth and thought about showing him the shotgun, but decided it would be better to let him think he had the advantage, and he had some more things to say first. 'I didn't put everything together until I walked through that door and saw you all here.' He spoke to Diane over his shoulder, his eyes still on Roth. 'It was an idea lurking around in the back of my mind, but I guess I didn't want to look straight at it.'

Diane's eyes were wide, her cheeks flushed. 'They didn't tell me about the robbery.'

'But you let it happen. You were happy to let me disappear. Is it different now, when I'm standing in front of you, under these lights? Standing in front of our daughter? Was it easier when it was just some mercenary doing it for you out in the desert, some barren place over the horizon? Was it an abstract concept then?'

Diane's eyes showed tears. 'No, it wasn't like that.' Her voice was barely audible.

He heard Chadwick breathing heavily on his other side and wondered whether he had a gun too. McCann had put an arm around Ellen, who looked scared; now he put his other arm around Diane, and began walking them towards the stairs to the Learjet. Diane kept a firm grip on Grace's hand.

'So what went wrong?' said Ford, loud enough to make McCann turn and scowl at him. 'You salt the drill cores, then salt the internet with rumours of your big find, let the stock market get greedy, set up Walsh to take the fall, but then it gets out of hand. You went too high too fast, flew too close to the sun. The stock market takes an interest in unexplained price fluctuations, trims your wings. Then the big boys start sniffing around, buying up stock, talking of takeovers, and they want to see the samples. They want their own geologists to assay the drill cores, want to put their own drill rigs out there. You need to cool things off. Lucky for you the Vipers are around. They've already threatened you. Maybe you get Roth to offer them something they want, then rob your own gold. The market gets a nosebleed from going so high so fast, and when it starts to fall, you short sell your own stock and make as much on the way down as on the way up. Now you're leaving the country. What's the angle there? You going to claim you're running scared from the Vipers? Where's the gold, McCann? Is it on that plane?'

'There's no gold here,' said Roth. 'You need to go ask those biker buddies of yours.'

'Where did you take it? Is it out of the country already? Lost in transit somewhere between here and Afghanistan?'

Chadwick's voice came from behind him. 'You've got nothing, Ford. You're talking to yourself. No proof of anything.'

'So what did you get, Chadwick? A reason to stamp on the Vipers once and for all?'

'Why are you here?' asked Chadwick. 'There's nothing you can do to change this. Look around. You're on your own. I'm amazed you got this far. You've got nothing going for you except dumb luck.'

'Yeah,' said Ford, 'but that counts too.' He looked quickly from Chadwick to Roth and back again.

'Just put your hands in the air and we'll end this here,' Chadwick said.

Ford shook his head. 'You remember when you were a kid, and you'd be running down a hill that was just a bit too steep for you? You're going too fast to stop, and you might fall over at any minute. You keep taking longer strides, but you know you'll trip and fall soon enough. You think about throwing yourself to the ground, trying to roll, but you know it'll hurt. The longer you put it off, the faster you'll be going, the more it's going to hurt, and you think maybe your legs will hold out till the bottom. Momentum is all I've got. It's the only thing kept me going. You can keep your gold. I don't care where you've hidden the profits from your little pump-and-dump scheme. You can all fuck off to some tax haven and cash in your trust funds and your numbered bank accounts.'

Grace stepped out from behind her mother. Ford looked at her and smiled. The look of love and trust in her eyes was the one last true thing left to him.

Catching sight of movement, he turned to see Roth stepping towards him, only ten metres away now, his hand on his shoulder holster. Ford gripped the shotgun and his finger found the triggers.

'You keep moving towards your gun and I'm going to shoot you.' Ford swung open his coat and raised the shotgun. Jamming the heel of it into the hollow of his hip he took a step back to brace himself.

Roth stopped and grinned, shaking his head. He took another step forward and pulled the pistol free of the holster, but before he could raise it Ford shot him.

The spray from the shotgun caught Roth across the right arm and shoulder. The hand holding the gun went limp and dropped, blood dripping down the fingers. Roth took a step backwards, looking at his useless arm as though he couldn't believe he'd let himself get shot. He glared at Ford and muttered something in Afrikaans, then transferred the gun to his left hand.

Before he could raise it Ford shot him again. The second barrel hit him across the chest and left shoulder, and Roth slumped to one knee. He managed to raise the gun and fire one round wildly into the air before he fell sideways onto the concrete, his eyes still staring at Ford.

The roar of the shotgun still echoed around the bare walls of the hangar. As it faded, Ford heard the scream. Grace had broken free of her mother's hand and was running towards him. Diane took two steps after her, but the look Ford gave her made her stop.

Grace's hair streamed behind her as she ran, her face filled with such terror that Ford wanted to close his eyes. Instead he dropped to one knee, held his arms open wide and she ran into him with such force that it almost knocked the wind out of him. He wrapped his arms around her, pulled her to him and buried his face in her hair, inhaling the smell of her until the pain in his ribs made him sob. He looked into her face and kissed away her tears.

He heard the sound of a gun being racked. Looking up, he saw Chadwick standing over Roth, gazing down at him as if trying to work out how long he might have before he bled out. The police Glock in his hand was pointed at Ford. 'Let the girl go,' he said calmly.

Ford looked at the empty shotgun in his hand. He dropped it but didn't release his grip on his daughter. He whispered in her ear, trying to stop her crying, telling her softly that it was all over now.

Chadwick raised his voice. 'This isn't how it ends, Ford. These people are getting on that plane and leaving. Let the girl go and come with me. You've no justification for detaining these people. You've got nothing.'

'He's got me,' said Kavanagh. She was walking across the hangar towards Chadwick with her gun drawn.

Chadwick looked from her to Ford and back again, his face in a snarl, weighing up his options, and turned his gun towards her. 'Detective Constable Kavanagh,' he said. 'We did all wonder what happened to you. I thought I had that little prick Butcher shadowing you but he continues to be a disappointment to me.' He looked behind her, seeing if she had back-up, smiling when he saw she was alone. 'Ford might have you, but what have you got?'

Kavanagh nodded towards Roth on the ground. 'I can link the gun in his hand to two murders and maybe to the robbery.'

'Well, let's just consider this man to be under arrest,' said Chadwick, grinning as though he'd discovered a way out. 'I think he'll live. If we can get an ambulance here quickly, I might just have an arrest to show for all this. So put your gun down and we might be able to salvage the situation.'

Ford straightened up slowly, his daughter's arms clamped around his neck, her legs wrapped around his middle, squeezing herself against the breastplate in his vest. 'My daughter stays here,' he said, looking at Diane. She was still at the bottom of the steps to the plane, hesitant, tears streaking her face. 'I don't care about McCann,' said Ford. 'Whatever he cooked up, it doesn't affect me anymore. My family stays here.'

McCann took Ellen by the hand and guided her up the stairs. She paused at the top, her face as blank and remote as the first time Ford had seen her at the races, then stepped inside the plane. McCann walked slowly back down the stairs, then stepped behind Diane and grasped her arms, his fingers digging into the material of her suit, and turned her towards the plane. She resisted at first, but then her head dropped and she allowed him to push her up the steps.

Kavanagh stood with her feet apart, both hands on her gun, sighting down the barrel at Chadwick. He seemed more relaxed, but his gun stayed trained on her. 'Just let them go,' he said. 'You've done all you could.'

Ford looked at Diane again, standing with McCann in the doorway, saw the distress in her eyes, the tears stained with mascara. 'So you can cry,' he said. 'I thought you were all dried up. You can stay here, or you can get on that plane. You've got that choice right now. For the last four days, nobody gave me much of any kind of choice.'

He held his daughter close, kept her head pressed into the hollow of his neck, not daring to let her look at her mother. McCann had both his hands on Diane's shoulders now. He turned her away from the door and guided her inside the plane. The door closed and the engine noise rose.

Ford watched the plane pull away, his lips close to Grace's ear. He didn't know what to say so he just hummed to her, bouncing on his knees and swaying from side to side, rocking her as he used to do when she was a newborn. She leaned away from him and he tried to look into her eyes and smile for her, but his eyes were misted with tears. All he could see of her was the bright golden halo of her hair, lit from behind by the runway lights. He felt her fingers reaching around his neck and pulling the chain free of his shirt.

Ford heard the rush of the jets as the plane accelerated away down the runway. As it faded, the roar of motorcycle engines filled the hangar.

Kavanagh smiled. 'Sounds like my back-up has arrived.'

THIRTY-FOUR

Ford lay on his back on the sand, feeling the sun on his face, the water lapping around his chest. He ran his fingers over the scar on his shoulder, the skin puckered around the bullet hole, red and angry. He splashed water over it, letting the salt water heal him, the sun purify him. He sat up and brushed the wet sand off his chest.

Grace was swimming in the calm water near the beach, sheltered from the waves breaking beyond her on the reef. She was staying within her depth, waiting for him to watch how her stroke had improved.

The roar of a motorcycle made him flinch instinctively, and he turned towards the road running along the top of the cliff. He recognised Kavanagh's Ducati by the racing colours on her helmet. She parked it on the kerb next to his Vespa, the two red bikes side by side, and took off her helmet, running a hand through her short blonde hair to slick it back into place. He watched her walk down the stone steps to the beach. Her only concession to the summer heat was to ride without her jacket. She wore the black leather pants he knew well, and another tight white T-shirt that showed off the pallor of her skin. She frowned at her boots as she stepped onto the sand, and her expression didn't change when she saw Ford.

He stood to meet her, held his arms out wide to embrace her, but she looked at him dripping sand and salt and shook her head. She took a slim envelope from her back pocket, unfolded it and tried to smooth out the creases.

'I asked them to let me deliver this to you personally,' she said. 'I reckoned you'd have had enough faceless cops and lawyers by now.'

Ford picked up his towel and wrapped it around himself. He started walking up the beach towards the benches in the shade, and waved to Grace as he sat down. He looked at the envelope, wiped his hands, and took it.

'It's a summons,' Kavanagh said. 'Coronial inquiry. Court date's next month.'

'No trial?' he asked, putting the unopened envelope in his beach bag.

'They're still investigating. Depends on whether Roth recovers enough to stand trial. There's still not a lot of evidence against him. The gun didn't match: he was smart enough to ditch the dirty one. No real eyewitnesses. The frame against Little Jimmy might hold together and they'll just pin it all on the dead.' She looked at the scars on Ford's shoulder and leg. 'How are you healing?'

'Well enough. Doc didn't do too bad a job, and the doctors fixed up most of it.' He spread his fingers, only the slightest tremor to them. 'Been off the booze since I left hospital. I should be off the painkillers soon.'

'How's Grace?' Kavanagh put her hand to her forehead to shield her eyes and watched the girl striking out into deeper water towards the reef.

'She's finding it difficult. I think she understands, but she's still sleeping with me.'

'You sleeping alright?'

'Not so much. I hold her until she's asleep and then I wander around the house all night. Been watching a lot of late-night television, and that's not good for anyone.'

'Any problems with the house?'

'Should there be? It's still in my name. I've been paying the mortgage since I bought it. I haven't heard Diane asking for her share. The only part that's all hers is the wallpaper and the bedspread, and she can come claim them whenever she likes.'

'They reckon she's in Macau with McCann. His lawyer occasionally gets in touch with the department to offer excuses as to why he won't be coming back into the country any time soon. He says McCann still fears for his life. As long as there are Vipers out there, he's not coming home. Walsh is missing and McCann's lawyer continues to insist he orchestrated the fraud and that McCann won't come home till Walsh is brought to justice.'

'You reckon Walsh's corpse is rotting somewhere in the Indonesian jungle?'

'Who knows. It's not like we'll be sending officers to Macau or Indonesia to look.'

'Lots of good horseracing in Macau,' said Ford.

'Lots of opportunity to launder his money, too,' she said. 'The local outfits run those chip scams at the casinos, wash your money for you. If you're a rich player, the Macau government isn't in too much of a hurry to talk about extradition.'

'When you've got as much money as he does, you can buy yourself a whole new life.'

'But only if you know where to shop,' she said.

'Did they find any of his money?'

'The receivers appointed a trustee and recovered whatever assets the business held, but most of McCann's own money was hidden away. Alannah's been doing some digging, trying to make a story out of it. All the trading he did in his own shares was through offshore constructs, nominee companies and trusts in Labuan, Macau, the Bahamas. The trail went cold in Liechtenstein, and neither the receivers nor Alannah's paper had the money to send anyone there. When McCann's daughter was in rehab she signed over power of attorney to him, and he set up a number of trusts in her name. His houses, boats, and a whole heap of cash were parked there. Some of it is in Diane's name.'

'We got a visit from some men in suits,' said Ford. 'Accountants, I think, maybe lawyers. Not sure who they worked for, but they found a trust in Grace's name. They said it was too small to make it worth their while trying to recover through the courts. Nearly a million, they said. I don't know what kind of world they live in, where that's considered small.'

'Current estimates are that McCann made over a hundred million trading his own shares.'

'Not bad for a weekend's work. I guess my conscience won't be troubled by Grace getting a piece. They say we can live on the interest until she comes of age.'

'So what does trouble your conscience? What's keeping you up at night?'

'I worry about what I've done to Grace, taking her away from her mother. And I feel bad about Doc losing his club.'

'I hear they still ride together.'

'Maybe, but he lost his clubhouse, they outlawed his club.'

'They always called themselves outlaws. Now they got their wish. Those Vipers who escaped jail after the raids have mostly gone over to other clubs. Doc's still got a group of old-timers he rides with. Just him and Banjo and a few old veterans. He talks of forming a new club, though I think that's mostly just to yank the Gang Squad's chain. A club is the people. The rest is just window dressing.'

'You riding with them?' asked Ford. 'A band of martyrs together?'

'I'm no martyr. I'm enjoying the time off.'

'Working on your tan?'

She smiled for the first time. 'They're rushing through my disciplinary hearing. I should be back on duty before the inquest.'

'Is Chadwick going to testify on your behalf?'

'That was the deal. We let him arrest Roth and keep quiet about his involvement with McCann, and he forgets about you and me and Doc and Banjo.'

'Didn't save me from hours of questioning, though. What if Roth decides to speak?'

'Chadwick seems confident he won't.'

'Chadwick's not the sort to leave any loose ends.'

'Like me and you?'

Ford watched Grace come out of the water and bend down to pick up a shell from the sand. 'I doubt Chadwick's got any problem with me,' he said. 'He made that bogus statement disappear. I'd have thought he might still have unfinished business with you, especially if they find those bodies in the bush.'

'Doc took care of that. Sent some of his boys out into the bush to find those dirt bikes and dig up the bodies. They'll have ended up down a disused mine shaft somewhere.'

Grace came running up the beach to them, shivering a little, shaking the water from her hair. Ford held open the towel and she ran into it. He folded it around her and hugged her to him, rubbing her dry. He pulled a sweatshirt down over her head and helped her on with her sandals, then dressed himself and scooped up the bags.

'You ever find that gold?' he asked, taking Grace by the hand and leading her up the steps, one at a time.

'Not a sniff,' said Kavanagh. 'We think Roth knows where it is, and that's why he's not talking. If he manages to walk free, it'll be waiting for him.'

'You think it's still in the country?'

'I doubt it. Roth had access to a boat and a plane. He would have been using them to bring in the guns and maybe drugs. The gold could have left the same way. My guess is when McCann took his boat offshore he was transferring the gold to a bigger vessel.'

Ford put the bags on the back of the scooter. Kavanagh put her helmet back on and threw her leg over the Ducati.

'Where to now?' she said.

'Home, I guess,' he said, as if he had some idea now where that might be.

'I meant, what's next for the two of you?'

'I guess it's time for the other life,' he said, 'the one without the mistakes.'

He lifted Grace onto the seat of the Vespa and put her helmet on, fixing the strap under her chin. It was still a size too big and fell forward until it rested on the bridge of her nose. She giggled and tilted her head back. He adjusted the helmet and swept the golden hair away from her eyes, held her chin in his hand and leaned close to whisper to her:

Rest, for your eyes are weary, girl—you have driven the worst
   away—
The ghost of the man that I might have been is gone from my
   heart today;
We'll live for life and the best it brings till our twilight shadows
   fall;
My heart grows brave, and the world, my girl, is a good
   world after all.

ACKNOWLEDGMENTS

The following works by Henry Lawson are quoted in the book: 'The Good Samaritan' (page 90), 'Up the Country' (page 228), 'City Bushman' (page 254), 'That There Dog of Mine' (paraphrased extract, beginning 'That there dog . . .', page 263), 'Down the River' (pages 263–4), 'The Drover's Wife' (page 279), 'Faces in the Street' (307–8) and 'After All' (page 371).

✪

I have a lot of people to thank: my agent, George Karlov, to whom I owe dinner and a lot more; Sue Hines for liking the pages; Richard Walsh, Clara Finlay and Sarah Baker for making them so much better; Colleen Egan and Jo Paul-Taylor for advice and encouragement; and first readers Matthew Saxon, Lance Collins, Tony Cockerill and Duncan Collins for all their red ink.

Most of all I want to thank my ever-loving wife Jacqui, for putting up with this book and with me; and Jackson, Charlie and Emma for being too young to notice the time I spent on this when I should have been with you. I love you.